HOW STILL WE SEE THEE LIE

**Allana Martin
Tom Mitcheltree
Connie Shelton
Elizabeth Gunn**

WORLDWIDE®

TORONTO • NEW YORK • LONDON
AMSTERDAM • PARIS • SYDNEY • HAMBURG
STOCKHOLM • ATHENS • TOKYO • MILAN
MADRID • WARSAW • BUDAPEST • AUCKLAND

HOW STILL WE SEE THEE LIE

A Worldwide Mystery/November 2002

ISBN 0-373-26437-2

THE CHRISTMAS BONUS Copyright © 2002 by Allana Martin.

A MERRY LITTLE CHRISTMAS Copyright © 2002 by Tom Mitcheltree.

HOLIDAYS CAN BE MURDER Copyright © 2002 by Connie Shelton.

TOO MANY SANTAS Copyright © 2002 by Elizabeth Gunn.

Printed in U.S.A.

Praise for the Texana Jones series by Allana Martin

DEATH OF THE LAST VILLISTA
"Allana Martin is my kind of writer. You're going to love this book—and her earlier ones, too."

—Tony Hillerman

"A compelling story, beautifully written and not to be missed."

—*Booklist*

DEATH OF A MYTHMAKER
"There is never a dull moment and the ending holds a major surprise for everyone…"

—*Mystery News*

"…spicy with Southwestern atmosphere."

—*Publishers Weekly*

DEATH OF A SAINTMAKER
"It's hard to find a better book about the Southwest…"

—*The Poisoned Pen*

Praise for *Katie's Will* by Tom Mitcheltree

"…more compelling with each turn of the page…eloquent writing, intriguing twists and turns…"

—*The Snooper*

"A complex, engrossing plot and highly recommended."

—*Mysteries By Mail*

"…keeps the reader guessing right up to the end…you do not want to put it down."

—*Electric Book Reviews*

CONTENTS

THE CHRISTMAS BONUS

by Allana Martin

Cuéntale tus penas a quien te las pueda remediar.
(Tell your sorrows to someone who can help you.)
—Mexican proverb

ONE

IT WAS Thursday, December 12, the feast day of the Virgin of Guadalupe and the official start of the Christmas season. Already this morning I'd strung multicolored lights across the roof, hung a plastic *Feliz Navidad* wreath on the sign that reads Texana's Trading Post and hidden a suitcase full of cash in the wellhouse out back.

The day had begun normally enough.

Because most families in the Rio Grande borderland would spend the day putting up holiday decorations, I expected few customers, but had taken my place behind the counter as usual. I'd unfolded the closest thing we have to a local newspaper, the Presidio *International*, which covers Presidio and Ojinaga, the U.S. and Mexico sister cities that lie fifty miles downriver. I'd gotten halfway through a story about the latest score-settling in Ojinaga between two rival drug smuggling capos when a man walked in. He closed the door behind him and stopped, black eyes scanning the room.

Along our isolated stretch of the river, I know almost everyone. He was a stranger. Black-haired, thin and medium height, he wore a red shirt and jeans. His heavy upper body seemed to overbalance his short bandy legs. His tooled leather boots had cost good money and were worn down on the inside heels. He might have been any *ranchero* had it not been for the suitcase.

It was a vinyl box, sixteen-by-sixteen and about eight inches deep, the kind you see in stores all over Mexico. I assumed he'd crossed the river and stopped to buy food before trekking north. Presidio County fronts the Rio Grande for 140 miles. There are few fences and many isolated crossings, making it tempting for immigrants. Crossing the river is easy; crossing the territory beyond is not. Presidio County climbs out of the rift of the river, over the Vieja and Chinati mountains, crosses a mile-high prairie basin and ends against volcanic upthrusts that line the horizon. It is a sparsely populated, rough county, meaning it can kill you by exposure, thirst, snakebite.

At intervals along the river, the Border Patrol has posted signs in Spanish, warning of the dangers of trying to cross this vast mountainous region of the Chihuahuan desert on foot. This man, like so many others, had probably ignored the warning.

He approached the counter, his face washed of any expression.

"Señora Texana Jones," he said, giving my name the soft pronunciation of Mexico—Tay-ha-na, rather than Tex-anna, as my parents intended.

He put the suitcase flat on the counter and opened it.

I nearly fell off the stool at the sight of the suitcase's contents: money, bundles of cash.

"A Christmas bonus, Señora Jones," he said. "My *jefe* wishes to use this trading post for twenty-four hours. You will arrange to be away for that time."

Fear squeezed my throat and churned my stomach. Having lived all of my life on the border, I knew exactly what, if not who, he represented. A drug trafficker on the other side of the river who wanted access on this side. By any measure, this was trouble off the scale. Say

"No," and I was as dead as the men I'd been reading about in Ojinaga.

He closed the suitcase and shoved it against me.

"Be ready," he said. "The *jefe* will send word of the date he wishes you not to be here. *Feliz Navidad.*"

Merry Christmas, indeed.

The wall clock ticked loudly in the quiet after the stranger closed the door. It seemed a long time before I got a grip on myself, went to the door and locked it, then returned for the suitcase. The instant my fingers closed on the handle, I broke into a sweat.

I rushed through the trading post like a madwoman, frantic to find a hiding place for the suitcase, putting it here and there and moving it immediately. Nowhere was safe enough. No hiding place would make the danger go away. I envisioned DEA agents breaking in to arrest me in some misguided sting operation.

I ended up in the wellhouse, a crudely built structure, walled with sheet metal, that housed the pressure tank. I peeled back part of the pink fiberglass insulation that Clay had loosely stapled to the two-by-fours at top and bottom and the one diagonal brace, shoving the suitcase behind it and repositioning the insulation.

After that, I went straight into the kitchen, downed a shot of whiskey, took a Pepcid and prepared iced tea with spoonfuls of sugar.

Better people than I had been bought by drug capos. I knew some locals who'd been caught: two ranchers, one Border Patrol agent, a sheriff, each now doing time in federal prison.

I would fight back. In 1888, my great-grandfather, Franco Ricciotti, had built the original wood-frame trading post on the same site as my present adobe building. I was a fourth-generation borderlander. I intended to stay.

Now, fortified with Dutch courage and against acid stomach and shock, I carried my glass of tea to the porch where I could see anyone coming. I wanted no more surprises.

The noon sky was pale with sunlight and nothing moved. The liquid mercury of the rusted thermometer hanging from the back wall of the porch touched 75° Fahrenheit. I set the dripping glass of iced tea on the metal table by my chair and watched the slick sweat pool, trying to collect my thoughts.

The cry that came from the river might have been anything, a bird, a fox, a raccoon, a human. I detected neither pain nor fear in the sound, yet I propelled myself out of the chair. In our isolated area, curiosity is second nature.

Rimmed by thickets of salt cedar, the river flows silently in a channel about as wide as a stream and knee-deep. As I approached the riverbank, my tennis shoes sank slightly in the sand. Out in the shallow, sluggish water, what looked like a pile of debris, caught among sodden branches and small rocks, rolled over with a groan. This movement released a ripe, unwashed human scent. I made my way carefully to the source.

John Henry Curzon's bleary eyes rolled up at me.

"Can't gerrup."

I grabbed his belt with both hands and pulled. He thrashed his arms, nearly toppling me.

"Give me some help here, John Henry."

He struggled to his feet, the stench of sweat and something more potent encircling him like an aura.

"*Pulque* is a mean drink," I said.

Everyone in Polvo knew of John Henry's taste for the cheap raw liquor.

"I'm not drunk," he said. "I'm wounded."

He lifted his shirt to reveal a narrow chest of flaccid

white skin sparsely covered with gray hair. I've seen uglier sights, but not many.

"Ri' there. See where he shot me."

He pointed a yellowed finger to a raw furrow across his lower rib cage.

"What was it, a .22?" I asked, rubbing my hands with wet sand to remove his clinging odor.

He smiled, nodding happily now that I was taking his plight seriously.

"If the *pulque* doesn't kill you, crossing to Huachito to get it will," I said, glancing at the tumble of shacks on the Mexico side. "Let's get out of here before they send a reminder shot that they don't like visitors."

He dug into the sand beneath the water, freed a worn pair of cowhide boots and tugged them over his bare feet.

"The shooter grazed the top of your head, too," I said.

He touched his bald scalp gingerly.

"No wonder I got a headache. Is it gonna leave a scar?"

"It won't matter if you die of infection from this filthy water. Come on. I'll clean that wound."

We turned our backs to Huachito, one in a string of tiny villages that hug the riverbank along a sixty-mile stretch of the Rio Grande. The villages are connected to one another by rutted roads. They smell of dust and sewage, have Honda generators and contaminated wells. Normally, children appear in abundance.

Huachito is different. It is a village of men, slight Mixtecs arrived only ten months ago from Oaxaca. They had thrown together shacks of scrap sheet tin and used wood and erected an open-air cantina, which would have been John Henry's destination. The village appeared abandoned except for the smoke of wood fires that curled toward the sky. At the river's edge the men had nailed a hand-painted sign to the thick trunk of a tree. It read NO MAS AQUÍ, crude Spanish that may be interpreted either as KEEP OUT or DON'T COME BACK. The men were equally unfriendly toward the locals on the Mexico side, according to my old friend Pete Rosales, who lives on the other side.

It was Pete who'd dubbed the village "Huachito," slang used by Northern Mexicans referring to small-statured *indios* from southern Mexico. Now, both sides of the river use the name as if it were mapped, and refer to the men who lived there as *huachitos*.

By twos and threes, never alone, the *huachitos* occasionally cross over to this side to buy groceries and loose tobacco and cigarette papers at the trading post. I greet them in Spanish. They keep silent, though among themselves I sometimes hear the murmur of the Mixtec language. They quickly collect what they need from the shelves, pay in pesos and leave.

John Henry followed me as far as the porch, where he tried to see the graze on his head in the reflection of the window glass while I went in to get disinfectant.

I dampened a cotton ball and liberally applied hydrogen peroxide to his rib cage and head.

"So why did the *huachito* shoot at you?" I asked.

"Meanness, I reckon. Bought my bottle at the cantina, I'm walking back to the river, some little guy in a doorway opens fire. Busted my bottle with the first bullet."

"Why don't you just go to Ojinaga to buy your drink?"

"Too far. 'Sides," he said seriously, "I don't believe in driving under the influence."

"There is that to consider," I agreed, taping a gauze bandage over the graze.

"You got a mirror so I can see how bad my head is?"

I fetched a hand mirror, knowing John Henry would fret until he could see the wound, as slight as it was. Staring at himself in the oval mirror, he prodded the tender mark.

"It's gonna leave a scar for sure," he said gloomily.

He handed me back the mirror. I offered to drive him home.

As coarse as John Henry is, he has his moments of sensitivity, exhibiting one when he climbed in the bed of the pickup instead of bringing his body odor into the cab with me. He rode looking in wistfully through the back window, like a dog watching his master drive.

Polvo is two miles up the road. Its heart is the small chapel dedicated to Our Lady of Candeleria that sits on a hillside behind the adobe-walled cemetery. Once, the two-room school had been the center of community life, but it had been closed by the State Board of Education three years ago. Now we use it for community meetings. Past the post office and parallel to the river, flat-roofed adobes line both sides of the pavement. John Henry's trailer sits on a lot at the end of a dust-padded street that forks away from the river. It is almost hidden by rusting car parts, old stoves and other scrap metal. The minute I stopped, he eased over the tailgate and came alongside my window.

"Watch out for yourself," he said. "My opinion, those *huachitos* are up to no good. They start shooting across the river at you, my best advice, shoot back." Then he made his way through the debris of the yard and into his trailer.

Consumed by my own troubles, I thought of little on the drive home except the fears inside my head.

TWO

THE TWO VEHICLES parked in front of the trading post couldn't have been more in contrast: a pink 1955 Cadillac Fleetwood in pristine condition and a 2001 black Mercedes-Benz with darkened windows.

The two men who stood talking beside their cars were equally different in appearance. Charlie, Vietnam vet, free spirit and friend, is pear-shaped, with thin brown hair and benevolent eyes. He was wearing a wrinkled knit shirt, jeans faded almost white and black tennis shoes. Charlie's golden Great Dane, Max, filled much of the front seat of the Caddy, even with his head hanging out the window.

My new neighbour, Clemente Gamez, the powerfully built man beside Charlie, had coarse red hair, blue eyes and skin the color of ale, traits reflecting his genetic ties to the Irish soldiers who fought with Mexico in the Mexican-American War. He was wearing a navy turtleneck under a black leather jacket and gray slacks, all casual but expensive. His boots looked new and had unusually thick soles. Given his modest height, I suspected lifts. He cradled a tiny dog, a bright-eyed long-haired Chihuahua named Nippy.

"You've introduced yourselves?" I said to the men.

"We have. Charlie has been telling me about his travels along the border,'' Clemente Gamez said pleasantly. "I came to ask you to post this."

His round face beaming, he handed me an eight-by-ten sheet of heavy paper. The poster invited the citizens of Polvo to a Christmas party at the home of Jovita and Clemente Gamez on Friday, December 20, from 2:00-6:00 p.m. Casual dress.

In the form of his invitation, Gamez had adopted the local custom. With only 125 people in Polvo, everything is democratic. *Quinceañeras, posadas*, weddings and funerals, everyone is invited. We display notices at the trading post and post office, the two places that, sooner or later, everyone visits.

The Chihuahua squirmed in her master's arm. Gamez put his face close to her head.

"You're a good girl, yes, you are," he cooed.

The tiny dog licked his face enthusiastically.

Gamez's watch played "Dixie" on the hour.

"Time for daddy to take baby home," he said, getting into the Mercedes. "Charlie, if you're here on the party date, please join us. Our house is yours."

Charlie and I watched the black car drive away.

"When I tried to pet the dinky dog," Charlie said, "it bit me."

"He should have warned you. That's how she got her name. She even bit Clay when he vaccinated her."

Clay is my husband and one of only two veterinarians in Presidio County. His office and clinic is in a trailer behind the trading post, but since he works mostly with large animals, he's out on the ranches much of the time, as he was today.

Charlie gave me his gentle smile and patted Max. The big dog quivered with affection and stared up at him. Max had been an orphan when Charlie adopted him. The

two lived out of the Caddy, "Bess," as Charlie referred
to the car. The trunk held camping equipment; Charlie
could set up home wherever there was open ground.

"We've been up to El Paso, but Max and me didn't
enjoy it much," Charlie said. "That town's gotten way
too big."

Over the years I've known Charlie, he's worked for
me many times. In the old days, before the fire that had
destroyed the original trading-post building, Charlie
would simply unfurl his sleeping bag in the big front
room. During the rebuilding with adobe, I'd added a tiny
guest room with its own entrance. Charlie had already
stayed there once.

I hesitated, then offered Charlie our usual hospitality.
"Make yourself at home. I'll fix us something to eat."

Charlie lifted a duffel bag and Max's cedar-chip pad
out of the Caddy's trunk. He went toward the guest
room. I crossed the porch and went inside the trading
post. As I passed the front display table, Phobe made a
flying leap out from underneath and grabbed my leg with
both paws.

Phobe is our pet bobcat, so named because strangers
are afraid of her, but she's really just a pussycat. She
adores humans and dogs, and tolerates domestic cats.
When I failed to stop and play, she followed me through
the arched doorway into our private quarters. I sat on
the couch. Phobe leaped up beside me, bumping me with
her head in typical bobcat greeting. I ruffled her thick
tawny fur, leaned my head back and closed my eyes. I
felt shaky. I needed to eat whether or not I wanted to.
And there was Charlie to feed. I was glad of his presence. I felt less outnumbered.

Charlie and Max joined us as I was microwaving frozen enchiladas and mashing avocados for the guacamole.

Charlie offered to chop onion and grate Monterey Jack cheese.

Phobe and Max spent some minutes sniffing around each other respectfully, reacquainting themselves. Then Phobe flicked the tip of her stubby tail, made a chirping sound that is her greeting, bumped Max with her head and brushed her body the length of his. Max fell in a heap and rolled over. Phobe leaped on him, and the two tumbled this way and that in a fit of exuberance.

"I heard Gamez bought the Birley ranch," Charlie said, as he used the knife expertly.

Charlie is not only good company and a good cook, he also knows more about what is going on along the border than just about anyone.

The ten-section ranch that Gamez now owned touches on the back of my own one section, 640 acres. My parcel is one mile square and fronts the river on one side.

Gamez had bought his ranch from the First National Bank. For four generations it had belonged to the Birley family, lastly to Cletus Birley, who had placed the land in trust, thinking that would allow his two sons to maintain and live on the property while protecting them from heavy inheritance taxes, or as the old man called it, "The government." Three years after Cletus died, the banker in charge of the trust informed the two sons that the bank's only obligation was to grow the trust; the simplest way to do that was to sell the land. The only cash the Birley brothers got was from the herd liquidation of their cattle, which Clemente Gamez also bought.

Immediately, he'd had a new house built, employing nearly a hundred men from Ojinaga.

"Special work permits, everything legal and aboveboard," he had said on one visit to check on the building's progress.

In a region where adobe, stucco and stone are the primary building materials, the Gamezes' gray brick home looked out of place sitting in the middle of yucca, prickly pear and ocotillo. For a few weeks after completion, the house stood empty.

Then, six months ago, moving vans had been spotted on the Pinto Canyon road, spotted again passing Cemetery Hill above the river road. Since the vans never passed my place, we assumed they'd turned off onto the new road Gamez had cut just outside the eastern boundary of my land. He'd bought the deeded rights to the access from an absentee landowner, a retired surgeon who, in the early eighties, had built an underground house on a two-acre parcel of land a few miles above the river. To build the road to Gamez's new ranch home had taken two bulldozers working four days. So many loads of gravel were hauled in that the road from Presidio was damaged. Reportedly, Gamez had offered to reimburse the county for the costs of repairs.

"Have you seen his house?" Charlie asked.

Max came up behind him, making feed-me noises.

"Clay keeps dog food in the pantry," I told Charlie.

I got out two pet bowls and Phobe's food log, horse meat with vitamin and mineral supplements. She gets a half pound twice a day. I cut off a chunk. As I chopped it up, I described for Charlie the open house that the Gamezes held when they first took up residence.

"Everyone went. There was lots of Tecate beer, soft tacos, and, would you believe, Russian caviar. Mrs. Gamez took anyone who wanted on a tour of the house. All five bedrooms have private baths, walk-in closets, and built-in television and video cabinets. There's a cathedral ceiling in the living room and those beautiful square-block bookshelves, the kind you see in the homes in Mexico. That's where Mrs. Gamez displays her collection of antique Spanish fans and clocks from Switzerland. She told me that was her favorite country.''

''What's Gamez do for a living?'' Charlie asked.

He'd finished cutting up the onion and slid the plate down the counter to me. I added some to the guacamole.

''He's *not* a Houston lawyer,'' I said.

It was a regional joke that so many of that city's attorneys had bought ranches in our area that soon we'd be designated a suburb of that huge coastal city.

''He owned a specialty food company near Monterrey,'' I told Charlie. ''He said he sold out to an American firm so he could get out of Mexico. Remember that famous Mexican actor whose father was kidnapped and ransomed for a million bucks? That made Gamez decide Mexico was too dangerous. His kids go to college here, the daughter at Berkeley and the son at Brown. Or is it the other way 'round?''

''I heard that his wife's father was a supplier to Pemex,'' Charlie said. ''Drilling equipment.''

''So there's money on both sides of the family,'' I said.

''If the father got paid before oil prices went bust in the eighties,'' Charlie said.

A dusty green pickup rolled past the window and stopped by the trailer.

Fifteen minutes later, Clay came in the back door. His hair was damp from the shower in the trailer, where he cleans up after his work and changes into fresh clothes. He welcomed Charlie warmly, then went to drop his dirty clothes in the washer. My husband is tall; his vet work with cattle and horses keeps him fit and slim. I felt better just seeing him.

I left the bad news until after we'd eaten and Clay had poured whiskey for the three of us.

"We have a problem," I said.

My tone must have spoken volumes. Clay emptied his glass. Charlie said he'd take his drink to his room if we wanted privacy.

"I think we could use an objective opinion from an old borderhand like you," I said.

By the time I'd finished telling the story of the man with the suitcase, Clay looked as depressed as I felt. We batted around solutions, but they were all strikeouts.

"If you don't go along," Charlie said, "this *jefe* will send someone to hurt you. Drug capos don't ask twice."

"Let him use the trading post once and it'll never stop," I said. "Until we get arrested by the DEA or Customs."

"We can't go to the Feds for help," Clay said. "If the smuggler gets wind of it, we're dead."

"So basically, we're either fugitives from the drug smuggler or from our own government's agents," I said. "Charlie, you know you're welcome, but it's not safe here."

"You don't know yet the date the smuggler wants to use your place," Charlie said. "We've got some time."

I blessed him for that "we."

Clay got up and put away the whiskey.

"We're going to need clear heads from now on," he said.

"Let's count that money," I said, "to find out how deep we're in."

We went together. Clay held the flashlight, and I uncovered the suitcase. Charlie watched our backs.

We worked at the kitchen table, each with a slip of paper for tallying. As we counted, we made neat stacks of bills by denomination. None was larger than a twenty, all were used.

Or as Charlie said, "It's already been laundered."

I took their slips and added the totals to mine. Twice. "One hundred thousand."

"That's bad. For five hundred dollars," Charlie said, "any *chavo* will bring a couple of kilos across the river on horseback. Buying your cooperation at this price means the capo's a big operator."

Clay stood and started replacing the cash in the suitcase.

"Where are we going to put it?" I said, helping him.

"Right where you had it," Clay said. He shut the suitcase. "I'll take care of this."

Charlie rousted Max from the couch, where dog and bobcat had been dozing in a tumble of legs.

"See you in the morning," he said.

I don't know how Charlie slept, but for Clay and me, it was the longest night of our lives. Even Phobe, perhaps picking up on our stress, rested uneasily.

THREE

ONE DAY IS much like another on the river. Rarely do I notice time slipping by. Friday, I did.

At six, I unlocked the front doors and prepared the twelve-cup coffeemaker for the group of ranchers who regularly gather here to gossip and talk cattle.

By eight, the ranchers had departed.

I tuned the radio to a powerful station in Chihuahua that broadcasts *Norteño* ballads and personal messages to family members in the United States. The station also runs numerous ads for Dr. Scholl's foot pads, aimed at those who arrive in Northern Mexico as the first part of a journey of passage to the U.S. side of the river. Despite the harsh terrain of our wild land, the big ranches are ribboned with footpaths worn deep from decades of use. Probably the *huachitos* would be traveling those trails, sooner or later.

It took courage and money to make the journey into what was, for them, the unknown. Driven by desperation, the courage came easier than the money, needed to live on while waiting for a guide to help them cross, needed to live on at some farther destination while waiting to find work. Their waiting was as perilous as their traveling, it seemed.

At 8:15, Charlie came in with Max. He sat at the table

the ranchers had vacated, turning his chair to face the doors. Max stretched out at his feet.

Friday was Clay's day to man his vet station in Presidio. He'd left at seven, after arguing that he should remain here with me. He'd been unable to persuade me that a change of routine would help our situation. I thought we should keep our lives as normal as possible. Clay had agreed, reluctantly.

Charlie, I knew, was keeping watch for Clay, waiting for the next message from the smuggler. Without seeming to, he kept his eyes on the front doors. His big body was still but alert, reminding me of the soldier he had been.

By ten, three customers had pumped gas. Between eleven and three, I sold groceries to two people, rented three videos and sold one ten-minute phone card. At three-thirty I hung a CLOSED sign on the hook out front and locked up.

"Is that a good idea?" Charlie asked.

"I didn't promise the *jefe*'s gofer I'd keep open house for him. I want to move that money off the premises. Will you come?"

"What if the smuggler has someone watching," Charlie said, "to make sure you don't talk to the wrong people?"

"He doesn't need to have me watched. He knows we're stuck between a rock and a hard place."

Charlie threw up his hands in surrender.

"Let's go."

We took Max with us. "He'll let us know pretty quick," Charlie said, "if anyone is around."

I didn't expect there to be anyone where we were going. If there was, we'd be able to spot them from a long way off.

I put the suitcase in the back of my '99 white Ford supercab. We drove up the low hill behind Clay's office, following a track of sorts.

In the days before overgrazing and severe drought, the rocky scree had been lush with grasses. Now creosote and mesquite held the soil, and barren mountains climbed the horizon.

Charlie didn't ask where we were going. His trust gave me courage.

The village site is on the high spot and nearly dead center of my 640 acres. The scattering of adobes were built over forty years ago for a movie location. Hurriedly put up, it had never been intended to last, but thanks to our dry climate and sparse rainfall, it looked almost the same as when I'd played there as a child. No one had any reason to come here. In summer there were snakes. In winter, skunks, sometimes even javelina, sheltered from the cold desert wind. I'd never found a trace of any human occupation.

In one of the buildings there was a hollow in a wall where the film crew had placed a camera. That's where I intended hiding the suitcase.

"This is something," Charlie said, as we got out.

Max jumped from the truck and put his nose to the ground, following a scent. I hoped it wasn't skunk.

I carried the suitcase.

"I'm going to put this in that building over there," I said. "I think I can cover it with some of the loose adobe bricks from the other buildings."

"I'll start collecting them," Charlie said.

It had been some time since I'd been here. Inside the one-room adobe, part of the ceiling had collapsed, letting in the sunlight. I'd counted on shadow to obscure the bricked-up hiding place. Would it be too obvious? I stepped carefully across the rubble-littered floor to the north wall. I wedged the suitcase into the opening halfway up the wall. I decided to stack bricks over it and then judge how it looked.

It was quiet. Here, where no sounds but nature's intruded, I should have heard Charlie and Max moving around. I didn't.

I stepped outside. The pair were straight ahead of me and more than fifty feet away. Max sat on his haunches, Charlie was on his feet, looking down at something. He saw me coming and pointed.

"Is this an old migrant trail?" he said.

Loose rocks had worked aside, and the light-colored soil showed in scattered patches. It looked like a goat path, but I run no livestock on my place. The trail had been made, not by livestock moving in single file, but by people, and recently, since all the plant cover wasn't yet worn away completely.

"This is new," I told Charlie, "since the last time I drove up this way."

I looked south toward the river. If the trail originated from there, I couldn't tell from here.

I walked a few yards in the direction of the back boundary of my land. At one point I thought I could see something that might have been a footprint, but I was unsure. The hard ground gave away little. I pointed out the faint impression to Charlie. He thought it was the print of a shoe, but neither of us was knowledgeable enough about reading sign to interpret much from it.

Max seemed keen on whatever scent the trail held and bounded ahead of us, but Charlie called him back.

"How long since you were up here last?" he asked.

"Maybe a year," I said. "I drove up this way after Gamez started building. I wanted to see how the old fence across the back was holding up. The Birleys never worried much as long as the fence would turn cattle, but I figured Gamez might expect me to go halves for new fencing.''

"Did he ask?" Charlie said.

"No, thank goodness. I'd have been hard-pressed to come up with the money."

"Would you have noticed the trail?"

"Not along here," I said, "but I drove the entire length of the back boundary. This trail has to cross over into the Gamez place somewhere."

"He's got a surprise coming, then," Charlie said.

"Maybe it's illegals," I suggested, "heading for Valentine."

The small town twenty-five miles from the border has a freight yard where Mexican nationals hitch rides to Houston.

"Or small-time smugglers," he said, "walking across a few pounds at a time."

Smuggling is an old habit on the border. In the early days, the contraband was cattle and mules going both ways. During Prohibition, kegs and bottles of liquor moved north. From the fifties until the NAFTA agreement opened trade, everything from refrigerators to toasters had gone south. The modern commodities were marijuana, cocaine and heroin, moving north even as guns, illegal in Mexico, went the other way. Sometimes, in the early hours of the morning, I would hear a solitary vehicle passing the trading post going toward Presidio. In some other place, I might have thought it innocent travel. Here, I knew it was likely not. We borderlanders were used to the trafficking of goods, but the corruption that accompanied the drug culture was something else, as I was learning firsthand.

"Charlie, stay here with the suitcase. I want to trace this trail to the back fence line."

"We'll put the suitcase in the pickup and drive it together," he said.

"The tire tracks will show. They flatten everything. I'm going to walk a couple of feet away from the trail. I don't want whoever's using it to know anyone's found it."

"No way you go alone," Charlie said firmly. "Clay would kill me. We can lock the suitcase in the pickup."

"Can you keep Max off the trail?"

"Yes, but we'd better get some brush and wipe away the tracks he's made along here," Charlie said.

After we cleaned the trail of paw prints, it took us twenty-five minutes of hard walking to follow the weaving route across to the point at the northeast corner of my land. There, I discovered that three of the fence posts had been sawed through at the base, an old rustler's trick. The barbed-wire fence could be flattened to let a horse or cow cross. The fence was then raised back up, leaving the landowner unsuspecting.

Beyond the fence, the trail continued into the Gamez ranch.

I checked my watch. Clay would have returned from Presidio by now, and I needed time to think about what to do next.

"Let's get back to the pickup," I told Charlie.

I made sure we didn't retrace our steps. I wanted no hint of our journey for sharp eyes to see.

"What do you know about Mixtecs?" I asked Charlie, as the pickup bounced along on the drive home.

"I know there's a couple of thousand of them living in the hills above the dump in Juarez. They sell crafts to tourists, when the other vendors aren't chasing them

off,'' he said. ''The Mexicans resent *indios* like the Mixtecs for moving into Northern Mexico. *Mixtecos* are so
poor, they can probably carry all the money they ever
earned in their shoes.''

I told him about the village of Huachito.

''What are they living on?'' he said.

''I don't know, but they have enough to buy food and
cigarettes from me,'' I said.

''You think they made the trail?'' Charlie asked.

''It could be anybody. I've got to find out where that
trail begins and ends, and what it's being used for.''

As I parked behind the trading post, Clay pushed the
back door open so hard it slammed against the outside
wall.

''Where have you been? Why didn't you leave a note?
I've been worried sick.''

I didn't blame him for being angry. Usually, we don't
worry about each other's independent actions. Our present situation being anything but usual, I apologized and
explained. Clay wouldn't let me out of his sight while I
put the suitcase full of cash back in the wellhouse.

I made coffee for the three of us, and we sat down to
talk things over.

''Are we saying the men across the river are connected somehow to the smuggler who's threatening us?''
Clay asked.

He was on the couch. I sat in one recliner, Charlie in
the other. On the floor, Phobe happily chewed on Max's
ear.

''I don't know,'' I said, blowing on the coffee. ''But
we'd better find out before the Border Patrol spotters see
that trail from the air.''

The agency used Cessna 182s, the pilots acting as
spotters for four-wheel-drive vehicles on the ground.

"Right. The last thing we need right now," Clay said, "is to draw attention to ourselves."

"We need someone who can read sign to look at that trail," I said.

"You're thinking of Pete?" Clay said.

I nodded. Pete Rosales is a lifelong friend, as honest as he is independent and feisty. More than once I've watched Pete walk with his head down, checking the dirt for tracks and finding them where others see nothing. He can read the slightest disturbance, an overturned pebble, a bent blade of grass, a ripple in the sand.

"We shouldn't tell him about the cash," Clay said. "It's dangerous knowledge."

I agreed and reached for my pickup keys.

"Not now," Clay said. "It's nearly dark. I don't want any of us on the other side after dark."

In all the years I'd been married to Clay he's always deferred to my knowledge of the border because it's based on a lifetime of experience. Nor has he ever questioned where I went or when. It was a measure of his anxiety for me, for our way of life, for our lives, that he did so now. I sat back down.

"Tomorrow will be soon enough," I said.

FOUR

THE ROSALESES have no telephone. Charlie manned the trading post while I went to see Pete. This time, Clay insisted on going with me.

Access to the Rosaleses' *rancho* is two miles south, where the foothills that line the Rio Grande recede a yard or two. The river is too sandy at this point to drive across. We parked beneath the trees and, one at a time, walked across the footbridge built by Pete. The frayed rope rail offered little support as the bridge swayed and dipped to almost touch the water.

On the other side, beyond the greenbelt, the ground is level. The thin soil supports just enough scrub and grass to sustain the mottled Spanish goats Pete raises. It was here, as a boy, that Pete learned to track. His father raised mules and horses that were left to run loose. Pete's job was to go out and find them whenever someone came to buy. By age ten, he was an accomplished tracker.

The Rosaleses' dogs, a baker's dozen of mongrels, had raised a warning from their dog compound, a fenced area where they could run but not chase goats. Pete and his wife, Zeferina, waited on the porch of the two-room adobe, shaded from morning sun by the delicate leaves of a honey mesquite tree. With them was a pit bull terrier named Gringo, a fat old animal whose temperament was mellow and sweet.

"*Hola,*" Pete cried. "*¿Qué pasa?*"

He had on a felt hat with a limp brim. His stocky figure was clad in a blue shirt and brown pants lightened from many hand washings by Zeferina, and sandals.

Zeferina, who Pete always said could make a peso stretch further than anyone he knew, is a tiny woman, barely five feet tall. Her long hair, graying slightly now, was tied back with a bright scarf. Her white blouse and red skirt were covered by the long apron she wears for housework. As we approached the porch, she untied the strings, folded the apron and placed it on the table by the door where a stack of tin cooking pots were air-drying.

The Rosaleses, married when Zeferina was sixteen and Pete twenty, have seven children and many grand-children. Their youngest son lives at home.

"Where's Alejandro?" I asked.

"Out with the burro and the goats," Pete said. "He loves to take his rifle and stay out all day."

"Like his father," Zeferina said.

When I first met her, Zeferina was so shy and quiet she rarely spoke. Over the years she has grown comfortable with me, first as Pete's friend and, finally, as her own.

We sat on the porch in metal Corona beer chairs that had come from the trading post. Zeferina had hung silver tinsel across the open windows, and it rustled in the breeze. Our first conversational topic was the weather. We moved on to the Rosales children, their jobs and Christmas plans, Polvo's holiday *posada*, and lastly, the health of the dogs, beloved by Pete only slightly less than his children.

I brought up the subject of the Rosaleses' Mixtec neighbors, asking Pete how he was getting along with them.

"I know they speak Spanish," he said indignantly. "Three of the goats went missing. I walked over there to see if they'd strayed in that direction. One of those *huachitos* warned me off. I bet they ate my goats."

"That's why Alejandro goes out with the herd, now," Zeferina said.

I told Pete and Zeferina about the trail I'd found across my land.

"You're thinking the *huachitos* made it?" Pete said. "I'm the best tracker the Border Patrol *don't* have working for them. You want me to take a look?"

"That's exactly what we want," I said.

"If the *huachitos* are crossing your place, I'll find their tracks," Pete said.

He agreed to come the next day, around noon.

"First thing in the morning," he said, "I want to scout around the village. Maybe find some of the *huachitos'* tracks for comparison."

"I wish you wouldn't do that, Pete," I said.

"It's the smart thing to do," he replied.

"They did warn you off," Clay said.

"John Henry went there to buy *pulque*," I said, "and one of them took a shot at him."

"I'm not that old *borrachón*," Pete said. "I'm not going to be drunk and stupid."

I kept quiet. Pete can be touchy about having his judgment questioned.

Our business settled, we turned the talk back to lighter subjects. It was an hour before Clay and I left for home.

Pete and Gringo accompanied us to the bridge.

"Anything you want to tell me that you didn't want to say in front of Zeffy?"

"Just be careful," I told him. "You know as well as I do that illegals and smugglers can be one and the same."

"Maybe we should leave Pete out of this altogether," Clay said gravely.

Pete gave him a long look.

"Trust old Pete. I can look two ways at once, and I've got ears like a free-tail bat." He paused. "If those *huachitos* fired at John Henry, they may decide to take a shot at Alejandro when he's out with the goats. If they're up to something, I want to know. It's my side of the river they're living on."

Clay and I were quiet on the way home, locked in our own thoughts.

The answering machine message light was flashing. Clay returned the call. A horse had eaten some bad hay. Clay left immediately for the outlying ranch.

Morning at the trading post had been routine, Charlie reported: a handful of customers.

"Mrs. Gully called in with a list of groceries she needs delivered," Charlie added. "I've got everything bagged."

I deliver to locals if they're sick or without transportation. I hadn't given any thought to what I should do about such orders while we were in this mess. Charlie caught my frown.

"I'll run them out to her," he said. "By the way, some cowhand came in for a cattle prod. I couldn't find one in ranch supplies."

I explained that I never carried them. Clay said if a cowboy couldn't work cattle without shocking them, he should find another line of work.

Charlie left with Max to deliver Olivia Gully's groceries.

I was dusting the canned goods when Jovita Gamez walked in with Nippy tucked into one arm.

"*Buenos días,* Señora Jones," she said. "Is your husband in? I didn't find him in the trailer."

At the Gamez open house, I'd caught Clay discreetly admiring Jovita Gamez. She's that kind of woman: glossy black hair, good skin, subtle makeup, expensive clothing worn with style, and plenty of social grace. I'd guess her age at midforties, but she looks ten years younger.

"Clay's out on a call," I said. "May I help?"

"It's about Nippy," she said. "But you're busy...."

"Is the dog sick?"

"No. I wish to board her with you," Mrs. Gamez said. "I have to be away for some days. Clemente also will be very busy. The maid, I don't trust."

I wanted to say no. The last thing we needed was something else to worry about. Assuming we had a future, I had to think of it. The Gamezes had brought in the Chihuahua for her shots and a checkup as soon as they'd moved into their house, proclaiming themselves elated that a vet for their "precious baby" was so close and convenient. Few borderland pet owners rely on veterinary care for their animals. Clay needed good customers as much as I did. And there were three hundred head of Gamez cattle to consider.

"Of course, we'll take her," I said, reaching out for the dog. "The kennels are empty—"

Jovita Gamez hugged her pet closer.

"Not the kennels. Nippy would be lonely. She pines without attention. And the nights are too cold. She's very sensitive to cold."

"We have heated pads," I said. "She'll get regular attention."

"Please, no. Nippy hates to be alone. I'd hoped you'd keep her here with you, inside."

I looked at the tiny dog. Her long silky hair and bright eyes gave her a winsome appearance.

"All right," I said. "She stays in the trading post with us. As long as you don't think she'll mind Phobe."

The bobcat picked that moment to drop down from the upper shelf onto the display table next to Mrs. Gamez.

The woman stepped back and clutched Nippy to her tightly. I'd forgotten she had never been inside the trading post, only Clay's clinic.

Phobe stretched, yawned and sniffed delicately at the air. Mrs. Gamez wore a heavy perfume.

"She's quite tame," I told Mrs. Gamez. "She was raised around children. If you'll let me hold Nippy..."

"You're sure...."

"Phobe loves dogs."

Mrs. Gamez edged closer to me and handed over Nippy. Knowing the dog's habit of snapping at hands, I was prepared to be bitten, but Nippy, intent on the bobcat, let me take her without incident.

I moved toward the table slowly. Phobe opened her eyes wide and leaned toward the dog Nippy barked fiercely. Phobe's round eyes half closed, her tail twitched and her big paw shot out.

Nippy's sharp little teeth made contact. Phobe leaped off the table, raced toward the counter and vanished behind it.

"As you can see, she's not dangerous," I said.

Mrs. Gamez was laughing.

"If you want to leave Nippy," I said, "I'll put her in a carrier until the two of them get used to each other."

Mrs. Gamez opened the purse strapped over her shoulder and took out a plastic bag of small doggy toys and a slip of paper, and handed them to me.

"I listed the foods she'll eat," Mrs. Gamez said. "I'll be at the telephone number at the bottom. Please don't disturb my husband about anything. Call me."

"How long do you want us to keep Nippy?"

"I'll be back to get her in one week. Goodbye, precious baby," she said, coming close to run her hand over Nippy's head.

I could see tears in Mrs. Gamez's brown eyes.

NIPPY DID NOT LIKE the carrier and after a few minutes of listening to her barking, I released her. She paid no attention to the other animals, but made straight for Max's feed bowl, which she dragged under the desk. Max wagged his tail and opened his mouth in a friendly smile.

Phobe, used to encounters in which she was the dominant animal, had decided to ignore the intruder, contenting herself with tearing open the bag of Nippy's doggy toys and batting them around the room. When Max joined her, she scrambled up to the back of the couch and leaped on his back. Then they both went off to chew on the rug.

Nippy spent the next three hours chewing, pawing and rattling the empty bowl on the floor. When Clay came home, all three animals were asleep, Nippy in the feed bowl, Phobe curled against Max on the rug.

"They're peaceful now," I told Clay, "but Nippy bit Phobe. I had no idea she'd be so aggressive with a bigger animal."

"If you weighed two pounds and stood eight inches high you'd bite first, too," Clay said. "The smaller the animal, the more ferocious they have to appear in order to protect themselves."

"Did you check the wellhouse as you came in?" I asked.

We'd failed to come up with a better idea of where to hide the suitcase, but were paranoid with worry, fearful of the unlikely event that the cash would be discovered.

"We've got to stop running out there every hour," Clay said, "or someone may notice and get suspicious."

"You're right," I said.

All the same, as soon as Clay left the room, I couldn't stop myself from going to the kitchen window and looking out at the wellhouse and its padlocked door.

Clay had missed lunch, so I heated chili from the freezer. Charlie joined us. Over the steaming bowls, we tried to talk of topics other than the most pressing one, but mostly we lapsed into silence. It was an exhausting evening.

PETE CAME ALONG to the trading post at two the next afternoon, a pleased look on his face.

Clay opened a fresh bottle of Jack Daniel's and brought a glass. Pete asked for stick baloney, crackers and cheese to go with it. I tried to get him to eat before talking, but he was eager to reveal what he'd discovered.

"I couldn't get too near Huachito," he said disgustedly. "They've taken machetes to the tree limbs and brush all around the village. But I found footprints in the sand near the river where they dump their garbage. Maybe eight different shoes, all slick soled. Some boots, some sandals. I found the crossing point on this side of the river right by the first Border Patrol warning sign northwest of here.''

''That's only a couple of hundred feet away,'' I said.

''I also found a tire mark,'' Pete said, ''right above the waterline.''

''They're driving across?'' I said, surprised.

I'd never seen a sign of a vehicle in the whole village, never heard a truck start up. And when the *huachitos* came to the trading post for groceries, they came on foot.

''Walking,'' Pete said. ''It's an old trick to keep your feet dry. You lay down tires like stepping-stones. The last man in line picks up the tire behind him and passes it up the line. All you need is one more tire than men.''

Pete had our full attention.

''The trail itself is pretty clean, because the earth is so rocky and hard,'' he said, ''but I made out ten different footprints. All waffle soles, like tennis shoes.''

''Not sandals or boots, like you saw by their dump site?'' Clay asked.

Pete shook his head.

''So maybe it's not the *huachitos*,'' Charlie said.

''It's them, all right,'' Pete said with satisfaction. ''These footprints are little. Like kids' shoes.''

''They're changing shoes,'' I said. ''Just to cross?''

Pete nodded somberly. He knew, as we all did, that illegals wore what they had, but smugglers nearly always wore waffle-soled tennis shoes or hiking boots. The knowledge was part of border lore.

''How long's the trail been in use?'' Clay asked.

''To disturb the hard pack that much,'' Pete said, ''six months, at least, if they use it fairly often.''

He paused to wash down a cracker and chunk of baloney with whiskey.

''Thing is,'' he said, looking grave, ''they're going

both ways, up and down the trail. And they're going up heavier than they're coming down.''

I put my head in my hands. Worse and worse.

"Looks like these *huachitos*," Pete said, "are smuggling. The trail goes northeast across your place and, like you told me, onto the neighbor's. I almost followed it over, but I had no excuse to be there. If it had been the Birley's place still, I'd have gone, but I don't know this new man."

"Gamez doesn't run the place himself," Clay said.

"He's got a ranch manager," I said.

"Anybody I know?" Pete asked.

"Nobody knows him," I said, "but he must be a hard worker, because I haven't heard of anyone who's seen him off the ranch."

"Good thing I didn't go over the fence, then," Pete said. "Being an outsider, this guy might have called the Border Patrol to drop me back on my own side."

He was joking. The Border Patrol agents knew all the locals like Pete who cross the river to buy at the trading post or visit relatives in Polvo. They don't waste time with those who return to the other side on their own.

Clay held out the whiskey bottle, and Pete placed his glass under the rim. After he finished the glass, Clay handed him the bottle.

"Take it home. You earned it."

"We're grateful for your help, Pete," I said, getting up to walk him to the door.

Pete gave us both a long look in which there was much assessing of whatever he saw in our faces: fatigue, worry, fear. Pete was adept at reading people, his judgment keen.

"On my side of the river," he said, "we don't call in the cops, 'cause who knows the smugglers better than the people who run with them. Over here, you can do things different. But this close to the river, even on this side, you got to be careful who you talk to. You know what I mean?''

''We know, Pete,'' I said. ''We'll be as careful as we can.''

He lifted the bottle. ''Thanks for the whiskey. You need me, you call. If I learn any more, I'll let you know.''

Clay drove him home. I'd packed a Christmas basket for Zeferina, including clothes and books for Alejandro.

Charlie sat with me, waiting for Clay's return.

''What you need,'' he said, ''is an airplane.''

FIVE

THE PAVEMENT ENDS at the edge of Polvo. Beyond that, for those willing to risk damaged shock absorbers, there is a lava-rock track that runs for five miles farther before impassable foothills squeeze the river.

Monday morning I was driving that track with a careful hand on the wheel.

I knew six or seven ranchers who used either planes or helicopters to reach their land or locate far-ranging livestock, but most were newcomers, absentee owners with homes in places like Santa Fe, Houston, and New York. I needed not only a plane, but an older borderhand to pilot it, one who would not ask too many questions and who would keep quiet about the answers.

Seventy-year-old Barton Howard had been born on the Curling A ranch and had lived there all his life. He had a plane. What he didn't have was a telephone.

At the point where the track runs out, I turned the pickup away from the river and toward the Vieja Mountains. I slowed to a crawl to cross a dry creek that during rain would flood faster than a jackrabbit could run. On the far side, the track climbed past the creosote bush and yucca of the low desert and into the mesquite and scrub of the foothills.

Two slow miles farther and I turned left across a cattle

guard and into windblown pasture. The barbed wire and juniper post fence stretched into the distance.

Barton's five older sisters had married and moved away. Barton, who never married, had gone away for four years, returning home with a degree in philosophy from Yale and a determination never to leave West Texas again. After the deaths of his parents within six months of each other some thirty-odd years ago, Barton had moved out of the eighteen-room house in which he and his siblings had grown up and into the bunkhouse. Small houses, he was fond of saying, put the mind aright.

Howard had a passion for books and spent much of his time reading. During season, he hunted. He ran the ranch single-handedly except for twice a year when he hired extra cowhands to help him work the cattle.

Sound travels far and fast out here in the big silence. You can hear a pickup crossing a cattle guard at five miles and an engine at two. Barton was on the bunkhouse porch in a rocking chair, hands patiently crossed over his stomach, waiting and watching as I drove up.

He smiled when I called his name.

"Is that you, Texana?" he said. "Thought I recognized the pickup."

Barton is a small man, trim and neat in his appearance.

"I don't know what brings you all the way out here, but you're mighty welcome," he said. "Sit down."

Barton settled back into the rocker and watched the horizon. His quiet was comforting. I felt entirely at ease with this man who had known my parents.

"I've got some trouble, Barton."

"I'm sorry to hear that. You want to tell me about it?"

I told him about the trail, about Pete's discoveries.

"You've got trouble, for sure," he said. "Something like this happened to me in '82. The Border Patrol spotted a trail on this place. Started flying over day and night, helicopters coming in low, spooking the cattle. I lost two good mother cows that broke their necks running into the fence. It got so the agents came on the place whenever they pleased, drove all over like they owned it. Finally I told 'em to get off and keep off."

He paused, cooling his remembered anger.

"Then they caught five Mexicans sleeping in one of the line shacks. They processed them right back to Mexico. After that, they came after me. Harboring illegal aliens, they called it. I'd made them mad, you see, telling them to get off my place. I knew Mexicans were crossing. I fed some of them and let them fill up their water bottles at the well. What was I supposed to do? Let them starve or die of thirst? But harboring, no. The agents knew the truth. They just wanted to make trouble for me. I had to hire a lawyer. Fellow from Midland. You need his number? I've got it written down somewhere."

"It may come to that," I said, "but right now, I need you and your plane."

It didn't take long to explain what I wanted.

"Will you do it?" I asked.

"You know the definition of a crazy person?" he said. "It's someone willing to go flying with a seventy-year-old pilot."

WE DROVE IN BARTON'S Jeep to the grassy airstrip.

The Skyhawk lifted into the air and turned southeast. Barton would follow the river.

"The Border Patrol is used to seeing my plane," he said. "As much as I riled them, I doubt they'll bother us, if they spot us. We'll keep low, off the radar like the smugglers do.''

"Have you ever seen a smuggler's plane crossing from Mexico when you're flying?'' I asked.

"Once, up at Valentine, I saw one shadowing a train to avoid radar. He stalled and burned. Mostly though, they fly at night or in thunderstorms when the Customs planes are grounded. A few years ago one passed over my place at two in the morning with lightning strikes going off like fireworks. Those pilots are risk takers.''

From five hundred feet the chocolate-colored river was a trickle in the middle of a cracked mud strip. Meager Polvo huddled against the rugged mountainside looking forlorn. It might have been a ruin except for the dozens of dogs and pickups. Everything was in hues of brown. Ahead, I could see the trading post, its metal roof reflecting the sun like a strobe.

Barton took the Skyhawk lower.

"There it is,'' I shouted, pointing.

The trail looked like a series of irregular scars in the rock-strewn earth. We cruised over the adobe village site. This is what I'd wanted the plane for: to follow the trail as far as we could.

Barton kept the trail on his side, spotting its traces as he flew.

"Looks like it's going to cut through the southeast side of the old Birley place,'' he said.

In the manner of locals and land, the Gamez ranch would never be called anything but the "old Birley place,'' until after it changed hands again. Then it would be called the "old Gamez place,'' the name always one behind the current owner.

We flew on.

"What's that?'' Barton said.

"Where?"

"Wait. I'll get in closer."

He swung the plane around and jockeyed it into position so I could see what he'd spotted.

"Whatever it is, it's big," I said.

An almost rectangular hummock of disturbed earth showed against the ground cover of rocky scree.

"From the looks of it," Barton said, "that mound must have been turned years ago. Let's take another look."

He turned the plane in a tight circle.

"The trail looks like it runs right into the east side of the mound," I said.

"Let's go out a few miles. Maybe we'll pick up something," Barton said.

But all we saw was Clemente Gamez's new entrance road, shining like a white ribbon curving around the rocky prominences of the land toward his house, itself not visible, hidden in a cup-shaped valley to the northwest.

"What now?" Barton asked.

"Back to your place."

It wasn't until we were ready to land that I realized what the hummock had to be: the underground house the long-gone doctor had built and abandoned.

With the ease of experience, Barton set down the plane.

A man of few words, Barton remained quiet on the short drive back to his house. I appreciated his reticence. There was no need to say what we both knew, that my troubles had just multiplied geometrically.

Had the trail passed across the Gamez ranch and beyond, it was likely being used by the *huachitos*, smuggling or not, to make connections with either Interstate

10 or the rail yard at Valentine. But the trail stopped at the underground house. I didn't know why it stopped there, but I did know it probably wasn't a good thing.

Barton parked the Jeep by my pickup.

"Don't go just yet," he said. "I want to give you something."

I leaned against my truck and waited.

In less than a minute, Barton was back.

"I've got a pair of binoculars, Barton," I said, staring at what he held in his hand.

"Not like these," he said. "Night vision. Ordered them out of a hunter's catalog so I could watch wildlife. On a real dark night, I can sit on the porch there and see every kind of creature."

"Are you thinking…"

"You might find them handy," he said.

SIX

A LIGHT BLUE PICKUP pulled up in front of Clay's clinic as I was getting out of my truck with Barton's night-vision binoculars.

I leaned back and dropped the binoculars onto the seat before walking over to greet Lucy Ramos, the postmistress, who was carrying a fat squirming puppy.

"Christmas present?" I said.

"For my youngest grandson," she said. "The pup's here for his shots."

"He's a sweetie," I said, patting the excited animal.

"Will you save a big box for me to put him in on Christmas Day?" Lucy said. "I'll get it at the sale."

Promising her I would, I waited until she was inside the clinic before retrieving the binoculars.

Until Lucy had mentioned tomorrow's sale, I'd almost forgotten my annual Christmas event, though the notice had been posted on the front door for two weeks. Each holiday season I reduce prices on all my inventory except hardware and ranch supplies.

Customers come from both sides of the river, and the day is one of my busiest. I had to unpack Christmas merchandise, stick price markers on each item and put up the tree.

I made pimento cheese sandwiches for a quick lunch, wrapping two for Clay and leaving them on the counter.

While Charlie and I put together the puzzle of the artificial tree, I told him what Barton and I had learned from our aerial scouting.

"Why do you think the trail ends at the underground house?" I asked Charlie.

"Maybe these *huachitos* are using it as a hideout from the Border Patrol, someplace to stay on this side until they learn the route north."

Illegals who made it to border cities of Mexico often didn't know much about where to go once they got into the United States, so those who could afford to hired men called *polleros* to drive them across and drop them in big cities well beyond the border checkpoints. The poorest, like the Mixtecs, lacked the means to do this. Nor did they have enough information about West Texas to know which way, beyond north, to go. Some illegals simply hid out by night, working day jobs until they accumulated a little cash, moving north by increments.

"The question is, what if the *huachitos* have something to do with this drug *jefe*," I said. "I don't have an answer, and I can't afford to guess wrong."

"Then we've got to find out what they're up to for sure," Charlie said.

I opened a box of bows, my only decorations for the tree. The first Christmas we'd had Phobe, I'd trimmed the tree gloriously. The bobcat, entranced by the bright balls and lights, had climbed it and brought it crashing down. The bows worked fairly well, though she occasionally tore off and shredded the lower ones.

After we finished the tree, I went to the storeroom for the Christmas merchandise I'd bought months earlier: photo-novellas, Spanish language melodramas; glass jars of brilliant candies in flavours like mango and chili powder; toys and nativity figures carved by a local man;

boxes of ornaments in green and red, the colors of Mexico's flag.

By four, I'd priced each item and arranged them on a table, thinking all the while of what Barton had intended by giving me the night-vision binoculars.

When Clay came in at four-thirty, he found Charlie and me at the coffee drinkers' table leaning over a topography map of Presidio County that I'd taken out of my map display case. I sell a few of the geological survey maps to the few adventurous bird-watchers who journey this far up the river.

"What are you two doing?" he asked.

"Plotting the best place to spy on the *huachitos* as they cross," I said.

"What are you talking about?"

I caught Clay up on what I'd learned from the flight with Barton and showed him the binoculars.

"You're not doing this," he said.

"No, we're doing it together, you and me," I corrected him.

"Us," Charlie said.

Clay had opened his mouth to protest, by the stubborn look on his face, when we heard the front doors open.

"I come bearing a gift," a big voice said.

Heavy steps crossed the brick floor of the front room and a bearlike figure appeared in the arched doorway to our quarters.

Father Jack Raff, his red beard streaked with white, stood there in black T-shirt, jeans and sandals, smiling and holding up a bottle of Jim Beam.

"Jack!" Clay and Charlie and I said in unison. Max ran to the priest and licked his hand.

"He thinks I'm a bishop, bless him!" Jack said. "Break out the glasses and let's toast my retirement."

Jack Raff, an Irish priest out of Chicago, had lived among us for five years before the Church moved him to an inner-city diocese back in his home state. For the past two years Polvo had lacked a resident priest.

"Retirement?" I said.

"I turned sixty-five in October," Jack said. "The archbishop suggested I minister to a convent of elderly nuns in Fort Worth. Hearing the confession of nuns is like being pecked to death by doves, so here I am. I'm staying at the Three Palms in Presidio until I find somewhere to live. Then, I'll grow tomatoes and propagate cacti."

When he first moved here, someone had given Father Jack a strawberry cactus plant as a housewarming gift. He'd been fascinated and soon the low front wall of the priest's house had been lined with pots of cacti he'd bought at the Chihuahuan Desert Research Center, which propagated them for sale. When Jack had left, he'd given the cacti to me. Most were endangered species that were disappearing from the desert on both sides of the border because of collectors who dug them up and carted them off in shoe boxes. Occasionally, a plant thief would be caught at one of the Border Patrol checkpoints, but not often enough to save the vanishing flora. The plant thefts had become so serious and well orchestrated that the federal Fish and Wildlife Service had put a special agent in place to try to stop them.

"I guess this means you want your plants back," I said.

"No hurry," Jack said. "The Houstonites have driven up real estate prices beyond a priest's stipend."

Clay got the glasses and Jack poured generous tots. After the first glass, I microwaved three frozen pizzas. We chomped down on food and caught Jack up on what had been happening during the two years he'd been away.

As the evening wore on, Phobe climbed onto my lap and fell asleep with her head on my arm. I stroked her absently, thinking of the many federal agencies I could name that were trying to catch drug smugglers. They were helped by the sheriff's department and state troopers, not to mention the special task force group. Even the Border Patrol admitted its first priority was drug interdiction. Big seizures were rare, and everyone involved got to claim credit and share the proceeds. And all of them might be watching Clay and me. I concentrated my thoughts on what Jack was saying and tried to relax as I listened to his self-deprecating story about his first months back in Chicago.

I rejoiced in the friendships of these good people, Jack and Charlie, across the river Pete and Zeferina, and on his mountainside ranch, Barton.

The border, the isolation and interdependence of life here, had forged our friendships. Nowhere else would the dynamic have been the same as in this place of many miles and few people. I could envision living nowhere else. My life was here, among these people. Without them I would never be the same. Jack had gone and now was back. Would Clay and I have to leave? Would we be able to return?

At the sound of gunfire and breaking glass, Phobe dug her claws into my legs for a leveraged leap halfway across the room. Clay dropped Nippy and bolted past me toward the bedroom and his revolver in the bedside table. Jack stared at the whiskey bottle as if he thought it had exploded. Charlie and I ran for the front, Max with us, and hunkered down behind the counter from where we peered at the windows and doors.

Clay passed Charlie and me, roaring, "Stay there."

Jack was on his heels. We jumped to our feet, and the four of us moved in a body to the front doors.

The windows on either side were broken. The one on the left had a small round hole and radiating cracks; the other had shattered completely. Charlie walked over and picked up something from the floor beneath the shattered window.

Clay opened the doors. Gun first, safety off, he stepped out onto the porch, Jack and I with him.

It was nearly dark. The front parking lot and the river road were empty.

As Jack and Clay walked out into the lot, I checked out the front of the building. Only the windows were damaged.

Charlie came out, closing the door carefully behind him to keep Max inside.

"We've got the date," he said, handing me a piece of paper. "It was wrapped around the rock that shattered the window."

He handed me a creased slip of paper.

22 *diciembre*, the printed message read.

"Come here," Clay called to us.

Charlie and I walked out to the spot where Jack and Clay stood looking intently at the ground.

"See the tire track where they turned around," Clay said. "They drove up from the direction of Presidio."

"I bet they positioned themselves to get away first, then shot out the windows," Jack said.

"The second window was broken with a rock," I said.

"I'm sure there were five shots," Jack said.

"Fired into the air, maybe, to intimidate," I said.

"Why would someone want to intimidate you?" Jack asked.

Clay and I looked at each other.

"I've no wish to intrude," Jack said, "but a trouble shared…"

"May be deadly in this case," I said.

"Then you definitely need a priest," Jack said.

I handed him the piece of paper with the date.

"Six days from now," he said. "The significance?"

Clay looked around cautiously.

"Let's talk about this inside," he said, putting the .45 on safety.

Max and Nippy stood immediately inside the doors and Charlie nearly stepped on the tiny Nippy, who barked fiercely and ran in circles.

I had to hunt for Phobe. She'd burrowed into the burlap bags in her basket in the laundry room. When I spoke her name, she shook her head free and looked at me, her big eyes more round than ever. I sat down beside her; she trembled under my hand. I made soothing noises and stroked her until the trembling stopped. When I left her, I closed the door so that she would feel safe.

Clay and Jack sat together at the kitchen table, Clay talking, Jack listening with concern on his face.

I went back to the front to see what needed to be done about the shattered window. Charlie had beaten me to it. The broken glass had been swept into a mound, and he'd cut a sheet of opaque plastic to fit and was taping it in place.

"Where'd you find the plastic?" I asked.

"Painter's tarp from your stock."

I helped him finish the taping, collected the glass in the dustpan and then we rejoined the others.

Jack looked at me encouragingly.

"I'm with you on this," he said. "I understand why you can't ask the authorities for help. It would be like

me asking the bishop for permission to leave the priest-
hood to marry. Even supposing he granted it, I'd be long
dead before we worked through the red tape.''

"The process can kill you," I said.

"Just so," Jack agreed.

"Do you have any suggestions?"

"It will take more than prayer, I can tell you," he
said.

He picked up the night-vision binoculars.

"The more you know and understand, the better," he
said, "provided you do everything you can to safeguard
your lives."

"Texana has our suitcases ready," Clay told him.

"I'm glad you're both realists," Jack said. "Now,
how can we find out when the *huachitos* will be on the
move again?"

It took us the better part of an hour to finalize our
plans. When Father Jack left, we went to the door with
him, making a show of his departure in case of watchers.

"Many thanks for the mighty fine food and drink,"
Jack said, giving his words a faint slur. "Give me a call
if you hear of a place I can rent."

SEVEN

TUESDAY MORNING, Clay had a ranch visit scheduled to help cull cattle, which means cutting from the herd cows and bulls past their reproductive prime. He canceled it, along with all nonemergency work.

I opened the doors at six, then cooked pancakes and bacon for three. Charlie and Clay were going to visit Pete and bring him in on our plan. It was too late for me to cancel the Christmas sale, so I would remain at the trading post.

I put down the pets' food bowls and joined Clay and Charlie at the table. We ate hastily and without conversation, still digesting our decision from the night before to determine, if we could, why the *huachitos* were crossing to the underground house. At this point any information seemed valuable. If they were bringing drugs across, they might or might not be connected to the *jefe* who threatened our way of life and our lives. We hoped that any information gained would help us find some way out of our dilemma. As Jack had pointed out, we had few options.

"Don't forget to put Phobe in the kennel," Clay said, as he and Charlie were leaving.

Too many people excited the bobcat, and children always wanted to play with her. Clay discouraged rough-housing with any wild animal, however tame. Bobcat play involves tooth and claw, used with a force that is natural to the bobcat, but painful to humans.

"Max can keep her company," Charlie said.

I let Phobe ricochet around the trading post, chasing Max and playing with her squeaky toy, until I finished the dishes. Then I brought out her carrier, big-dog size because Phobe is thirty inches long and weighs twenty-five pounds. She seems to think being put out is punishment, as it prevents her from participating in all our activities, which she takes as her right. If I tried to carry her out to the kennels in my arms, she'd jump and run.

After a wrestling match to get her into the carrier, Max trotted over to see what was going on and I called him to follow me.

Max ran inside the kennel as if he approved of the whole idea. I opened the carrier inside the run, but Phobe wouldn't get out, so I set the carrier down and left her to exit in her own time. I made sure the pair had plenty of fresh water, then I went back to get Phobe's squeaky mouse and her favorite stuffed animal, a teddy bear. I hunted for Max's rawhide chew, finally locating it under the table with Nippy, who couldn't get her tiny mouth around it, but had draped herself over it possessively.

She growled when I tried to take it.

"You have to go out, too," I said to her.

No matter what I'd promised Mrs. Gamez, the Chihuahua was sure to get stepped on if I left her inside during the sale. I could see Mrs. Gamez's face if she came back and found her dog's leg in a cast. Carrying dog and toys together, I returned to the kennel. Phobe still sulked in her carrier. I put Nippy in the run and tossed in the toys.

I hurried through last-minute chores, putting a box of plastic toys under the tree for the toddlers to play with while their mothers shopped, and stacking my old box record player with recordings of Christmas music. The sale began at eight. In a matter of two hours most of Polvo had come and gone, along with nearly as many people from *ranchos* on the other side, including Zeferina, who said she'd left Pete, Clay and Charlie poring over an aerial map. Between ringing up sales, I spent most of my time gift wrapping purchases.

Lucy Ramos came in at ten-thirty.

"I've got a letter for Clay," she said.

She reached into her pocket.

"Mail delivery? You'll spoil us," I said, joking.

Polvo's post office is a wall of wooden boxes in the front room of her house. We can pick up our mail from eight until ten Monday through Friday.

"You didn't come in on Friday to clear your box," Lucy said. "I thought it might be important."

Another thing I'd forgotten under the stress of events. I usually stop in at the post office twice a week. So much for sticking to routine.

"It wasn't mailed," Lucy said, handing me the envelope. "See, no postmark. Somebody put it straight into your box."

"I hope it's someone's payment for vet service," I told her, putting the envelope aside for Clay.

I gave her the box I'd saved for her. We picked out a wrapping paper with dogs and cats in Santa hats. Lucy bought puppy food, a leash and collar, and doggy toys. I wrapped them for her in a second box.

My last two customers of the morning were leaving as Clay came in from the back.

"Everything go okay?" I asked.

"Pete is ready," he said. "You forgot Phobe, didn't you?"

"What do you mean?"

"You forgot to put her in the kennel."

"No, I didn't."

Charlie walked in saying, "Where's Max?"

"You two must be blind," I said. "Phobe and Max are in the kennel together. Nippy, too."

"They're not," Clay said.

I was already moving and so were Clay and Charlie.

"I put them in right after you left," I said, staring at the empty kennel. "Phobe wouldn't get out of the carrier. Where are they?"

Clay went into the kennel. He reached down and picked up Phobe's teddy bear. A piece of paper was tacked to the front.

"I don't believe it," he said. His tone was black.

"What?"

Clay walked out clutching the stuffed bear in one hand, the paper in the other, looking miserable and shocked.

"This is a ransom note."

I snatched it from his hand. Charlie ran to look over my shoulder as I read.

$5,000 gets the dog back. Tell Gamez to get the cash ready. Someone will collect it. This is the only message.

"What about Phobe and Max?" I said.

"The kidnapper didn't expect them to be there," Clay said.

"This was planned? How could anyone know I'd have Nippy in the kennel?"

"The kidnapper either watched and waited for an opportunity," Clay said, "or—"

"Took advantage of the situation," I finished. "So it might not have been planned."

"Five thousand dollars is planned," Clay said. "Someone knows Gamez is rich and loves that little dog."

"I'll pay to get Max back," Charlie said.

I could hear the tears in his voice.

"We'll get demands for Phobe and Max, don't you think?" I said, watching Clay's face.

"I know people get kidnapped," Charlie said, "but dogs?"

"I'd read about a couple of cases in the vet journal," Clay said. "A pet disappears from a fenced backyard and the owners are notified that someone has found their pet safe but wants a reward for returning it. No one can prove the person returning the animal stole it, but the cops and the owners certainly think so. That's in cities, but this, here…it's no joke to take someone's pet."

"Maybe it's somebody who followed Gamez from Mexico," Charlie said.

"We'll have to call Señor Gamez," I said.

Clay just looked at me.

"All right, I'm the one who agreed to keep Nippy," I said. "I'll call."

"What about Mrs. Gamez?" Clay said. "You told me she said not to bother her husband."

"This is an emergency. He has to know. The note says get the money ready," I said. "Besides, you know Mexico's telephone system. It takes half a day just to get through to an operator. This can't wait."

I was afraid that Señor Gamez would be out, given his wife's instructions, but he answered on the first ring.

I identified myself. His voice was warm, his tone courteous.

"Señor Gamez," I said, "I'm so sorry to tell you this. Someone has taken Nippy from our kennel. They left a ransom note."

"What!"

"Yes, I'm sorry but it's true."

I read him the note.

"Of course I'll pay whatever this crazy person wants."

"Whoever it was, they took our pet bobcat and another dog—"

"Others! Why would they take… Five thousand, did you say? I'll have the money ready immediately. My wife, my poor wife. She'll be distraught. You know where she is?"

"Yes, she gave me her number in Mexico City. I thought she should hear about this from you—"

"No! You must call her. I can't tell her such terrible news."

"I understand. I'll call."

"Tell her to come back right away and all will be well. Tell her my exact words, please."

He hung up.

I called the number Jovita Gamez had given to me. The operator in Mexico City said she would ring me back when the connection was made. I settled down to wait.

At 5:43 the operator called and I was connected to Mrs. Gamez.

"How could you let this happen?" she said.

I made no excuses. I had none. I tried to reassure her by repeating her husband's words. "He said to come home and—"

"You called him?" she yelped into my ear.

"As soon as we found the note. He has to get the—"

She hung up.

For the rest of the day, we held out hope we'd get a call or another note asking for money for Phobe and Max. Charlie, clutching Max's rawhide chew, paced the aisles of the front room. Clay looked out the front window every ten minutes. Without mentioning the missing pets, I made a few calls to some of my regular customers to ask if they'd seen anyone around the kennels. No one had.

If anyone I knew had seen Phobe with someone else, they'd have called me. The whole community knew the bobcat at the trading post.

Just after dark, Father Jack and Pete arrived, dressed in dark shirts and pants. Clay and Charlie and I had already changed into similar attire. In spite of Phobe and Max having gone missing, we still had our plan to enact. I cooked spaghetti. We ate, then waited. Pete and Clay had agreed that nothing would happen probably until after midnight, but we'd decided to be in place by eleven, in case.

We looked comical, but I didn't laugh as Charlie used charcoal to blacken our faces. He and Pete and Jack took two river stones apiece from a pile on the counter.

Pete had selected the stones that morning and taught both Clay and Charlie how to use them properly. Father Jack had spent the afternoon with Pete, practicing.

"If you strike them together right," Pete told them, "the sound will carry half a mile. Our people used to warn the *ranchos* this way when the Rangers crossed looking for cattle they claimed were stolen. It's an old Aztec trick."

Pete's son Alejandro would strike the first signal from

the other side, if and when the *huachitos* crossed the river.

At ten, our usual bedtime, I cut off the light and we sat silently in the dark. At ten-forty-five, we left by the back door and divided, Pete and Father Jack and Charlie to move into place at intervals well away from the trail. It would be their job to pass by turns Alejandro's signal along to Clay and me.

We took his pickup, less noticeable in the dark than my white Ford. Clay drove, lights out, along the river to the new access road to the Gamez ranch. At the turnoff, he put the parking lights on, the way game wardens do when they chase a poacher. He kept to the gravel road for only two miles, cut off the parking lights and headed across country toward the underground house.

He stopped at the point, determined by Pete's aerial map, where a ridge would hide the pickup and allow us to overlook the trail's approach to the house. From here, we walked.

We moved out across a flat. The cool wind smelled of earth and creosote bush. Scattered clouds slid over a quarter moon. The ridge was a jagged black edge ahead of us.

The loose rock and tangle of lechguilla, cacti and yucca made it slow going. I could feel every aching joint in my feet, and my mouth was as dry as a cotton ball.

Just this side of the ridge there was a ravine. I stepped into it before I saw it and felt my feet slip. Only the rough contours saved me. I dug in my heels to slow my descent. It took both hands and feet to make it up the other side and onto the ridge top.

There, we positioned ourselves as comfortably as we could to keep watch in the quiet and the dark.

Over the next hour it grew cold. The wind dropped

off. A coyote began to yelp and howl, and the land came alive with a hundred high-pitched answers. The singing lasted for minutes and then died, letting the silence sweep back in.

I clutched Barton's night-vision binoculars and wondered if someday we would laugh about all this.

EIGHT

THE SOUND WAS resonant, high and ringing, fading as quickly as it came. Clay squeezed my hand. This was it. The *huachitos* were on the move.

By the luminous readout on my watch, it was an hour and twenty-two minutes before we heard the slight sounds of movement: the scratchy brush of ocotillo thorns against something, a breathy exhale that might have been a mule deer.

I lay immobile on my stomach, my chin in the dirt, and raised the night-vision binoculars to my eyes. The *huachitos* moved in a line, bent forward under the weight of packs made of canvas sacks tied together. Not one of the men was over five feet tall, yet the burdens under which they labored were nearly as large as they were. I guessed each man carried one hundredweight. Of…what? Heroin or cocaine was my borderwise guess. As the *huachitos* passed along the trail and closed in on the hummock that marked the underground house, I counted sixteen men.

I passed the binoculars to Clay and felt him tense as he took in what was happening.

Moments later, a narrow line of light broadened into a rectangle as a door opened on the exposed side of the house. I almost stopped breathing. Silhouetted against the light stood a man with disproportionately short bowed legs.

I reached for the binoculars so fast the cord was still around Clay's neck as I pulled them to my eyes to confirm what I knew was a certainty. The man in the doorway was the *jefe*'s gofer, the stranger who had come to the trading post.

Taking turns with the night-vision binoculars, we watched as one by one the *huachitos* filed into the underground house and then exited, without backpacks, and turned back down the trail, all in silence, like the night.

When the last of the *huachitos* had gone, the light went out. There was a rasping sound as the door closed, then the faintest click, like a padlock snapped into place.

I felt Clay's hand on the back of my head, pressing me flat. I counted five seconds before I heard another sound. Bow Legs was taking a pee. Sixty-two more seconds and a door slammed, followed by an engine starting.

As soon as we were sure the vehicle was moving away from us, we raised our heads, but, as we had done, the stranger drove without lights. I caught only the weakest gleam of the sickle moon's pale light on the chrome of the bumper as the vehicle vanished over a rise.

We waited, keeping still and quiet until the *huachitos* moved well out of earshot. Forty-five minutes after they had gone, we moved, easing our cramped legs upright and walking stiffly back to the pickup, careful to ease the doors closed. As we drove through the dark, I told Clay I'd recognized Bow Legs. When we reached the cutoff, Clay parked off the road, under the heavy shadows of the trees.

"You nap," Clay said. "I'll keep watch."

"You think he might cut back this way?" I asked.

"It's one possibility."

"And the others?"

"Pete's aerial map shows two old ranch roads crossing the Gamez place that originate from Pinto Canyon road. Just because the driver headed into the ranch doesn't mean he belongs there."

"Where did Pete get this map?" I asked.

I stock maps of the county, and the only ones available to me are topography maps and road maps.

"He wouldn't say, but it's got United States Air Force stamped on it," Clay said, a grin in his voice.

"Knowing Pete, I'll bet it's classified," I said.

"Do you think Gamez knows what's going on?" Clay asked.

"Just because the underground house is now part of his ranch? The *huachitos* are crossing our place to get there, but we aren't involved. But people—"

We froze at the sound of a vehicle coming from the southeast.

"It's Annie Luna's car," I said with relief, as a light-blue Honda Civic pulled up beside us and stopped. The young nurse, who lived at Polvo but worked in Presidio, rolled down her window.

"You two okay?" she asked, recognizing our pickup as we had her car.

"We're fine," Clay told her. "I had an emergency call. We were on the way home." He nodded toward the river. "I thought I saw a mountain lion moving through the brush."

Annie looked away then back. "I guess I scared it off. Do you know, I've never seen one."

She waved as she drove off.

"You're a pretty good liar," I said. "She's really late getting home. It's nearly daylight."

"Then we may as well go home," Clay said, starting the engine. "Bow Legs won't be going anywhere he can be seen."

At the trading post, Pete, Charlie and Jack waited for us inside, anxious to know what we'd seen. I explained while making coffee and piles of buttered toast. Clay scrambled a dozen eggs.

"So we know the *huachitos* are moving drugs," Pete said, as we filled our plates. "It won't be on their own. I've never heard of *indios* being more than tools for the smugglers."

"Forced labor, more like," I said. "I know the Tarahumara in Copper Canyon have had their crop terraces taken over. They grow opium poppies because they have no choice."

Newspapers in Northern Mexico like *La Jornada* asserted that at any one time thirty to fifty thousand pounds of cocaine were stashed in warehouses, truck trailers and underground bunkers around Ojinaga or sitting at clandestine airstrips in Chihuahua state. If someone wanted to shift a major load, there was plenty to go round.

"Think how little the capo is probably paying those Mixtecs," Charlie said. "In Juarez, they make maybe nine or ten bucks a day selling trinkets to tourists. Pay them twenty a load for hauling cocaine, and they'd have heavy pockets."

"So what we're saying is that instead of bringing one tanker across the border filled with thousands of pounds of cocaine," Father Jack said, "some guy has hired this bunch of men to haul one hundred pounds each as many times as it takes to get…how much?"

"The *huachitos* have been here ten months," I said.

"If they only crossed one night a month, that's sixteen thousand pounds."

"Some of it has to have already been moved out," Pete said emphatically. "So, small transactions may have been going on, but this time, on the twenty-second…"

"It's going to be a very big transaction," I said. "The *jefe* is meeting someone here at the trading post on the twenty-second who will hand over enough cash for however much is in the underground house."

"But why the trading post?" Father Jack asked. "Why not sell from that house?"

"Neutral ground," I said. "The *jefe* doesn't want his buyer knowing where he keeps his stash."

"Someone might shift it for him without paying," Pete added.

"Buyer and seller will make the exchange here," I said. "That way, the *jefe* can keep using the underground house for long-term storage."

"Is there anything else we can do?" Jack said.

"Pete, is there *any* chance some of the *huachitos* might talk to us?" I asked.

He shook his head. "They don't trust any of us *ladinos*."

Literally, the word means "foxes." It's what the *indios* of Mexico call anyone of mixed blood, meaning Mexicans and Anglos alike.

Our conversation stopped. We knew we'd uncovered part of the truth, but not enough to solve our problem. Smuggler, *jefe*, capo, whatever you called the man who operated the drug network, it was ugly. For the first time, I felt like I might lose this battle to save our way of life and our lives.

Our little group broke up. Jack would drive Pete to

the river crossing and drop him off. Charlie said he was
going to take a nap, though I knew he was thinking as
much of Max and Phobe as I was and would probably
sleep little.

When we were alone, Clay brought out an unopened
bottle of Crown Royal. Every year, my father gives Clay
a fifth of the premium whiskey for his birthday. The rest
of the time we drink the modest brands.

"I thought you were saving that for a special occa-
sion," I said.

"I think we need it now," Clay said, "don't you?"

He poured us fresh coffee, topped it up with whiskey
and joined me on the couch.

"Using Crown Royal for Irish coffee," I said. "Dad
would call that a sacrilege."

"Think what Jack would call it," he said, laughing.

"I don't know what to do," I said.

"I know. It's okay. I don't either."

"I thought I knew the border too well to misstep, but
this…"

"We'll be okay, whatever happens," he said, slipping
his arm around my shoulders.

"Right now," I said, "I'd give up everything if we
could just get Phobe and Max back."

"Me, too."

I sat up and turned to look at him.

"Do you think this kidnapping has anything to do
with the other, the *jefe*?"

"How do you mean?" Clay said.

"Some kind of insurance that we don't do anything
stupid, like call in the DEA."

"Why the ransom note for Nippy, then?" Clay said.
"Why not just take Phobe and say we'd get her back
after the twenty-second?"

"You're right, I'm too tired to think clearly."

"Why don't you take a couple of aspirin to help you relax?" Clay suggested.

"I think I will," I said, getting up and going to the kitchen cabinet where I keep aspirin handy. I filled a glass with water and tossed down the pills. That's when I saw the letter Lucy had delivered. I'd left it on the desk for Clay, but with all that had happened, he hadn't noticed. I picked it up and carried it to him.

"What's this?"

"Lucy brought it. Someone put it in our box, last week probably. I forgot to collect the mail."

Clay tore the end off the envelope and took out a letter. As he read he sat up, the expression on his face as much puzzled as worried.

"What is it?" I asked.

"Damned if I know," Clay said. "It's from Jovita Gamez."

He handed me the letter. It was handwritten on stationery embossed with the writer's name, the script fat and rounded, almost childish.

Señor Jones—Should I be unable to return to pick up Nippy within the week, under no circumstances are you to hand her over to my husband. She is my dog. She was given to me as a birthday present. I make this request to you as her veterinarian. I will return as soon as I can. Charge whatever you like, but keep her safe and do not let my husband know where she is.

"I'll bet she's leaving him," I said, "and she's afraid he'll fight her for custody of the dog."

"Why didn't she just tell you this when she was here?"

"She probably thought I'd ask awkward questions," I said. "Or refuse to take the dog, which I probably would have. I like both of them and even if I didn't, we don't need to be caught in the middle."

I crumpled the letter and tossed it onto the coffee table.

"No matter," I said. "It's too late now. They'll be lucky if either of them sees Nippy again."

Then I started crying. I was afraid we'd never see Phobe or Max again either, and after Sunday we might lose our home, too.

"Damn the *jefe*," I said, burying my face in Clay's shoulder.

I SLEPT FOR THREE HOURS and woke feeling as tired as if I hadn't rested at all. A hot shower helped. I blamed the tears of the morning on stress and fatigue, preferring to think I remained indomitable in the face of disaster.

It wasn't until Clay left on an emergency call about a dog trapped in a hole that I decided to take action.

I went to ask Charlie to watch the front, but I heard snoring through the guest-room door. Relieved that I had to account to no one for my actions, I put the CLOSED sign on the hook, locked the front doors, left a note for Clay and Charlie that I was going to the post office, a lie, and went to the wellhouse and opened the suitcase.

One hundred dollars is a lot of money to me, so my hand shook as I removed five bundles of bills totaling ten thousand dollars. I replaced the suitcase, stuffed the bundles into the pockets of my windbreaker and left.

NINE

FROM THE ACCESS ROAD to the Gamez gates took five minutes. As I passed over the cattle guard, the pickup broke a thin beam of light. The Gamez security had been enhanced since the open house. I had thought the drive from the gates to the main house would take more than ten minutes, but the new road, not yet washed by rain nor rutted by cattle trucks, was fast.

The road circled in front of the two-story building and ran back to the three outbuildings: a steel-sided equipment shed, a frame bunkhouse and a brick miniature of the main house that I assumed was a guest cottage. The house itself was distinguished only by size, being massive without grace or proportion. I parked beside Clemente Gamez's black Mercedes, got out and stepped under the twin-columned portico to ring the doorbell, wondering if the maid Jovita Gamez had mentioned would admit me or if her busy employer had left orders not to be disturbed.

Gamez opened the oversized glossy green door himself, smiling a welcome that seemed genuine, though concerned.

"You bring news," he said, "about my Nippy?"

"No, no," I said, as he stepped aside to let me in. "I came to see if you'd heard anything. The kidnapper's note said they'd be in touch with you."

"Let's go into the living room and sit down," Gamez said, going through to the wide white-paneled room with a row of French doors that looked out over the back of the property to the blue mountains beyond.

I sank into a crimson armchair; Gamez took its twin. We were in what the fancy house magazines call a "conversational area," one of several in the room. I've never lived in a big enough space to have more than one "conversational area," or more than two armchairs for that matter.

"I haven't heard anything," Gamez said, "but I have the money ready. Not to worry. And you, have you had any news of your pets?"

"None," I said tightly, trying not to tear-up again.

"Ah, coffee," Gamez said, as a heavyset middle-aged woman came in with a tray and served us.

While Gamez stirred sugar into his cup, I tried to control my emotions by scalding my tongue with hot coffee. It tasted of cinnamon, like the brew of Mexico.

After the maid had left the room, Gamez said, "I have faith that all will be well and Nippy—and your pets—will be returned."

"That's why I'm here," I said.

I set my cup and saucer on the mosaic-topped table next to my chair. Before I could explain myself, a telephone rang in the next room.

Gamez rose. "Please excuse me. I was expecting this call."

I nodded. He left the room. I felt too twitchy to sit still in the deep chair. I walked over and stood in front of one of the French doors and looked out at the deck and, beyond a line of desert willows, the outbuildings.

A Steller's jay flashed his blue wings from the branch of a mountain laurel growing in a huge pot on the deck.

I followed the bird's line of flight as it winged toward the sky until a greater movement caught my eye.

Someone had exited the bunkhouse and was coming in a straight line toward the deck.

I backed away from the window, spun on my heel and headed for the doors to the hall before I realized that leaving abruptly might give me away. I willed myself back into that crimson armchair.

My heart beating so hard that it hurt, I listened for all I was worth for any sound of those doors opening. Surely there was another entry for employees; I counted on it. I rested one hand over my eyes, as if I nursed a headache, and peeked between the fingers, all the while thinking frantically of how I should handle Gamez. The French doors remained closed.

I jumped when Gamez returned, apologizing for his absence.

"Now," he said, his voice revealing noting save polite concern, "you were telling me why you'd come."

"To ask if you'd had news," I told him, mustering a smile and trying not to jabber. "And to tell you how responsible we feel about the dog."

I got to my feet.

"You mustn't feel bad," he said. "I think things happen for a reason."

Amen to that, I thought, as he escorted me to the front door.

I drove home without regard for flying gravel. It gave me great satisfaction to think I left the son of a bitch's road rutted. At the moment it seemed the only damage I could do him.

I skidded into the trading-post parking lot and jumped out of the pickup almost at a run. Charlie came out the door and met me on the porch, his face lined with worry.

"What's wrong? Didn't you see the car? We've got a—"

"I know who it is," I said.

I grabbed his elbow and swung him around with me as I pushed through the doors.

One customer, a man in a khaki uniform, sat at the table drinking a Coke. I stopped my forward momentum instantly and put a smile on my face.

"Afternoon, Dennis," I said.

"Hey, Texana," Deputy Sheriff Dennis Bustamante said. "How'd the Christmas sale go?"

"Great."

"Glad to hear it," Dennis said, finishing off the last of his soft drink and getting to his feet. "One thing I like about the Christmas season, things are quiet. Even the smugglers take time off. Makes a change."

"Yes, quiet is good," I said, moving behind the counter to accept Dennis's money.

At the door, he turned around to wave, saying, "Merry Christmas."

Charlie and I stood still, listening until the deputy's Grand Marquis drove away, back toward Presidio where he lived.

I turned to Charlie. His face was sweaty with anxiety. I touched my forehead and felt matching beads of perspiration.

I took a deep breath. "The *jefe*," I said. "It's Gamez."

IT WAS HOURS before Clay got home covered with dirt from having had to dig the puppy out of a sinkhole. After he showered and changed, I explained all over again.

"I took some cash from the suitcase. I was going to

ask Gamez to offer it to the kidnappers if they would return Max and Phobe safe. Bow Legs was there. He walked right out of the bunkhouse, looking right at home.'

Clay skipped right over my trying to use drug money to buy our pets back, instead getting to the heart of the problem.

"I don't see how this information helps us."

"Maybe it doesn't," I said, "but I like knowing who my enemy is," I said.

Charlie left us after that, saying, "You guys got things to talk about."

"We can't stay here. We can go to Dad's place," I told Clay.

My father lived in a two-bedroom frame house on three thousand acres just beyond the Border Patrol checkpoint on Highway 67, which runs from Presidio to Marfa.

"That's not a long-term answer," Clay said. "We'll have to leave the county, probably the state."

"I know, but right now, until we know if Phobe is alive, we have to stay close. Later, we'll decide where to relocate. You be thinking about what you want to do. You have more options than I do. There's not much call for trading posts anywhere else."

"Maybe we can go to New Mexico, or Arizona."

"I've read it's easy to get a new identity. Think we can find someone with a computer to help us pick up new names from dead people?"

THURSDAY MORNING I packed our clothes. I'd lost all my family memorabilia in the fire that destroyed the original trading post, which made deciding what to take simple.

Thursday night Father Jack came by. We discussed the situation with him, but, like us, he could find no way out.

"If you go to the authorities, you'll get the satisfaction of seeing Gamez arrested," he said, "but that doesn't keep you alive long enough to testify." He turned to Charlie. "What are you going to do?"

"Hang around close to see if Max shows up," he said.

"Do we go to the Gamez party?" Clay said.

"Of course we do," I said. "If he gets Nippy back, maybe whoever took her will return Phobe and Max at the same time. At this point he's the only contact with the kidnappers. We have to keep up a front with him, don't you think?"

"I do," Charlie said.

"I bet one of Gamez's own people grabbed Nippy," I said. "Probably someone who wants a bigger cut than what he's getting."

Friday morning crawled by. I couldn't sleep, eat, or concentrate, and Charlie and Clay were no better. I spent most of the day washing windows, vacuuming and dusting, as if making things neat would make things better.

I knew I was in real emotional trouble when I started to repot Father Jack's cacti. I packed the two dozen pots into five boxes that Clay loaded into the bed of the pickup. Jack had said he'd see us at the Gamez party, intending his physical presence to provide moral support. I would turn over his precious cacti to him there. We'd decided to go on to my father's for the night. Who knew when or if we'd be back.

At one, we dressed for the party. Clay wore gray slacks and a twill shirt. I wore a moss-green jacket over a yellow blouse and pants. Charlie, whom I've never seen except in the most casual clothes, unearthed from the Caddy's capacious trunk a tweedy sports coat that he put on over his usual knit shirt. With his Levi's and tennis shoes, he looked like a college professor. Just as we were getting in the Caddy, Jovita Gamez arrived in a Presidio taxi.

She paid the driver, who did a U-turn in the parking lot and was gone before she walked over to where we stood staring in surprise.

"Is there any word about Nippy?" she asked.

"Not to us," Clay told her. "The kidnappers said they'd contact your husband."

"That's where you're going?" she said, seeming to notice us at last. "May I ride with you?"

"Of course," I said, introducing her to Charlie, who offered her a seat in the Caddy.

She thanked him gravely. Clay and I went to the pickup and followed Charlie and his passenger to the Gamezes.

TEN

EVERY KIND of vehicle, from ancient pickups to new Suburbans, filled the driveway and overflowed into the adjoining pasture.

Ahead of us, Charlie's hand came out of the Caddy's window, motioning to us to follow as he moved out of the parking line, apparently being guided by Mrs. Gamez, and drove around to the back of the house.

"Looks like the whole county showed up," Clay said as we parked adjacent to the deck.

As we got out, I glanced at the bunkhouse, but saw nothing except empty windows and a closed door. If Bow Legs was here, I assumed he'd keep out of sight.

Mrs. Gamez climbed the steps to the deck. Charlie waited for Clay and me to catch up.

"Mrs. Gamez said we could go in by the French doors," Charlie told us. "She's gone to find her husband. She asked me to hang around and drive her back to Presidio if she gets her dog."

Charlie's words seemed to confirm my idea that Jovita Gamez was leaving her husband, but being right about the Gamezes' domestic situation hardly mattered. We were here to find out if Nippy had been returned and hopefully our pets.

The party had yet to move out to the deck, where a buffet and tables had been set up. We crossed to the house and went inside. Mariachis played with loud enthusiasm. All of Polvo and much of the ranching community seemed to be in this one room, even John Henry, in a new flannel shirt and clean pants, clutching a large whiskey and staring at the drinks bar as if it were heaven. Father Jack waved at me from across the room, where he stood talking with Barton Howard.

Charlie hung back by the French doors. Clay moved into the middle of the room, saying he was going to watch out for our host and keep his ears open. I looked for where Jovita Gamez might be and followed my nose and instincts toward the door through which her husband had gone to answer the telephone the day before.

The room had a partners desk in rosewood, three leather chairs, a well of television screens for multiple viewing and another door opposite that was half-open.

I heard a high-pitched whine followed by Jovita Gamez's voice saying, "My precious."

I was at the door in an instant, eavesdropping without shame.

"She's perfectly fine, Jovita," Gamez said consolingly. "She's been right here with me the whole time—"

"You stole your own dog!" I said, shoving the door open.

Gamez didn't flinch, though his wife involuntarily tightened her hold on Nippy, who barked furiously until Mrs. Gamez quieted her.

"It was the only way to bring Jovita home," Gamez said.

She raised her head from kissing the dog. "I'm not going to stay. I have a plane waiting in Marfa—"

"Where are Phobe and Max?" I asked.

"Safe, as far as I know," Gamez said.

"Phobe? Your bobcat?" Jovita Gamez said, looking from me to her husband. "What have you done?"

"Nothing, my love," Gamez said. "A mistake. My *amiguitos* didn't expect there to be other animals with Nippy. Unfortunately, not being very intelligent, they took all three."

"Are they dead?" I said.

"Not as far as I know," Gamez said.

"You keep saying that," his wife said. "What does it mean? Where are these people's pets?"

Gamez, obviously irritated by the question, said petulantly, "I could hardly keep a huge dog and a bobcat here. The maid would have quit, for one thing, and it would have been impossible to keep secret for another."

I stepped forward. "Please. Where are they?"

"I've no idea," Gamez said.

"Where?" his wife said insistently.

"Jovita, please!" Gamez said.

Looking defiant, his wife crossed to the desk and reached her hand under the rim.

"Don't," her husband warned.

They stared at each other. I didn't know what was going on until a cold voice spoke from behind.

"*¿Jefe?*"

Gamez tried to wave him away, but I'd already turned.

Bow Legs stood there staring as if uncertain what to do.

Jovita Gamez said, "Carlos, where are the dog and bobcat?"

"Leave us," Gamez snapped.

Bow Legs, Carlos, backed out, closing the door behind him. I turned to face Gamez.

"I see you remember him," he said. "Keep quiet and

cooperate as arranged on Sunday, and I'll tell you where to look for your animals.''

I nodded, not trusting myself to speak.

''You can go now,'' Gamez said, and I did.

I found Clay leaning against the rail of the deck watching as white-coated waiters served barbecue.

''Where's Charlie?'' I asked, shouting over the noise. The mariachis had moved outside with the crowd.

Clay pointed. Charlie sat hunched on the bottom step.

I grabbed Clay's arm and pulled. ''Come on, let's go.''

Clay moved without question. I love the man for knowing when not to ask why. I touched Charlie's shoulder.

''I think we can get Max and Phobe back.''

Charlie jumped to his feet, his face brighter than it had been in days.

I kept moving as I explained what I'd learned and what I speculated. By the time we reached the Caddy, Charlie had his keys out. We drove as close as we could get to the front door. There was no one in sight. Charlie unlocked the trunk. We each lifted out a box of Father Jack's cacti.

''Group them around the front door,'' I said.

''Won't the Gamezes notice?'' Charlie said.

''Those two have other things on their minds. And none of the staff is going to question the Gamezes about potted plants. We can do this so quick no one will notice.''

We tossed the empty boxes into the trunk.

''We've got to get our pickup,'' I told Charlie. ''Meet us at the trading post and get the suitcase out of hiding.''

Charlie drove away. As calmly as we could, Clay and I walked back to the pickup and got in.

Clay didn't say anything until after we'd cleared the gates and were safely on the river road.

"How do you know Gamez used the Mixtecs for the kidnapping?"

"He referred to the kidnappers as *amiguitos,* little friends."

Clay's eyes left the road to give me a stunned look.

"You're betting a lot on one word," he said.

"I'm betting more than that. Our lives are at stake here. He knows I can name him for what he is."

"But you're sure?"

"Yes."

"Mind telling me why?"

"It's the border, it's Spanish, it's how the language works and the mind behind it thinks. *Amiguitos* is descriptive and derisive. The Mixtecs are little, but they're not his friends. He's contemptuous of them and the word shows it... Okay, so this is no time for a linguistics lesson. I just know. It's knowledge based on experience. Trust me."

The trust was the easy part. Getting Clay to let me go to Huachito alone was the hard part.

"Absolutely not," he said.

We stood in the trading post parking lot beside the pickup. Charlie gripped the suitcase, ready to put it in the truck if Clay gave in.

"They know me," I said. "They won't see me as a threat. That gives me time to explain what I'm doing there."

"They shot at—"

"John Henry kept going over there. They had to stop that. Gamez would have told them to keep people out. They didn't shoot at Pete."

It took some time, but finally Clay agreed to park his pickup right by the crossing and wait there.

"If I yell you can be across in seconds," I told him.

Charlie set the suitcase on the seat beside me. I made the crossing so slowly the pickup barely stirred the water. As I neared the far side, I honked the horn three times to let them know someone was coming, then pulled up onto the bank and stopped.

The men moved out of the village huts one by one until they had gathered into a knot that inched toward me like a threat, then stopped ten feet away and stood staring with their round black eyes.

I opened the door and stepped out.

"*Buenas tardes, señors. The jefe* sent me with a message. Your work is done. You're to be rewarded. But first you have to give me the dog and the bobcat that you took, on his orders, from the kennel behind the trading post."

The men looked at one another and muttered. One man, carrying a .22 rifle, stepped forward a pace, removed the cigarette from his lips and flicked it away.

"How do we know you come from the *jefe*?" he said.

I reached into the pickup, pulled out the suitcase, set it on the ground and opened it so they could see the contents.

One of the group stepped forward. Rifle Man pushed him back with the barrel of the weapon and advanced on me. The others followed a few paces behind and crowded around us. Rifle Man knelt, lifted one bundle, looked up at me and grinned. He slammed the lid shut, lifted the suitcase and handed it to another man that might have been his twin. Saying something I didn't understand in what I assumed was Mixtec, he motioned toward the village. Three of the men trotted off.

The man with the suitcase moved off after the runners. The others turned and followed him.

Rifle Man and I stood there looking at each other.

I heard spitting and snarling. Two of the men were returning with an animal carrier between them. The third man followed, leading Max on a rope leash. I had to make myself keep still and not run to get Phobe. Max had no such reservation. He gave one piercing bark, broke from his keeper and ran straight to me. Standing on his hind legs, front paws on my shoulders, the dog licked my face soggy.

I told Max to sit. I looked in the door of the carrier as the men set it down. Two glowing round eyes stared back. I opened the pickup door, and Max leaped into the front seat. I turned to get the carrier, but two of the men were already lifting it into the bed of the pickup. I forced my legs to hold me up for five more seconds until I could get in beside Max. As I closed the door, Rifle Man came close to the window.

"We can go home now?" he said.

"Yes, señor, you and your friends can go home now."

He nodded.

I started the engine, reversed, turned and crossed to the other side.

On the riverbank, Charlie sat behind the wheel of Clay's pickup, engine running. Clay stood in front of the truck. He'd been watching through a pair of binoculars that he keeps in his vet bag, handy for finding sick livestock, which tend to go off by themselves.

I gave them a thumbs-up as I drove past. I kept going until I parked in front of the clinic. Charlie pulled in right behind. Clay came around and removed the carrier.

Max was so excited to see Charlie that he tried to climb through the window instead of waiting for the door to open, but Charlie stopped him before he could get stuck.

As badly as I wanted to see Phobe out of that carrier, I had one more vital chore.

I ran for the door and went straight to the telephone on the wall by the kitchen counter.

"Let him be home," I said as I dialed Billy Deed, whom I've known all his life. His mother, Maria, until her death six years ago, had been my best friend since childhood.

But Special Agent Billy Deed, with the federal Fish and Wildlife Service, wasn't home. His machine picked up. I left a message: "Billy, you know those shipments of endangered plant specimens you've been trying to stop? I think I've identified the shipper. His name is Clemente Gamez, the man who bought the Birley place. There are pots of rare cacti lining his front steps. He owns property in Mexico, so it would be easy for him to smuggle plants across the river, too. There's one thing, he may leave town tomorrow. I heard his wife say a plane was waiting at the Marfa airport. Be careful, Billy, I think this man could be dangerous."

As I hung up, a smiling Charlie came into the kitchen to open two cans of dog food for Max, who hugged his master's side for reassurance. I went out to the clinic, where Clay was shampooing Phobe in the dog bath. Bobcats by nature love water, and in this Phobe was no exception to her feral relatives. She tentatively batted a paw in the suds swirling around her legs as Clay rinsed off the soap.

"How is she?" I asked anxiously.

"Filthy," Clay said adamantly. "Evidently, they were afraid to let her out of the carrier or feed her. She's lost some weight, but not too much. Mostly, she was thirsty.''

"But no permanent harm?"

"None," Clay said. "Did you make the call?"

"I got the answering machine and left a message telling him everything I could."

It was vital to our safety that Gamez not associate Clay or me with any drug raid, but he had no reason to associate us with a search by the Fish and Wildlife Service looking for endangered plants, nor would he have a clue where the plants had come from. The attention of any federal agency would keep him from following through with the drug deal set to go down at the trading post in one day's time.

"So we keep the bags packed until we hear something," Clay said.

"We wait and we hope."

WE DIDN'T HAVE to wait long. At eleven-forty-five the next morning we heard the throbbing of helicopter rotors and ran outside to see three Hueys flying low and fast to the northwest.

The telephone call from Billy Deed came at six-thirty that evening.

"I got your message." Billy said, his tone elated. "He had cactus plants sitting right on the front steps, all on the endangered list. Gamez couldn't show us even one receipt to prove that he'd bought them. But you won't believe what else we found."

"Tell me," I said.

"We had a search warrant ready for the house and outbuildings, based on finding the endangered species. What really got us curious was this bowlegged guy who tried to run. Turns out one of the closets in the house was stacked floor to ceiling with cash. The Customs agents actually cheered. It looks like we've got more than a plant smuggler. We called in the DEA, and they got a warrant for the whole ranch. We already found a hidden landing strip in the mountains.''

"What about Gamez?"

"We've got him and the bowlegged guy in custody."

"That's amazing, Billy," I said, feeling like cheering myself. This was better than I'd dared hope.

"The DEA has moved to have Gamez's bank accounts frozen if we find more than cash," Billy said.

"You know, I seem to remember an old abandoned underground house in a notch of land along the southeast boundary of the ranch," I told him. "Gamez bought it for the river road access."

"You know something you're not telling me?" he said.

"Call it local rumor."

"That's good enough for me. And, Texana, thanks."

ELEVEN

"I KNOW YOU'RE CLOSED Sundays," Deputy Dennis Bustamante said, as I answered his knock at the door, "but you might want to open up today. I'm not going to be the only one needing gas."

"What's going on, Dennis?" I asked.

"Big news," he said. "Billy Deed's made a huge drug bust. Black tar heroin stashed head-deep in some bunker owned by that Gamez guy."

"No kidding," I said, turning on the pump switch so Dennis could fill his dual tanks with diesel.

"The DEA is trucking it out today," Dennis said. "Everybody in law enforcement is out there taking a look. Billy's going to get a promotion out of this. They'll confiscate the ranch, all the vehicles, furniture, everything. They found a million in cash in the house."

He started toward the door, stopped and turned to say, "Wonder who'll buy the old Gamez place?"

"I wonder," I said, smiling at him.

After he'd pumped gas and paid, I locked up again, then went to the back. Charlie was in the yellow recliner; Clay was stretched out on the couch.

"Who was that?" Clay asked.

I explained. He lifted his feet, and I sat down beside him. We watched as Phobe rocketed from table to chair to couch, where she nestled against me, shoulder to shoulder, purring. Max rolled on his back on the floor like a puppy, then settled in his favorite place, at Charlie's feet.

"It's early, but I'd like to break out the whiskey for our guests," I said to Clay.

"Are we expecting company, or do you mean Charlie?"

"I invited Father Jack and asked him to pick up Pete and Zeferina."

Clay got out the Crown Royal and six tumblers.

When the others arrived, I put out the casserole dish of sirloin hash with eggs, which Charlie had cooked, a plate of biscuits and a pot of coffee. Clay filled the tumblers and handed them around and I made the toast.

"To enduring friendship."

We drank.

"To prayer and preparation," Jack said.

Everyone filled their plates. Clay and Charlie and I caught the others up on what had happened since Friday and the Gamez party. When the hash was gone and the coffeepot empty, I handed out envelopes to Pete, Charlie and Jack.

"Christmas presents?" Jack asked.

"Bonuses," I told him. I could smile now at the word.

Pete gave his envelope to Zeferina to open. She looked astonished when she took out the cash.

"What is this?" Jack said, opening his.

"Three thousand three hundred and thirty-three dollars."

"Is this your money?" Pete said. "'Cause if it is—"

"It was part of the suitcase cash," I said.

"But you told us you gave that to the *huachitos*," Jack said.

"I did."

"And they're gone," Pete said. "The village is deserted. I can graze my goats anywhere I like now."

"But I forgot about the ten thousand dollars I'd stuffed into the pockets of my windbreaker," I said.

"Without your help," Clay said, "we'd have lost everything. So no arguments about not taking it."

"None given," Pete said, grinning.

Someone pounded on the front door of the trading post.

"I'll get it," I told Clay, who had risen. "It's probably somebody else needing gasoline."

As I walked to the front doors, I could hear Clay telling the others to put the money in their pockets.

Looking handsome and authoritative in his uniform, Billy Deed stood on the porch holding Nippy in his arms.

"I need a favour," he said. "This is Gamez's dog. He asked if you would take it."

"For how long?" I asked.

"He won't be out of jail in the dog's lifetime," Billy said.

"What about Mrs. Gamez?"

"Gamez says his wife left Saturday morning and is probably in Switzerland by now," Billy said.

I took the Chihuahua from Billy, who had to get back to work, and rejoined our guests.

"What's that dog doing here again?" Clay said.

"I guess you could say she's our Christmas bonus."

He reached out to take her and she bit him.

"We've got to break her of that habit," he said.

"Then she'll need a new name," I said.

"Why don't you call her *Jefe*," Jack said.

A MERRY LITTLE CHRISTMAS
by Tom Mitcheltree

ONE

HE COULDN'T HELP from giggling to himself, the idea of it all so delightful that it had to escape from the merry thoughts that danced in his head. Life was usually such a tangle with little sense to it, so that when something so spectacularly perfect came along, he couldn't let it slide by. Not something like this. Not something so layered in irony that it only could be contrived—but it wasn't contrived, and that made it incredibly precious. He giggled again. Oh, what fun he would have with this, he thought.

He stumbled about in the dark until he found the spot. The full moon had faded behind clouds, but this area was in the open. He could see now to walk from mound to mound, while he sought out the right grave. The grave was in a distant corner of the cemetery, on the side of the open area the farthest from the town of Jacksonville, which was laid out below the hill where the Pioneer Cemetery was located.

This field held the remains of the disenfranchised: the early settlers too poor or too unfortunate to afford a plot in the cemetery proper where headstones were required. The remains of many a gold miner, dance-hall girl and crooked gambler were buried here, temporary residents of Jacksonville when it was a booming, gold-mining town nearly a century and a half ago. Most had met grief by crossing paths with a knife or a bullet, some meant for them, some gone astray.

The Chinese laborers had been buried here, too, at one time, until their relatives had earned enough money to send the bones back to the homeland. As best anyone knew, all the Chinese buried here were now gone. The grave sites left were each recorded in a book faithfully kept over two centuries by people like Adam Shipper, the man who now stood over an oblong indentation in the soil. He was on the cemetery board, and he took pride in the fact that he had found and identified every grave in the cemetery, making sure that the records were straight, or straightening them out if they were wrong. That was how he discovered this grave. It was the only unrecorded grave site in the cemetery, and finding the identity of the man who occupied it had grown from a curiosity to an obsession for Adam.

Not anymore, though. He'd finally solved the riddle. The answer to it had delighted him. When he had known what it was, he had laughed with such childish glee that he'd actually wet himself. He'd been so pleased with the perfection of the answer that he hadn't even bothered to be embarrassed by his wet drawers.

Tonight was the reward for his efforts. He was going to have a lot of fun with this. By the time he was done, his invited guest would squirm, and he would take infinite pleasure in the squirming. Not until he'd had his fun, and his guest had suffered the angst of it all, would he tell that he planned to keep the secret. To share it with the rest of the world would devalue the pleasure. Yes, he'd probably get some recognition, and, yes, there might be a brief moment of glory, and, certainly, all would have a good laugh as he had had, but then it would, like these sorts of things do, fade away. Besides, he wasn't out to hurt anyone by it.

If he did share it with the rest of the world, the pleasure would be short-lived. As long as he could keep it a secret between the two of them, then the pleasure would last the life of each.

He heard a noise behind him. He turned to see a familiar figure walking toward him, the shape a little sinister emerging from the shadows of the cemetery in the dead of night, but far from frightening because he knew who it was.

He smiled broadly and gestured toward the grave. "I wasn't sure you could find it."

His guest, arriving with a cane in hand, walked to the spot and looked down at the sunken grave site with its deep, dark scar running its length, the illusion created by the shadow that filled the indentation in the earth.

"A credible piece of research you've done, Adam."

Adam smiled, pleased at the compliment. It was all of that and more. The work he'd done was brilliant, and the solution to the puzzle, the name of the occupant of the unregistered grave, was derived from genius. *Genius is,* he thought, *the right word—not an exaggeration.*

The call he had made to his guest was the thrust of the knife. He couldn't help now, considering the joy he felt, to keep from twisting the blade a little. It wasn't often he could make a person like this quiver in fear, lest someone else knew what Adam knew. Few others would take this kind of thing to heart or fear its revelation. That's where the fun came in with his guest. He would push his friend's discomfort to the limit before he admitted his intention to keep the secret between the two of them.

"Better your family than mine," Adam said, fighting to keep a straight face.

The visitor stared at the sunken spot of earth. "What are your intentions?"

"My intentions?" Adam laughed. "Nothing illegal, I assure you." If the light had been better, the other person would have caught the twinkle in Adam's eyes and known the joke for what it was, but the light was not good; the moon, though full, was pale and distant. "I'll have a good time telling the story. I suspect I'll be telling it for years to come, and I suspect those who have heard it a dozen times won't be tired of hearing it a dozen times more, as perfect a tale as it is."

Adam did manage to stifle a laugh, but his face twisted with the effort, and what the other person saw in the shadows was something that resembled a sneer.

"Yes, I'll love the telling of it...."

The cane came around quickly, with force, and when it slammed into the side of Adam's head, it was with enough power to leave him standing, but stunned and nearly senseless. He struggled to push through the shock of the blow and the scrambling of his senses. He opened his mouth to protest, but before he could, his body finally caught up with the assault on it, and his knees slowly buckled so that he sagged to the earth, first coming to rest on his knees before toppling over sideways and then rolling into the indentation of the grave on his back.

Looking a bit like a fish out of water, his mouth tried to form words, but instead it simply repeatedly puckered while nothing issued forth but air and a spray of spittle.

Still, something untouched deep in his brain was still having a chuckle, recognizing that this addition to the story would be the cherry on top of the ice cream sundae.

His eyes slowly refocused and his thoughts began to clear. He was seconds away from finding his voice again, so that he could get out the words that would reassure his guest of his harmless intentions. Before all of that could happen, though, he saw a flash of moonlight on a shiny surface and then he watched with fascination as the tip of a blade, the end of a sword that had been cleverly sheathed in the barrel of the cane, came to rest on the soft spot between the top of his breastplate and the bottom of his Adam's apple. With a concentrated effort that brought all of his addled senses together, one word managed to explode from those puckering lips: "Wait!"

His friend did not wait. The visitor leaned against the handle of cane attached to the blade of the sword, driving the tip through the soft flesh of the throat, between two vertebrae in the neck and a foot down into the grave below.

Adam thrashed about and thought the last thoughts that rushed through the minds of men who knew they were soon dead. With the blade of the sword thrust through his throat, he could not speak the final words that came to his mind, something to the effect that this hadn't been a very good idea after all.

From somewhere in the town below, a Christmas carol drifted up to the cemetery, and a few flakes of snow began to fall.

TWO

BUNDLED UP for the cold weather, Paul Fischer sat on a bench next to the duck pond in Lithea Park in Ashland, Oregon. He sat quietly and stared at the ripples on the surface of the pond, a cup of coffee cradled in one hand, a newspaper folded on the bench beside him and a cinnamon roll in a white paper bag resting in his lap. At this moment he was thinking nothing. That is to say, he was thinking the word ''nothing'' while attempting to reach a state of zero thought. This was both a failed exercise and futile. Paul Fischer would have to stop breathing in order for him to stop thinking. Thought was at the core of his being.

He shifted his attention briefly to the black water of the pond that stood out in sharp contrast to the three inches of white, white snow that had accumulated overnight.

Paul was bored. Not only was he bored, he was also depressed. Christmas vacations had never been this way for him before. First of all, he didn't have his boys with him. This was the year they spent Christmas with his ex-wife, and even though she talked of moving to Oregon so they could all be closer together, she still hadn't made up her mind to do it. The boys were spending Christmas in New England.

Second of all, he was caught between two women.

Yes, he had finally settled in with Pam Livingston and had thought he was comfortable with that, until last summer. He met a widow with a young daughter and suddenly his emotional life was turned to turmoil. He still didn't know if he loved this new woman or not, but he did know that something wasn't right between himself and Pam.

Pam handled it as she handled most things in life, with a quick, determined decision. She invited him to leave and not come back until he knew for sure that she was what he wanted. The other woman, whose father had died recently, said she needed time and space to put her life in order. She hoped that she and Paul could try again the following summer. In the meantime, he was left out in the cold, he thought, and then laughed, because he was out in the cold both literally and figuratively.

Finally, he was pushing forty. He wasn't there yet, but the idea of being so close and his life in such disarray didn't help an already bleak Christmas holiday.

He tried to think of something positive. Okay, he was still trim at six foot and two hundred pounds. His blue eyes were still his best feature, and his light colored hair still hadn't produced a gray hair. The coeds on campus still flirted with him. He thought those positives might delay a midlife crisis, except he felt as if he had been through a full-life crisis already.

He was back to being bored.

He considered writing something. As an associate professor of English, he still lived by the rules of publish or perish, but with two biographies to his credit and a dozen articles on the secrets to good research printed in a variety of educational journals, he was well ahead of his fellow department members. Besides, he had been brought in to help the department revamp its curriculum to a level that matched the school's recent transition from a college to a university. "No more party school of the south," his department chair had said. "Southern Oregon University students will now have to work for a living."

When Paul wasn't in the classroom teaching, he was cloistered in the faculty library revising goals, rewriting curriculum and evaluating possible new textbooks. He had written more in a year than he had written in the past five, and now he was tired of writing. He needed a break from it.

For the first time since he had come back to Southern Oregon, he actually questioned his choice to tie his life so closely to that of Pam Livingston's. He had made few friends. He had dated no other women. He had participated in no social event that wasn't tied directly to the university or to Pam's job as a lawyer. His fellow faculty members finally stopped asking him to socials, finally stopped sending him invitations.

He was about to reach for the newspaper beside him when the unmistakable tinkle emitting from his pocket ruined the moment. "Not here, not now, not ever," he mumbled. Certainly not in the shadow of the Shakespearean theater that loomed above him, over his left shoulder. He reached in his pocket and pulled out the cell phone to answer the call.

"Paul Fischer," he said into the thin, plastic mouthpiece.

"Mr. Fischer, I'm sorry to bother you, but I've nowhere else to turn."

Close the gates. Load the cannon. Raise the flag. His defense mechanisms switched on. The last time he'd been asked to help someone in this valley, he'd been the pawn in the midst of another's agenda. Not again, not now, not ever. Fortified with his rectitude, he cautiously asked, "And who might this be?"

"Minnie Shipper."

All those defenses to the ready, and he didn't have a clue. "Have we met?"

"No," she said.

"Then I'm at a loss."

"Nora Ryan recommended you."

Everyone to his battle stations, his mind screamed. Nora Ryan was the curator of the Jacksonville Museum, and she had been in the middle of two episodes in his life that he was ready to forget. He couldn't imagine Nora recommending him for anything unless she had developed a misguided sense that she owed him something.

"And just what was it she recommended me to do?"

The woman's voice faltered as she said, "Find out who murdered my husband."

He found himself staring into the mouthpiece of the phone, trying desperately to see the woman on the other end. What kind of a joke was this, and what did Nora Ryan have to do with it?

"Again, I'm at a loss," he said.

"My husband was killed two weeks ago. His body was found in the Jacksonville Pioneer Cemetery. He had been stabbed to death."

"Certainly the police..." Paul let the words trail off. He had read the story in the paper, but not very carefully. The man's name had not rung a bell.

"The police haven't a clue."

"I doubt that I could do better," Paul said. "Besides, I'm a college professor not a sleuth."

"But Nora said this would be just your sort of thing. She said that if anyone could figure it out, you could."

"A murder?"

"My husband discovered something. A secret from the past. He said it was too good to be true. I think that's what got him killed."

Now he was beginning to understand. "Something from Jacksonville's past?" he asked.

"Yes."

One of the biographies he had written had for its subject a doctor from Jacksonville who lived at the turn of the last century. His research had led him into a fascinating story about three sisters who lived at the same time. By the time he had finished researching both stories, he had learned a great deal about the deviant behavior of Jacksonville's pioneers. He didn't see, though, how that knowledge could help in a murder case.

"I don't think I can be of much help."

"Please!" she begged. "My husband had a heart of gold. He couldn't hurt a fly. Everyone liked him. I need to know." She broke into tears, the sobs clear on the phone.

He hated tears, his more than anyone's. "I'm sorry," he said.

"Just meet with me. Let me explain face-to-face. You are, truly, my last resort. I can't stand the idea of someone killing such a wonderful man and getting away with it."

He was beginning to cave in; he could feel it. He threw up one last line of defense. "Has Pam Livingston got anything to do with this?"

"Pam Livingston?" Mrs. Shipper sounded truly surprised. "The businesswoman?"

"The lawyer."

"Of course, the lawyer. Why would she have anything

to do with this? I've never met her before, and I doubt that my husband knew her, either.''

He relaxed. He had spent a nervous five months staying on his side of the valley, avoiding both Medford and Jacksonville. He wasn't ready to run into Pam. That was childish, he knew, but he also knew he had unresolved issues with her. Right now it was easier to hide from them.

''Can you come to Ashland?''

''I don't drive.''

The sinking feeling sucked at his innards. He would have to go to Jacksonville, a place he swore to himself to avoid.

''I will meet you anywhere in Jacksonville but at the museum.''

She named a coffee shop/bakery on the main street. He agreed to see her later in the afternoon.

He turned off the cell phone and stuffed it back in his pocket. A murder? He really didn't think he could help, but the idea of it beat being bored.

THREE

SINCE HE HAD MOVED OUT of Pam's house and rented a small place of his own in Ashland, this was the first time that Paul had crossed the valley to Jacksonville in those five months.

He knew it was silly to keep distance between him and Pam. She knew where he was because she forwarded his mail to him. She had his phone number. She could keep up on his activities just by calling any number of shared acquaintances. He could follow her exploits in the newspaper. She had just finished a case in which she had kept a killer off death row who by all rights belonged there. He had murdered a lesbian couple because he hated lesbians. Although the victory on her part didn't gain her a lot of popularity in the community, it gained her respect in the legal profession. Her firm was expanding. It was moving into several cities. She had plans for it to move into other states. Pam was an ambitious woman. She thought Paul came up a little short in that category.

As he turned onto California Street, the main road going through the heart of Jacksonville, he felt comfortably at home. He couldn't see that anything had changed in the small town nestled into the corner of the valley. It still clung to its quaint, mining town heritage, with many of the buildings original to the 1800s still in place and with others built as nice reproductions to keep the theme alive. The town was now an attraction to tourists, and it had everything from a jazz festival to a pioneers day celebration to draw people to this corner of the valley.

Paul had fallen in love with the relaxed character of the town. He had enjoyed walking down the sun-baked streets and smelling the history that seemed to radiate back from the soil. Small towns with character were a disappearing breed. The city fathers seemed to recognize that fact, and now the main focus of the town seemed to be to keep its character.

By the time he found a place to park a block and a half from the bakery where Mrs. Shipper said she would meet him, the sun had already turned the snow to slush. The valley didn't get much snow, and when it did, the snow didn't stay around very long.

As he walked up the sidewalk, he spotted two bookstores that he had liked the last time he was here, and another shop that specialized in collectibles. By the time he reached the bakery, he was kicking himself for taking so long to get back to a place he truly liked.

Mrs. Shipper was waiting for him when he walked into the bakery. She sat at a small table, the only other person in the room besides the woman behind the counter. She stood as soon as he entered, and she greeted him. "Mr. Fischer," she said, stepping forward to offer her hand to him.

Round. That was the first thought that came to Paul's mind as he took the hand and shook it. Her face was round, accented by graying hair cut short and curling in at the ends to hug the near-perfect oval of her head. Round also was her body. She reminded him a bit of a snowman, round stacked on round stacked on round. Even her fingers were pudgy and round.

She sat back down and he slipped into a chair opposite her. "You really must have some pastry," she said. "Everything here is good. You can't go wrong."

"I think I will start with coffee and perhaps a cinnamon roll," he said. He turned toward the counter where the girl behind it motioned him to stay seated. She would bring his order. He turned back to Mrs. Shipper. "I am flattered," he said, "that Nora Ryan can find it in her heart to recommend me to you, Mrs. Shipper, but I'm afraid I'm not the expert she has made me out to be."

"First," she said, poking at a cheese croissant that sat on a plate in front of her with a fork, "you can call me Minnie. Second, you weren't recommended for your knowledge of the obvious. Whatever got my husband killed wasn't generally known, or the police would have found the killer by now. Adam had discovered some information that almost no one else knew."

The coffee and roll were slid in front of Paul by the girl. She set a receipt next to him, but before he could do anything with it, Minnie reached across and took it from him. He could have argued with her about who was to pay, but already he sensed the Minnie was a much stronger woman than she looked.

"Perhaps you should tell me more. You are making some assumptions...." He let that trail off.

She responded. "Adam Shipper was a good man. He was a good father and a good husband. He was on the school board, he was on the church board of directors, he was on the library board and he was on the city council. He was even on the cemetery board. He was well-liked by everyone, which helped him to be successful in business. He had a one-man realty office, but he was so good at selling homes that people from all over the valley used him. He was a great provider not only for me but for our four children. I don't know of a person who didn't like him.''

Paul could think of one person, but he let the thought slide. "You are saying, then, that no one had a reason to kill him."

"I'm saying that whoever killed him probably liked him, too."

Paul couldn't keep a short laugh from slipping out. Mrs. Shipper smiled at him, also appreciating the irony. "The police have ruled out a stranger-to-stranger attack?"

"Adam was wonderful about leaving messages. I'm on the library board. On the night he was killed, I was at the monthly meeting. He left a message on our answering machine saying that he would be home late, that he had a wonderful joke to play on a friend. That was the last that any of us heard from him. He was found the next day in the cemetery."

"And the police think he met the friend there?"

"Jacksonville Cemetery is a lovely old cemetery, but in the dark of night it is not a warm and friendly place to be. Even our children stay out of it at night. If those of us who know and love it stay out of it at night, I can't imagine a stranger wanting to go there alone. Adam went there to meet someone. We're all very sure about that."

"A friend."

"As I said, Adam was loved by everyone. Because of his involvement in so many things, his friends numbered in the hundreds. The police have not been able to get a handle on this case because of a lack of suspects. Unlike most people who might have an enemy or two, Adam had none. Whoever killed him was indeed a friend, and those Adam had by the gross.''

Paul nodded. He didn't doubt what she was saying. People feared attacks by strangers, but more than likely a murder would be committed by someone they knew: a family member, a relative, an acquaintance or a friend. ''If indeed the police have so few potential suspects, I'm not sure what I could do that they couldn't do better, considering my limited resources.''

She reached across the table and patted him on the back of the hand. ''The reason you will have it so much easier than the police,'' she said, ''is that you will not be looking for people, but you will be looking for the wonderful joke that Adam discovered. Find that and you will find the person who killed him.'' She leaned back in her chair, beaming.

How simple it was, he thought, for her. ''If I were to do this,'' he said, ''I'd need a starting point. I assume Adam left some papers behind.''

''Adam compartmentalized,'' she said. ''When he worked on the cemetery board, his records remained in the little administration building in the cemetery. He kept a desk at the district office for his school-board duties. He had another desk in a storeroom at the church. Of course he has a space at city hall, and another one in Nora Ryan's office at the museum. His real-estate papers stayed at his Realtor's office. He never brought anything home, by design. When he was at home, he wanted to focus only on me and the children.''

''Would I have access to all these spaces?''

''Each has been emptied out, boxed up and the items sent to me. The realty office is as he left it. Since you are not on the board, the cemetery's private records won't be available to you, but most of what is in the private records is available in the public records."

"And how do you know that?"

"Because that was Adam's goal when he was selected to the board. He made the records available to the public."

"All of them?"

She folded her arms on the table and leaned toward him. "Something got him killed. I doubt that it was a public record. Adam was a good man. His killer needs to be punished for taking this good man from us."

Paul looked for something in the face across from him that would give him a reason to say no. He wanted to see grief so consuming that it defied reason. He wanted to see an obsession for vengeance. He even would have settled for a hint of stupidity. Instead, he saw intelligent eyes. He heard a simple appeal for justice. He sensed that this woman had complete faith in his ability to find the answers for her. He found nothing that he could hang a "no" on and feel good about it.

"This really isn't..." he started to say.

She held up a hand to stop him. "Adam was a successful businessman. That alone left me financially comfortable. Adam also was a worrier when it came to the welfare of his wife and children. He carried far more insurance than he should have. I can and will pay you handsomely for your time. If you don't think you can help, I will understand, but I won't understand if you don't at least try first."

Paul, too late, realized that Mrs. Shipper was a very clever woman who understood that the simple and direct approach in life was often the most rewarding, a fact that Paul himself had never been able to master. "I'll look into it," he said. "But no promises. Let me poke around for a day or two and then I will get back to you. And I'm not interested in making money on your misery, Mrs. Shipper, but if I have expenses, I will ask for those to be reimbursed.''

"That would only be fair," she said.

He nodded in agreement. It was fair. And besides, what else did he have to do with his time?

FOUR

PAUL HAD ONE ABILITY in his career that was both the prerequisite for his success as a student and a teacher and the vital ingredient for his professional success as a writer: he was a master at research. If the key to Adam Shipper's murder was recorded somewhere, Paul was the one likely to find it

He said his goodbyes to Mrs. Shipper at the door of the bakery, promising to meet with her soon to go over her husband's papers, and then strolled back toward his car. He changed directions before he reached it. In those few paces he realized he had to do something he had been avoiding. He needed to bring himself back into contact with some of the people whose lives had been nearly fatally mixed with his. On top of that list was Nora Ryan, the curator of the Jacksonville museum.

Once again he stood in front of the museum, a two-story brick structure that dated back to 1883. The complex had character. The museum and the old jailhouse next to it, now an annex of the museum, sat on their own block, surrounded by a low wall that was stone-capped. Old, giant oaks and alders shaded the lawn in the summer; pathways and picnic tables surrounded the buildings. Nothing had changed here in the two years since Paul lasted visited the museum. He doubted if much had changed here in the past fifty years since the museum was opened. He climbed the steps to the front entrance, walked between white columns and entered through the double doors.

To each side of him were curved staircases that met in a landing in the middle and led to more steps to the second floor. He walked over to the set of stairs on the right and glanced up to see if the portrait was still there. It wasn't. A painting of three sisters had hung on the wall halfway down the staircase, and it was this painting that had drawn him into a series of adventures here.

He moved to an open door that was set back under the second staircase. Nora Ryan sat at a rolltop desk with her back to him, busily reading through some papers in front of her. As he watched her, she suddenly put the papers down on the desk and slowly turned in her swivel chair to face him. She hadn't changed at all, Paul thought. Her hair was still cut short, and, despite its gray, the style made her look much younger than he knew her to be. And, yes, she was still an attractive woman, nicely dressed, and by her bearing still supremely confident in herself, despite the fact that it wasn't that long ago that she fled the valley for fear of her life.

"I thought you were going to retire," he said.

She slapped a hand on a knee and laughed, a habit she had when she was about to say something sarcastic. "Thanks to you, I didn't have to."

They both had a smile on their faces. Paul realized for the first time that he was actually fond of this cantankerous old woman who'd helped make his life miserable at one time. "How are you, Nora?" he asked.

"My main battle right now is fighting retirement. They keep trying to shove me out the door, and I keep digging my fingernails into the doorjamb."

"That bad?"

"No, not really. The effort is halfhearted on their part, while my resistance is lionhearted. They quake in fear of a real battle, so they let me stay."

He didn't ask who "they" were. Nora, like Don Quixote, would find an enemy to battle even if one didn't exist. She was a woman who was not at peace unless she was in turmoil. "I'm sure they are no match for you."

"I'll use you for a reference," she said. "A word from a hotshot college professor ought to be worth something. How's your return to the valley been?"

He laughed. "Like you, I seem to be able to create chaos where none existed before."

"Life must be treating you pretty well. You look as handsome as ever."

That was a stretch on her part. He'd spent too many hours locked away in his office or his classroom, and he hadn't gotten the kind of exercise he was used to, nor had he taken in much sun. In his mind he was pale, out of shape and on a downhill slide toward forty. Handsome wasn't a word he would use for himself.

"I suppose you know about me and Pam."

Nora's face always reminded Paul of an owl with its wide, round eyes. The smile remained on her features, but he could see the eyes take on a hard focus. "The only thing that surprises me is that it lasted as long as it did between the two of you."

"I suppose you're right."

The eyes kept their focus, looking for whatever clues might be hidden in the features of his face. "She's a busy woman. She hasn't got time to be a wife or a mother—she hasn't got time for a man."

He didn't come to talk about Pam. Nora couldn't offer a thought he hadn't had himself. He turned the conversation to the point of his visit. "I actually came to see you. I've just left Mrs. Shipper, and I understand you recommended me to her. I'm not sure what to think about that."

The smile faded from Nora's face. "Adam Shipper was a silly man who people loved to love. He was totally dedicated to both his family and to his community. He'd loan you a buck if you needed it. He'd give you the shirt off his back if you asked. He'd volunteer for anything if it had Jacksonville's best interest in it. He was on the museum board. He was the reason they couldn't ease me out at sixty-five. Like his wife and everyone else in the community, I want to know who killed him. As you already know, the police in Jacksonville are damned near helpless unless it involves a parking ticket."

"I may be equally effective, but tell me everything you know about Adam Shipper and what happened to him anyway. I've been blessed with dumb luck, so who knows...." He let that trail off intentionally. He wasn't yet confident that he could do anything to help.

"Come in and sit down then. This will take a while."

He looked around for a chair. As usual, the office was overflowing with everything from old weapons to old tools, from paintings leaning against the wall to boxes filled with papers. He finally found a chair under an ancient wedding dress that had been draped over it. After looking unsuccessfully for a place he might hang the dress, he finally settled on draping it over a stack of cardboard boxes filled with books.

As he slid the chair across from Nora's, she began to tell him about Adam Shipper. In the end, the story was like the one told by Mrs. Shipper. Nora added a few more details. Adam headed a Boy Scout troop. Adam was deeply involved in bringing Gold Rush Days back to Jacksonville, a popular celebration fifty years earlier. Adam headed a food and clothing driving for the less fortunate during the Thanksgiving and Christmas seasons. Adam was involved in the blood drive.

When Nora finished her narrative, Paul asked the only question that came to mind. "Can anyone be that good?"

Nora laughed. "Not from where we stand," she said. "Adam, on the other hand, came from a different mold. He was blessed with enthusiasm and energy, and, bless his heart, he wasn't the most intelligent man on Earth. That's not necessarily bad. Everything was pretty simple and straightforward to him. Black and white. He didn't let himself delve in the gray areas, because, to be honest, I don't think he knew that there were gray areas. Simple heart, simple soul."

"Enemies?"

"I can't think of a person who didn't like Adam. A few have been exasperated by his simplicity, but that same simplicity of soul endeared him to them. The only one he crossed horns with was Thelma Clay, but that was a pretty common practice and it was done in a good-natured way."

Thelma Clay. He remembered the name from some place, but it wasn't Clay. "Thelma Clay?"

"The former Thelma Clay-Harrison. Her husband died about ten years ago and left her a tidy fortune from car dealerships. She's gone back to Clay. Henry Clay started the first Presbyterian church in town during the gold rush. He was named for Henry Clay, a distant relative, the famous statesman and orator. Thelma's pretty big on her pioneer connections. She thinks that's the only thing that really counts."

Now he remembered the name. Henry Clay. His name

had come up somewhere in his research, something interesting tied to it, but it hadn't anything to do with the Bakers so he had passed on it. He wondered now what it was. "Any serious disagreement between them?"

"No, no," Nora said, chuckling. "She either didn't like what Adam was proposing, or she wished she had thought of it. With one of her boys running the Presbyterian church now, and the other being groomed for state politics, she hasn't been as active in civic duties as she used to be. She's too busy pushing her boys."

"Could a stranger have killed Adam?"

"Paul," Nora said, "you got a good look at this community when you were here before. We're tucked up in the corner of the valley, out of the mainstream. We get a summer crowd, but this isn't summer. Tramps and bums don't come this way. Besides, no one in his right mind would hang out in Jacksonville Cemetery late at night."

"Adam was up there, and from what I understand, he was murdered there. He either was taken there against his will, or he went there voluntarily."

The owl eyes blinked; Nora slowly nodded. "That's why I thought of you. You have a way of seeing things clearly."

Paul got up. "Where do I start with this Adam thing?"

Nora shook her head. "I wish I could help you there. The only thing he told Minnie was that he was going to play a joke on a friend. A couple of hours later he was dead."

"It must have been a hell of a joke," Paul said, and then he walked out of Nora's office.

He walked from the museum, but not back to his car. He didn't stop until he reached the entrance gate that led to the cemetery. The cemetery had been there for more than 150 years. It contained the remains of most of the notables from Jacksonville's history, famous and infamous alike. Even Adam Shipper, killed in the cemetery, was buried there as well.

Paul followed the steep road that curved around the hillside to the cemetery on top. Despite the cold, he was sweating by the time he reached the graves. The front part of the cemetery contained the remains of early residents of the town. The family plots were laid out in squares that might contain the remains of a dozen or more ancestors. Deeper in, the cemetery branched off in two directions. One was a modern burial ground that lacked the ornate headstones, statues and monuments that gave the older site its character. In the other direction was a ragged ground where the Indians, the Chinese laborers and the poor had been buried. Many of the graves had been marked simply by an indentation in the ground where cheap coffins had long ago collapsed. Few had headstones.

In the center of all of this was a small building that was part maintenance shed, part office and part guide to the location of burial plots. Paul started here. It took him a while, first getting his bearings with a map of the cemetery that indicated plots by number and then by tracking numbers and names. He wasn't looking for the remains of anyone in particular. He was trying to locate the spot where Adam Shipper had been murdered. From what Mrs. Shipper had said, and from the newspaper accounts he had read before coming to Jacksonville, he had a pretty good indication of the spot.

It took him a while to find what he was looking for. What looked neatly arranged on the map wasn't quite the same in reality. One family plot ran into another without a divider between them. As he worked his way back through the cemetery, he discovered it was bigger than he remembered, mainly because he had stayed in the oldest part the first time he was here.

Finally he found the open area. Here the ground was pitted with indentations. The fact that he could find the spot at all, and then that he could find the exact grave site where Shipper had died, was a credit to Adam. As a member of the cemetery board, he had painstakingly researched every grave in the cemetery, and, where there were no markers, he ordered white stakes with numbers on them that were then driven into the ground at the head of each burial spot. He had then put together a complete registry that was located in the office and available to the public.

Paul stood next to the spot where Adam died. Even in the light of day with the warmth of sunshine, the location had a chill to it. The spot was in an open area, but it was near a line of trees that even now had deep shadows to them. At night, with just moonlight, the trees would have easily obscured anyone, even someone a few feet from Adam.

This was not a spot that a man would go to late at night to meet someone he feared, Paul thought. And Nora was right. This was not a place where a stranger would seek refuge at night.

The mystery was clear. Why this spot? Why late at night? Why did he want to meet with the person who killed him? A joke? Was there really a joke?

Paul didn't doubt for a minute that it was meant to be a joke. Shipper was too transparently simple to be malicious. On the other hand, someone had apparently missed the joke and concluded, totally against character, something else. A threat? A dark secret? Blackmail?

Something to kill for. Whatever Adam knew, it had to
have been a huge threat to someone, Paul thought.

When he reached his car, he spotted a folded slip of
paper under one of the windshield wipers. He glanced
around, looking for a sign that would explain a parking
ticket. No signs. He slipped the piece of paper out from
behind the wiper and unfolded it. On it, written in childish print, were the words: STAY OUT OF THIS!

Paul refolded the paper and stuck it in his pocket.
Again he scanned the sidewalk and street up and down
the block. He wondered if someone was watching him
at that moment. He saw nothing suspicious. As he slid
behind the wheel of his car and shut the door, he made
up his mind. He'd look a little deeper into this.

FIVE

PAUL RENTED a small house in Ashland, far enough from campus and a few blocks from the main drag to give him some privacy. Fortunately, the house had once been a guest house for a large Victorian home, and it was nestled in a neighborhood of old, restored and expensive houses. The owner of his house, who lived next door to him, rented exclusively to college professors.

The expensive homes guaranteed for Paul that he would not have to live surrounded by his students, under their eyes, so to speak. With his own driveway and a tall screen of arborvitae between himself and his landlord, he didn't have to worry about prying eyes at all, not that he had anything to hide. He'd kept himself in solitude for these past few months, licking his wounds, as he liked to think, but in reality completing a grieving process for a marriage lost, for love lost, for family lost and for life as he knew it lost. When the time came, he would reemerge into the social life. That time, though, was still in the future.

His driveway ran between a six-foot fence and the arborvitae. At the end of the drive was a rectangular area large enough for the small house, a parking space next to it and a deck in back. This, too, was surrounded by either a fence or arborvitae. He liked it. In the middle of the town, he was enclosed in an urban garden, the fence lined with trellises that supported wisteria and honeysuckle. In the summer the deck was layered with potted plants that were tended by the wife of the owner, who would call and arrange a time with him to care for the flowers.

When the weather was good, he enjoyed sitting on the deck at night in the dark while nursing a glass of wine. For a man who still needed time to heal from what life had thrown at him so far, this was the perfect spot for it. Nights were quiet. The neighbors, cultured and sensitive, never let loud voices cut through the night, nor did their televisions or stereos blare. Instead the night had a quiet hum to it, some of it electrical, some of it human, but none of it distinguishable.

The house was small, but it didn't lack the essentials. The galley kitchen was open to the combination dining and living room, separated by a counter that acted as a breakfast bar on one side. At one end of the kitchen was a door that opened into a combination pantry and laundry room. The front door of the house opened onto the living room. At the other end of the room, just beyond a small dining table, were the French doors that opened onto the deck. In the center of the wall of the living room, just opposite the kitchen entry, was an alcove with three doorways in it. Two led to small bedrooms. The third led to the bathroom that separated them.

One bedroom Paul used for a study, with a sofa that unfolded into a bed for when his boys came to visit. He kept a computer there on a desk, but this he used for e-mail and correspondence. The computer was also loaded with games for the benefit of the boys. He kept a laptop for work. When he needed to print something or needed to connect to the Internet, he would bring the laptop into the study and hook it up to the printer or phone line there. Most of his work he did at the dining-room table or on the deck when the weather was good.

On this night he had the dining-room table covered with the papers he had collected from Mrs. Shipper. Adam was a busy man, active in too many things to keep track of in his head, so he was a note taker who relied on half a dozen planner notebooks to keep himself organized.

Mrs. Shipper was a big help. Paul counted on the town's sympathy to get the things he wanted from her. For that reason, instead of going after them himself, he sent her. She was surprised by the request at first and then delighted, because it meant that Paul had decided to help her out, and it also gave her something meaningful to do. She was able to provide Paul with more information about Adam's involvement in the school, library and cemetery boards. The city council records were public and easy to come by. Nora Ryan provided information from the museum board meetings.

Paul made stacks on the dining-room table. Each stack represented Shipper's work on each board, and an additional stack represented his work with the scouts, charity drives and clubs. Simply sorting the material had taken Paul several hours and then when he was done, he had to stand back and marvel at how much Adam had done. The man had been a dynamo of social responsibility. Paul hoped something on that table would explain why Adam was murdered.

Paul had learned his lesson well the last time he was in the valley. Back then his house had been broken into and research material stolen. The first thing he did was make copies of everything on the table, using the copier he owned in his study, and then he scanned the material into the computer and stored that on a read/write CD.

Everything would be preserved in triplicate, and none of it would be stored in the same place. One copy would remain here. Another copy would go into the file at his office on campus. The CD would go into his safety deposit box at his bank.

Once organized, Paul took one stack at a time to a comfortable chair in the living room and began to read. He had begun his reading with one notion of Adam Shipper, and by the time he had finished the last stack of information, he had arrived at a different one. Adam Shipper was a dynamo, but that came with a price. Although most found it necessary to work with him because he was the driver and doer, not many liked him for it. Adam stepped on toes. Lots of toes. He would slap backs, cajole and humor to get his way. And most of the time he would get his way.

Of course he would. To defy Adam came with a risk. With so many fingers in so many pies, Adam had influence. Anger him and you weren't honored by the city council for your work in the community. Anger him and you did not sit on the budget committee for the school board. Anger him and your name was overlooked when invitations went out for the church social. Yes, he had a smile for everyone, but he also kept a scorecard for everyone he knew.

Paul finished the last stack late in the evening. He poured himself a glass of wine and sat for a long time, thinking it all through. Social slights didn't get Adam killed, he was pretty sure, but other things that Adam did incited temper tantrums.

While on the library board, he took offense to a highly popular series of books that were the rage among young readers. He felt that beneath the surface of the plot were themes too adult for sensitive young minds. He never explained in detail what those themes were, but he did get the librarian to put the books on a closed shelf and require a parent to check them out for a child.

He had more success on the school board. He got the books removed from the library altogether. The protests to both boards were vocal and heated, but Adam prevailed. He didn't ride out as well the next protest to the school board. Adam had pushed through a proposal for mandatory summer school for students who fell a few points behind the state standards. Parents supported this at first, until they found out that Adam set a mark so high that nearly half the students would be required to return for summer school. The support among parents faded quickly, especially when they found their child on the list.

Adam tried to bully the board into maintaining his stand, but the political body that it was collapsed under public pressure. They tabled the issue until the following school year, over Adam's protest. Adam was angry because of the weakness of the board, but he wasn't as angry as some of the parents were with him.

On city council he managed to stir up a mess first when he insisted that the city hire a part-time animal control officer and then rammed through a leash law for dogs. In this community it had been the tradition, in the pioneer spirit, of letting the dogs run free. Not only did he get a leash on the dogs, he next set out to require cats to be licensed. He argued that a licensing of cats would raise enough money for a full-time animal control officer. This enraged more than one family who not only found that their dog had been hauled off, but now Adam wanted them to pay for the privilege of having a cat. Adam's enemy list grew.

Still, Paul couldn't see the man being murdered for

any of these reasons. Even when confronted with the angriest of citizens, Adam had a knack for deflecting the anger with humor. Someone steaming with anger usually walked away laughing after a confrontation with Adam.

Paul nursed the glass of wine. Something Adam had done apparently had turned someone murderous. He would look at real-estate transactions in the morning. A book in a library wasn't likely to get someone killed, but a transaction worth thousands of dollars would do it. He fell asleep in the chair with that idea in mind.

SIX

HE WAS ON HIS THIRD CUP of coffee for the morning, again reviewing Adam Shipper's papers, when his phone rang. Sometimes his boys or his ex-wife called at this hour because they knew they would catch him at home. He picked up the phone, deciding as he did that it had to be the boys.

He couldn't have been more wrong. "Paul Fischer?" a pleasant female voice asked.

"Yes it is," he said.

"Could you hold for a moment. Pam Livingston would like to talk to you."

Something close to panic swept through him. He and Pam had not talked much since he moved out, and they hadn't communicated at all in the past three months.

When she came on the line, she simply said, "Paul." Her voice was as it always was, filled with confidence.

"Pam," he said, trying his best to give away nothing in the tone of his voice.

"Is there any chance you could stop in and see me this morning?"

No, he thought, but there was every chance he would. "I'm kind of busy, Pam."

She got to the point. "The past is the past, Paul. I just picked up a client, and I am going to need your help defending him."

A short laugh escaped him. He didn't know what caused it. Was he incredulous? Was he suspect? Or was he just surprised? Whatever, his mind was still searching for the catch. "I don't know how I could help you."

"The client's name is Jimmy Cross, and he's been accused of killing Adam Shipper."

Paul's brain raced through the information he had just reviewed. Jimmy Cross? He didn't remember the name. "I don't even know who Jimmy Cross is, but even if I did know, I don't see how I can help you."

"Come in and see me and we'll talk about it. The police have focused on Jimmy because they can't think of a single reason why anyone else would want to kill Adam. That's where you come in. If anyone can find another reason, you can."

"I'm sure even Medford has private investigators. I still don't see how I can—"

She cut him off. "I think you can help, and I think this is a good time to put the past to rest."

"What time?" he asked. Face it, he thought. If her client did do it, he didn't need to run around playing investigator for Minnie Shipper.

"I'm free at eleven. We could have lunch afterward."

"I'll meet with you, but we'll have to see about lunch."

"Good. I will see you at eleven."

As soon as she was off the phone, Paul dialed a number. When Nora Ryan answered at the library, he asked, "Who's Jimmy Cross?"

"Word travels fast," Nora said.

"Pam Livingston."

"Yes, I heard she got the lucky draw."

"Lucky draw?"

"The lawyers in town do a rotation of court-appointed

attorney for those who can't afford one. Pam usually shuffles it off to someone in the firm, but I heard she decided to take this one.''

''And you haven't talked to her?''

''Is that skepticism I hear in your voice? Pam and I are not close. We never have been. We were united once by a common goal, but that's in the past. I might run into her at a public function now and then, but we don't spend hours on the phone sharing girl talk.''

That brought a smile to Paul's face. He couldn't imagine either one of these women as ''girls.'' Both, he thought, were honed from the same marble slab, one with few imperfections. He brought the conversation back to the purpose of his call. ''Jimmy Cross?''

''Adam made more than a few people mad at him in his day. He had a narrow view and never harbored a doubt that he might be wrong about something. That could get to you if you had to work with him, and lots of people had to work with him. None ever got mad enough to kill him. Jimmy Cross, though...''

He waited, but she just let the words trail off. He was forced to prod her. ''Jimmy Cross?''

''Jimmy Cross was in Adam's Boy Scouts troop. He accused Adam of making sexual advances.''

''Why does that sound all wrong, even to me who never met Adam?''

''Because it does sound all wrong. Nobody believed Jimmy for a minute, and the humiliation that came with it for him drove him out of town. His parents had to take him out of the high school here and put him in one in Medford.''

''Is there any evidence that ties Jimmy to the murder?''

''You'd have to talk to the police about that.''

"One more thing." He didn't expect an honest answer, but he thought he might learn something from a dishonest one. "Pam and I are meeting at eleven. Should I be worried?"

Nora was quiet for some time. When she did answer, she sounded almost thoughtful to Paul. "You know, Paul, if I were a single man, half good-looking, I'd run down the street clicking my heels and shouting for joy if Pam wanted to see me. You've got lots of good reasons for feeling differently. But, again, that comes from the past and now it's time for you to reevaluate your feelings. Don't ask me to do it for you. Pam's a complex woman. It takes a man to appreciate that."

The phone went dead in his hand. Typically of Nora Ryan, she hung up without saying goodbye.

When he arrived at Pam's office, an attractive woman sat at the reception desk. "You must be Paul Fischer," she said, standing to reach across her desk and offer him a hand. The hand lingered in his.

"I am Paul, yes," he said, reluctantly letting go of the hand, letting it fall away, the fingers slowly dragging through his.

"I'm Pam's new legal assistant, Jenny Ahrens. She has talked a lot about you, and now I can see why."

Jenny directed him to double doors where she tapped lightly and then opened one enough to stick her head into the office. She said, "Paul is here." She then pushed both doors open.

When Paul walked in the room, Pam was already up from behind her desk and walking toward him. She took his hand and dragged him to the sofa. "Come over and sit. We have some catching up to do."

He followed along, offering little resistance, but he still was alert. Once they were seated, she took one of his hands again in both of hers and said, "Relax. You don't have something I want, except a good knowledge of Jacksonville history and a nose for good investigation. My client may need both of those talents."

"I think you might be giving me too much credit."

She squeezed his hand. "I think you might be giving yourself too little credit. Why don't we have lunch together, and I will detail everything I know for you. Then you can decide."

He could smell her perfume. She was still the most beautiful woman he had ever known, and he still marveled at the thought that they had spent two years together. He had to remind himself once again that during those two years he was allotted only a small part of Pam's life, and it hadn't been enough. She, on the other hand, expected complete dedication.

Pam walked them to a nearby restaurant that was neither fancy nor expensive, but it was crowded, and once he had his meal served and eaten, he understood why. The food was excellent. Pam arranged for a table in a corner, one that was set back from the rest. As she explained, a lot of lawyers and city officials ate here, and this table was intentionally set back from the others for private conversation. That consideration was another reason it was a popular spot.

As they ate, Pam outlined the case against her client. He had accused Adam of inappropriate sexual advances, he held a grudge against Adam because the boy was made out to be a fool for bringing the charges, he had made threats against Adam's life and he had no alibi for the time that Adam was killed.

"All that is circumstantial," Paul said. "Do they have any physical evidence?"

"Not that they've shared with me yet, but they do

have the boy locked up and have convinced a judge that he is a flight risk, so he stays locked up. My client claims to me he is innocent, and I'm sure we will go to trial."

"Why would the DA push such a flimsy case?"

"We have a new DA. He and I are not close. I won't even pretend to tell you I know what motivates him."

"What is it you want me to do?"

"I need you to come up with alternate theories for Adam's death. Not just wishful thinking, but concrete reasons why someone might be mad enough at Adam to want him dead. I can make a circumstantial case go away in a hurry if I can find a few other people who might want Adam dead."

"According to Jacksonville lore, Adam was a saint."

"And according to Paul Fischer?"

"He was a saint, but…"

She tilted her head back so that her hair fell away from her face. This was when she was most beautiful, Paul thought, when her features were fully exposed. Her face was perfect: the shape, the creamy complexion, the crystal sheen of her blue eyes, the rich lips and of course the blond hair. She hadn't been given an imperfection. He should know. He had spent a lot of time looking for one.

"You will do it?"

"I will discuss it with Minnie Shipper. If she wants me to keep looking, I'll keep looking. If I find something useful to you, I'll let you know."

She nodded. With the meal complete, she picked up the check and paid it on the way out. They walked back to her office and stood outside the front doors. She offered a hand and then she walked to the doors. She stopped just long enough to turn back and smile as she said, "You're still in love with me." She laughed and then disappeared inside.

He walked back to his car. There it was. Like a good lawyer she had taken it from a briefcase and placed it on the table. Yes, he was still in love with her, but that didn't make him foolish enough to return to her.

SEVEN

HE WAS an English teacher, he reminded himself as he drove from Pam's office. He wasn't a cop. He wasn't an investigator. At best he was a researcher, but his research led to articles in English journals or to biographies. He didn't know the first thing about catching a murderer that didn't involve a lot of luck.

Having convinced himself he was traveling in a direction he should not go, he began to think of where he would begin, if he were to travel in that direction. One question kept coming back to him. Why the cemetery? No one seemed to think that the Jacksonville Cemetery was a place that any sane person would go late at night. By all accounts, Adam was sane. On the other hand, he was on the cemetery board and he was probably more comfortable being in it than most people, night or day.

Maybe the cemetery was a conveniently private place to meet, as was suggested. If that were the case, then almost anything could bring Adam and his killer there. Something with the school board? Something with the library board? Something with city council? Something with real estate? Something with church? A charity drive? Scouts? By the time he got back to his house, Paul had a headache just thinking about it.

Inside, he walked around his dining-room table, looking at each stack of papers that dealt with the life of

Adam Shipper. "She loves me, she loves me not," he said. "She loves me, she loves me not." His hand came to rest on a stack of papers. He lifted his fingers. The school board. He had to start someplace. He took the stack of papers to his armchair with a cup of coffee and read through them again.

When Adam died, he was the chairman of the board. He was one of five members. He tended to lead the board, but from the information that Paul had he could see that Adam didn't always get his way. The teacher union, for one, had some power. The superintendent was not a rubber-stamp man. Some parents were influential members of the community. That all sounded pretty healthy to Paul and unlikely to produce a motive for murder. Still, he had to take a look at everything. He called the superintendent of schools' office to make an appointment to see Dr. Robertson. After that he made another phone call and arranged to meet with a school board member.

After a bite to eat, he was back in his car, this time to take the back roads to Jacksonville, following a path that skirted along the hills that lined the west side of the valley. He smiled at the thought of it: mild-mannered English teacher Paul Fischer, driving in his nondescript midsized American passenger car, cruising through middle-class America on his way to investigate the murder of a man he had never met. He'd played action hero twice before in this valley, and he had surprised himself by his resourcefulness at the time, but it always seemed to him that he was standing outside himself, and the man he was watching was not Paul Fischer. He doubted that this incarnation of Paul Fischer would have the resources needed to find the killer of Adam Shipper.

As he followed the final twists of Old Stagecoach

Road that brought Jacksonville into view, he wondered how he could feel so comfortable in this valley. He was an East Coast man, and he was a New Englander. As old as the West was, and as prominent as Jacksonville was to Oregon history, this was still new territory compared to New England, and it came up short a couple of hundred years of history.

Nor did the valley remind him of where he had come. This was too sun-baked and golden in the summers. The sky was too prominent. The towns were too far apart. The people were too casual and relaxed. They didn't even have an accent, or at least they didn't have one that could be identified with any region of the country. Yet when the chance came to come back here, he had jumped at it. And during the time he had been back, he never once felt that he had made a mistake or that he had come out west to run away from something he had left behind.

He had come back to this state and this valley because he liked folks who were friendly and didn't treat him like an outsider because he hadn't been born there. He liked his students because they weren't driven to succeed the way Ivy League students were driven to succeed, and he liked them because neither class nor wealth mattered as much to them as it did from where he came. He liked working with professors who did more to work together than to compete with one another. He liked being in a university that knew it was far from one of the best around, but was driven by an administration that wanted to improve on that. Despite what he had run into from Pam Livingston and Nora Ryan before, here he had discovered a certain degree of honesty that seemed to underlie everything.

He drove to the school administration office located

in a complex at one end of one of the high school, and there he parked his car.

Dr. Robertson was not just a big man, he was a huge man. Paul guessed the superintendent was as least six-four and weighed close to three hundred pounds. Robertson also had a boyish face, and movements light and quick that defied his weight.

After shaking his hand, Robertson said to Paul as he led him into his office, "I read your book on Doc Hollingsworth. I thought it was pretty good considering the limits of the subject matter."

Paul entered the office and sat in a chair he was directed to that was opposite the superintendent's desk. "I'm surprised. The biography of the good doctor didn't exactly burn up the charts."

"It never would have. It's the type of book an educator like you writes to further his career. Sales are irrelevant. When I thought it was pretty good, I meant that I thought it would put a gold star next to your publication credits."

Publish or perish wasn't what it used to be in the academic world. Now a professor could get by with a nutty idea, as an expert witness, as a guest on a talk show, or a good quote in a newspaper article. Celebrity carried as much weight as accomplishment, just like the rest of the world. Paul might be one of the first to complain, but he had no doubt that celebrity played a part in the job offer he got from the university.

On one wall was the superintendent's celebrity. It contained framed degrees, certificates, awards, honors and pictures of Dr. Robertson with other modest celebrities: one with the mayor of Medford, one with a state senator, one with the governor. One picture, though, was an eye-grabber. It was a picture of Robertson in a New York Jets football uniform.

Dr. Robertson followed Paul's stare to the picture, and then he offered an explanation. "Out of college, I got a tryout with the Jets. I lasted a few weeks until the big boys showed up. First I got knocked on my butt on a regular basis, and then I got cut. That's when I thought an advanced college degree might be nice."

It was hard for Paul to imagine anyone big enough to knock the superintendent on his butt. "We're all caught in the food chain," Paul said.

Dr. Robertson let out a laugh that was close to a bellow. "Spoken like a true educator."

"I've come to talk about Adam Shipper."

"I know. His wife called and greased the way for you, otherwise I wouldn't be finding time for you. Minnie is a good woman, and Adam was a man of good intent. Closure for everyone means finding out who killed him."

Praise for the wife; mild praise for the husband. "Good intent? That doesn't sound like you and Adam had a perfect relationship."

Dr. Robertson leaned on his desk so he could draw closer to Paul. The good humor on his face and the sparkle in his eyes were real, Paul thought. Paul amused him in some way. He was about to find out how. "I understand you to be a fair English teacher, but that doesn't come close to giving you the right even to hint at the idea that I might somehow be involved in Adam's death."

Was the superintendent being overly sensitive, Paul wondered, or was he being defensive? "I don't think I accused you of anything," Paul said. "I've already done some preliminary research, and I don't find you and Adam, at least publicly, at odds with each other.''

"That's not the issue," Robertson said, still leaning on his desk. "Adam and I didn't agree on much. He was a tail wagged by the dog of educational reform. He was blind to a lot of the reform's consequences, and engrossed in the idealistic purity of it. That's why he and I did not get along. Fortunately, he couldn't do much to make what the state had already done any worse than it was.''

Over a decade before, the state legislature in Oregon had tossed out the latest educational reform, and came up with a replacement that demanded that students be tested on standardized tests at certain grade levels until they reached a degree of competency by their tenth grade. That was when they would earn a certificate of master in each of the areas such as reading, writing, math, et cetera. For educators, students and parents alike, the reform came with its own nightmares. A public report card was issued each year to let everyone know how the school was doing. Unfortunately, the report card did not take into account demographics, but only bottom lines. Students were stigmatized because only a small percentage were able to pass the tests the first time. Parents had their faith in their schools and their faith in the educational system shattered by the public reports. What seemed to go unnoticed in all of this was that Oregon was consistently at the top with SAT score results and listed as one of the best states in education when it came to national standardized tests even before the reform effort.

"You disagreed about the educational reform?"

"Adam was a political creature. He saw our test scores as both a threat and an opportunity. Although we did fairly well on the tests, fairly well still had half our students failing to get mastery the first time around. Adam worried that would be a reflection on him as board chairman. On the other hand, he thought if he could push through a program that would create immediate gains on those tests, then that would boost his standing in the community.''

''That's why he wanted students held back if they scored low on bench mark tests, and forced into summer school programs to bring them up to speed. Is that such a bad idea?''

''No. It's a great idea unless you are one of the kids held back or one of the parents of those kids. What Adam didn't understand was that one political disaster can be less evil than another. Retention was a greater embarrassment than scoring below the state average on the tests.''

''Did that make anyone mad enough to kill him?''

Robertson pushed away from the desk and leaned back in his chair. ''I'm going to do something that I will deny I ever did,'' he said. ''I'll give you the names of a couple of parents who were enraged because of Adam's proposals. And then, I'll tell you flat out that none of them killed Adam, that I didn't kill Adam and that nothing to do with the school board got him killed. You will come to that conclusion yourself eventually, but I expect you to take a look anyway.''

''I appreciate the help.''

''You should. I may be the most friendly person you will talk to in Jacksonville.''

''As long as you are being friendly, let me ask you a question. Understand that I'm not with the press or with the police, that I simply am honoring a request by the widow to look into the death of her husband and that whatever you tell me will stay between us. With that in mind, can you tell me what you really thought of Adam Shipper?"

Dr. Robertson shrugged. "I could repeat the line you've heard a dozen times. Adam was a saint."

"Saints get martyred not murdered."

"Yes, I forget you have your doctorate, too." He took a moment to gather his thoughts, his fingers pushing together into a steeple. Finally, Robertson said, "Adam had a great need to be loved by everyone. Unfortunately, he also lacked long-range vision. He would wade into things, throwing into it his considerable influence, because he thought people would really appreciate his efforts. That was the case with retention of students and summer school. He thought parents would see him as a hero for doing something about poor test scores. He never once thought that most parents would be enraged because their child was being held back. Adam was too busy going for the glory to think that far ahead."

"One more question. Adam was about to propose that your contract renewal be tied to a percent of improvement in test scores. What did you think of that?"

Robertson stood up straight so his whole bulk hovered over Paul. "You're a good researcher, Mr. Fischer. I've given you honest answers. Now's a good time to leave before my goodwill disappears."

Paul smiled, offered his hand, shook with the superintendent and left the office feeling lucky to get out in one piece. He had touched a nerve. Was it a sensitive enough a nerve to turn a man into a killer?

THE FIRST NAME ON THE LIST would be easy to start with. Arnie Ambrose was the board member he had arranged to meet with after he saw the superintendent. He and

Adam apparently did not get along at all, and that wasn't much of a secret to anyone. In fact, as Paul had learned from Pam, Arnie was one of the first people the police had interviewed.

Despite the cold, he found Arnie flat on his back on a dolly under an old Jaguar Mark II sedan. The Jag was in the parking area of Arnie's gas station and garage, located on California Street in Jacksonville, the main road through town. Considering the number of cars in the lot waiting for repair, Paul guessed that Arnie did a pretty good business. The fact that a number of the cars were older sports cars and exotics, he could see that Arnie also had to be a pretty good mechanic considering the odd selection of autos.

Paul walked over to admire a sleek sports car, one that had all the classic lines of models from the sixties and seventies. He hadn't heard Arnie approach when the man walked up next to him. ''That's a Fiat 2000 with fuel injection. Folks joke that Fiat stands for Fix It Again Tony, but one that is well maintained, like this one, will be as reliable as any car. By the way, this one is for sale.''

Paul admired the car. It was dark blue with a tan interior. It had a small back seat, big enough for a set of golf clubs or a tight fit for a third person. This would be a great summer car, Paul felt, but totally impractical.

''How much?'' Paul asked.

''Three thousand.''

''That sounds cheap. What's the catch?''

''Fiats have a reputation. Folks down here are suspicious of most things made in Europe. This isn't sports car country. Pick one. If I took it to Portland, I could sell it for more, but, then, I'd have to take it to Portland.''

Paul extended his hand. "I'm Paul Fischer."

Arnie wiped his hands on a rag and then shook Paul's. "I know," he said. "For a foreigner, you've managed in a short time to make yourself part of Jacksonville's mythology."

"A foreigner?"

"For some, that's anyone from outside the valley."

Paul took his eyes from the car long enough to look at Arnie. Even in coveralls, the school board member was an imposing man. He was shorter than Paul, but he had the build of a boxer with wide shoulders and powerful arms. He was a handsome man as well, with dark, curly hair, brilliant blue eyes and striking, white teeth. If he had a summer tan, he would look a bit like the actor Dean Martin, but he was far from as relaxed. Paul could see the tension in the body language and in the eyes.

Paul said, "I need to talk to you about Adam Shipper."

"Come on into the cffice."

Paul followed Arnie into the office of the service station. The station itself was right out of the fifties, with a four-bay garage off the office and gas pumps under a portico. Arnie moved behind the counter and poured two cups of coffee from a Mr. Coffee and slid one of the foam cups across the counter to Paul without asking if he wanted one.

Paul took the cup. Ask or not, Arnie got it right. Paul liked his coffee black. Each of them leaned on opposite sides of the counter. "Adam?" Paul asked as a reminder.

"Adam was an idiot. He got himself involved in too many things, and then he stretched himself thin. More often than not that led to a half-assed job of it. Adam counted on people being in awe of him because of his civic dedication, so he never gave a shit if something worked or not, just as long as he didn't get the blame if it failed. He made sure he got the credit if it worked.''

"You didn't like him.''

"I didn't like him at all. I thought he stirred up a mess for the school district unnecessarily, the only purpose behind it to glorify Adam Shipper. But then, nothing ever stuck to Adam, unless it was praise. When things went wrong, he had a way of shifting the blame to some-one else. He tried to tie low test scores to the superin-tendent and to make me out as the bad guy for the sum-mer school disaster.''

"Is that why the police questioned you about his death?''

"Is there an accusation in there someplace?''

"You seem to have disliked him enough to wish him harm.''

Arnie unbuttoned the top two buttons of his coveralls. He didn't have on a shirt underneath and thick, black, curly hair filled the opening. "I did wish him harm. I wished that some of his failed scheming would finally come back to bite him on the butt, and it did piss me off when that didn't happen. On the other hand, I would have punched him in the nose in a public place while making a public denouncement. I wouldn't have skew-ered him in the dark of night in a cemetery.''

"Did you ever punch him in the nose?''

"I tried once, in a board meeting, but Robertson got between us. Now there's a man big enough to make even a hothead like me think. So, the answer to your question is, yes, the police did interview me, and, no, I didn't kill him, although I'm not sure the cops haven't counted me out yet.''

"Who do you think killed Adam?''

"I think Adam made one misjudgment too many with a person he totally underestimated. That would be par for the course, for Adam. This time it got him killed."

Paul asked, "Do you have any suspects?"

Arnie said, "I can't think of a single suspect in Adam's murder. On the other hand, I can think of a hundred, because whoever did it, if it is one of us, hasn't given a hint in the past of murderous intent. That means it might well be any of us."

"One last question," Paul said. "I understand from his notes that Adam was going to propose that your station be shut down. He was concerned about your old gasoline storage tanks and feared they might leak into Jackson Creek. How'd you feel about that?"

Arnie struggled for control. His whole body tensed and leaned toward Paul, aggression written all over it. With a smile he struggled to keep on his face, he said, "I think it is time for you to leave."

One look at Arnie's body language convinced Paul it was time to leave, too. He had parked his car on a side street off California, Jacksonville's main street. Only a few days after Christmas, the decorations in the town were still up. Windows were covered with painted Christmas trees, jolly Santas and precocious elves. Many of the windows were lined with Christmas lights that shone brightly. Jacksonville was still in the holiday spirit, a fact that seemed to contrast sharply with the death of a leading citizen. Paul had seen no signs of mourning. It was as if the town were sending out a message to Mrs. Shipper. That message was, have a merry little Christmas.

As soon as Paul turned the corner and spotted his car, he knew he was in trouble. A uniformed police officer was waiting for him, leaning against the front fender of the car. Paul considered a cup of coffee in a nearby restaurant right at that moment, but the cop had moved away from the car and stepped toward Paul. He didn't even have to look at the nametag to know who this was. His name was Daryl Hollis, and Adam had mentioned him more than once in his notes.

Paul stopped in front of the cop. "You wouldn't be waiting for me, would you?"

Hollis moved half a step closer to Paul and leaned into him, speaking softly so his voice wouldn't carry. Paul was tempted to step back. Hollis was big, but he filled his uniform with bulk not muscle. He looked a bit like a giant doughboy stuffed into a uniform two sizes too small for him. Nonetheless, a man pushing six-two and weighing about 275 pounds wasn't one to fool with, even if he was out of shape. Still, Paul held his ground.

"I hear you've been playing PI without a license. That's against the law, and I'm thinking I'm going to have to arrest you."

Paul smiled up at the fat face with tiny, tiny, nearly black eyes. "I'm just helping out a friend."

"And who would that friend be?"

Hollis's breath was bad, and now it took a great deal of will for Paul to hold his ground. "Mrs. Shipper."

Hollis smirked. "By all accounts, Mrs. Shipper had a pervert for a husband. And by all accounts, she can't make you a licensed investigator. I think maybe you want to hop in your car and maybe head back east where you belong."

"Try this on for size, then," Paul said. "I'm gathering information for the lawyer Pam Livingston for her defense of a client. I don't believe you need a PI license for that."

Wrong thing to say, Paul had just enough time to

think, as he was whirled by Hollis and slammed against the side of his car. Hollis's whole bulk was pressed against him and his face was in Paul's. "I don't think you got the message, asshole. You're out of here or you're in jail."

"And I think that maybe you should go read a law book."

"That's it," the cop growled. He roughly spun Paul and pinned him by the back of his neck to the roof of his car while he groped for his handcuffs.

A female's voice cut into the scuffle. "I'm only a third-year law student, but even I know he's right. I also know police brutality when I see it."

The pressure eased on Paul's neck, and then Hollis's weight moved away. Paul turned slowly, rotating his head on his shoulders to make sure everything was still attached.

She was wearing tight jeans and a bulky sweater, and her hair was longer now. She'd gone from being very cute, with the short haircut she had worn the last time he had seen her, to very beautiful. "How's law school going for you, Liz?" he asked.

Liz Mendoza had been Pam Livingston's legal secretary when Paul had returned to the valley the second time. She had been in the middle of that chaotic episode, and afterward she had decided it was time to get on with her career ambitions. She had been accepted to law school at the University of Oregon. Paul hadn't seen her since, but he did get updates on her from Pam, at least until they had separated.

"Fine, Paul. I think Officer Hollis could use a little law school, though."

Hollis had turned scarlet and was sweating profusely, despite the cold. Paul wasn't sure if it was from anger or overexertion. Either way, the man didn't look well. "Adam Shipper didn't have you in mind when he introduced a resolution about the physical fitness of police officers in Jacksonville, did he? In fact I think he was about to recommend that you be fired."

Hollis went from scarlet to purple. "Do a California stop, spit on the sidewalk, jaywalk—your ass will be mine."

Hollis did the best he could to make a graceful exit, but it consisted of a wobbly turn and a bit of a stagger down the street.

Paul finally allowed himself to let out a long sigh of relief and collapse with his back against his car. "Officer Hollis wasn't a man I wanted to be alone with. Thanks for the rescue. I owe you."

"Good," she said. "I'm hungry. Why don't you buy me something to eat."

"My pleasure. What are you doing here?"

She reached out a hand and took one of his, and then she held it as they walked back to California Street to look for a place to eat. "I'm staying with my parents for the holidays. They live in Jacksonville. And I'm feeling pretty lucky, just when the holidays were getting boring, to run across Paul Fischer."

Paul was feeling pretty lucky, too. Lucky that Hollis hadn't done much damage, and lucky that he was holding hands with a woman with whom he had once shared an attraction. It wasn't one that either of them had acted upon, but sparks had been there. Considering that he could damn near feel electricity traveling through their hands, he had no doubt that the sparks weren't gone, either.

EIGHT

BACK AT HOME later that afternoon, he dialed a number from a notebook he brought with him. He had written down all the names of school board members. He wanted to hear from one more before he moved on to another activity of Adam Shipper's. He'd learned a long time ago that in research, all sources needed to be contacted. He never knew when one of them might spring a surprise on him.

He caught Mondo Alvarez at work at the Jacksonville fire station. He was one of the full-time firemen who specialized in training the volunteers and organizing contact between the fire department and schools, presenting fire-safety workshops. Because he had so much contact with the schools, he was an excellent choice for the school board, but Paul had learned that he had run for the position against two others, and the election had been close and the politics in it unpleasant. The message was pretty clear. The other board members had run unopposed. But not Mondo. Some people in the community were not ready for a Hispanic to be on the school board. It didn't help, either, that Adam Shipper had supported both of the candidates running against Alvarez.

When he got Mondo on the phone, Paul introduced himself, using a line that seemed to work best with the people in Jacksonville. "Mondo, I'm Paul Fischer, and

I'm looking into the death of Adam Shipper at the request of his widow.''

Mondo's first question was surprising to Paul. "Have you talked to Arnie yet?''

"Yes, I have. Do you think Arnie had something to do with this?''

"No. Arnie and I were the first two called in by the police after Adam died. They were smart enough to interview Arnie first so there'd be no hint of racism. I just wondered if you were as smart.''

"Is racism an issue in Adam's death?''

"Since I don't know who killed him or why, I'd have to say that I can't answer that.''

"But you think it could be. Why?''

"Don't get me wrong. Adam wasn't some flaming racist. I don't even think he was a closet racist. He was just racially insensitive.''

Paul poured himself a cup of coffee. "What makes you think that?''

"That whole issue of summer school. Most of the kids who would have been held back would have been poor kids and minority kids. Those are the ones who need summer to work the fields and orchards, or they don't have new school clothes for the next year. His response to that was they were the ones who needed schooling the most or they'd forever be working the fields and the orchards.''

"That's not a totally invalid point," Paul said, "especially if they were deficient in basic skills.''

"I have a college degree, Dr. Fischer, and I'm not a stupid man serving on a school board. I know, though, that if those kids can't come to school in new clothes, if they can't keep up with the other kids socially, not academically, then they won't stay in school, so they won't get an education anyway. I argued for the lesser of two evils. Adam often argued for the glory of Adam."

Paul began to see a pattern emerge, if only in relationship to the school board. Several people had now told him that they felt Adam's main interest in what he did was in the best interest of Adam. He wondered if the pattern would hold up in the other activities Adam was involved in.

"You didn't like him, then."

"You couldn't dislike Adam. He'd perfected friendliness the way a Saint Bernard perfects it. You couldn't help liking him to some degree, but that didn't mean you didn't get mad at him when he peed on the carpet."

"Can you think of anyone who might have been mad enough at him to kill him?" Everyone he talked to would get that question from Paul. He doubted if many would give an honest answer, even if they did suspect someone, but the way they answered the question might be enlightening on its own.

"They arrested a kid for the murder," Mondo said, avoiding an answer to the question.

"The kid accused Adam once of unnatural attention. Do you know anything about that?" That was a question that Paul hadn't even bothered to ask the superintendent, and for good reason. As a school official, the superintendent would have had to act legally on any suspicion of child abuse. If he had admitted to a suspicion, one he had not acted on, then he faced criminal liability in the state of Oregon. Educators and health officials were required by law to make such a report or they faced possible fines and imprisonment. As a board member, Mondo wasn't in the clear, either.

"I can only respond to that after the fact. At the time I didn't think much of it."

"Why is that?"

"Adam tried to get to as many high school sports events as he could."

"That, I would think, would be a credit to him."

"He made it to the wrestling matches, the soccer games, the basketball games and baseball games."

"So?"

"The ones played by the boys."

"You're saying that he didn't go to the girls' games."

"I've got two daughters at the high school, both out for team sports. I never saw Adam at any of their events."

"Maybe he just thought the boys were better athletes and more entertaining to watch."

"Maybe."

"But you don't think so."

"I don't know. Like I said, it was something that occurred to me after the fact."

"Thank you for your help. Would you mind if I called you again?"

"Probably, but if it helps to find out who killed Adam, then I'll put up with it."

"I admire your dedication to finding out the truth."

"Bullshit. I just want people to stop thinking I might have done it." The phone went dead.

That, Paul thought, was about as honest an interview as he was going to get. Still, it wasn't as helpful as it seemed. If Adam had an affinity for boys, he would have had to do a great job of hiding it. No matter how involved in his community he was, because he was active in scouts, church youth groups and the school board, no public official from the superintendent to the police chief could have ignored even a suspicion of perversion on his part. He wondered what the police chief might have to say about that issue.

He settled back down in his chair in the living room with a stack of papers in hand. He was curious. Although she and Adam were major players in the town of Jacksonville, both of them with a great deal of influence, Paul was surprised that Thelma Clay's name hadn't been mentioned by any of the people he had talked to yet. He needed to give that some thought. He didn't have a lot of time to think about it, though. Liz Mendoza was coming over for a late dinner. The best part about it was she told him not to do a thing. She would bring everything herself and cook for him. The last woman who had cooked for him, Terri Drexler, had damned near stolen his heart.

NINE

AT THREE IN THE MORNING Liz was still there, they were still awake and they were in Paul's bed. He hadn't expected it, but then again he couldn't complain. She was a beautiful woman. She had lovely, smooth skin that was pale despite her Hispanic heritage. He liked her hair long. He liked the feel of it as he let it slip through his fingers. He especially liked her eyes. If diamonds could be brown, he thought, this is what they would look like.

And he liked making love to her. With her, sex was about pleasure and fun. She was in no hurry. She liked her pleasure and fun.

She turned away from him, and then she scooted up against him and drew one of his arms around her. "Thank you," she said.

"Shouldn't I be thanking you?" he asked.

"I think we both can say thank you," she said. "First times aren't supposed to be so good, are they?"

She didn't expect an answer, he was sure, but she was right. First times were rarely this good, at least in his experience. "And thanks for taking my mind off Adam Shipper."

"Not having much luck?"

"Too much luck. Everyone I've talked to so far seems to have a good reason to kill Adam."

"I didn't know the man, so I don't think I can be much help."

He enjoyed the feel of her body pressed against him. Nothing could replace the comfort that came from the warmth of another human being's body. "Maybe you can help," he said. "Tell me what you know about Thelma Clay."

She laughed. "I don't know much about her at all, and most of what I do comes from my father."

"Why is that?"

"I really don't know why, but my father has never liked her. He says that because of her name alone she expects the little people to kiss her feet. That she's not satisfied that one son runs the biggest church in town and the other manages the largest auto dealership in the valley. No, she won't be satisfied until one of them runs the whole state. She'd prefer that it be her, but she'll settle for her oldest taking control. Since she runs both of their lives now, she'll be running the state by proxy if one of them gets elected governor. But that's just my dad. He gets that way about things. Why'd you ask?"

"Curious, I guess," he said. "Nora Ryan told me that Thelma and Adam were pretty much at odds wherever they butted heads. No one I've talked to yet has mentioned her name. I was just wondering why that was."

She snuggled deeper into his arms so he couldn't help but notice that he shared a bed with a woman who was not only beautiful, but who had the body to go with it. He was pretty sure this conversation wasn't going to last much longer.

"Maybe you talked to the ones who Thelma backed."

He had to admire the logic in that. The superintendent still had his job. A school board member still got elected even though Adam supported two other candidates running against him. An incompetent, overweight cop still had his job despite Adam's efforts to get rid of him. Arnie's gas station was still located in town. The only other person in town with the power to thwart Adam's will was Thelma.

She began to move her body against him. "You know, as silly as it seems for a woman in her early thirties, I'm going to have to crawl out of this bed pretty soon and go back to my parents. They would be shocked if they found out I had stayed out all night."

"But you're not thinking of crawling out of this bed right this minute, are you?" he asked, as he slowly slid a hand over the slight swell of her stomach.

"Oh, no!" she said. And she meant it.

An hour later he watched her car back out of his drive and then pull away. He returned to the house, but he didn't go back to bed. Not yet. Instead he poured himself a glass of wine, played a CD softly on the stereo and sat in the dark to think.

His mother would have called it a wait-and-see date, although she would have been shocked to learn that it had ended up in bed. Over dinner Liz had discussed her plans. Although Pam had offered a position in the law firm when she passed the bar, Liz didn't think she would take the job. She simply had said, "Being her personal secretary is one thing. Working for her as a lawyer would be another." Paul didn't probe, but he knew what she meant by it. Pam was hard on other lawyers.

Liz was saying, in a nice way, that she wasn't likely to be around in the future. He didn't know if anything would change because of what happened after dinner. That was the wait-and-see part. He did notice, though, that she had not asked him about either Pam or Terri.

That was probably good. He doubted he could have

told her much. He had talked to Terri and her daughter on Christmas Day. Terri was finally in a place where she could put to rest a dead mother, a dead husband and a dead father. The grieving wasn't yet done. The future was yet something just over the horizon.

Pam? Life was black and white to her. Whatever she saw as gray, she didn't share with anyone. The relationship between the two of them fell into that gray area. She had told him before they separated that she knew what she wanted, but he was the one who needed to know what he wanted. As far as he could tell, that hadn't changed.

A slight sound on the patio froze the wineglass on his lips. He slowly lowered the glass and turned his head toward the patio doors. The large shadow of a man slid through the moonlight and then merged with the man himself just outside the doors. The man's hand reached for the door handle and slowly turned it. The door was locked, but Paul knew it wouldn't take much to pop out a panel of glass on the French doors and reach in to undo the lock from the inside.

Paul reached back his hand with the wineglass in it as far as he could, and then he lobbed the glass over the dining-room table toward the door. The glass shattered against the door at face level. The man jumped back away from the doors, and then he, followed quickly by his shadow, disappeared into the darkness of the yard.

Paul went from the chair to the phone and called the police. By the time they arrived a few minutes later, the man was long gone. Paul had already grabbed a flashlight and searched the yard by the time they arrived. In those few minutes he had found out everything he needed to know about the intruder. He didn't share the information with the police because he was pretty sure it wouldn't do any good. On the other hand, he was now convinced he knew who was trying to discourage his curiosity about the death of Adam Shipper.

Despite the hour, he called Pam Livingston at home. She wasn't very excited about the phone call, not at four-thirty in the morning, nor was she very enthusiastic about the question he wanted her to ask her client.

TEN

BY TEN THE NEXT MORNING, after a couple of hours' sleep, Paul was back in Jacksonville. He wasn't quite sure what he was looking for. He knew that three amateurish attempts had been used to discourage him. A silly note on his windshield, the bullying on a public street by a not-too-bright cop, and the rattling of his French doors by a less than lionhearted intruder certainly were not the brainchildren of a rocket scientist. On the other hand, he couldn't be sure the three events were related, nor could he even be sure they had anything to do with the death of Adam Shipper.

He had already found a handful of people who might not want Adam's agendas revived. Each probably would be delighted if Paul stayed on his side of the valley. But murder?

He parked his car at the bottom of the hill on the street, and then he walked the steep, winding road up to the cemetery. He needed the exercise, and he needed the time to think. As he neared the top of the hill, he paused at the short brick wall that separated the road from the hillside and looked out over the town of Jacksonville. The snow was gone now, and the dark clouds heavy with rain hovered low over the valley. Jacksonville was a quaint town blurred a bit by the mist, and little of the holiday season was obvious below. No Christmas music.

No Christmas lights. With Christmas Day behind them, it was as if everyone had packed up their holiday spirit and gone back to business as usual. Only, Adam Shipper was no longer aboveground to enjoy it. Apparently, Paul thought, the reason for that had to have something to do with the cemetery. Why else would he have chosen this spot for a meeting?

He walked again to the spot where Adam was killed. He stood for a long time next to the depression in the earth where Adam's body had settled and looked in each direction, trying to find something that would give him a clue as to why Adam Shipper had come to this spot. He even moved into the depression itself, as if this new perspective would give him the clue. And it did, finally, when he realized he had been asking the wrong question. He had wondered what was here that could have led to Adam's death. Lateral thinking. When an answer doesn't come, look at the question in a different way. What wasn't here that might have gotten Adam killed? The answer leaped up at him.

He walked away from the depression in the ground, sure he had the right question, but he also knew he didn't have the answer.

Back at his car, he used his cell phone to call Pam Livingston. The secretary put him right through to her, and she answered the phone with, "I mentioned the name, and I got a reaction, but he's not talking."

Paul nodded to himself. He said, "The boy's not too bright. He probably figures he's in more trouble if he tells you the truth than he is letting things stand the way they are."

"Are you going to share this insight with me?" Pam asked.

"In time, but right now I've got to sort it. I've got a

vague notion of what, but I know none of the details nor do I know by whom. I am sure, though, that your client didn't kill Adam Shipper. I suspect he had a lot to gain with Adam alive, and a lot to lose with Adam dead.''

''You're talking in riddles, Paul,'' Pam said. He recognized the familiar tone of impatience in her voice that she used on him when he was getting in the way of her black and white thinking.

''I need to talk to some more people. Should I ever get this into focus, I'll get back to you.''

''Don't get me wrong, Paul,'' she said. ''I appreciate you sticking around to help me out. I would have thought you'd have been off to Florence for the holidays.''

Cheap lawyer trick, Paul thought, smiling to himself. Did Pam want to know if things had gone sour for him and Terri Drexler, the woman he had met in Florence, Oregon, who led to their separation? ''I talked to Terri and her daughter on Christmas Day. She needs to go it alone for now, and I'm respecting that.''

''I see,'' Pam said, and he could imagine her smiling to herself.

He ended the call and then drove across town to the Presbyterian church. He had arranged to meet with Thelma Clay and her son Lexington at the church at ten. Lexington and Dallas were her two boys. Dallas Clay—he, too, had dropped his father's last name as had Lexington—was mounting a run for the state senate. Paul wasn't sure who would take over the car dealerships if he won, but he knew it wouldn't be Lexington. Lexington had the church to run.

He found the two of them standing at the top of the tall set of steps that led to the double church doors, waiting for him when he walked from his car. This was his first look at Thelma. As he climbed the stairs, he could see that she wasn't very big. Short, solid if not stout, white hair with a slight blue tinge to it, and cool, blue eyes. When he reached the top of the stairs, she offered a hand to him, gave him a firm handshake and nodded toward the open church doors. He followed the two of them inside.

Lexington only vaguely resembled his mother. He was tall and thin, his dark hair going gray over the ears. Paul put him around forty-five. Little about him would draw attention, except for his eyes. They were large and dark, as were the circles under them. They gave the man a look of being haunted by ghosts.

The church had two rows of straight-backed, wooden benches that faced a slightly elevated pulpit at the other end of the room. Behind the pulpit was a choral loft. On either side of the pulpit were doors that led into a room. He followed them through the door on the right and into a small office. Like the chapel itself, the office was Spartan. He was directed to a wood chair across from the plain desk that nearly filled the space. Lexington took a seat behind the desk, and Thelma stood next to a wall of bookshelves that were overflowing with books.

He had been seated for no more than a second when Thelma said, "I understand you want to see us about Adam."

Paul took a moment to answer. In the parking lot had been a new Mercedes and a new Cadillac. Thelma wore rings on both hands, and to his untrained eye they looked expensive. He knew more about suits. The one worn by Lexington was tailored to fit and was made from a wool blend. He had looked at one once, but he couldn't afford it on his income. Either car sales or soul saving was profitable, if not both. Having money wasn't a problem to people who had it, but losing it certainly was a concern. He wondered if another motive might exist that he hadn't considered.

"Mrs. Clay, you worked closely with Adam on a number of boards and councils, and Lexington worked with him on the church board. I understand that all did not go smoothly between the two of you and Adam."

"Excuse me, Mr. Fischer," Lexington said. "I had no problems at all with Adam on the church board. He was a dedicated member and a good Christian. He performed wonderful service to the church, and he was admired and respected by all."

"But…" Paul said, leaving it hanging. Everyone he had talked to so far had heaped praise on Adam before dropping the other shoe of condemnation.

"But nothing," Thelma said.

"That's refreshing," Paul said. "Adam actually served on something without making anyone mad at him. Of course that wasn't your experience with Adam, was it, Mrs. Clay?"

"Of course it was," she snapped. "Adam and I didn't always agree on everything, but we worked it out between us. I found Adam to be sincere in his beliefs and dedicated to doing the best for everyone."

She actually said that with a straight face, Paul thought, and she didn't even wink. He decided that maybe he needed to refresh her memory. "When Adam tried to tie test scores to the superintendent's job, it was you who worked behind the scenes to thwart Adam's efforts. You guaranteed Arnie that his gas station wouldn't have to move if he supported you. You got support from another board member, Mondo Alvarez, because you supported his election to the position. I know you have Nora Ryan in your pocket, too, because she didn't like some of the proposals Adam had for the museum. I also know a cop who exceeds the weight requirements and the education requirements for the job who still has his job because you wouldn't back the initiative for weight and education requirements proposed by Adam if it didn't have a sunset clause. It seems to me that every day was a battle of one kind or another between you and Adam Shipper."

Thelma Clay smiled. "You've been misinformed," she said. And that was it. Thelma picked up her purse from her son's desk where she had left it when she walked in and then squeezed by Paul and left. Lexington stood and reached across the desk to shake Paul's hand. "Thank you for the opportunity to clear up a few things," he said. "You will have to excuse me now. I've a sermon to prepare."

Thelma's car was gone by the time Paul reached the parking lot. He left his car in the lot and walked the short distance to the Jacksonville Museum. He didn't go in. Instead he sat on a picnic table under the branches of a huge oak tree that was missing its leaves but was still green because of the moss that draped from its branches.

He ran through his mind the things that he knew. Adam Shipper's body was found in the indentation of a collapsed, unmarked grave. Unmarked was the key. Adam prided himself, as a member of the cemetery board, that he had sorted out all the graves in the cemetery and arranged a marker for those that did not have one. In the papers that he had found, Adam had made it clear that he had identified all the graves. Why, then, did this grave not have a marker?

He knew that Thelma and Adam had battled on a lot of fronts for years. Neither was incapable of dirty tricks.

Adam had supported two different candidates on the school board to try to keep Mondo Alvarez from being elected. Adam was no saint. He probably didn't want a Hispanic on the board.

Mondo stepped forward to suggest that Adam was a closet homosexual. He had no proof, of course, but in conjunction with Jimmy Cross's accusation and then his arrest, the town had suddenly dropped its interest in Adam's murder. If he was one of those people, well, maybe he deserved what happened to him seemed to be the town's attitude now.

One name changed that for Paul. He asked Pam to talk to Jimmy about Thelma Clay. He had reacted to the name, but he kept his mouth shut. More dirty tricks? The battle between Thelma and Adam had heated up over the years as Shipper became more involved in the community. Was it possible that Thelma, in some kind of desperate act, had convinced the boy to make his claim against Adam? Just the rumor of it would hurt Adam; the public accusation would destroy his influence in this conservative community.

Finally, he knew who had rattled his patio doors the other night. The bulk wasn't hard to miss, nor were the huge footprints that had settled deep in the soil of the flowerbed. He had noticed those big feet when the cop had him pinned to his car.

All of it had the Clay family written all over it. The final piece, though, was the fact that the Clays claimed they had no issues with Adam. That was obviously a lie, but Paul got the message that he was to accept the lie because it came from them.

He got up and headed back to the parking lot. Maybe it was time he thought about buying a new car. The one he had was nothing spectacular, and Paul was a man who liked a good car. Besides, he hadn't met Dallas Clay yet, the one family member with the most to lose if Adam knew a secret about the Clays. Paul was pretty sure now that it was something about the Clays that Adam had discovered.

ELEVEN

PAUL FINALLY TRACKED DOWN Dallas on one of his lots just outside of Ashland. He had four different dealerships on this strip. He had another half dozen in the Medford area. He had four more in Roseburg. Altogether the family owned twenty dealerships in Southern Oregon. Each was successful.

Dallas Clay looked successful. He favored his mother. He, too, had the blue eyes, and he had the same solid build, only it looked better on his six-two frame. Like his brother, he also had a taste for expensive suits. He didn't seem to be the least bit surprised when Paul introduced himself in the Subaru showroom. He learned quickly why not.

"My mother said I'd probably be hearing from you." He said this while looking over Paul's shoulder. Paul was forced to turn to see what he was looking at. He was looking at Paul's car. "That's a decent car new, but it doesn't age very well. A man like you needs a little more flash than that, anyway. I've got a little Subaru on the lot that's based on a rally car. You'll have to give it a look before you leave."

That was one way to divert Paul's attention, he thought. Sell him a car and maybe he'd forget about Adam Shipper. "I appreciate your interest, but I'm really here to ask some questions about Adam Shipper. How well did you know him?''

Dallas smiled. He was the best looking of the lot, Paul thought. He had the friendly smile down pat, he kept himself trim despite his bulk and the cut of his jaw gave him both a look of strength and a look of integrity. He was the perfect choice for a politician. He answered Paul's question with, ''Not at all. Oh, I've heard my mother complain about the man often enough, but I don't live in Jacksonville, don't have a dealership there and usually see my brother and my mother at my place in Medford. It's a bit nicer than either of theirs.''

''So you've never met him?''

He waved away the question with one hand while brightening his smile a few watts. ''Of course I've met him. My mother insists that her boys attend the important functions in Jacksonville, but I've never gotten to know him.''

''And you haven't talked to him recently.''

''I don't think I've talked to him in the past year.''

Paul watched Dallas's eyes. He was pretty good at reading a lie in a man's eyes, but he knew he wasn't going to get any clues here. Dallas was already a pro on the campaign trail. Paul wouldn't know any more about him than Dallas wanted him to know.

He'd done his research first before catching up with Dallas. He knew he had played football both in high school and in college. He liked to hunt and fish. He worked out to stay in shape. Pushing fifty, he looked more like forty, and he had the look of a fit man of thirty. Of the three, Paul would say that Dallas was the most likely to have the physical strength to kill a man like Adam, who was not a small man himself.

"Would you know if Adam had some information that the family might find damaging?"

Dallas chuckled. "I've got an ex-wife who will tell you I work too much and play golf too much. My brother is working on sainthood. My mother is already there. We don't cheat on our taxes, kick dogs or spit on the sidewalk. If Adam Shipper dug in our family dirt, he'd come up with his hands clean."

Paul had to appreciate the man's smoothness. He really seemed to believe what he was saying. "Your mother and Adam didn't always get along."

"Neither do Democrats and Republicans, but they don't generally kill each other over it."

Paul smiled in defeat. He wasn't going to get anything but quick-witted answers, and if he stayed for that he might end up liking the man. He offered a hand to Dallas. "I appreciate your time," he said.

Dallas took his hand, and then he didn't let go of it. Instead he pulled Adam toward the door leading to the lot. "Next door I've got a Honda dealership. I think I have just the car for you." He let go of the hand, but then he secured Paul by and elbow and gently let him to the next lot. "This is a beauty," he said. "It's a Honda S2000 with less than ten thousand miles on it. A friend of mine traded it in for a new red one. His wife didn't like the yellow. We've done all the service on it, what little there was to do…"

TWELVE

HE WOULD MAKE a lousy private investigator, Paul decided. Dallas had not only talked him into a test drive of the Honda, he had knocked a couple of thousand off the asking price and had quoted a high blue-book trade-in for his car. It took all of his willpower to walk off the lot without making the deal, but then Dallas had given him three days to make up his mind. His mind was made up. He loved the car.

Liz had returned that evening to cook for him again, this time authentic Mexican tacos. He would have liked to think that she was heading to his heart through his stomach, but at the end of another evening that had ended in bed, she made it clear again that she wasn't likely to be returning to the valley on a permanent basis. The message seemed to be: enjoy it while you can.

Liz had left before dawn again to appease her parents, and he had slept in late. That next morning, once up, showered, shaved and fed, he sat in the living room with the radio tuned to a jazz station and lingered over a cup of coffee. His mind bounced back and forth between the mystery of Adam Shipper's death and the sound of the Honda winding through the gears.

He finally gave up. He could think of only one way to be able to focus on Shipper's death. He called Dallas and said he would take the car. Dallas took some information from him over the phone and then said he would have the paperwork ready by noon if he wanted to stop by then to pick up his new car. Paul hung up the phone and said, "Merry Christmas, Fischer."

He was not a man to agonize over a decision once it was made. He had indeed freed up his mind to think about Shipper's death. He wasn't exactly impressed with the results. A big piece of the puzzle was missing. He needed to know who was buried in the unmarked grave. He had looked just about everywhere he could for the answer. Liz had helped him go through Adam's records of the cemetery. Adam hadn't recorded the mystery there. While Liz cooked, he had reviewed his own records from the research he did into the lives of the Baker sisters. Finally, because something nagged at him in the back of his mind, he had Liz pump him with questions about Jacksonville, the Bakers and the other settlers of the town. He had hoped that the questions might trigger something, but they had not. Besides, it was only the questions that separated him from another trip to bed with Liz. Needless to say, he might not have concentrated as hard as he could have on the answers.

Today he would stop by to get his car, and then he would head back to Jacksonville and to the museum. If he had run across something before that might explain the unmarked grave, then it had most likely been in the museum.

THIRTEEN

NOTHING. HE HAD GONE through the filing cabinets that Nora Ryan kept containing historical documents related to the history of Jacksonville, and then he had gone through the computer database again that she had accumulated over the years about the town. Nothing.

He had even gone to the Internet, one of his last choices, to see if he could find some information. He didn't like the Internet because no one could be quite sure who really was on the other end of that electrical impulse, nor could anyone easily verify the information gained was accurate or not. Still, something could come up, a piece of information buried in an electronic file attached to a museum, a university or a state archive. In the end he came away with the same result. Nothing.

In desperation, he even tried Nora Ryan. He asked her who she thought might be in the unmarked grave in the cemetery. Her reply was typical Nora. She said, "As long as it is not me, why should I care?" She said it with her reading glasses down on the end of her nose and her owl eyes pecking over the top of them. Paul thought he saw a smirk on her face when she replied, but he knew from experience that if Nora knew something she didn't want him to know, then he wouldn't know it.

He walked outside of the museum and stood under the

barren trees to think. The temperature had dropped again, and the clouds had a shiny darkness to them that threatened snow. In fact snow was in the forecast for early evening. He wanted to be home by then. He wasn't ready to drive his new car in snow. Besides, he promised to pick up Liz at five and take her back with him. She had told him on the phone that morning that she was ready, finally, to declare her independence from her parents and spend the night with him.

He was already getting tired of Adam Shipper. He knew he ought to have more sympathy, but Christmas vacations did not last forever, and he had no intention of pursuing this matter after the holidays, regardless of the sympathy he still had for Adam's wife. Adam Shipper was a toe stepper. He'd stepped on lots of toes in order to get his way. This time he had stepped on the wrong toes. Paul was losing hope of finding out whose toes those were.

He wasn't a man to give up, either, as he had proved to himself too often. Paul would push it until he was sure he couldn't find the answer. The question was how to push it. He had nothing concrete, a town full of suspects, a dozen motives and no front-runner for the crime. In a card game, this was the time to fold. Paul smiled to himself. In a card game, a man could fold—or he could bluff. Why not a bluff?

He pulled out his cell phone and scrolled to a number he had entered a few days earlier. He pushed a button and listened for a ring. Within a few seconds he got an answer. "This is Paul Fischer," he said. "I've discovered something interesting about the unmarked grave where Adam Shipper's body was found. If anyone is interested in talking about it, I'll be at the grave site at three." He ended the call before Thelma Clay had a chance to respond.

He wasn't a foolish man. He stopped in town for a late lunch, and over the meal he made a couple of phone calls. In each case no one answered, but he was able to leave a message on an answering machine for Liz and a message with her secretary for Pam. He wanted to make sure someone knew where he was going and whom he would meet.

That was a problem though. He wasn't sure whom he was going to meet. He had a tough time imagining Thelma Clay hiking to the cemetery in the middle of the night with the threat of snow to kill Adam Shipper. Her style was to have someone else do the dirty work. Lexington seemed unlikely. Too pious. Dallas was a possibility, but killing Adam Shipper would have put him at risk too much. Dallas had a lot to lose, and Paul doubted that Adam could know anything that would have brought more than a grin to Dallas's face. He was a rich man with a comfortable life with or without politics. He could lose an election and still be a happy man.

Who else was there? The fat cop was a strong possibility. He did show up at Paul's house late at night to do a little intimidation. He wasn't smart enough to do it on his own initiative. He supposed Arnie might be talked into it. If Adam had managed to close down his station, Arnie probably would have faced bankruptcy. The superintendent of schools? A stretch at best. Maybe the boy really did do it.

Paul would go to the cemetery and wait to see who showed up. He'd just have to wing it from there and hope that daylight kept him out of harm's way.

Paul left his car at the base of the hill, on the street, and walked up the steep drive to the cemetery. He didn't want both himself and his car to be in an isolated spot. That would leave him too vulnerable when he walked back to the car. It took him fifteen minutes to get to the grave site, and then he waited.

He didn't have to wait long. He could hear the sound of a car engine working hard to make the steep grade of the cemetery road. A few minutes later the car came into view and stopped as close as it could get to the grave site. Thelma Clay climbed out of the car. She was alone.

She walked toward him slowly, using a cane to help her along. She hadn't used one before, Paul noted, and he was surprised to see her with one now.

"I'm surprised to see you here," he said to her when she was across from him, the indentation in the ground separating them.

"I believe it was you who called me," she said.

"I thought you might send someone else."

She gave him an odd look. "Why would I send someone else?" she asked.

"Maybe you wouldn't," he said. "Maybe I got that wrong. Why the cane?"

"Arthritis," she said. "The cold is a killer to my hip joints."

"I'm sorry to drag you out in the cold, then," he said.

"No, you're not. You're delighted because you figured it out about the Indian, and now you want to rub my face in it."

The Indian? The Indian? Then it came back to him. It had been interesting at the time he read it, but it hadn't been about the Bakers, so he had put it aside. In the late 1860s an Indian had come into Jacksonville to see his mother, a washerwoman. A few days before, a party of travelers had been attacked by Indians and three killed as they crossed the mountains on their way to the Rogue

River Valley. A small, angry mob of about a dozen men grabbed the boy and strung him up from a branch on the oak tree behind where the Presbyterian church was now located. They said they were sending out a message to the Indians who had attacked the travelers.

"Kind of an embarrassment for Jacksonville, wasn't it," Paul said. "The boy probably wasn't much more than sixteen at the time, and he certainly hadn't been involved in any attack on settlers."

"That's why getting rid of the records of the lynching was so easy to do," Thelma said. "The day after, folks were indeed pretty embarrassed by what happened. They wanted to forget it, not keep track of it."

Paul made a guess. "Especially Henry Clay."

"You're every bit as good as Nora Ryan said you were. She said that even though we had purged all the records, you'd still come up with the information. How'd you do it?"

He smiled. There she was again, Nora in the mix. "I'm more interested in how Adam did it," he said.

"Blame that one on Nora," she said. "She gets lazy sometimes. She got behind on donations to the museum. She says she hates going through it because most of it is garbage. She let Adam help her catch up. He's the one who found the journal with the account of the lynching."

"And he found out that Henry Clay led the mob."

She frowned. "Well, you're not that good. He was in the mob, but he didn't lead it. And, because of his shame for that day, he dedicated the rest of his life to bringing organized religion to Jacksonville."

"Is that what you told Adam at the cemetery that night?"

The frown slowly shifted into a grin. "You think I

came up here and killed Adam? I was so knotted up with arthritis that night I couldn't have gotten out of bed.''

Guessing had worked well so far. He tried a big one this time. ''And that cane you have there in your hand, the one you've been waving at me for the past two minutes, doesn't have a sword blade attached to the handle?''

She seemed surprised to find herself waving the cane, and then she held it still in the air and stared at it. ''It's just a cane,'' she said. Something though changed the expression on her face. Paul saw a hint of worry there.

''Can I see it?'' he asked.

She handed it across to him. ''Be my guest.''

As soon as he had it in his hands, he knew it wasn't a weapon. This was too light.

He had wondered how someone could have gotten that close to Adam to stab him. The idea of a sword blade hidden in a cane had come to him because he had seen several in the Jacksonville museum and that type of blade would have been consistent with the injury that killed Adam Shipper. They had been a popular weapon for defense in Jacksonville after the gold rush days and before the town finally became civilized.

''My mistake,'' he said.

''If you think I killed Adam, then that's your biggest mistake. He made me mad more often than not. He worked against me more than I liked. And he wasn't as nice as everyone made him out to be. I admit in the end I didn't like him, and I admit I might have been ambitious in my methods to stop him. But I didn't kill him. I was having too much fun battling with him.''

Paul nodded. She was an unlikely suspect, he had to

agree now. "Adam did call you that night, though, didn't he?"

"He called. Said he wanted me to come to the cemetery and meet him at the grave site. I told him over the phone just what I told you. Henry Clay did a dishonorable thing, but he made his amends for it. I wasn't about to go out on a cold night to discuss it in a graveyard, though."

"And you weren't worried about what this information would have done to your reputation?"

She laughed. "Over the years I've pretty much spent the value of Henry Clay's name. When I mention it now, people cringe. I milked all I could out of my ancestry long before the night Adam died."

"What about the damage it might have done to Dallas's political hopes?"

"If I weren't pushing him, Dallas wouldn't walk across the street. He's fat and happy, and he could do without politics, but he does it to please me. Folks know that. Henry Clay's sins wouldn't stick to him."

She was right, Paul thought, and now he was running out of suspects. "I told Minnie Shipper I'd help her out, but it looks like I'm not getting anywhere."

She stuck out her hand. "The cane?"

He handed it back to her. "I'm sorry if I've treated you unfairly," he said.

"At least you're sorry." She turned and walked back to her car, slowly, painfully. "I'm heading back to my electric blanket."

He waited until she was almost to her car when he asked, "You wouldn't have anything to do with a fat cop harassing me or a boy claiming that Adam was a homosexual?"

She stopped short of the car and turned back slowly

to him. She had a broad smile on her face. "Adam always thought of this conflict between us as being a game. He didn't seem to get the idea that it was only a game if both people were playing. I might have done something to elevate the give-and-take beyond game status to send him a message, but this is the last time you will ever hear me say it. And I might have told a fat cop, one who thinks I saved his job for him, that you are an aggravation. What he did with that information I don't know." She chuckled, continuing to smile as she nodded in agreement. "Yes, yes, I will miss the give-and-take between Adam and myself." The smile faded as sadness shoved it aside. "Tragic, tragic," she said as she turned back to her car.

He watched her get in her car and drive away, but he still had one nagging thought. What was that shadow that crossed over her face when she mentioned the sword in the cane? She did know something. He tried to imagine what that might be as he walked through the cemetery to the road that would take him back down to his car.

He doubted now that he would ever figure it out. The least likely to kill Adam still seemed the least likely. The most likely seemed less likely now. He was out of good suspects.

As he walked out of the cemetery, he worked his way through the list again: the superintendent, Arnie, Mondo, the fat cop, Thelma, Dallas, Lexington, the boy... Any of them could have done it. None of them seemed to have. He was so engrossed in his thoughts that he didn't hear the noise behind him until it was almost too late. He sensed the movement. As he turned to see what it was, instinct told him to duck. Because he did, something slammed down across his shoulders, sending a searing pain through his body, instead of catching him on the back of the head and knocking him senseless.

Slowed by the pain, he turned but could not get out of the way of the next blow that came slicing down onto his right shoulder. His legs buckled with the blow, and his whole right side went numb. He dropped to the road and rolled up against the low wall, a move that saved him from the next blow. He watched the tip of the weapon, a cane, catch on the wall and bounce away from him.

He had his back wedged tight into the crook between the road and wall, and he held his left hand out to protect his face. He heard the sound of metal sliding across wood, and then the tip of a sword blade slid through the gap between his fingers and came to rest on the soft spot just below his Adam's apple.

Above him hovered the face of rage. The lips were curled back to bare teeth, and a little spittle oozed from one corner of the mouth. The flesh was scarlet. The eyes bulged, and the pupils were dilated. The voice screeched at him, "You couldn't stay out of it! You couldn't stay out of it!" Above him was the face of a madman. Above him was the face of Lexington Clay.

The tip of the sword pinched the skin of his neck. He knew the slightest pressure would drive it straight through, and he, too, would suffer Adam Shipper's fate. To delay the moment, he managed to whisper, "Why?"

"Why?" Lexington seemed to grimace in pain. "Why? Isn't it obvious?"

The only thing obvious to Paul was that here he was again facing death. Was this the time his luck finally ran out, he wondered? His right arm was still numb, and his left arm was partially pinned between his body and the wall. He had managed to wrap his hand around the blade, but it was so thin and sharp that he had cut his fingers doing it. He couldn't keep the blade from sliding through his grip. He couldn't keep the tip of it from pushing through to the ground.

"No, it's not obvious," Paul said, his voice surprising him because of its calm.

"Adam had found out about Henry Clay. He was already working behind the scenes to get me ousted from my ministry, and now he knew the secret that could destroy me."

"Your mother didn't seem to think the secret would do much damage."

"My mother wasn't thinking about me. She has thoughts only for Dallas." He leaned forward, and Paul felt the tip of the blade slice into flesh. He could feel a warm trickle of blood on the cold skin of his neck. "Would she have the dealerships run by me if Dallas were elected? No. They were going to hire a manager. Did she try to stop Adam from talking about me behind my back to create support for my dismissal? No. Did she do anything when he called me bland and uninspiring on the pulpit? No. Did she even care about the church? No. She said I was a grown man, and she was tired of taking care of me. The church, she said, was mine to win or lose."

Lexington's free hand came up to rub across his eyes, as if he were trying to wipe away an image or maybe to wipe away the rage.

Paul was aware of something else now. He listened intently, and then he knew he had to keep Lexington talking. He thought of suggesting that Lexington take this out on his mother, but then decided that was sure to get him killed.

"How were you so sure that Adam meant you any

harm?'' he asked, and then he strained to hear the sound
that went with the vibrations he felt coming through the
road.

Lexington raised up, and the tip of the sword lifted
from Paul's throat. He laughed, a laughter that sounded
almost normal if it weren't for the slightly hysterical
warble to it. ''The man was mad with glee. He couldn't
keep it in on the phone, and he was just as mad with
glee when I met him at the cemetery that night. I
couldn't let him live, not with the piece of history he
had that would make me a laughingstock in my own
perish. How could I face my people? The name Henry
Clay is as close to a religious icon as we have in this
town.''

Paul heard it clearly. First came the surge of engine
noise as the car started up the steep road, and then that
was followed by the hum of the tires on the asphalt. He
even heard the slight squeak of the brake and the unmistakable sound of car doors unlatching. As loud as
this was to Paul, deafening almost, Lexington seemed
oblivious to it. ''You see why I have to kill you, don't
you?'' He lifted the sword up, both of his hands on the
handle as he readied to plunge it into Paul's throat. Paul
tried to twist away, but his body still could not move.

The next sound was like the crack of thunder, and it
was followed almost immediately with an explosion that
seemed to shake Paul's world. Suddenly Lexington's
body flew away from him while the sword hurled into
space and spun through the air before it, too, disappeared
from view.

''Deus ex machina,'' Paul whispered, and then he
lifted his head. Down the road about thirty feet was a
sheriff's patrol car. Two deputies stood at an open door
with guns drawn. One barrel had a wisp of smoke rising

from it. Behind their car was another car. Liz stood at her open door with her fist pressed to her mouth and her eyes wide with fright.

The two men moved slowly toward the body of Lexington, their guns still trained on him. Paul twisted his head so he could see Lexington. He knew that Clay wouldn't be a threat to anyone again. Gore fanned out on the road above his head. The deputies rolled him over and cuffed him anyway.

Liz dropped to her knees next to Paul with her hands out, but she seemed afraid to touch him. "I look worse than I am," he said.

"You look awful," she said.

"And you are the loveliest thing I've ever seen. Thanks for calling the cops and coming to my rescue."

"Oh, Paul," she cried out, "I wish I had, but I was just driving up to see if you were okay after I got your message on the answering machine."

FOURTEEN

HIS HOUSE DID NOT have a real fireplace, but instead it had a gas stove with ceramic logs that glowed realistically. They were close enough to the real thing for Paul. He sat now in an overstuffed chair with his feet on a footstool, warming them with the heat from the stove. Liz stood behind him, gently soothing with her fingertips the tender muscles of his neck and shoulders.

Once again he had been lucky. He'd walked away with some minor injuries. The tip of the sword had penetrated the skin of his neck but not his airway. The cuts on his left hand stung, but only one of them required a few stitches. The bruising on his back was still sensitive, but the muscles were beginning to loosen up, especially because of Liz's soft touch.

It took a few phone calls, but he finally found out who called the sheriff's office. Thelma Clay had not believed Lexington capable of murder. In fact she had not considered him capable of much of anything. He had pursued the ministry because he knew she admired Henry Clay and he wanted to please her. What he didn't know was that it was the man's name she admired, but not the man. Being a Clay was useful. Being married to a successful businessman was even more useful. Yes, she doted on Dallas because he was like his father. The most she did for Lexington was to work behind the scenes to get him the ministry at the Presbyterian church. In truth, though, she didn't think he was a very good minister and failed to support him after the appointment.

Lexington was not a stupid man, though. He saw that his mother's affections were directed toward Dallas. He felt rejection from her. He knew the only reason he was able to keep the church was because of the Clay name. And he knew that Adam Shipper had the power to destroy that name.

The truth hit home for Thelma when Paul mentioned the sword in the cane. She knew that Lexington possessed the very sword cane that had once belonged to Henry Clay. On the way from the cemetery she spotted Lexington's car parked at the bottom of the hill. She had called him to let him know where she was going and why, much as Paul had done when he left a message for Liz. She hadn't trusted Paul any more than he had trusted her. She was the one who called the sheriff's office from her cell phone to have them check the cemetery, worried about what Lexington might be up to.

Paul thought it was funny that she hadn't even trusted the Jacksonville police, the ones she was so very good at manipulating, to check the cemetery. Perhaps she thought they would do something stupid and hurt Lexington. She would have the rest of her life to think that one through.

Minnie Shipper had called earlier in the evening to thank him. She had been concerned, though. She had said, ''Adam's death nearly killed the holiday spirit in Jacksonville. Lexington's death will certainly finish it off.''

Paul had said nothing. His holiday spirit nearly had been snuffed out. Now, in front of the fire, he had a little bit of it back, but that was tempered with a touch of sadness. Pam had called, delighted that her client would be free. She expressed some concern about his injuries, but she had not offered to come to visit him. "After all," she had said, "you are not in the hospital or anything."

Although he was sure the story had made the evening news, he had not heard from Terri Drexler, either. He had Liz, of course, for compensation, but even that had its own sadness attached to it. She'd be gone in a few days, and both had agreed that this Christmas interlude came with no strings attached.

He closed his eyes and enjoyed the touch of Liz's fingers and the warmth of the fire, and he thought that next time he would say no when someone needed his help. Each time he had said yes he had found his life in danger, and, afterward, each time he had found himself a step further away from being in love.

HOLIDAYS CAN BE MURDER

by Connie Shelton

Biscochitos

1/2 cup sugar
1 cup shortening
1/2 tsp anise seed
2 cups white flour
1 cup whole wheat flour
1/2 tsp salt
1 tsp baking powder
about 1/3 cup water
sugar-cinnamon mixture

Cream shortening and sugar. Beat until light and
fluffy. Add anise. Sift flours, salt and baking powder
together and add gradually to the shortening mixture.
Add just enough water to make a firm dough. Roll
1/4" thick and cut with cookie cutters. Dip cookies in
a mixture of sugar and cinnamon. Bake at 350° F for
10-12 minutes.

ONE

THE HOLIDAYS BRING OUT the best in all of us, and the worst. Between crowded shopping, endless cooking, and hosting a variety of visiting relatives, many a normally rational person has been driven to desperation—sometimes even murder.

I'd been to the mall—something I don't relish at the best of times—and the holiday crowds, traffic and surly temperament of my fellow shoppers had served to put me in a less than charitable mood. Rusty, our red-brown Lab, greeted me at home with his usual I-love-you-no-matter-what exuberance. By the time I'd dropped my shopping bags on the sofa, shed my winter coat and received a few doggy kisses from him, my attitude had begun to ease.

"Hey, you're home," Drake said, emerging from the kitchen. He carried the portable phone and extended it to me now. "Want to say hello to Mom?"

My mother-in-law and I haven't exactly established a rapport just yet. In the fourteen months I've been married to Drake I've met her only once, on a quick trip through Flagstaff, when we flew our helicopter there, on our way to a charter job at the Grand Canyon. During that visit, and a few other phone calls, she and I had probably not exchanged more than two hours' worth of chitchat. To be fair, the conversations had all been pleasant, with the only hint of coolness coming when she discovered that I hadn't taken the Langston name when I married her son. Drake was holding the phone out to me.

"Catherine! How are you?"

"Hi, Charlie, I'm doing just great. I'm so excited about the visit." She got high marks for her bubbly voice and general enthusiasm for life.

"Visit?" Somewhere in there I must have missed something.

"Oh, Drake didn't tell you yet? Well, we've decided that I'll come out there and spend Christmas week with you guys."

We have, huh? I glanced over at Drake, but he'd gotten very busy scratching Rusty's ears.

"I can't wait," Catherine continued. "He tells me how special New Mexico Christmases are, and I'm just dying to get in on some of the traditions."

I took a deep breath. "Well, we can't wait either," I said. "What day will you arrive?"

"The twentieth—that's the Friday before Christmas Day. I can stay a week. And Drake said I should bring Kinsey. Charlie, are you sure that's okay with you?"

Catherine's three-year-old blond cocker spaniel, named for her favorite mystery character, had been absolutely adorable when we'd visited their home. I felt sure she would be as well behaved when traveling and would get along with Rusty.

"Sure, she won't be any problem." I looked toward Drake again, but he'd disappeared into the kitchen. Catherine ended the phone call with love to all and I hung up, ready to track my husband.

"Your mother said thanks for the invitation," I told

him when I found him at the kitchen sink, peeling potatoes for dinner.

He turned around sheepishly. "I hope you don't mind," he said. "It kind of popped out. See, she originally called to invite us to her place for Christmas. And, well, you know how it is with the helicopter service. I could get a call anytime, and I can't really afford to leave town. So, I suggested she think about coming here instead. Guess I thought she'd take a few days to think about it, and I could check with you in the meantime."

"It's okay. I mean, a little warning would have been better, but I don't mind. It'll give me a chance to get to know her better."

He pulled me into a hug, "You're terrific," he mumbled into my ear, giving a little nibble.

I pulled back to arm's length, eyeing the project on the kitchen counter. "So, what are those potatoes going to turn into?"

"Homemade French fries, smothered with chile and cheese?"

"Umm…consider yourself forgiven for anything at all." Drake makes the best homemade French fries ever.

I turned back toward the living room. "I think I finished the last of the shopping. I'm going to put all this stuff in the guest room. That way I'll be forced to finish wrapping it before your mom gets here." I mentally ticked off other things on my to-do list as I carried my bags into the newly remodeled section of the house, hoping I could fit it all into the following week. The baking for the annual neighborhood cookie swap could wait, as would the final touches on the luminarias for the yard decorations.

We live in the old Albuquerque Country Club neighborhood, and a big tradition in the city is that our neighborhood is decorated to the max so everyone else in town can drive through and stare at us. My parents did it when I was a kid, and apparently the tradition goes back at least a generation beyond theirs. My neighbor to the south, Elsa Higgins, is like a surrogate grandmother to me, and she's decorated her yard annually for the fifty-some years she's lived in that house. The tour thing has grown over the years. It used to be that folks just climbed into their cars and drove around. Now there are city bus tours, sold out weeks in advance, and the police place barricades so the tour can only follow certain streets—ours being one of them.

"Hon? Telephone." Drake handed over the portable to me. I hadn't even heard it ring. He shrugged to indicate that he didn't know who it was.

"Hello, Charlie, this is Judy. Judy Garfield. Next door."

Our newest neighbors, a couple of mild-mannered Midwesterners, had moved into the house north of ours two months earlier. The adjustment from life in one of the better suburbs of Chicago to the Southwest was coming as a bit of a culture shock to them.

"I just heard about the decoration requirements," she said. "I don't know what some of this stuff is."

It's probably only in the Southwest that a brown paper lunch sack, some sand and a votive candle can be considered beautiful, but that's how we do it. I explained to her that they could either make their own or buy them ready-made and delivered from the Boy Scouts or other groups that sell them.

"Well…" She hesitated. "Wilbur is really getting into the holidays this year, with everything being so different and all. Could you show us how to make them?"

I added one more thing to my to-do list. "Sure. I think

Drake wants to make ours too. We can have a lesson on it in the next few days.''

We hung up after setting a time to work on luminarias the next afternoon. I closed the door to the guest room, leaving the pile of shopping bags in the middle of the bed, out of sight. I changed from the wool slacks and fluffy sweater I'd worn shopping into jeans and a sweat-shirt before rejoining Drake in the kitchen.

Rusty was supervising the dinner preparations, making sure any tidbits that fell to the floor were swiftly dispatched.

"Boy, those fries smell good," I told my husband, wrapping my arms around his middle and resting my face against his back. "Are they almost ready?"

"Five more minutes. I poured you some wine." He indicated a glass standing on the counter.

I sat at the kitchen table and took a sip while he stirred the green chile sauce simmering in a pan on the burner. I watched him pull the basket of fries out of the deep fryer and prop them on the side to drain. He set two dinner plates on the counter and reached for a bag of grated cheddar. Rusty whimpered, but I managed not to.

"Forgot to tell you—Elsa called while you were out shopping."

"Busy day with the telephone, huh?"

"Wish they were business calls instead," he said. He divided the fried potatoes between the two plates, then shook the shredded cheese over them. It began to melt instantly against their heat. He ladled a good-sized dose of green chile sauce over the top of the heap, making a small mountain in the middle of each plate. I pulled flatware and napkins from a drawer and met him back at the table.

"Wow, am I ever hungry," I told him. "Braving the mall during the Christmas season is tough work."

"Hey, the least I could do is have dinner ready," he said. Shopping is not Drake's strong suit.

"I should probably get a little something extra for your mom, now that she'll be here," I said.

"I hope that was all right, my asking her without checking first."

"Just don't ever do it again," I teased, poking at him with a cheese-coated French fry. "As punishment, you have to help with everything that needs to be done before Christmas." I told him about Judy's call and the planned sacks-and-sand operation for the next day.

"I'll go get the supplies," he promised. "And some spare lightbulbs. Everything looked okay when I checked the strings in the garage this afternoon, but it never hurts to have extras."

We usually decorate the house and trees with red bulbs, offset by the soft golden glow of the luminarias lining the sidewalks. When fire claimed part of our home more than a year ago, we lost our supply of light strings but were, fortunately, able to replace them at last year's postholiday sales.

We finished swabbing the sauce off our plates, and Drake put the dishes in the dishwasher while I returned Elsa's phone call.

"So, red or green?" she asked, after we'd checked on each other's state of health.

"Green, of course," I told her. Not being much of a cook, I have my old favorite green chile stew recipe I fall back on every year for the annual Red and Green Chile Cookoff. New Mexico's two flavors of chile lend themselves so well to the holiday season, that the cook-off has become an annual fund raiser for charity. Between my regular work as a partner at RJP Investigations and my occasional hand in Drake's helicopter service, I have to confess that there isn't much time to give back to the community. The holidays are one time when I make a little extra effort.

"The Cookoff is just a week from today," Elsa reminded. "I think I'll do my grocery shopping tomorrow. Need anything?"

I gave her a short list of ingredients for my stew. Now that it looked as if we'd spend the upcoming weekend decorating the yard, time was about to become crunched. I'd also promised Ron at least two full days at the office next week, the gifts would need to be wrapped, the tree set up in the house and Catherine would get here the same day I had to be down at the convention center cooking chile stew all day.

I glanced up at the wall calendar and noticed that today was Friday the thirteenth.

TWO

THE SKY TURNED WHITE on Monday morning and tiny flakes of snow fluttered onto my windshield as I drove to the office. Sally, our part-time receptionist, was already there. Her car sat in the parking area behind the gray-and-white Victorian that houses the private investigation agency I own with my brother Ron.

"Hey, there," Sally greeted me as Rusty and I blew in through the back door. "Weather's kind of taken a turn, hasn't it?" Her normally ruddy cheeks were pinker than usual, but her shaggy blond haircut didn't look any more ruffled than it usually does.

"Whew! I'm just glad it wasn't doing this yesterday. We hung 143 strings of lights all over the outside of our house. Covered the trees with them, too. And Saturday, I can't even begin to guess how many paper bag tops I folded down. Drake's got them all over the floor of the garage so he can fill them with sand over the next few days."

"By next year he'll probably be more than willing to buy them ready-made," she said with a chuckle.

"Who knows? He's very much a do-it-yourself kind of guy. And he offered to help the new neighbors with theirs, too. I don't think any of them knew what they were getting into."

"Ron's upstairs. Left his car off for an oil change,

and he wants you to take him out at lunchtime to pick
it up. Looks like the only case in the works right now
is one of those spouse-spying things. Can you imagine?
Wanting to track your spouse during the holidays so you
can get divorce ammo on him?''

I raised one eyebrow. Things people do to each other
never cease to amaze me.

''Probably her way of saying 'Happy New Year!'''
Sally finished stirring creamer into her coffee and headed
back to her desk at the front of the converted old house.

I found my favorite mug and poured the last of the
coffee from the pot, switching it off as I added sugar.
Rusty stared expectantly up at the countertop, waiting
for me to get him a biscuit from the tin we keep there.

Upstairs, I peeked through Ron's doorway and gave
a little wave when I noticed he was already on the phone.
He swears that ninety percent of an investigator's work
is done on the telephone, and I'm beginning to believe
it. I rarely see him without it pasted to his ear. In my
own office across the hall, a stack of new mail awaited,
which I quickly sorted by categories: bills to pay, letters
to write and circular file.

I WAS INTENT ON ENTERING expenses into the computer
when I became aware of Ron standing in my doorway.

''Ready?'' he asked.

''For what?''

''Sally said you'd take me downtown to get my car
from the lube place. Hello? Remember?''

''Jeez, is it noon already?'' I glanced at my watch and
saw that it was.

''Time flies when you're having fun?''

I growled.

Rusty opted to stay at the office with Sally, who was

microwaving a cup of hot chocolate. Thirty minutes later, I returned with a bag from McDonald's, and the dog was more than happy to turn his affection back toward me. I was still intent on my fries when Sally came through, announcing that she was done for the day and going home to relieve her husband, Ross, of baby-sitting duties. I spent a couple of hours sending dunning notices to delinquent accounts and answering miscellaneous correspondence.

When I arrived back home, Drake had made little progress on the luminarias. He was slipping on his jacket as I took mine off.

"Got a call for a charter photo job," he said, brushing my lips with a quick kiss. "Been on the phone with this guy half the afternoon, planning the logistics of the thing. Wants to catch the sunset on the Sandias. I told him the light was terrible today, with this gray sky, but he wants to give it a try. Guess I'll buzz him around the west side for an hour or so. If he doesn't get decent pictures, the forecast is better for tomorrow and we'll try it again."

"Flight time?"

"No more than an hour. I'll call as I'm taking off."

The FAA requires a commercial aircraft to file a flight plan or provide someone within the company to monitor each flight. In Drake's business, that was me. I gave him a quick kiss and watched him drive away.

A faint tapping at the back door drew my attention.

"Got your groceries," Elsa said, coming into the kitchen. "The pork tenderloin looked wonderful. It's gonna make yours the winning stew."

I smiled and thanked her. Bless her heart, she has a lot more faith in my cooking abilities than I do. I heated a kettle and made us each a cup of tea. Drake called to give his takeoff time, which I jotted down, then Elsa and I settled back with our tea and several cookbooks to choose our recipes for the neighborhood cookie swap.

"Well, I'm doing my spritz," Elsa said, before we'd delved very far into the books. "They go over pretty good every year, especially the ones I decorate with those little candies."

"They're fabulous," I agreed. "Nothing like a cookie with tons of butter in it to get my loyalty."

I flipped aimlessly through the cookbook. "You know, I think I'll make biscochitos this year. They're Christmasy, and not nearly as much work as some of the frosted, decorated, fancy things other people bring."

"Oh, yes," she agreed enthusiastically, "those are wonderful. Do them."

I'd already filled her in on all the projects I had to accomplish within the week, and the fact that my mother-in-law would be here, now only three days away. We finished our tea, and Elsa headed back to her house through the break in the hedge that's been there since I was a little girl. I used to duck out the kitchen door and try to get through the hedge before Mother could catch me and make me come back. Then I'd sit in Elsa's kitchen and be fed cookies and milk. When my parents died in a plane crash, Elsa Higgins took me into her home and kept me out of trouble until I could move back into the family home and be on my own. Anyone who'll take in a teenager for a couple of years should probably have "Saint" stenciled above her doorway.

I flipped aimlessly through the cookbooks for a few more minutes but didn't change my mind about my choice. Drake phoned to say he'd landed and I noticed that the gray day was dying, becoming a gray twilight.

THE NEXT THREE DAYS FLEW BY, filled with gift wrapping, freshening the guest room and setting up the tree in the living room. By Friday morning, I'd made about all the preparations I could for a mother-in-law visit. I gathered my ingredients for green chile stew and headed downtown to the convention center and the cookoff. The plan was that Catherine would arrive about midafternoon and Drake would bring her downtown to sample the results.

I was well into dipping out my four hundredth ladle of stew into someone's bowl when I glanced up to see my husband grinning at me. Next to him, Catherine stood as regal as ever, her sleek page perfect and her makeup freshly retouched. I pictured how I must look—wilted hair, sweaty upper lip and tomato stains on my white apron. Makeup isn't something I do much with anyway—a touch of lipstick and maybe mascara on a good day—so I knew that department was lacking.

Catherine waited until my customers walked away, then she came over to gather me into a hug.

"Charlie, you look great!" she greeted.

My expression must have shown my skepticism.

"Well, okay, not the *best,* but really, dear, I'm so glad to see you."

I took the compliment as graciously as possible.

"Can we have a taste?" Drake said, eyeing the nearly empty pot.

"Did you buy a ticket? Gotta have your official tasting bowl, you know."

He produced two of the generic bowls and I gave them each a dipper full. He rolled his eyes as he tasted; my green chile stew is his favorite dish.

"Charlie, this is wonderful!" Catherine exclaimed. "Really, really good. I vote for it to be the winner."

I had to chuckle. "You haven't tried any of the others yet," I said.

"That's okay—I still vote for yours."

I smiled at her. "Doesn't look like there's going to be any left to take home. Otherwise, we could have it for dinner."

"Looks like we'll just have to go to Pedro's," Drake said, shrugging. As if eating out at our favorite little spot was a big sacrifice.

I glanced at my watch. "Cookoff's over in another fifteen minutes," I told them. "If you want to check out the other booths before everything's gone, go ahead."

"I think I'll save space for Pedro's," Drake said. "Need help carrying anything out to the car?"

I gathered most of the utensils and ingredients I hadn't used and let him carry them away. Catherine wandered down the long row of booths while I finished wiping up a few stray spills. The crowd had thinned considerably.

"Looks like they raised quite a lot for the homeless," Catherine said, coming back.

"Good. I'm glad it helped. This event has become quite a tradition. Gets bigger every year."

Drake came back and carried the remaining gear outside, and I folded my apron. Fifteen minutes later we were parking both vehicles in front of Pedro's tiny establishment near Old Town. The little parking lot contained only three other vehicles, making it nearly full.

Inside, three of the six tables were occupied, one by Mannie, a grizzled old man who eats chile hotter than most people can stand. He raised his gray-speckled chin in greeting as we took our usual table in the corner.

Concha, Pedro's other half, was in the process of setting heaping plates of tacos on one table. "Margaritas?" she asked as we passed.

"Three," Drake said.

Pedro stood behind the bar, whirring the cool green drinks in his blender. Concha wiped her hands on her apron and picked up the glasses. Balancing a small cocktail tray, she threaded her way toward our table. Drake introduced his mother and the Spanish woman gave Catherine a warm smile.

"I thought you were getting a waitress," I asked her as she set down my drink.

She made a sound that came out like "Pah!" and pulled out her order pad. "Kids. Can't get any of them to do any work. Easier to do it myself."

I noticed that Pedro had headed back to the kitchen while she wrote down our order. Easy enough, since Drake and I usually have the same thing—chicken enchiladas with sour cream. Green. Catherine followed suit.

"I'd forgotten how you get a choice of red or green chile here in New Mexico," Catherine said after Concha had left. "Most places make up these weird concoctions called sauce, and you really don't know what kind of chile is in it."

I could tell I was going to get along just fine with her.

THREE

SUNDAY MORNING DAWNED clear and cold. Frost was thick on the grass and trees, but the hoped-for snowfall from a few days ago seemed to have vanished. Albuquerque rarely gets snow for Christmas—only an inch or two when we do—and it was looking like this year would be no exception.

"Is there more cinnamon, Charlie?" Catherine was helping me bake the biscochitos and we were running out of the cinnamon-sugar coating we'd mixed up earlier.

"Check that upper cabinet," I told her. "I'm pretty sure we're not out."

So far the co-baking project was going along fine. We had two good-sized batches of the traditional Mexican cookies almost done. Catherine and I worked well together in the kitchen, with Rusty and Kinsey supervising as only dogs can. The big red-brown Lab and the little cocker both sat with ears perked and deep brown eyes staring winsomely at our every move.

The cookie swap is our neighborhood's way of getting together socially for an afternoon and for everyone to take home a variety of holiday cookies without having to bake for days on end. Later this afternoon we'd all meet at the country club and have a couple of glasses of sinfully rich eggnog and indulge in far too many calories. I couldn't wait.

Drake eased into the kitchen and slipped one star-shaped cookie from the cooling rack.

"Uh-uh," I scolded. "You're supposed to come to the party to get some."

"That doesn't make any sense," he complained. "You're going to bring home a box full anyway. Why can't I just have some now?"

I shot him a look.

"Besides, I probably won't be able to go. That photographer who got lousy gray pictures the other day wants to try again this afternoon now that the sky's cleared. Looks like I may have to be out with him most of the afternoon." He tried his best to look underfed, so I gave him another cookie and was rewarded with his gorgeous smile and a kiss.

"By the way," he said, "did you notice some guy cruising the street in a dark blue car a while ago? Thought he might be casing the place, so I took down his license number." He reached into his pocket and pulled out a scrap of paper.

The phone rang, interrupting.

"Charlie? It's Judy. Judy Garfield. Next door."

I wondered if she'd continue to identify herself so completely every single time she called. I stuck Drake's note to the refrigerator with a daisy-shaped magnet.

"The cookie swap this afternoon? Is it okay to bring a guest?" Judy asked.

"Sure. Catherine's coming with me. Drake may not be able to make it."

I could hear her taking a deep breath on the other end. "Well, Wilbur's mother dropped in, and we'd like to bring her if that's all right."

"Really? You hadn't said anything about having company for the holidays. That's nice she could make it." I brushed sugar off my hands. "I'm sure it's no problem to bring her along. We'll see you there—about four?"

"See you then." Her voice sounded tight, like she was talking with her teeth clenched.

THE COUNTRY CLUB'S dining room was dressed in all its holiday finery when we arrived. Twin spruce trees at each end of the room were laden with bows, pinecones and bunches of sugared fruit. Red and gold satin ribbons draped the cookie tables, set up along three walls. Already, platters of cookies filled two of the long tables, beckoning with their loads of butter and sugar. I set down my plates and turned to see who was already here.

Elsa stood across the room, a dainty basket hanging from her arm, her puff of white hair freshly styled. She seemed intent on a plate of some kind of cookie with bright red maraschino cherries in the centers.

"Let's go say hello," I said to Catherine.

"Oh, that's your neighbor, isn't it? The one who's also your grandmother."

"Almost, that's right."

Elsa remembered Catherine immediately. "And where's that husband of yours?" she asked me.

"Got a flight and couldn't make it. He'll consume his share of the cookies later, I'm sure."

A commotion at the entry grabbed our attention.

"Oh! I'm so sorry," a woman was saying. Her voice came through the room clearly, as though amplified. "Judy, here let me get that."

I looked beyond her to see Judy Garfield, looking mortified, standing just inside the vestibule.

"Judy! Did you hear me? I said I'll take that for you."

Unfortunately, everyone in the room heard her and all eyes were watching the little scene play out. Judy and Wilbur each carried a heavy-looking platter covered with plastic wrap, and the woman was attempting to take a plate in each hand, something that clearly was not a good idea. Wilbur said something quietly into her ear, and she finally settled for carrying only one of the platters.

She tottered into the dining room on red four-inch heels. The shoes were complemented by a strapless red satin dress, formfitted to the waist then blossoming out in a tulip-shaped skirt. Her short-short black hair was pulled back on the right side and held in place by a monster of a red poinsettia. The whole effect was a bit much for a neighborhood gathering at four o'clock on a Sunday afternoon.

I was beginning to figure out why Judy's voice had sounded so tense this morning.

Wilbur placed a guiding hand on his mother's elbow and ushered her toward the tables at the far right wall. Judy followed meekly, looking as if she wished the floor would swallow her up. As Wilbur and the red woman set down their platters, all eyes stayed on that end of the room and conversation had not quite picked up again.

"Well," said Elsa. "That's certainly interesting."

Catherine and I both chuckled at her estimation of the situation.

I caught Judy's eye and gave a little wave. She smiled and practically trotted across the room toward us. She wore a gray pleated skirt and a gray-and-pink sweater. Her straight brown hair was pulled back with a pink headband.

"Your mother-in-law?" I asked hesitantly, nodding toward the other end of the room.

"Oh, yes." Her eyelids dropped for a moment, as if she had a headache.

"She's certainly colorful," Elsa offered.

"Oh, yes," Judy said again. "That she is."

Wilbur had spotted us and was steering his mother in our direction. His scalp blushed extra pink through his thinning, sandy hair. As they approached, I noticed that the woman was really rather petite, no more than five-two, even in the high heels. Her hair was deep black, and her brows were penned in to be the same color. Lipstick the same shade as the satin dress served to highlight the fact that there were deep creases beside her mouth, and the crow's-feet at her eyes were the kind caused by heavy smoking.

Wilbur spoke up. "This is my mother, Paula Candelaria."

"Charlie! I'm just so *glad* to meet you," she squawked as he introduced me. "Judy's told me so much *about* you. A private *eye*—that must be so *exciting!*"

Her voice came out at least a dozen decibels louder than anyone else's. Heads turned again.

"Well," I murmured, purposely bringing my own voice lower, "I'm not really a private investigator. Just a partner in the firm."

"But you solve *mur*ders and *every*thing," she went on, not taking my hint to lower her voice.

I shrugged, scrambling vainly for another subject. "That eggnog sure looks good," I suggested.

Paula's head whipped toward the end of the long table. "Oh, my, yes. That does look good. I sure hope they made it strong enough."

She began a sprint toward the opposite end of the room and stumbled in her spiky heels. Mr. Delacourte, a Methodist minister who lived two streets over from us, reached out instinctively to catch her elbow. She turned and placed both hands against his chest.

"Why *thank* you, kind sir. You saved me from embarrassing myself."

Mrs. Delacourte turned three shades whiter, and I could swear I heard her sharp intake of breath.

Mr. Delacourte removed Paula's hands from his lapels and mumbled some kind of gracious reply.

Paula turned with a swish of her red tulip skirt and headed again for the punch bowl. I caught myself holding my breath as I watched her maneuver the ladle shakily toward her cup.

Beside me, Judy took a deep breath and squeezed her eyes shut. Wilbur headed to the end of the cookie table, where gold boxes with tissue linings waited for residents to fill with their choices of goodies to take home. Conversation in the room began to return to normal, and Elsa had resumed her browsing.

"I'm so sorry," Judy murmured. "I had no idea she'd make such a scene. I suspect she got into Wilbur's special cognac before we left the house."

"Hey, it's not your fault," I assured her. "Is she going to be staying through Christmas?" I tried to make the question sound polite.

"Ugh, yes. I hope I make it."

"Judy, I don't want to sound rude, but is she always like this?"

Her eyes rolled. "Her behavior is very off-and-on. It's just that it's been 'off' much more frequently since she left husband number five a few months ago. I just had this feeling, this dreadful feeling, that she'd show up and want to spend the holidays with us.

"See, she latches on to Wilbur in every crisis. In our twelve years of marriage, she's been through two husbands and I can't even guess how many boyfriends. It'd be sad if I could watch it from a distance, but every time she lands on our doorstep I just grit my teeth.''

"You're right, it is sad,'' I sympathized.

"And now, with the baby, I just don't want her around. Can you imagine how you'd feel if she were your grandmother?''

"A baby? Judy, you didn't tell me!''

She blushed. "Well, we've wanted this for so long and had a couple of miscarriages. I hadn't planned to make it public until I got a little farther along.''

"It's okay, I won't tell anyone—except Drake. Would that be okay?'' I reached for a cutout Santa on a platter near me. "Does Paula know?''

"No! Sorry. I really don't want her to find out yet. I just hope Wilbur can keep it quiet awhile longer.''

A crash and the tinkle of breaking glass grabbed our attention. Paula stood at the punch bowl, ladle in hand.

"Hey! Watch it, lady.'' The abrasive male voice came from Chuck Ciacarelli, one of the richest men in town, with a reputation for being nasty tempered. We called him Chuckie Cheese behind his back.

Paula was staring at the floor with a puzzled expression. Two women nearby knelt to pick up broken glass, while another reached for a handful of napkins.

"Careful, you're bleeding,'' the napkin woman said.

"Oh my gosh,'' I said to Judy, "it looks like Paula's cut her hand.''

"At this rate we'll be lucky if she doesn't kill herself,'' Wilbur said, handing Judy his partially filled cookie box and heading toward his mother.

"Or lucky if she does,'' muttered Judy.

FOUR

I GAZED OUT at the early morning, trying to determine whether it was cloudy or merely too early for the sky to show any color yet. Christmas Eve. It was going to be a busy day, and I really wanted nothing more than to snuggle in with Drake and wake up three days later to find the holiday hoopla all behind me.

We'd spent all day Monday setting the luminarias along the sidewalks and driveways. Paula had been much subdued after her antics at the cookie swap Sunday afternoon. Drake and I pitched in and set Elsa's sacks out for her and then helped Judy and Wilbur do the last of theirs. A plan had evolved that the three households would get together for dinner tonight, then we'd go out and look at the lights.

One downside of living in the most popular section of town for Christmas light displays is that the police barricade our streets and the traffic is so solidly packed that there's no hope of getting out of our own driveway anytime after late afternoon. We've learned over the years to settle in and plan on Christmas Eve at home. I decided to make another batch of my green chile stew, since Drake had hardly gotten a taste of the last one. It could easily feed the whole group. Elsa would contribute corn bread and Judy planned to bring a salad. Paula said something about making eggnog, but Judy quietly nixed that. Paula without alcohol would definitely be easier to handle.

I nestled into Drake's shoulder for a few more minutes but finally decided I was too wide-awake to actually get any more rest. I kissed his bare chest and rolled off the bed. Ten minutes later, quick-showered, dressed and with a hasty swipe of the hairbrush, I padded to the kitchen in my socks. Rusty trotted along and Kinsey, hearing him in the hallway, nosed the guest room door open and followed us.

I let the two dogs out into the backyard while I started coffee. By the time it finished trickling into the carafe, Catherine had emerged from her room, hair freshly brushed, wearing a cozy burgundy velour robe. We good-morninged each other while I pulled two mugs from the cupboard.

"I hope I don't live to regret my offer to Paula," she said, taking her mug and adding a slight drizzle of cream.

Catherine, with the patience of a saint, had offered to take Paula shopping for a few last-minute things. They planned to leave shortly after breakfast this morning and come back midafternoon.

"I'll watch Kinsey while I make the stew," I offered. "Or maybe it's the other way around."

"I think you've got that right. Once she smells something cooking, she'll be right in your face."

"It's okay. I'm used to it. She's such a little sweetheart. Easy to have around." I opened the kitchen door and the dogs raced in. They both headed for the food dishes I'd set out.

Catherine and I toasted a couple of English muffins and finished our coffee.

"Guess I better get dressed. The sooner we hit the stores, the sooner we'll get back," she said.

Drake shuffled into the kitchen wearing pajama bottoms I'd never seen before and his favorite old robe. Catherine gave her son a quick kiss and headed toward her room. I gave him a much longer kiss and settled him at the table with a mug of coffee.

"Woo-hoo! Anybody home?" Paula poked her head into the kitchen.

I shot Drake a look. He shrugged and held up the newspaper he'd carried in. *Yeah,* I tried to convey, *you forgot to relock the door.*

"Coffee! I smell coffee," chirped Paula. "Do you mind?" She'd already begun opening cabinet doors, looking for the cups.

I handed her a clean one.

"Judy and Wilbur don't drink coffee," she said. "Can you believe it? God, I can't believe there's a household in America where they don't make coffee in the morning."

She took a long sip and let out a satisfied sigh. "Man, I needed that." She settled into the chair across from Drake and reached for his newspaper. My husband is too well-mannered to actually swat her hand, but I could tell the temptation was there.

Paula wore a pair of skintight black jeans, high-heeled boots and a fluffy sweater in a bright shade of magenta. Her short black hair was slicked back from her forehead with some kind of gel and would have looked model-like except for the patch in back that still had a little sleep tangle in it.

"Catherine's getting ready now," I told Paula. "She mentioned that you were going shopping this morning."

"Yeah, silly me." She did a little forehead knock with

the heel of her hand. "Here I show up at Christmas without any gifts. When I saw all the stuff Wilbur and Judy have under their tree, well, duh, I figured I better get with the program."

"I'm sure they weren't really expecting much," I offered gently. *Least of all were they expecting you to show up unannounced.*

"Guess I've just had a few other things on my mind. This hasn't been an easy year, I'll tell you. Divorce. That's really hit me hard." Her voice had turned from perky to teary in an instant. "And my job—huh, that's a joke. *Downsized,* they're calling it. Truth is, they're cutting out everybody who might be getting close to collecting any of their precious retirement fund."

She took another deep sip of her coffee.

"Hah! Guess that'll teach me to trust those corporate types." A cackle started down in her throat and turned nearly hysterical on its way to her lips. "Lucky I had kids to come home to."

I glanced at Drake. He was intently studying the stockmarket pages.

"Um, maybe I should let Catherine know you're here." I refilled her mug and dashed toward the bedrooms.

"Gosh, are the stores even open yet?" Catherine asked after I tapped on her door.

"Take your time," I said. "I can always send her back to Judy's for a while."

When I got back into the kitchen, Paula was rummaging through my refrigerator. "Got any jam?"

I pointed to the jars sitting in the racks on the door. I noticed that she'd helped herself to a couple of slices of bread, which were browning in the toaster oven. Drake had abandoned his newspaper, probably deciding to get dressed and find something to do outside. The dogs were sitting in front of the toaster, their bright-eyed gazes traveling between the food and Paula. She didn't appear to notice them.

I busied myself rinsing Drake's mug and putting a few things into the dishwasher. Paula made herself comfortable at the table with her toast and our newspaper.

"Are you thinking about staying here in Albuquerque?" I asked. A quick image flashed through my mind of Paula coming over early every morning, helping herself to my coffee, some breakfast and our newspaper. I dropped a knife into the sink with a clatter.

"Hmm? Oh, I don't know yet," she answered. "Maybe sometime after New Year's I'll start checking out the want ads."

Poor Judy.

Catherine came in, dressed in a pair of tailored gray wool slacks and a deep blue sweater that gave a rich tone to her sleek, dark hair. She took in the scene and raised an eyebrow toward me. Paula mumbled a "good morning" through a mouthful of toast and turned back to the horoscope section of the paper.

"Well," said Catherine, trying to work some cheerfulness into her voice, "I guess we could get going anytime."

Paula brushed crumbs off her hands onto her jeans and stood, leaving her plate and mug beside the rumpled newspaper.

"Don't worry about those dishes, Paula. I'll get them." Like she'd planned on cleaning them up. As they left, I glanced up at the clock. She'd been here a whole twenty minutes. It was going to be a long week.

FIVE

DRAKE WAS BUSILY CHECKING the outdoor lights once more when I opened the front door to look for him. The sky had turned white again, an ominous indicator that there might be snow later in the day.

"Hon, I think those bulbs haven't had time to burn out yet," I teased.

"It wasn't the bulbs I was saving," he said, peeking around the huge blue spruce by the dining-room window.

"Your mother is really a doll. Anyone who would voluntarily spend a day shopping with Paula..."

He walked toward the front porch and put his arms around my waist. His face was red and chilly. "Hey, do you realize we're alone? For probably the only time this week."

"Uh, not exactly." I spotted Judy Garfield walking across the lawn toward us, bundled up in wool slacks and a puffy car coat.

He groaned, dropped one arm and turned to face her.

"Oh, Charlie, I'm sorry Paula came over so early this morning," she began. "I thought she was still in her room—it takes her forever to get dressed and made up in the mornings."

"It's okay. Catherine was almost ready." I glanced

up at Drake, who was eyeing the neatly placed luminarias along the sidewalk.

A dark blue car cruised by, the driver looking at addresses. I got an impression of a male with longish dark hair and wraparound sunglasses. When he realized the three of us were staring at him, he sped up and took a left at the intersection. I glanced toward Drake, but he was still staring after the car.

Without a jacket, I was feeling the chill in the air. I'd ask him about it later. I turned to Judy. "Want some coffee—or how about a cup of tea?"

"Tea would be great," she said, pushing a wisp of mousy hair behind her ear.

In the kitchen, I set a kettle on the burner and found two muffins left from earlier in the week. I gathered the scattered newspapers into a relatively neat pile and set out mugs and tea bags. Judy slumped into one of the chairs.

"I tell you, Charlie, I'm whipped." She sighed. "Having Paula around is like inviting a tornado into your home. She's a bundle of energy, the kind that needs to be the center of attention. And the phone rings constantly for her. What did she do—tell everyone she knows that she's visiting us?"

I didn't mention Paula's comment about possibly making it more than a visit.

"'Course, I guess that also describes what having a child must be like." She laughed. "Maybe this is good practice for me."

"Well, at least a baby starts out small and unable to get into everything," I offered. "You have a little time to get used to it."

She dunked her tea bag four times and wrung it out

by twisting the string around a spoon. Placing the wet bag on a saucer, she began to peel the paper off a muffin.

"I'll tell you, though," she said, her eyes narrowing to slits. "I won't *ever* get used to having Paula around. Wilbur won't do anything about her. He's…well, she's ingrained a lot of intimidation into him. But I will. And pretty soon."

I sipped my tea and watched her rip the muffin paper into tiny shreds.

By four o'clock that afternoon I'd stuffed the last of the packages under the tree, helped Drake straighten the luminaria sacks and had the pot of green chile stew simmering on the stove. Catherine had come home around three, looking somewhat frazzled. She'd opted for a nap before the evening festivities and, thinking that sounded like a pretty good idea, I crawled onto our bed and pulled a quilt over myself.

Drake's gentle hand on my shoulder woke me. "Hey, you gonna sleep all night?" he teased.

I mumbled something incoherent.

"Elsa just showed up at the back door with corn bread, and I have a feeling the others might arrive anytime."

"Oh my God, what time is it, anyway?"

"Almost six."

I realized the windows were dark and couldn't believe I'd slept nearly two hours. I whipped the quilt aside and stood up too fast.

"Take it easy," he said. "I turned on the outdoor lights. Cars are already coming up the street. The stew is doing fine, and Mom and I set the table in the dining room. I think everything's under control."

The doorbell rang. "Uh-oh, get that, okay? I'll brush my teeth real quick and get the tangles out of my hair."

He blew me a kiss from the doorway. "No rush."

I emerged five minutes later to a houseful of people. Catherine was setting food on the table, and Drake had managed to satisfy everyone's needs drink-wise. I slipped past Judy—looking a little tense around the mouth—and Paula—dressed in green leather pants, a tight red sweater and red flats—and made my way to the kitchen. Tasted the stew, just to be sure it had turned out all right, before we began ladling it into bowls.

"How did the shopping trip go today?" I asked Catherine, keeping my voice low.

"Interesting."

"Just…interesting?"

"Well, I'll tell you, I learned more about Paula than I ever wanted to know. She gave me the whole lowdown on what was wrong with each of the five ex-husbands, and a few juicy tidbits about some new young hunk she's seeing."

"Oh boy, I'll bet that was fun."

She rolled her eyes and began carrying the bowls of hot stew into the dining room. I followed with another batch and called everyone to the table. I noticed that Catherine chose to sit by Drake's side at one end, staying as far from Paula's chair as possible. Wilbur sat near Paula, probably at Judy's insistence, although from what she'd told me, if Paula got out of hand Wilbur would be the last person to do anything about it. Judy seated herself on the other side of her husband, undoubtedly for the proximity to his shins.

Actually, dinner went quite well, with Elsa entertaining us with stories of Christmases in the fifties. When she got to the point where she was about to reveal some of my crazier antics as a kid, it looked like a good time to start our tour of the neighborhood lights.

While I have to admit that having the neighborhood barricaded and watching bumper-to-bumper traffic snake its way down our street until the wee hours of the morning doesn't sound like an appealing way to spend Christmas Eve, we local residents have discovered a nice side benefit. We get to slip behind the barricades and walk the closed-off streets, enjoying a private show of our own.

"Looks like it could snow a bit," Drake said, peering out between the bedroom drapes as I slipped on heavy socks and walking boots. "That sky's awfully white."

"Better caution everyone to bundle up," I said, remembering Paula's attire.

Out in the living room, everyone had put on heavy coats, gloves and caps. Rusty and Kinsey were waiting by the door expectantly.

I eyed Paula's leather slacks and thin leather flats without socks. "Paula, I'd be happy to loan you some sweats and some socks," I offered.

"Oh, thanks, Charlie, but that's okay. I'll be fine in these." Her chic winter jacket of red faux fur just wouldn't have been the thing with sweats, I guess.

I clipped a leash on Rusty's collar, and Catherine did the same with Kinsey. By default, because we were being dragged ahead by the dogs, she and I ended up leading the little procession. I glanced back to see Drake lock the front door behind him, then offer Elsa an assisting hand on her elbow.

We walked past Elsa's house and the next one, holding our breath against the exhaust of the tour buses. At the corner, we turned left, slipping past a barricade that kept traffic off the side street as well as two other blocks behind ours. By the time we were one street over from our own, the difference was incredible. The traffic noises and smells faded away, and we strolled leisurely down the middle of the streets enjoying our own private show of all the homes not on the regular tour.

Catherine exclaimed over the number of luminarias lining the sidewalks and driveways. "I can't imagine how much work went into all this," she said. "And the lights, look how beautiful they are!"

"Oops!" cried Paula. "I sure didn't see that crack in the street."

Wilbur reached out and grasped his mother's arm, steadying her. I wondered how many martinis she'd made for herself after the one Drake had given her. I reined in Rusty and held him back until Drake caught up with us. He slipped his arm around my shoulders.

"Merry Christmas, sweetheart," I whispered to him. No matter how crazy the rest of the holiday got, I was glad we had each other.

"Hey, look," he said. "Told you it looked like snow."

A big, fat white flake drifted in front of me and landed on Rusty's back. Soon, there were thousands of them and the street had a thin white cover. I smiled, remembering Drake's and my first Christmas together last year at the Taos Ski Valley. There'd certainly been no shortage of snow there. I tilted my face up to the sky and let the flakes land on my eyelids. I would ignore Paula and do my best not to get involved with my neighbors' problems.

Well, it was a good intention, anyway.

SIX

I AWOKE TO GRAY LIGHT filtering around the edges of the drapes and utter silence outside. My first thought was: the buses have gone away. I rolled toward Drake and he pulled me into his arms. The next thing I knew he was planting little nibbles along my neck and shoulder, and the rest became a pleasant blur of sensation as we pulled the covers over ourselves and enjoyed each other.

I awoke for the second time to a brighter gray light. I reached for Drake again, but he wasn't there.

"Snowed about three inches," he whispered, emerging from the bathroom.

"Really?" I was instantly awake and wanting to go out and play in it. He pulled me back into his arms and wrapped the comforter around both of us.

Rusty sat by the edge of the bed, signaling that he'd soon require attention. We ignored him.

"I'll make breakfast if you want to go out there and build a snowman or something," Drake said. "I can tell you're itching to get up."

"Well…if you're sure." I was up and rummaging in the closet for my ski pants almost before he'd finished the offer.

He laughed out loud and tossed a pillow at me. I

dashed into the bathroom and brushed my teeth in record time, then slipped into ski pants and boots.

"C'mon, Rust, we're gonna have some fun."

I heard water running in the guest bath, so I opened Catherine's bedroom door and let Kinsey dash out. "You, too," I told her. "We're gonna play!"

The two dogs beat me to the back door by a long shot and bounded ahead of me. Kinsey leaped through the fresh powder, her stubby little tail pointing straight up. Rusty made his usual rounds of all the trees and sniffed to make sure intruder dogs hadn't used them during the night. I packed a bit of the powder and tried for a snowball, but it was pretty hopeless. The stuff was as dry as shredded cotton. I had to be happy with running around the yard, tossing handfuls of white powder at the two dogs and watching them try to bite at it as it hit their heads.

"Breakfast!" Drake called from the doorway. He batted at the dogs' fur with an old towel, knocking the powdery white off them. Kinsey had loads of it embedded in the long blond hair around her legs and belly and in her long, curly ears.

"Your cheeks are red," he said to me.

"Umm, feels good. Don't worry about the dogs—they can't hurt the kitchen tile too badly."

An hour later, we'd finished a fabulous breakfast of eggs Benedict and fresh fruit and were well into the loot under the tree in the living room. Catherine had given us matching robes, and Drake gave me a heart-shaped diamond pendant and my very own .380 automatic. He'd been teaching me to shoot at our local range, where I usually used his 9 mm Beretta. This would be lighter to handle and small enough I could carry it in my purse. My gift to him was a set of aviation references—lacking the romantic element, but something he'd been wanting for a long time. Together, our gift to Catherine was a vacation trip she'd been wanting to take to visit her elderly aunt in Vermont. Drake had told me that Aunt Ruthie was a real pistol at eighty-nine years old, but just couldn't quite manage a two-thousand-mile-long journey.

"This is the best," Drake sighed, plopping himself on the couch, gazing fondly at his mother and then at me, while stroking one of the reference books in his lap. I wasn't sure which of the above made him the happiest, but it didn't really matter. I stretched out in one recliner and Catherine took the other. I had an instant's déjà vu as I remembered holidays in this same room when I was a kid.

"Well, if we're going to have turkey tonight, I think I better put it in the oven," I finally said, pulling myself out of my little haven.

The phone rang just as I walked into the kitchen.

"Merry Christmas, Charlie." It was Judy. "If you're not terribly busy right now, could I come over for a minute?"

"Sure. We're pretty much just lying around, fat and happy," I told her. With eggs Benedict for breakfast and a full turkey dinner coming up—fat and happy was a pretty good description.

A couple of minutes later, I heard Drake open the front door, then Judy came into the kitchen.

"Thanks so much," she breathed, sinking into one of the kitchen chairs. "I just had to get out for a little while."

"Coffee?" I offered, belatedly remembering that she didn't drink it.

"Please. Strong."

I raised an eyebrow. "I could make you some tea, if you'd rather."

She waved her hand back and forth. "No, it's okay, really."

She accepted the mug I handed over and doused it liberally with sugar and cream while I put the turkey into the roasting pan and set it in the oven.

"You don't look like you're having such a great day," I offered tentatively.

She made a low growling sound. "Oh, it started off all right. Paula was so hung over from last night—apparently she'd restocked her hidden supply and managed to duck into her room several times throughout the evening. Anyway, she slept till nearly eleven this morning, and Wilbur and I finally had some time to ourselves."

She sipped at the coffee and grimaced. "The fun started after that. She came dragging into the kitchen and informed us that she plans to stay in Albuquerque and that she'll be living with us until she gets a job and a place of her own. Not more than a couple of months—" Her voice cracked and she put her forehead on the table. A sound came out that sounded like "no, no, no."

"Staying?" I'm afraid my own voice sounded frightened.

Judy raised her head. Her eyes were red-rimmed, her face blotchy. "I can't handle it, Charlie, I really can't." She raised the coffee mug and put it back down. "And the worst part is that Wilbur won't say anything. He doesn't want her here, either. We've talked about this when we're alone. But he just can't stand up to her."

I microwaved a new mug of water and got out a tea bag.

"Here. I don't think that coffee's doing you much good."

She did the dunking and squeezing ritual and took a sip before she spoke again. "What am I going to do?"

"Change the locks? Move to Zimbabwe?" I offered helpfully.

"Have plastic surgery so she won't recognize me?"

"Go into the Witness Protection Program?"

"Bump her off?"

"But only in the most painful way possible."

"Oh yes, only that would do." She giggled and took a good pull on her tea. "I better get going. I've got a few things to do around the house and I'd love a nap. Wilbur and I are invited to a dinner party tonight. And Paula's *not* going."

"Hey, at least we put a smile back on your face," I said. I walked her to the front door and watched her move lightly down the steps. The sun had come out early and melted the snow from walkways and street, leaving only the lawns and shrubs in frosty white.

A nap sounded pretty good to me, too, but I first called each of my brothers to wish them Merry Christmas. Paul's household in Mesa, Arizona, was raucous with the shrieks of his two kids and a series of electronic blips in the background. Distracted by all of it, Paul was clearly not with me, so I ended the call after just the basics. Ron answered his phone with a note of hope in his voice.

"Oh, I thought it might be the boys," he said when he heard my voice.

"They'll call," I assured him. My heart goes out to my elder brother every other year when he faces this separation from his kids. Part of the price one pays for selecting the wrong spouse, then producing three munchkins before figuring out what kind of person she really is. Ron's divorce hit him hard, and Bernadette did nothing to make it easier, either for him or for the kids.

"Dinner's at five," I told him, repeating the invitation extended a few days earlier. "But come any time. You and Drake can play with your new Christmas toys." I didn't mention my new gun. Knowing my brother, he'd convince Drake to head out to the range immediately, and I wanted to be the first to fire it. Sometime in the next few days we'd find the time.

I AWOKE TO THE WEIRD sensation that something was way out of place. Before my eyes opened, the realization came that there were voices. I rolled over and moaned and squinted at the red numerals on my bedside clock. 12:37. No wonder, I was still into those first few really deep-sleep hours. After our early dinner, we'd sat around the table playing card games for several hours before calling it a night around eleven.

The voices rose and fell and seemed to be coming from outside.

"What's going on?" Drake said, his voice coming through clearly, like he'd been awake for a while.

I turned toward him and realized that I was seeing faint images of red and blue lights swirling across the ceiling. I swung my legs over the edge of the bed and slipped on my new robe. Spreading the miniblinds, I peeked into the backyard. Same eerie swirling lights, but no clue as to their source. I walked into our bathroom, whose windows face the side yard and the Garfields' house. The strobes were clearly reflecting off the side of their home.

"Something's wrong next door," I told Drake. "Let me see."

I nearly tripped over Rusty as he jumped up and tried

to race me to the hall. Drake was pulling on his robe as I made my way through the darkened house to the front door. I gripped Rusty's collar as I opened the front door and stepped out to the front porch.

Three police cars sat at the curb in front of the Garfields' house and ours. An ambulance was backed into Wilbur and Judy's driveway. It was the vehicle with the lights flashing. A small cluster of neighbors stood in front of the Johnsons', the house directly across from ours. Luminaria bags slumped in wilted mounds along their sidewalk.

"What's going on?" Drake said, joining me on our front porch.

"Can't tell. Something next door. Gotta get shoes," I gasped. My bare feet were nearly frozen to the concrete.

I ran back inside and dropped my robe, pulling on jeans and a sweatshirt, socks and my walking boots. Drake was right behind me, grabbing clothes and boots, too. I instructed Rusty that he had to stay inside, and I headed across the lawn toward the Garfields' front door.

"Hold it right there, ma'am," a sharp voice commanded. A rough hand gripped my shoulder and spun me. "Charlie?"

"Kent? What's going on here?"

He dropped his hand but stood firmly blocking my way.

"This is a crime scene. Neighbors of yours, I gather?"

"Uh, yeah. I live right here," I said, indicating our house with a vague wave. "What kind of crime?" I knew it was a stupid question the minute it slipped out. Kent Taylor worked only one kind of case—homicide.

SEVEN

"Who…?" My mind couldn't come up with anything more intelligent at the moment. I felt Drake walk up beside me and was aware that Taylor greeted him by name.

He consulted his notes. "A Paula Candelaria," he said. "Not a resident of the home, visiting her son and daughter-in-law."

"Right." Paula was dead? It took me a minute to process it. Then the floodgates opened and a thousand thoughts rushed through. *Couldn't happen to a nicer person. At least she can't move in and take over Judy's life now. What a pain she's been. What a pitiful person, so desperate for attention, her drinking out of control…* I found myself staring at the ground, waffling between feelings of relief that she was gone and horror that I would think that way.

"Do you…?"

I realized that Kent Taylor had said something to me and I hadn't caught any of it.

"I said, do you have any idea who might have wanted to kill her?" he repeated.

"Kill her?" I recited dumbly.

"Detective, maybe we could take this inside?" Drake requested. He slipped his arm around my shoulders and tried to rub some warmth into them.

"Tell you what," Kent said. "I've got some more questions to ask here, and I need to take a look outside before these snowy footprints get even more trampled. You guys go back into your own house, and I'll come over after a while and go over this with you."

"Good idea," Drake agreed.

"What about Judy? How's she doing?" I pictured this as just one more thing my fragile neighbor had to cope with.

"We're checking into that." He turned away, and Drake steered me toward our front door.

"That was a strange answer, don't you think?" I asked Drake as he opened the front door. The warmth of our living room felt so good, I rubbed my chilled hands together.

"What's going on?" A sleepy Catherine was just emerging from her room, zipping the front of her robe, her hair tousled wildly.

"There's been some problem next door, Mom," Drake said gently. "I think you could go back to bed if you want. The police may be over here after a while, so we're going to stay up."

"Police? Oh my God!" she exclaimed, instantly more alert. "Well, in that case I'm staying up, too. I'll make us some hot chocolate."

She hurried to the kitchen while I flopped on the sofa. I remembered the jokes Judy and I had made earlier in the day, about bumping off Paula as painfully as possible. God, I hoped she hadn't taken me seriously. I sat with elbows on knees, my face in my hands.

"Hon? You okay?" Drake asked.

I nodded but didn't trust myself to speak. He stuck his index finger under my chin and raised my head until he could see my eyes.

"Sweetheart, *what* is it?"

"What if I had something to do with this?" My throat suddenly felt tight.

"How could you poss—?"

"Judy and I talked about killing Paula," I blurted out.

"Wait…what?" Confusion mingled with horror on his face.

"Jokingly! I mean when she came over earlier today—well, I guess it was yesterday now. Anyway, she'd been telling me how Paula was driving her nuts, and we got into this little banter about ways to get rid of her. It was just… You don't suppose I gave her an idea, do you?"

He put his finger gently on my lips. "Hush now. *No,* you didn't give her any ideas. And no, Judy wouldn't have really hurt Paula. Saying you wish you were rid of someone is *not* the same as killing them."

His voice dropped as Catherine peeked in from the kitchen. "Marshmallows?" she asked.

"Cabinet beside the fridge." I answered in a surprisingly normal tone, but the minute she disappeared my head dropped back into my hands.

"Charlie, take a deep breath," Drake ordered. "Now, you're not going to say any of this to Kent Taylor."

"What if I'm concealing evidence?"

"This conversation between you and Judy is not evidence. Not yet, anyway. Just wait to find out what he finds at the…the…"

"Crime scene," I filled in. "I can't believe this. Our neighbors' house has become a crime scene."

"Whatever. Just don't impart this particular information to him unless it looks like it really might be relevant. And even then, be very careful what you say."

"Chocolate's ready," Catherine chirped from the

doorway. She hipped open the swinging door, her hands loaded with a large tray and three steaming mugs. Drake gave my hand a squeeze, then shoved magazines aside to make space on the coffee table.

We drank our hot chocolate and speculated as to what might be happening next door, with Drake periodically peeking out the front windows to report as various vehicles left. We'd fallen into an almost sleepy silence again when the knock came at the front door at two-thirty. Kent Taylor's appearance and the gust of wintry air he ushered in brought the rest of us around again.

"Do I smell chocolate?" he asked before he'd slipped off his overcoat.

Catherine immediately offered to get him a cup, and the rest of us decided we'd take refills, too.

He flipped to a new page in his spiral. "Okay, what does anybody know about the friction between the family next door?"

Nothing like getting straight to the point. I glanced at Drake, a move that I'm sure made it look as if I had something to hide.

"Wilbur and Judy appear to get along just great," Drake offered. "Haven't noticed any problems there."

"Well, I'm kind of looking more for information on who might have not been getting along with the victim, Paula Candelaria." Taylor's voice was only a tad short of sarcastic.

"Kent," I began, "I'm not sure there was actually anyone who *did* get along with her." I wrapped my chilly hands around the mug Catherine handed me. "I don't mean to speak ill of the dead," I added hastily, "but Paula was rather—shall we say, abrasive. The kind of person who just rubbed most people the wrong way."

"I'm kind of getting that impression," he admitted.

"Okay, I understand there was some kind of altercation over eggnog at some 'do' down at the country club?"

I tried to remember back to the cookie swap. It had been a busy week. "Well, there was an incident where Paula broke a glass cup and Chuck Ciacarelli yelled at her. But he's such a grouch, even on a good day. He'd probably yell at Santa for leaving footprints on the roof."

"I heard the exchange went a little beyond that. Ciacarelli carried it on outside and got into quite an argument with the victim and her son after they left the party."

Drake and I looked at each other. "I sure didn't hear anything about that," I offered. "They left before we did, but I never heard any more than what went on in the party room."

Catherine and Drake nodded in agreement.

"Any other incidents you know of?" Taylor asked. "Fights between family members, raised voices, things like that?"

I had a hard time imagining the mild-mannered Wilbur or long-suffering Judy ever having a screaming match with anyone. I shook my head. Judy's complaints about her mother-in-law's behavior were all secondhand; I'd never witnessed a nasty exchange between them.

"Who do you think would have a reason to kill Paula?" I asked Kent. "She didn't know anyone here."

"My question exactly. Woman comes to town to visit relatives. Meets a few neighbors. Hard to find someone with motive."

"Was there a break-in? Judy had mentioned that she and Wilbur were invited to a dinner party last night. Did it happen while they were gone?"

"Yeah, they were gone when she died. Supposedly. I'm checking alibis."

An uneasy tremor went through me.

"And what was the cause of death?" Drake asked.

"Looks like a single blow with a fireplace poker. It was lying beside her, bloody, couple of smudgy prints on the handle, but it looked like it was wiped down. She was lying in one corner of the couch. Could have been innocently napping or something. The blow caught her in the temple, so it's also possible that she saw her attacker and was standing when she was hit. Could have just fallen in that position."

"There's been a strange car in the neighborhood," Drake mentioned. "Let me get the license number." He headed for the kitchen.

"True," I said. "Paula'd had some bad relationships in the past, ex-husband in California and all. Maybe somebody tracked her down here."

"Yeah, I've got the ex's name," Kent said.

Drake handed him the note with the plate number on it. "New Mexico plate," he said.

"Thanks."

Kent set his mug on the tray and reached for his overcoat. "We'll know more tomorrow."

"Do you plan to do drug or alcohol tests on Paula?" I asked.

He raised an eyebrow.

"Paula drank quite heavily. And from her erratic behavior, I wouldn't be surprised if some drugs were in the mix, too." I shrugged. "Just a thought."

"I'm sure they'll look at all that during autopsy."

Drake walked him to the door and Catherine, who'd been yawning for the past half hour, excused herself to go back to bed. I felt wired. No way would I fall asleep anytime soon.

"I'm going over there," I told Drake.

He started to make some mild protests but didn't get very far with it. "Okay. I think I'll switch on the bedroom TV for a while. See you whenever."

I pulled on my down jacket and stepped outside. The air was still, the night black. All the official vehicles had left, and the snoopy neighbors had long since tucked back in and turned out their lights. Only our house and the Garfields' showed any sign of activity. Yellow tape still circled their side yard, protecting the patches of snow that hadn't yet melted. I blew out a deep breath, watching the white vapor puff into the darkness, then headed for the front sidewalk. I tapped tentatively on their front door.

"Oh, Charlie!" Wilbur seemed surprised to see me, but ushered me in immediately. He wore pale gray pajamas with a tiny pattern on them, topped with a blue-and-red-plaid robe. "Come into the kitchen. I'm trying to get Judy to have some hot chocolate."

His face seemed drawn, with a set of age lines I hadn't noticed before. His eyes were red-rimmed with dark smudges beneath. I followed him into the kitchen. Judy was rummaging through an upper cabinet, her back to the door, her quick movements masking the small whoosh of the swinging door. She was also clad in her nightwear—flannel floor-length gown with ruffles at the cuffs and neck.

"Honey, Charlie's here," Wilbur murmured.

She jumped visibly at the sound of his voice. A mug clattered to the countertop and she automatically reached out to catch it.

"Charlie! Oh, God, I'm glad you're here." She left

the mug lying on its side and slumped into a chair at the maple dining table. "I just can't think...I mean, I just don't know what..." Her fingers fidgeted with the top button of her gown at the base of her throat.

"I know," I said gently. Wilbur patted her on the shoulder as I sat down beside her. "I'm so sorry to hear about what happened."

They both nodded.

"Did the police have any answers for you?"

"Nothing yet," Wilbur volunteered.

"I couldn't keep up with them," Judy added. "I think they went all over the house and spread black powder on everything. I haven't had a chance to check. It's going to be a mess to clean up." She rubbed her index finger around in tiny circles on the table's shiny wood finish.

"Let me get us some hot chocolate," Wilbur offered. "The milk's already hot."

"None for me, thanks. We just drank a couple at home."

He went to the stove and busied himself with the mix and the milk, making two mugs.

"Would it help to tell me about it? Did you come home from your dinner party and just...find her?"

"We went over all this so many times with the police," Wilbur said. His voice almost had a sharp edge.

"I'm sorry." I felt like a totally insensitive jerk. "I shouldn't—"

"It's okay," Judy said. "Wilbur, I really don't mind. Investigating is what Charlie does, you know. Maybe she could help."

"Well, I—" I'd told Judy about my brother being a private investigator, and that I was a partner in the firm. I didn't mean to imply that it was really *my* field.

"Yes," she interrupted. "I want to tell you about it and see what you think."

Wilbur picked up his mug and left the room.

"Judy, are you sure this is okay? I mean, well, Wilbur seems upset by my being here."

"You know, I don't really care," she whispered. She took a long swig of her cocoa. "I mean, I do care. I'm sorry Wilbur lost his mother. He's shaken up about it, but I don't think grief has really set in yet. It's just that I felt like the target of all those police questions earlier, and I don't care whether he wants me to tell you or not. I won't sleep the rest of the night anyway."

"Target? Judy, what do you mean?"

"I guess I'm their main suspect."

EIGHT

IT WAS NO SECRET that Judy didn't much like her mother-in-law, but to think she would have killed Paula seemed ludicrous. We *were* only kidding around.

"You're not serious, surely."

"Well, let's just say that the questions were going one way when they first got here—what time did we get home, where had we been, was Paula alone when we left, that kind of thing. Then one of the officers who'd been outside came back in the house, and there was a little whispered discussion between him and that chubby, bald cop."

Kent Taylor.

"And then the questions started being about my relationship with Paula. Did we ever fight? Did we have words last night? That kind of thing."

Oh boy. I guess I wasn't the only one Judy'd made little remarks to.

"Do you want to go over it again?" I asked. "Tell me what happened last night, the sequence of events?"

She drained her cup and shrugged. "Sure." She carried the mug to the sink and ran some water into it.

"Wilbur and I were invited to dinner at the home of some people we know from church. They live off Rio Grande, in that new subdivision west of Old Town."

"Okay."

"We left here at six. Dinner wasn't really ready, so we sat around and talked awhile, drank some iced tea. It was actually refreshing to be around people who don't drink, after the week with Paula's...you know.

"So, anyway, we ate about seven-thirty, I'd guess. Then we started a domino game that went on for quite a while. I developed a horrible headache. I thought it might be a migraine coming on. The game was really in high gear and Wilbur didn't want to leave, so Norma told me to lie down in their guest room for a while. I dozed off and must have been in there for an hour or more. But when I woke up the headache was gone."

She'd been pacing the length of the kitchen while she related all of this. Now she sat again.

"We left their house around eleven, eleven-fifteen. When we walked in the front door, there was Paula, on the sofa." She squeezed her eyes shut as if she wanted to erase the picture. "You know, at first I thought she'd passed out there. Her head was on a pillow, and one arm and one leg kind of hung over the edge. She was just, you know, sprawled out. Wilbur and I were just talking about whether to wake her up to go to bed when I noticed the blood."

She paused and swallowed.

"Wilbur wanted to revive her. He kept shaking her. I called 911 but she was already..."

"It must have been so frightening."

"It was. Charlie, I've only ever seen one dead person, and that was at a funeral home. This was...really..."

"It's okay. It's over now."

"I just...I can't figure out why someone did this."

"Like robbery? Did you check the rest of the house? Maybe they broke in to steal something." Aside from the fact that Paula was a real pain in the neck, I couldn't think of any motives.

"We glanced around a little. We really didn't have much chance. The police were here so quickly. I didn't notice anything missing, though, and they said there was no evidence of a break-in." She glanced nervously at the back door. "I think I'll just check everything one more time. What if we interrupted them when we came home? They might decide to come back."

I went around the house with her and checked all windows and doors. Everything looked secure, and I didn't notice anything major out of place, no missing TV set, no drawers left open with clothing hanging out. Wilbur was locked in the master bath with the shower running, but that was the only window we didn't test. I left a few minutes later, both of us trying to convince the other to sleep well.

I slid into bed beside Drake a few minutes later, but didn't actually close my eyes until gray dawn began to show at the windows.

The day after Christmas here in Albuquerque has become nearly the biggest shopping day of the year. Everybody has to rush out to exchange all the stuff they didn't really want for the stuff they could have just bought for themselves if they hadn't spent all their money buying other people stuff *they* really didn't want either. Knowing this, the last places I'd want to be were the malls or downtown. However, curiosity was going to get the best of me, and I knew I'd end up in Kent Taylor's office at the main APD downtown station.

I sat in a straight wooden chair across from him, having cruised a four-block area three times to get a parking spot. My excuse for coming was that Wilbur and Judy were too upset to ask about the autopsy report and had sent me to do it. My real reason was my usual one—I wanted to know the skinny on what the police were doing.

"Pretty much what we knew at the scene," Kent was saying. "Blow to the head with the fireplace tool. The indent matches the hook on the Garfields' poker. Beyond that, let's see...blood alcohol level pretty high. Way more than is legal for driving. But then, she wasn't driving, was she? Other drugs, pretty good amount of cocaine. The combination isn't a good one. But she'd probably been mixing them for quite a while and it wasn't enough to kill her. That's not the full, final report, but it's the important stuff."

"Was there a struggle at the scene?" I hadn't noticed much out of place, but there'd been time to straighten everything by the time I'd arrived last night.

"Not much, if any. Couple of chair cushions on the floor. The son told us he wasn't sure if the front door was locked when they got home."

"How could he not be sure?"

"Said he approached the door, used his key, went on in. Didn't really pay attention to whether the lock was actually engaged or not."

"So, Paula could have opened the door to her killer?"

"Or it could have been someone with a key."

"Who else would have a key but Wilbur or Judy?"

"Exactly. That, coupled with a few other things is pointing to her as the main suspect."

"Really, Kent. Judy?"

He ticked off points on his fingers. "One, she made no secret of it that she wouldn't mind seeing her mother-in-law dead. Two, she disappeared from the dinner party she was at for, let's see, the hostess told us, well over an hour. Three, there were more sets of tire tracks in the snow at the front of their driveway than they can account for. Said they went out twice all day. There are three sets of tracks.''

"All those tracks are from their car? For sure?''

"Looks that way. And, four, the only prints on the weapon belong to your neighbor Judy.''

"Well, whoever used it obviously either wore gloves or wiped it clean. Of course, there would be some partial prints of Judy's. The poker's in her home.''

His look told me I was getting a little too argumentative.

"Okay, okay, I'll shut up. But are you at least looking for other suspects, too? Kent, I can't believe this quiet, mild-mannered woman is a killer. She just isn't the type.''

"She's pregnant, you know. Hormones and all.''

"Kent! Oh, please!''

"Hey, I'm just saying there's a case right now where this woman's using raging hormones as a defense. Doesn't deny she did the crime.'' He shrugged and gave me a raised eyebrow.

I gritted my teeth and suggested I better get going. He didn't contradict me.

Outside, the sky was a clear, pale blue and the wind was sharp. I pulled on my knitted mittens and zipped up my parka to my chin. I race-walked around the block to dissipate a little energy. Back at the car, I fumbled with the key twice before getting the door open.

We'd be lucky if she killed herself. Hadn't Judy grumbled those very words to me at the cookie swap?

I could just kill her. Didn't she once say that to me, too? She must have said it to other neighbors too, because the police had obviously gotten some pretty strong ammunition in their queries among the crowd last night.

This wasn't looking good. I didn't have any idea how long it would take Kent to put together enough evidence to arrest her, but that sure looked like the track he was taking.

NINE

I CRANKED THE JEEP'S ENGINE to life and cruised the downtown streets before turning west on Central. Although we weren't officially open all this week, on an impulse I decided to stop at the office before heading home.

The gray-and-white Victorian sits in a neighborhood that's partly commercial and partly residential, and has been that way for many years. We like being on the quiet side street and the fact that there are some full-time neighbors around who keep an eye on the place. I pulled my Jeep into the driveway that follows the left-hand side of the property to the back, where a one-time carriage house serves as storage and the yard as parking area.

The old house was cool and echoey, lonely feeling in its holiday abandonment. The linoleum on the kitchen floor creaked as I walked across it, switching on lights, heading for the hallway to turn up the thermostat. A pile of mail was sprawled on the floor inside the front door, and I scooped it up and deposited it on Sally's desk. Absently, I picked up each piece and sorted them into piles—for Sally, Ron and myself. I'd become so engrossed in the mindless flipping of envelopes that I nearly jumped out of my skin when the phone rang.

Patting myself on the chest, I let it go four times so the answering machine would pick up.

"Charlie, are you there?" Drake's voice came through the tinny little speaker.

I reached for Sally's handset. "I'm here. How did you know?"

"Just a wild guess. I tried your cell, but it's turned off. So I took a chance that you'd stopped at the office."

I reached into my purse as he spoke and checked my little phone. The battery had gone dead sometime in the past few days.

"...taking her away right now," he was saying.

"What? I missed the first part of that."

"The police have just taken Judy Garfield."

A ball of lead settled in my stomach. "Damn that Kent Taylor," I railed. "I just saw him and he knew this was happening. Didn't say a word about it to me."

"Wilbur's over here now, out in the kitchen with Mom. He doesn't know what to do next."

"Has he called a lawyer?"

"I don't think so. They don't know many people here. Can you recommend anyone?"

"Let me put you on hold. I'll check Ron's Rolodex." I pressed the red button and trotted up the stairs.

Ron's office is on the left, with mine across the hall. His desk, as usual, was a hodgepodge of paper, piles of unopened mail mixed in with telephone messages and sheets from yellow lined pads. I'll never know how the man finds anything in here. I patted down the mountain of stuff until I felt a hard, square shape resembling the Rolodex.

Cradling the phone to my shoulder and stabbing the button for line one, I assured myself that Drake was still on the line.

"Hold on a second while I try to remember Ron's filing system," I said. "He doesn't do anything the way anyone else does." On a lucky guess, I flipped to the letter *L* and discovered several cards with "Lawyer" written at the top. I thumbed through them to see if I recognized any names.

"Might try Martin Palmer or George Collins," I suggested, reading off the phone numbers. "Or if Judy would feel more comfortable with a woman, I've heard Natalie Rice is good. Don't know if any of them will be in their offices the day after Christmas, but maybe there'll be a message with an alternate way to contact them."

I closed the Rolodex lid. "Did they actually arrest Judy, or just take her down for questioning?" I asked. I listened while Drake repeated the question to Wilbur.

"He's not really sure. They didn't put cuffs on her."

"Well, either way, she probably should have an attorney with her. I'll get off the phone so you guys can make some calls. There's not much to do here, so I should be home soon."

I switched off Ron's light, went back downstairs and finished stacking the mail. After carrying mine and Ron's upstairs to our respective offices, I scanned the empty rooms to be sure everything was in place, debating the wisdom of driving back downtown to see if I could help Judy. Decided they probably wouldn't let me see her, since I wasn't legal counsel. I locked the back door and headed home.

Wilbur, Drake and Catherine were sitting around the kitchen table when I arrived.

"Any news?" I asked.

"We reached Martin Palmer on his cell phone," Drake said. "He's on his way to APD to see if he can straighten this out."

Wilbur looked more helpless than ever, clutching an

empty mug and staring at a spot somewhere in the middle of the table. His thin, sandy hair stood out in tufts on the sides, as if he'd been running his hands through it repeatedly. Catherine looked up at me with a raised eyebrow, which I took to mean that things didn't look too great.

"Would anyone like a sandwich?" I offered, needing something to do besides stand around.

Catherine jumped up and headed toward the refrigerator. "Yes, that's a great idea. Let's put some lunch together for everyone."

The phone rang just as I was reaching into the bread box. We all froze in place. Drake reached for it on the second ring.

"Martin Palmer," he said, handing the receiver to Wilbur, whose hand shook visibly when he took it.

"Uh-huh, uh-huh." He nodded as the attorney talked. "Is that it, then? Uh-huh." He pressed the button to end the call and set the phone on the table.

We all stood in our frozen positions while he scrubbed at the sides of his hair some more.

"Well?" Drake finally asked in a remarkably calm voice. I wanted to scream.

Wilbur let out a huge sigh. "They've charged her." His voice nearly broke, and he swallowed deeply. His Adam's apple traveled up and down again before more words came out. "She has to stay there until a hearing tomorrow. The judge will decide whether she can be out on bail."

Catherine crossed to him and put her arm around his thin shoulders.

"Surely she'll be granted bail," I pressed. "She's certainly not a flight risk or a danger to society." I pulled slices of bread out of the loaf and began smearing them with mayonnaise.

"I can't believe this is happening at all," Drake argued.

That pretty well summed it up for all of us.

"Let me call Ron this afternoon," I said. "Maybe we can do a little investigating of our own and get some leads on the real killer."

"You know the police aren't going to take kindly to our interference in an active investigation," Ron told me when I finally reached him about four o'clock.

"Is it really an active investigation?" I asked. "They've got a suspect, and they're about to indict her tomorrow. I seriously doubt they're pushing real hard to find any other suspects."

He grumbled a bit but basically agreed. "So, what other leads do you have?"

I had to admit there really weren't any, other than my firm belief that Judy just didn't have what it took to swing a poker at someone and bash the person in the head with it. "I'm going to see what I can find out from Wilbur. And maybe from the other neighbors Paula talked to. Maybe somebody can give us some insight. Right now, her life is pretty much a mystery."

Drake had done a good job of distracting Wilbur from his problems for the afternoon. The two men had cleaned up the remains of the luminarias from both our yards and were raking a few of autumn's leftover leaves from our backyard. I donned a light jacket and went out long enough to suggest that I'd warm up the leftover green chile stew and that Wilbur should stay for dinner. In the meantime, would he mind if I took a peek through Paula's things in their guest room? My own guess, privately, was that the police would have removed anything of use, but there was no harm in looking for clues.

The Garfield house felt like a place that's been suddenly abandoned. There were dishes on the dining table, where Judy and Wilbur had been having breakfast when the police arrived. I carried them to the kitchen and ran some warm water over them in the sink, put away the butter and wiped off the countertops. Turned on a couple of lamps against the late afternoon twilight.

Their floor plan was similar to ours, three bedrooms off a hall on the north side of the house. It took only a minute to figure out which one Paula'd used. The rumpled bed had probably remained unmade during her entire visit, I guessed. The disarray of the comforter and blankets was complete. The tight red dress she'd worn to the cookie swap lay draped over a chair back, with her outfit from Christmas Eve piled on top of it. A suitcase was on the floor against one wall, the lid open and lacy underthings spilling over the sides. The bag had been thoroughly rummaged, whether by the police or by Paula herself, I couldn't tell. Of course, the other possibility was that the killer might have searched her room for something. What that might be, or whether he'd found it, was anyone's guess.

Knowing that I was probably just repeating someone else's moves, I ran my hands through the suitcase, but nothing incriminating jumped out at me. I took the time to pull out each item, give it a look and fold it neatly, making a little stack on the floor beside me. Two pair of jeans, three sweaters, an assortment of dainties—not much else. A tote bag, the kind made of canvas with handles of webbing, stood beside the suitcase and was crammed with shoes. I pulled them out—pink tennies, black pumps, black boots, silver flats—shaking each upside down in case any notes written in invisible ink or keys to bus depot lockers might fall out. No such luck.

Tentatively, in case something sharp reached out at me, I felt around the inside of the tote. It was exactly what it appeared to be, medium weight canvas with no hidden compartments. The suitcase was another story. It was one of those ubiquitous black airline bags with wheels and a pullout handle. Under the flimsy plastic lining, I felt the mechanism for the wheels. One side had just a touch more padding than the other and my curious fingers poked around, exploring that oddity, until I discovered a narrow slit in the lining.

With thumb and forefinger, I reached inside and came out with the corner of a zipper-type sandwich bag. A tug at the bag brought the whole thing out and I saw, not especially to my surprise, that it contained white powder. Now I know these things are usually referred to in grams or kilos or such, but that was completely outside my realm. I'd put the contents at about a tablespoon or two.

Probably the cocaine that had been found in her system. I wasn't about to dip my finger into it and take a taste. How was I going to know what it would taste like anyway?

I placed the small bag on the floor and proceeded with my search of the room. The nightstand drawer yielded a paperback romance and a pair of reading glasses that I'd bet Paula never wore in front of anyone. The adjoining bathroom vanity held a large makeup case with a mirror encircled by a row of Hollywood-style makeup lights. Everything in the case looked standard for a woman who took great pains with her face and hair. No more little sandwich bags. And if there had been, I was sure the police had thoroughly checked over this treasure trove and removed anything of use to them. I wasn't interested so much in her stash as I was in where she'd gotten it.

Since it looked as if Paula were crazy enough to travel with her powdered treasure hidden away in her airline bag, did that mean she'd brought it all with her? Or did she have a connection here in town? For a person who planned to move in and stay awhile, I couldn't imagine the tiny bit I'd found would last very long. And based on the behavior I'd witnessed the couple of times I'd been around her, she'd probably already dipped into it more than once.

I stood in the doorway between bedroom and bath, pondering what I might have missed.

A purse.

Every woman carries a purse, and it would surely be where she kept those items she'd want close at hand. An address book, photos, stuff like that. I crossed the bedroom again and pulled open the dresser drawers. The top two were empty, the next two held spare linens and towels—obviously things that belonged to the household, not to Paula. The bottom drawer was where I hit pay dirt. Under another stack of towels was a black handbag, not Paula's large everyday one, but a small quilted leather one about six by twelve inches, with a gold chain for a strap. Small and dressy enough that it could double as an evening bag, but large enough to carry the essentials. And inside, I found two very essential items: an address book and a wallet with a nice juicy section of photos. Why the police hadn't seen fit to take these, I didn't know, but I wasn't passing up a chance like this.

A quick glance told me that none of the names or faces—except one stiffly posed photo of Wilbur and Judy—meant anything to me. But maybe Wilbur could identify more of them and give me a whole load of clues.

I realized that it was completely dark outside now and since I'd volunteered to provide dinner for everyone, it was time I hustled myself back home. I'd just closed the drapes in the guest room and switched off the light, pulling the door closed behind me, when I bumped into Wilbur in the hallway.

TEN

"Oh! I DIDN'T HEAR YOU out here," I gasped.

"Um, I just thought I better check on you. See how things were coming along." He fumbled with a ring full of keys.

"You're coming back to our place for dinner, aren't you?" I sidestepped him and worked my way toward the living room. "I found a couple of items you might be able to help with, if that's okay." I held up the wallet and address book.

"Sure. Drake told me to come right back. I just thought I'd make sure the house was locked and some lights were left on. That's what Judy..." He glanced around uncertainly.

"Okay, then, let's go." I took his elbow and steered him toward the door. He gave one sharp glance toward the sofa where his mother had died, then followed me timidly.

I switched on the porch light and twisted the little thing in the middle of the doorknob to lock it. I made a show of checking it after I closed it behind us.

"All set?" I asked.

Wilbur nodded absently and followed me across the lawn to our front porch. I wasn't sure how much help he'd be when we started going through Paula's possessions. He was clearly still dazed by the dual shock of his mother's murder and his wife's being arrested for it.

Inside, the house exuded the warm fragrance of meaty chile stew, and Catherine had warmed some garlic bread to go with it. We served everything at the kitchen table, and the four of us took our places. Despite his glazed appearance, Wilbur put away two bowls of stew and perked up somewhat afterward. Drake and Catherine cleared the dishes and put coffee on while I pulled my chair closer to Wilbur's and brought out Paula's things.

"I could use your help now, Wilbur. Can you identify the people in these photos?"

He pushed his glasses farther up his nose and opened the wallet. His gaze caught for a moment on Paula's driver's license before he flipped to the photo section. The first was of a dark-haired man, probably Hispanic.

"That's Ray. The fifth."

"The recent ex?"

He nodded. "I'm not even really sure the divorce was final. She may have just left him when she showed up here."

"Really? I was under the impression that they'd been apart for a while." Something came back to me. Paula had said the past year had been hard because of the divorce. I thought she meant it had dragged on that long.

"No, I don't think so," Wilbur said when I mentioned it. "The split was pretty new. But, who knows? Mother sometimes came up with a variety of stories to suit her purposes."

It was the first time, I realized, that I'd heard Wilbur say anything negative about his mother.

"Now this picture? These are my brother's two girls."

"I didn't realize you had a brother."

"An older half brother, actually. He's from her first

marriage. I was from the second. After that, I think she dropped the idea that men would be permanent in her life. At least she didn't bother to have any more kids with the others.''

"Were they close? Your mother and half brother?"

He made a snorting sound. "Not at all. Amos wrote her off when the second marriage failed. He's a very traditional kind of guy."

And you're not? I clamped my lips together, hoping I hadn't actually voiced this aloud.

He was quiet for a moment, then seemed to realize he still had the wallet in his hand.

"This picture of his girls must be at least ten or twelve years old. These little kids in pigtails are now in high school. Doing really well, too. Judy and I get them birthday and Christmas gifts every year. Used to spend the holidays with them when we were all in the Chicago area.''

"Back to Ray," I said. "I'm thinking any clues that will be useful to Judy are going to be more recent. Did Paula tell me she and Ray lived in California? Is he still there?"

"Guess so. I have to admit, I followed my brother's lead in not getting too close to Mother's husbands. It just didn't pay." He was flipping idly through the photos. "Come to think of it, though, she had a phone call from him right after she got here. Could the phone company tell you where it came from?"

"Probably." If the police hadn't already checked this lead, they should have. Maybe Ron could pull some strings if the police wouldn't cooperate.

Catherine brought Wilbur a cup of tea, coffee for me.

"In fact, when she first got on the line with Ray, I

think Mother asked him something about how the weather was out in sunny old L.A.''

I'd pulled a notepad out of the kitchen drawer and made myself a note to find a number for Ray Candelaria.

"Was their divorce bitter?" I asked.

"I got the feeling it was. Like I said, I tuned out a lot of it. I know Mother wasn't happy with him for a long time. She hinted, but never really said, that he abused her. Of course, all that only came out after she'd left him. I overheard her telling Judy about an incident where Ray threatened her if she left, but she said she wasn't taking any sh— Well, any bad stuff from him. She left anyway.''

"Wilbur! Don't you see that this could be the whole story right there? Maybe Ray decided to make good on his threat. Maybe he couldn't stand her being gone, holidays and all, and he came after her.'' I felt myself getting excited that another suspect was turning up so quickly.

He looked skeptical. "Ray? Um, I don't know.''

Was Wilbur just one of those gentle types who didn't truly believe that a man would harm a woman? I decided I might have to set him straight on that someday.

He was pointing to another of the photos. "That was my dad,'' he said. "Too bad he died before he got to see our baby.'' His voice cracked slightly on the last word, and he looked at me with sorrow in his gray eyes. "What will happen if Judy—''

"Let's deal with one thing at a time,'' I told him. "I'm sure we're going to find out who really did this long before it's time for the baby to come.''

I sure hoped we would, anyway. We spent a few more minutes going through the address book, a cheap thing in a vinyl cover. Paula had even filled out the few lines inside the front cover with "This book belongs to:" information. At least I had her previous address and phone number in California now.

Wilbur didn't recognize most of the names in the book. He'd pointed out a couple of cousins from the Midwest, but didn't know any of her friends from her years in California. He let me take the picture of Ray Candelaria from the wallet and said I could keep the address book as long as I needed it. He was beginning to look faded again by the time he went back home.

ELEVEN

I SPENT A RESTLESS NIGHT pondering my next moves. I wanted to question Ray Candelaria and didn't think I'd learn what I needed to know over the phone. A trip to Los Angeles might be in order, but I wasn't sure I should just do it. Wilbur hadn't actually hired us to investigate his mother's death. As the accountant for our firm, I knew we were flush enough for the year that a plane ticket to L.A. and a night or two in a hotel wouldn't break us. We could consider it pro bono, but I wasn't sure how Ron would feel about that. The only conclusion I'd reached by two-thirty a.m. was that I would run it past him at a more decent hour.

Catherine was already up when I went into the kitchen. The smell of coffee pulled at me. I let the dogs out into the backyard and poured myself a cup, then sat at the table with her. Once again, I felt so thankful that my mother-in-law and I had a good relationship.

"So, what do you think?" she asked, fingering the address book.

"Not much idea yet. But I need to talk to Ray Candelaria. I think he'll know something."

"There's another name in this book I'd check if I were you," she suggested. "I think he might have sold Paula drugs."

"You know which one it is?"

"Gus," Catherine said. "Paula just dropped this on me that day we went shopping. It was so casual I almost didn't notice. She said something like, 'Guess I'll have to find me a Gus here.' I was driving, and I guess something pulled my attention away and I never did ask anything about this Gus. But later, when we stopped for lunch, she excused herself to go to the ladies' room and when she came back she seemed much more energetic. And her nose was kind of red. I thought, coke. She's doing coke. But what was I going to do? I couldn't ditch her at the mall. I just tried to get her home as quickly as possible."

"You never mentioned any of this! Was she, like, out of control or anything?"

"Oh no. It startled me at first, realizing it, but later I thought no, that's just what Paula's like. Not somebody I'd want as a friend, obviously, but I didn't think it was up to me to preach to her, either."

We'd both finished our coffee and I got up to refill the mugs. "I think I'll go into the office today, check some of this stuff with Ron, maybe do a little more investigating. Want a piece of toast or something first?" I had let Catherine fend for herself for much of her visit, and now I was offering nothing more than toast for breakfast.

"That's okay, Charlie. You go ahead and get ready for work. I can make something later."

Thirty minutes later, I'd had a quick shower, an even quicker kiss from my hubby and was on my way to the office. Ron had told me Christmas Day that he didn't plan to take the whole week off and would probably spend part of the weekend catching up on paperwork. His car was already there when I arrived.

The kitchen smelled of burned coffee, which is usually an indicator that Ron has made a pot of his killer-strong brew and let some of it dribble onto the hot metal plate on the coffeemaker. Having tasted this stuff in the past, I opted to make myself a cup of tea in the microwave.

"Anybody home?" I called as I climbed the stairs.

His voice came trailing from his office in a monotone. Phone conversation. I flipped on the light in my own office and realized that the pile of mail from the previous day hadn't magically disappeared. I sat down to sort through it.

"Thought you weren't coming in this week," Ron said.

I hadn't heard him approach and I nearly sloshed my tea. Recovering, I set the mug down on a coaster and shoved the mail aside.

"I didn't think so, either, but this situation with the neighbors has kinda taken over my time for the past couple of days. Wilbur is really devastated. He can hardly answer a question coherently."

"Well, who wouldn't be? The papers are full of it. Having his mother murdered, then his wife accused of the crime. What a mess."

"Pregnant wife. Did I tell you that?" I drained my mug. "Anyway, I've come up with a couple of clues."

He grinned with a knowing little twist to his mouth. "Couldn't resist, could you?"

"Well..."

"So, are we hired, or what?"

"That hasn't come up. Like I said, Wilbur's a wreck. And I don't know how much money they have."

"So ask a few questions. We can do a charitable deed now and then," he said.

"Would the charity include my making a quick trip to L.A.?"

He rolled his eyes and puffed out a big sigh, but he didn't say no. An hour later I'd made reservations for the 4:10 flight on Southwest and a room downtown. I rushed through some routine paperwork and gathered my notes before dashing home to pack and spend a little time with the family before leaving.

By 5:10 I was airborne, somewhere over Arizona. Glass of wine in hand, I was transferring names and addresses to my little spiral notebook and pinpointing places on my road map of the greater Los Angeles area, which was certainly greater in scope than anything I usually dealt with. By the time I picked up my rental car and headed into the maze of freeways, it was dark and the commuting drivers were even surlier than I. I was beginning to question the wisdom of the whole trip.

My research and mapping had indicated that Ray Candelaria's place was between the airport and my hotel, so it only made sense to stop there first. I exited and pulled out my map at the first stoplight. I happened to glance up and realized I wasn't in a great neighborhood and that reading my road map at the intersection definitely branded me as an out-of-towner. I laid the map down and locked my doors.

At the next well-lighted place, a twenty-four-hour medical clinic, I pulled in and parked under a lamppost. Getting my bearings, I discovered I was only six blocks from my goal. Ray's home turned out to be a white-stuccoed, red-tile-roofed, mission-style home in a decent neighborhood. The lawn was well-groomed, and elegant palms flanked the sidewalk leading up from the street. There were no cars in the driveway, but lights shone from inside the house. I pressed the doorbell and set off a short symphony.

A woman in her thirties, with long, dark hair and twelve ounces of mascara opened the door. She wore a red-and-gold caftan and strappy gold sandals. One hand held a martini glass and the other stayed firmly on the door frame.

"Is Ray Candelaria home?" I asked.

She appraised me slowly, top to toe. When she'd decided that a travel-worn woman with hair in a ponytail, wearing jeans with scuffed knees, a faded turtleneck and dingy Nikes wasn't a threat to her, she stepped aside.

"What was your name?" she asked, finally figuring out that she might have admitted a census taker or insurance salesperson.

I handed her my business card from RJP Investigations.

"Charlie? What kind of a name is that for a woman?"

I slipped on a tight smile. I really didn't want to go into the whole explanation of how I'd been named for two maiden aunts and that Charlotte Louise had never quite stuck to me. When I didn't answer, she turned on her heel and headed upstairs. I waited until she'd disappeared, then looked around.

The entryway was small and opened directly on the living room. Beyond that I could see the L of a dining room, with a kitchen and breakfast area directly in front of me. Everything was done in shades of blue and cream. I stepped into the living room and examined a group of photos standing in brass frames on a bookcase. There were plenty of Ray, some including the woman who'd opened the door. None including Paula.

Considering their divorce was only recently final, he'd

done a remarkable job of mopping up traces of her and installing her replacement quickly enough.

Voices from upstairs caught my attention. The male sounded grumbly and included something along the lines of, "...and you let her in?" Almost immediately, a door closed firmly and the woman appeared at the top of the stairs. Putting on a weak smile, she tottered down on her slender heels and approached me.

"What did you say this was about?" she asked.

"I didn't." I gave her a minute to come up with something, but she wasn't ready with anything quick. "It's something I have to discuss with Ray."

I walked over to a very straight wingback chair and sat.

"He's getting dressed. It'll be a few minutes."

"That's fine." I guess I looked prepared to camp there because she didn't say anything else. She went into the kitchen and rattled some ice cubes in a glass.

A good ten minutes passed, during which the woman disappeared into another room beyond the kitchen. Sounds of doors opening and closing and the occasional running water upstairs told me that Ray was making no haste with his toilette. I walked back over to the bookcase and continued my perusal.

Unfortunately, the reading material was limited to romance novels and a few volumes on how to improve your golf game. There were no scrapbooks or albums or other juicy stuff. The furniture was the midpriced kind you found at outlet places, and the art on the walls was of the starving artist variety. I was about to start toe-tapping when I noticed Ray at the top of the stairs. I wondered if he'd been standing there watching me give the place the once-over.

"Ray Candelaria?" I walked toward him and extended my hand as he reached the bottom step. He was in his midforties, probably ten years younger than Paula, or more. Black hair, razor cut to perfection, tailored gray slacks and a pink polo shirt, about two too many gold chains.

He held up my card and looked at it. "You're an investigator from Albuquerque?"

"That's right. Could we sit down a minute?"

He ushered me back into the living room, and we took chairs at opposite ends of a crushed velvet sofa.

"Have you heard about Paula?" I began tentatively.

His expression said "the bitch," although the words didn't come out. "What about her?"

"That she was killed a couple of days ago?"

His surprise seemed genuine. His face screwed up in puzzlement. "Killed? What happened?"

So the Albuquerque police hadn't considered Ray worth talking to.

"It was murder." I didn't know any other way to say it and still get to the point quickly. "She was visiting her son and daughter-in-law at the time."

"The one in Albuquerque."

"Yes."

"Think I met that one a couple of times," he said. "You know, Paula and I were together only a couple years. Fun while we were just fooling around, you know. Sailing up the coast, doing the sights, hanging out in some good clubs. But then we got married. Thing she had about 'commitment.' I don't know. The fun just kind of went out of it after that."

He shrugged and reached toward the coffee table, picking up a small wooden box with a hinged lid. He began flipping the lid open and shut, clicking it repeatedly.

"When did you see her last?"

"Oh, gosh—" he glanced upward "—way before the divorce actually went through. Probably been a couple months anyway. Maybe more than that."

"What was she doing during that time? I mean before she showed up at Wilbur's house."

"My guess? I mean, I don't really *know.* My guess is, hanging out in some flophouse." He snapped the box's lid loudly and set it back on the coffee table. Thank goodness, I'd been about ready to snatch it away from him.

He rubbed his hands through his hair and it fell perfectly back into place. His gaze met mine firmly. "Paula couldn't give up the drugs. I mean, heck, I'll smoke a little dope now and then, do a little coke at a party or something. But for Paula that was just the appetizer. She'd started with crack a few months before I finally told her to get out. Who knows what else she's tried by now."

"Who supplied her? Was there some guy named Gus?"

His mouth twisted into a grimace. "Oh, yeah. Gus."

I waited silently, sure that there was more to come.

"Met Gus at a party at my boss's house in Brentwood. We both did."

"Nice neighborhood. What kind of business?"

"Time shares. Sales have been good the past few years. I'm doing okay." I remembered a sales brochure I'd come across, tucked between two of the golf books.

"What about this Gus?"

He snorted. "The guy is slime. I have *no* idea how he got into the party, must have been on the arm of somebody connected. Paula gravitated right to him. Don't know how, but those types always find each other.

I had to drag her out of the kitchen to go home. But they stayed in touch, I know they did.''

"Any idea where he lives?" I'd found a phone number in Paula's address book, but nothing more.

He shook his head. "She probably never went there anyway. Probably just met him places."

"Know where he hangs out?"

He gave me the names of a couple of clubs, and I wrote them down in my notebook. The tinkling of ice cubes reminded me of the other woman in the house. I hadn't seen her cross the foyer. How long had she been listening in the kitchen?

TWELVE

It was completely dark when I emerged from Ray's house. I thought how odd it looked to see Christmas lights on palm trees and flowering shrubs. I spent a couple of minutes in the car studying the map to figure out where I was going next. One of the clubs was near my hotel, so I decided to check in and freshen up first. The real action probably didn't start until later anyway.

My room was on the sixth floor, giving me a swell view of the windows of an office building across the street. A surprising number were lit, considering it was Friday night. I took a quick shower and browsed my suitcase to see what I'd brought that might be appropriate for nightlife. Nothing, really.

I settled on a newer pair of jeans—ones without the knees worn white—and a white tank top. I'd brought it along thinking the California climate might be a lot warmer than ours, although it wasn't exactly tank weather. With a denim jacket, I might pass. I rummaged through my sparse makeup bag and found a pair of rhinestone earrings that had probably been in there for years. I could probably rinse the face powder off them. I looked at the ensemble spread out on the bed and really just wished I could put on my flannel jammies and watch TV before falling asleep early.

After a quick call to Drake to let him know I'd made

the trip okay, I decided I better keep moving while my momentum was up. I got dressed, put on way more makeup than I usually do and fluffed my hair to double its volume. Surveying the result in the mirror, I decided I would just avoid mirrors the rest of the evening.

The first club, known simply as Billy's, turned out to be in a not too bad neighborhood, luckily, since I had to park three blocks away. I carefully locked the rental car and clutched my purse against me, wishing I'd been able to bring my new pistol with me. These kinds of situations make me extremely edgy.

I used the three-block walk to work up a little hip shake and throw on some attitude. By the time I approached Billy's, I was ready for anything. It was one of those places where people line up outside to get in and a seven-foot-tall black guy with a shaved head and three gold earrings guards the entry. I could see that I'd never make the cut without a story. I strutted right up to him.

"Hi, I'm supposed to meet Gus here," I said, craning my neck to look him in the eye.

"Oh yeah?" His eyes traveled down to the dip in the front of my tank top. I forced myself not to reach up and close the gap.

"Yeah." I hoped I managed to make it sound saucy. "I'm a friend of Paula's."

Something shifted in his face. "Hold on. Let me check." He gripped the shoulder of a younger, shorter, white guy and whispered something to him. The young one disappeared inside.

"Wait right here," the guard said in a deep baritone.

He turned to the next couple standing in the line. I felt like I didn't quite know what to do with my hands. I moved a little to the beat of the music coming from inside and hoped I didn't look totally nerdy. Stares from the other people in line were beginning to become noticeable, but I refused to meet their gaze or apologize for skipping to the front.

It took about five minutes for the runner to come back. Apparently I'd been given the go-ahead. Interesting. Paula must have been a good customer. The huge guy moved the padded rope barrier aside and ushered me through. I didn't know where to find Gus, or what he looked like, but figured this wasn't the moment to ask.

I walked into an assault of deafening music, strobing lights, clouds of cigarette smoke and writhing bodies. I stood to the side for a minute, adjusting to it all, before making my way to the bar. I ordered a beer, which I usually don't drink, figuring that would make it easy for me to nurse one drink for quite a while and create no danger that I'd be too intoxicated to drive.

While the bartender drew it into a tall mug, I scanned the room. On the far side, a row of booths lined the wall, most of them filled with couples. One corner booth was occupied by a stringy looking white guy, flanked by two girls, one black and one white. Two other men sat on either side of the girls. They were getting with the music and clearly enjoying themselves. The white guy in the middle was more intent. Gus.

I confirmed it with the bartender as I paid for my beer.

Hiking my purse strap firmly onto my shoulder, I re-adopted my attitude, picked up my beer and headed his way. I hadn't yet decided on my approach, so I strolled between tables and dancers, smiling vacantly, pretending to really get into the scene. By the time I'd reached the row of booths, I noticed that Gus was eyeing me. I caught the stare and gave it right back.

"Yeah?" His voice was surly. His gaunt face showed

a couple of days' worth of stubble, and his streaky blond hair looked as if it hadn't been washed in a week. The black girl had her arm draped over the back of the booth behind him.

"Paula said I should come see you." I stood with my weight on one hip, going for a casual attitude.

His eyes narrowed. "Yeah. So?"

"She said you got some really good—" I hoped my eyebrows conveyed the message, since I didn't know the slang word for it.

"You ain't from around here," he said.

"Nah. Met her in New Mexico. Happened to be here on, let's say, business. Just lookin' for something to make the trip a little more enjoyable."

He turned toward the guy closer to me who was sitting in the end seat of the booth. "Clear out."

The man grabbed the hand of the white girl. "C'mon, let's dance."

They slid out of the booth, and Gus gestured for me to take the empty seat. I did, staying within jumping distance of the opening.

"Whatta ya want?" he asked, getting right down to business.

I shrugged. "Just a little grass, I guess. What'll twenty bucks get me?"

"That's *it?*"

"I'm only in town till tomorrow. Don't want to get caught with it on the airplane."

"So, going back to New Mexico?"

"Yeah. Back to the grind." I slid a folded twenty across the table toward him. He took a pinch from a zipper bag, put it in an empty one and slid the little bag to me. "I'll give Paula your regards."

Something in his face changed. "What're you up to?" His eyes had become slits.

I glanced around the table. The other two had suddenly taken an interest in me, too. "What do you mean, what am I up to?" I tried to dish it right back at him, but wasn't feeling overly confident at the moment.

"Paula's dead." He watched closely for my reaction.

"What! No way, man. I just saw her last week. She looked great." I shook my head back and forth. "No way could she be dead."

Apparently my feigned shock convinced him. He shrugged. "You'll see."

"Well...what happened? How'd you find out?"

"Let's just say a mutual friend told me. We got a short grapevine here."

The black girl forced a laugh and nodded agreement. I took a long pull on my beer to give myself a moment to decide how to handle this. When the chuckles died down, I shrugged.

"So, what? Accident, or something?"

"Yeah, let's just say she accidentally forgot to pay her bills." He grinned for the first time. The man really should invest in some good dental work.

"Too bad." I gave a couldn't-give-a-shit shrug. "Well, it's been real."

I stood and tucked my little purchase into my purse. Resisting the urge to look back at the table, I sauntered toward the ladies' room at the back of the club. It looked like I had the place to myself. I took one of the three stalls and slid the latch, blowing out a deep pent-up breath. I did a quick pee, dropped the bag of pot in after and flushed. At the row of sinks, I stopped to wash my hands, knowing that I'd want another shower back in my room before I could go to sleep.

"All right, bitch, the truth!" A hand grabbed me from behind, long nails digging into my bicep.

I whirled to find the black girl from the table. She shoved me against the wall, the electric hand dryer jamming into the small of my back. Pain shot down both legs and I struck out, whipping my arm free at the same time I rammed the heel of my hand into her chest. Her butt hit a sink, which rattled slightly, as if it might come off the wall.

"Slow down a second," I yelled before she could come at me again.

She braced herself against the sink, while I backed up to a flat place on the wall.

"What makes you think I'm 'up to something'? What's with all this third degree stuff from Gus, anyway?" I snarled the words, not faking the anger.

"You—prissy little white girl—come in here with that story about Paula sending you. Paula'd never be friends with somebody like you."

My mind whirled, searching for a way to handle this. "Okay." I slumped against the wall. "Okay, look, you're right. Paula and I weren't exactly friends."

She leaned back against the sink, crossing her arms under her ample breasts.

"Look," I said, "I know Paula was murdered. Okay, I wasn't surprised when Gus told me."

She tapped an index finger against her upper arm.

"It's just that a friend is accused of killing her, and this lady, well, there's just no way she's got it in her to kill anybody. So I'm just asking around, trying to figure out what really happened."

"And you think Gus got somethin' to do with it?"

"You don't?"

"I *know* he don't. Gus been here, in this club, at that

table, every night for the whole two years I known him. Gus, he may be sorta messed up. I mean, a dealer, he shouldn't be *doin'* the stuff, you know. He make some money if he jus' sell it. Gus, he dumb enough to use it, too.'' She uncrossed her arms and propped herself against the sink's edge, staring at the floor. ''It's jus'…he's my man. I don't know how to make him quit.'' Her voice cracked a little.

''Okay, look, I'll take your word for it. He does look like a fixture here.''

''Damn straight. B'lieve it or not, Gus ain't gonna get so worked up over a piece of junkie like that Paula Candelaria. What'd be his reason to kill her? Why'd he even care?''

'''Cause she didn't pay her bills?'' I ventured.

''Yeah, like she gonna pay 'em now?''

Good point. I stood and retrieved my purse from where it had landed beside a trash can. She grabbed my arm again, more gently this time.

''He's just a lotta talk. Leave him alone, okay?''

''Okay. Look, I'm not the law or anything. I can't actually do anything to him.''

She backed away and let me pass. As I walked out the door, she was checking her makeup in the mirror.

THIRTEEN

I FELT AS IF I WERE batting zero when I got on the plane the next day, heading back to Albuquerque. I'd left the club last night at a leisurely pace, casually inquiring of both the bartender and the doorman about Gus's habit of being at his table every single night. They both backed up the girlfriend's story.

This morning I'd called Luxury Resorts, the time-share company Ray Candelaria worked for and had been assured that he'd been at work Christmas Eve until six and again on the twenty-sixth at eight a.m. Wouldn't have been impossible for him to get to Albuquerque and back, but it seemed pretty unlikely.

So, I was short on ideas at this point. I still didn't give Gus credit for much in the brains department, and it wasn't entirely out of the question that he might have sent one of his "friends" to convince Paula to pay up and the guy might have gotten a little too rough. However, the evidence at the scene didn't quite work with that theory—no damage to the room, no sign of a fight, nothing stolen from the house. I'd run the idea past Ron when I got home, get his take on it, but didn't think it would exactly get the police hot on Gus's tail.

I settled back in my seat for the flight and two hours later had forged my way through the baggage claim in Albuquerque and retrieved my car from the lot.

It was pretty much on my way home, so I stopped at the office before heading toward my own neighborhood. Sally had left for the day and Ron was sitting at his desk, the phone against his ear. I waved hello and went into my own office to see how much mail and how many phone messages I'd missed. I was halfway through them when Ron appeared in my doorway.

"Back already?"

"And without much, I'm afraid." I laid down the phone bill I'd been studying. "Neither of my two suspects seem quite as likely, now that I've talked to them."

Ron pulled a stick of gum from his shirt pocket, unwrapped the foil and folded the gum twice before stuffing it into his mouth.

"I just don't see Ray Candelaria as a suspect," I told him. "The man appears to be getting on with his life and didn't seem to be harboring ill feelings toward Paula.

"Gus, the drug dealer, on the other hand, might have had reason to come after her. He just doesn't seem to have taken the opportunity. Several people swear he never leaves his usual spot. Maybe we could ask some questions around town, see if there's anybody who might know something about that dark blue car we noticed prowling around before Christmas. Gus could have very well have hired somebody to come after her. Or, Catherine said Paula was bragging about some new hunk in her life."

"I ran the plate on the car while you were gone," Ron said. "Johnny Domingo. Twenty-one years old. Got a rap sheet, petty stuff mostly. Started as a kid taking things from convenience stores. Graduated to house burglaries by the time he was fifteen. Supporting a mild drug habit by ripping off TV sets and microwaves."

"Hmm…seems a little young to be a boyfriend. All this time we've been looking for a connection to Paula, but maybe it was simply a case of this kid breaking in, thinking no one was home. Hoped to score a nice appliance of some kind and get out. Paula was there and he grabbed the first available weapon."

"With all the traffic in the neighborhood?" He knew a fair number of people would drive around Christmas night rather than take on the huge crowds Christmas Eve. His look was pure skepticism.

"That could be the perfect cover. He might have faked a breakdown and started walking. We were all out walking the night before, and no one questioned us."

"And he'd haul a TV set right out past the other drivers and stash it in the trunk of his car?"

"Nothing like that was missing. However, there are plenty of smaller treasures around. A camera? Jewelry? Come on, Ron, there are dozens of valuables he could have stashed into a pocket."

He gave a small nod of concession.

"Do we know where Johnny was Christmas night?"

"Haven't checked that yet," he admitted. "Let me contact a couple of people I know." The phone rang. "That's gonna be Leroy. I'll get it in here."

I fiddled with my mail some more, thinking I should answer a couple of letters but stalling while Ron made the calls. If we could at least send the police looking at Johnny Domingo, it would take some of the heat off Judy. Make their case against her look iffy.

Ron reappeared. "Well, Johnny Domingo wasn't in jail or the hospital, as far as I can tell. As to where he actually *was,* that's gonna take a little longer."

And it could have been a million places.

"I put a couple of guys on it," he said. "They aren't

exactly model citizens themselves, but they'll nose around a little.''

I didn't especially care, and certainly didn't want to know who these guys were. I was just happy that we'd found a direction to go that was leading away from Judy.

''While you're at it, know any hit men?'' I was only half joking.

He wasn't. ''Maybe.''

''I'm just wondering how we might find out if Gus hired anybody local to go after Paula. And who it might be.'' I twiddled a pencil in my fingers. ''I do think his girlfriend made sense—he wouldn't have anything to gain by killing Paula. But a hired gun might have gone beyond his duty. Done more damage than planned.''

''I don't know...this line seems pretty sketchy to me. But I can see what there is to learn. Never know.''

That's right, you never know, I thought as I gathered jacket and purse and headed for my car. I was ready for fresh clothes and a shower.

Drake and Catherine were out when I got home, but the two dogs greeted me happily enough. Drake had left a note suggesting dinner at Pedro's, so I shouldn't bother to make anything at home. As if I would have leaped right to the task anyway.

It was only three o'clock, and his note said they'd be back from their museum trip about five. I decided to go next door and see what had happened with the Garfields since I'd been away.

Wilbur answered the door after I'd rung twice. His normally pale face was pasty white. His thin, sandy hair lay plastered to his head in oily strands and his hands trembled noticeably. His pants and shirt looked as if he'd slept in them, and his navy cardigan hung lopsided from his shoulders. His wire-rimmed glasses had fingerprint smudges on the lenses. He greeted me with a grunt and stepped aside so I could enter.

The living room showed the lack of a woman's touch. Newspapers and unopened mail were strewed over the sofa and tables. Two beer cans stood on the end table next to his recliner, and a dinner plate on the coffee table had something tomatoey dried on it.

"Judy hasn't been released, I gather."

"No. The judge was taking a long holiday weekend and her lawyer hasn't pushed to be assigned to a different one. Her bail hearing is now set for Monday."

"Oh no. I can't believe that! She shouldn't be stuck downtown just because it's a holiday week. Want me to see if Ron can pull any strings? Call somebody, or get her a different lawyer?"

He didn't seem to know what he wanted. He shuffled over to his recliner and flopped down. I followed and sat on the sofa across from him.

"Ron and I are trying to follow the drug connection," I said. "I met the guy in Los Angeles Paula was buying from. But there must have also been someone here in Albuquerque. Do you have any ideas? Somebody who called her here at the house, or somebody she called?"

He sat lifelessly in the chair.

"I found her address book the other day, but didn't find any local phone numbers in it. Could there have been another place she wrote them?"

He picked at a thread on the arm of his chair but didn't respond.

"Wilbur, I'm trying to help get Judy out of jail for good. To avoid the hassle and embarrassment of a trial. Can you meet me halfway?"

"My wife did not kill my mother," he said slowly and deliberately. "I know this for a fact. I *don't* know anything about any drug dealers.'' His voice was rising shrilly.

''I'm not insinuating that you'd normally know anything about drugs, Wilbur. I'm just...''

The true meaning of his words sunk in and my voice skipped as I figured it out.

He saw it in my face.

''Oh my God. Wilbur...''

FOURTEEN

HE STOOD and hovered over me.

"Wilbur? What happened Christmas night?" I slid to the other end of the sofa and stood. "You and Judy went to the dinner party, but she got that headache and went to lie down. What were you doing then?"

I was backing away as I asked the question, but he was quicker. He snatched out at me and grabbed my wrist. Twisting it behind me in a sudden move, he spun me and moved behind me in a flash. The pain in my arm was unbearable.

"Too many questions, Charlie. You're getting too close, and I can't let that happen."

He yanked at my wrist until my knees buckled. "That way," he growled, steering me toward the connecting door to the garage. He kept me gripped with his right hand, opened the door with his left. "Down the steps," he ordered.

I stumbled and thought he might loosen his hold, but I felt my shoulder snap instead. I cried out.

"Stay there!"

I halted on the third step. He bumped into my back and began to pull me to the right, so I was stumbling backward while he headed toward his workbench. He grabbed a plastic tie, the long ones used to bind groups of cords together, and turned back to me.

"Put your other hand back here."

"No! Wilbur, wait. Think what you're doing."

"Now!" He yanked my wrist again. The pain shot through my weakened shoulder and up my neck. I slowly lowered my right hand.

"You never did answer my question," I said, trying to distract him from his work. "What were you doing while Judy was nursing her headache? You came back here, didn't you?"

He was fumbling slightly with the plastic tie, trying to keep a grip on me and operate both ends of it at the same time.

"You made some excuse and came back here, knowing Paula was alone and thinking the police would probably attribute it to a break-in. You knew you could get rid of her."

"I didn't plan it," he whined. "Not like you're saying."

"But you'd had enough of her, hadn't you? She'd never treated you like a man. Never listened to your opinion. And you'd never been able to stand up to her your whole life, right?"

"I just came back for Judy's migraine medicine. I'd told our hosts I'd run to the convenience store and get something for her, but then I remembered she had this prescription that worked really well. So I came back here."

"And the police never asked your hosts if you'd left the party, did they? They latched on to Judy and went with her as their suspect."

"I never thought that would happen. I *never* meant..."

I tried withdrawing my free hand, hoping he wouldn't notice.

"No, Charlie! Don't try it."

"So what happened when you got here, Wilbur? Paula started in on you, didn't she? She was nagging, giving you a hard time, wasn't she?"

"She...she said..." His voice cracked. "She wanted to stay here and show us how to raise our baby. Said Judy and I were so stupid we'd never be able to do it by ourselves. She'd had some drinks. I just couldn't handle it. The thought of her ruining one more little life. The thought of Judy leaving me—because I knew she'd never go for it."

"And then what? A nice guy like yourself doesn't usually just pick up a fireplace poker because someone insults him."

"She laughed." His face turned grim and I could see him reliving that horrible scene. "She laughed at me and I just snapped."

"Wilbur, let me go. I'm sure there's a way we could explain this to the police."

"Uh-uh. They might let Judy go but then our baby's father would be in jail. I can't have that. You're the only person who's come close to figuring it out, Charlie. I just have to think what to do with you. I already have a plan for getting Judy out."

"Wilbur, think about this. If you get rid of me, you'll have two mur—"

"Shut up! I mean it!"

Quick as a flash, he grabbed my free hand and was about to snap the plastic clip on me. It was now or never. I stomped on his instep as hard as I could and followed immediately by flinging my right arm toward his face. I only clipped him across the ear, but it was enough to make him drop his grip on my pulsing left wrist. I spun to face him, scanning the workbench behind him for a weapon, any weapon.

He'd had the same thought. He pulled open a drawer at his side and came out with a can of spray paint. I almost chuckled at the vision of myself with a green face, but checked it just in time. Women who laughed at Wilbur didn't last long. All he had to do was temporarily blind me, and I'd be bound and gagged and in the back of his car before I knew it. I ducked and ran behind the car.

"Wilbur, slow down. This isn't the way to do this. Getting rid of me will just be the beginning of your troubles."

He held the can above the roof of the car, ready in case I raised up. I watched him through the windows, staying on the opposite side. My mind whirled. I had no idea what time it was, but didn't realistically expect Drake for at least another hour. I couldn't fend off Wilbur that long. I edged my way around the car, coming up on the driver's door. I could always lock myself inside and make him break a window to get at me. Dumb idea, Charlie. He had the keys. If I could just…

I edged toward the front bumper. He'd been following my moves, trying to get closer to me. He was now at the rear bumper. I decided to make a run for it before he caught on to what I was doing. I ducked and ran around to the passenger side and up the steps to the house. In a flash I was inside and I snapped the dead bolt behind me.

The front door. I raced to it and locked that dead bolt, too.

Wilbur was still pounding on the garage door, but it would probably only be a matter of moments before he figured out that he could hit the electric opener switch and get out. If he had his key ring in his pocket, neither the house, the garage nor the car would be safe for me. I had to get out of there. I ran to the kitchen door. The pounding at the garage door had stopped.

I grabbed the kitchen phone and dialed 911, laid the receiver on the counter and screamed as I headed for the back door leading to the yard. I hoped the operator wouldn't talk to the empty phone too long before she sent help to this address. I peeked out the glass panes at the top of the door. No sign of Wilbur.

Then I heard the front door creak open.

FIFTEEN

THE FRONT DOOR CLOSED with a stealthy click as I fumbled with the locks on the back door. Finally. I yanked it open. A siren screamed through the house as the burglar alarm went off.

Wilbur had obviously set the alarm as soon as he came in, hoping to catch me if I tried to escape. He appeared at the kitchen door as I raced onto the back patio. I headed toward my own house and belatedly remembered that my purse and keys were sitting beside the sofa on the floor in his living room.

"Looking for this?" he taunted from his back door. My purse dangled from his fingers. In his other hand he carried a claw hammer.

Shit.

He sprinted across the patio. I raced away, trying to stay beyond his reach.

Think, Charlie, think. Where could I go? I thought of Elsa's, my safe haven for much of my life, but knew I'd never make it. He'd easily be upon me before she could shuffle to her door to answer my knocks. Besides, I would never put her life in danger too. No, it had to be somewhere else. I headed down the street, opting to leave the relative quiet of our neighborhood for busy Central Avenue. It was six blocks away, but at least there would be traffic and people. Somewhere in the distance a siren wafted lightly on the wind.

Two blocks later, I was beginning to regret my recent lack of exercise. I made a hasty New Year's resolution, the same one I'd probably made last year at this time. My legs burned and the air in my lungs felt like fire. Wilbur was keeping a surprisingly good pace for someone who looked like he never did anything more physical than punch buttons on a calculator. He was no more than fifty feet behind me.

Ahead, a cross street bisected my path and I prayed there would be no oncoming traffic because I wasn't going to have the luxury of stopping to take a look. Wilbur was closing quickly. My feet pounded on the sidewalk, my breath rushed in and out with a sound like a charging bull, and somewhere—much nearer than before—the siren entered my consciousness. The cross street was about thirty feet ahead of me. I made a snap decision. Just before I came to the intersection, I spun to my right and cut across the yard on the corner.

Wilbur's momentum carried him straight toward the street. The oncoming police car, with lights and siren wailing, was only going about thirty. His body smashed into the driver's-side fender and it flung him through the air and into the yard on the opposite corner from where I ran. I caught a glimpse of all this just before I collided with a huge blue spruce tree and found myself stabbed in the face with a thousand needles.

SIXTEEN

THE MESS WASN'T NEARLY as bad as I'd envisioned. My face felt like a pincushion and looked like I had a delicate rash for about a week. Wilbur was lucky, too. His injuries consisted of a concussion and a broken leg, both of which were treated with one night's observation in the hospital before he was released to the custody of the Albuquerque Police Department.

Judy came home as soon as I told the authorities of Wilbur's confession. She looked a whole lot better after a shower and good night's sleep at home. We spent several afternoons talking at my kitchen table. She'd decided to move back to her hometown. It turned out that Wilbur wasn't the only one who suffered intimidation at the hands of an oppressor. While Wilbur had taken his mother's belittling for years, he'd dished out much of the same to Judy. From my own experience, watching his personality go from docile to almost manic in a few moments, I could believe it.

Kent Taylor probably suffered the worst from the whole ordeal. It just about killed him to admit that he'd jumped to much too quick a conclusion about the perp in this case and that he should have conducted a more thorough investigation.

Drake and I are doing great—missing Catherine a little because she really was a good houseguest over the holidays—but happy to have our space back to ourselves.

TOO MANY SANTAS
by Elizabeth Gunn

ONE

"WHERE DOES the time go?" Trudy asked me Friday morning.

"No idea." I try to stay cocooned in the sports section over breakfast. Simple interactions like "Pass the sugar" are okay, but I shy away from tough questions like where time goes until later in the day.

"Well, Christmas is next Wednesday. Are you listening? This weekend is crunch time."

"You bet." I had two dollars in the department football pool for next Monday's game. The Vikings' coach was estimating his team's chances against the Giants as "better than fair," and I wondered, is that about the same as "good"?

"We gotta get our ducks in a row. Buy food, get the tree up, decorate the house—"

"Decorate?" I lowered the Rutherford *Times-Courier*. "What does that mean?"

"Earth to Jake Hines." She handed me pencil and paper. "We are speaking here of an ancient Judeo-Christian holiday—"

"Trudy, c'mon, now—"

"—for which we have invited nine people to dinner. In this context, decorate means spread jolly, bright-colored stuff around. Hang up some ho-ho-ho material."

"We're not gonna do that whole number with the angels and the tinsel, are we?"

"In a ninety-five-year-old farmhouse? Hardly. A wreath and a traditional tree. With maybe popcorn strings? Mama says she's still got some of the old ornaments—"

"But nothing with blinking lights, right?"

"Trust me. Quit looking stricken, Jake, okay? No blinking, no flocking. Come on now, time to make lists."

My list turned out to be mostly hardware store basics: tree stand, wreath hanger, a couple of extension cords. Outlet adapter.

"And a bottle of Elmer's Glue," she suggested.

"Which we will use for—?"

"Putting extra limbs in the tree. To fill in bare spots."

I groaned.

Trudy agreed to buy the things that took taste—tablecloth, wreath, wine glasses—and bring a pizza to eat while we put up the tree.

"I'll bring the beer," I said.

"Try to get home on time."

"No problem," I assured her, "long as it keeps snowing." She works at the state crime lab, so she knows as well as I do that bad weather holds down the crime rate.

I put my list in my inside jacket pocket, got into my pickup and eased carefully into traffic on US-52. Light snow had been falling all night, but the plows had just been through, so I arrived at the Rutherford Police Department on time, with no fresh dents.

I'm chief of the detective division in a rapidly growing town of just under a hundred thousand, eighty miles southeast of St. Paul. My job requires some tolerance for rude behavior and bursts of violence, but it's lively and unpredictable and it suits me. Not incidentally, it pays my share of the mortgage and upkeep on the farmhouse, with enough left over, usually, for a few extras. This Christmas was beginning to include more than a few extras, though, another good reason to wish it would go away.

I've explained to Trudy that my bearish feelings about Christmas are completely irrational and have nothing to do with her. I was born a foundling and raised in foster homes, so my childhood Christmases were meager affairs, cobbled together out of grudging private charity and skimpy municipal handouts. I've never quite buried the left-out feelings those memories generate, so the yuletide commotion that makes my peers merry puts me in a funk.

I try to stay harmlessly entrenched in the bah-humbug camp, debunking fake sentimentality and waiting for the hymn-singing to stop. My failure to embrace my ex-wife's vision of Martha Stewart holidays contributed as much as anything to the breakup of our five-year marriage; our most epic battles were waged in a living room adrift in taffeta bows and tinsel.

Last Christmas, Trudy and I had just moved in together, and easily agreed we had all we could do to keep warm and dry in our drafty farmhouse. We accepted her sister's invitation to Christmas dinner, left as soon as Bonnie's children started fighting over their toys, came home to a bottle of ice-cold champagne by the wood stove and made giddy love under many quilts. "The best Christmas I ever had," I told her next morning. "Let's make it a tradition."

But this year, with the house insulated and the furnace working fine, Trudy said, "It's really our turn, you know," and on the day after Thanksgiving, it seemed almost painless to agree. In fact for a while, planning the feast, inviting her family and a few of our friends, I persuaded myself that with this smart, sexy Swede sharing my life, even Christmas could be fun. Now that it was time to deck the halls, though, I was getting that familiar panicky urge to climb on a camel and journey afar.

Mounting the stairs to the Rutherford PD at three minutes to eight, I felt almost grateful for the harsh clatter of malfeasance I knew would be waiting inside. All through this raw gray morning, phones would ring and computers would clatter, transmitting a string of sordid complaints: he hit, they took, it wasn't me. The gritty misbehavior of dysfunctional citizens would be alleged and sworn to and signed, and with luck we might move one case, a needle out of this haystack, a little closer to the punishment it so richly deserved. It might not be pretty, I thought with grim satisfaction, but at least, by God, around here nobody's doing fool things with sleigh bells and tinfoil.

Well, hardly anybody. Schultzy, my pal in Dispatch, looked up as I went by her glass-walled space and beckoned me in so she could solicit money for the department Christmas party next Monday. "The eve of Christmas Eve," she said, grinning gleefully, snapping her gum. She had mistletoe pinned to her lapel, and her cubicle boasted a string of blinking lights and a poinsettia plant with ceramic elves. When she started to hustle her list of raffle ticket opportunities, I told her I could hear my phone ringing, and fled. My lie must have landed pretty close to the truth; by the time I got the door open, my message light was blinking and the tape was loaded with calls.

I answered the most urgent messages, waded through a thicket of e-mail and was duking it out with next quarter's budget when Bo Dooley appeared in my open door-way, saying, "Got a minute?"

"Come in." He's the vice cop for the section, an experienced investigator with great street smarts and no penchant for small talk.

"Ray said I better tell you," he said, standing just inside the door, cradling his elbows in his thin hands, "I got a little deal cooking with the DEA."

"Oh?" On paper, Bo's immediate superior is Ray Bailey, my head of People Crimes. In practice, Bo mostly rows his own boat and tells Ray when he needs any help. So this wasn't a request for approval, exactly; more like a heads-up. "Better you than me," I said, "what do they want?" Little deals with the DEA are my least favorite thing, except for big deals with the DEA, which I like even less.

"They're chasing a rumor about a shipment of pot." He shrugged. "Probably just fishing. It sounds like too big a score for here. But they're hot for local intelligence these days, so I said I'd help."

"You know if you find anything for those puppies they'll grab it and run for the cameras."

"Sure," he said, and allowed himself a two-second smile. "Good for us."

He's right, of course. Bruised egos to one side, in a town as small as Rutherford, it wouldn't take a whole lot of publicity to make Bo useless on the street. And where would we find another trustworthy loner like Bo?

"Okay," I said. "You need anything?"

"Nope. Just wanted you and Ray to know in case you don't see me for a while."

I worked another ten minutes on the budget before a call came in on my outside line. "Hines," I said, and Officer Vince Greeley yelled, against a background of many shrill voices, "Jake?" as if he suspected some stranger might have usurped my last name.

"Where are you?" I asked him. "What's all that screaming?"

"I'm outside the main entrance to Iroquois Mall," he said. "There's a crowd of little kids here with their mamas, waiting to get into Davidson's so they can sit on Santa's lap and tell him which pieces of overpriced crap they want for Christmas."

"Why'd you call me?" I said, to head off Vince's annual parenting lament, which is another part of Christmas I can live without.

"Well—boy, these little devils are makin' a racket, hang on, I'll move over here—" I heard the squinch of his padded clothing, the crunch of boots on icy snow-pack, and then he said, from some quieter space, "Dispatch sent me out here because the outdoor Santa, the Salvation Army one that rings the bell out front? Well, he's disappeared."

"Disappeared? Who says?"

"Captain Lyman, the local commander. He called 911. Said, 'My Santa's gone.'"

"Well, he probably just stepped inside to get warm."

"Captain Lyman looked all over the mall before he called the station. And I went through it with him again."

"Did you check the men's rooms?"

"Of course."

"How about his car?"

"It's here, but he's not in it."

"Call his wife?"

"She says Santa put his gear in the van this morning like always, took his lunch and said he'd see her at five. She's very concerned."

"Santa have a girlfriend?"

Vince laughed nervously. "Some Santas, maybe. But this one's Willard Chase."

"Wil... Our Willard Chase?"

"Yup. Mr. Flashlight himself."

Vince and I have called him that since we were young recruits and he was one of the paradigms we were told to imitate, a middle-aged cop well past amateurish mistakes. He was the designated backup one bright June day when we answered a call to a gritty fourplex where an elderly woman stood on the porch, shaking with fear, telling us devils had invaded her cellar. Trying to quiet her fears, Vince went inside while I walked around the outside of the house. I was looking at a broken cellar window near the rear of the building when Willard walked up behind me and said, "Where's your flashlight?"

"Oh...in the car," I said.

"Not doing you a whole lot of good there, is it?" he said. He pulled his big Streamlight out of its belt sling, stuck it through the broken window and switched it on. The darkness below was suddenly filled with glowing eyes. Just then Vince, having groped his way through the dim parlor and kitchen of the creaking house, opened the rickety cellar door and reached for a light switch, as two feral cats, howling bloody murder, streaked up the unlit stairs and scared him silly.

We crammed a board in the broken window, put the landlord on report for several counts of substandard housing, and found a neighbor to sit with the unnerved widow till she calmed down. Then Willard Chase invited us to a coffee break and gave us his Famous Flashlight Lecture.

"Always, always," he said, "keep your flashlight

with you, even on bright, sunny days, because you never
know when you'll end up in some dingy, unlit basement,
looking for a suspect or a victim. Or a cat,'' he added,
''which you would look very dumb if you shot by mistake and terrified the whole neighborhood.'' We twisted
in our seats and smiled sheepishly. ''Always carry your
flashlight in your nonshooting hand, even in the most
benign-appearing situations, because if something suddenly goes to hell, you won't get to call time-out to
switch hands.''

We thanked him and drove away in our own squad,
sharing a defensive laugh at this geezer cop who thought
the whole secret of good police work was hanging on to
your flashlight, for God's sake. But I never got out of
my squad without my Streamlight again, and his advice
about which hand to carry it in saved my life once, when
I followed a whimpering noise up a darkened stairwell
and an abusing husband came out of the dark swinging
a pipe wrench.

''Ol' Willard's in the Salvation Army now?'' I asked
Vince.

''He just does this one volunteer job at Christmas
since he retired, his wife said.''

''How'd this Captain Lyman find out he was gone?''

''Says he was out checking on his volunteers like always. Found the bucket and bell here, but no Santa.
Looked all around the mall for him and then called us.
Ordinarily I'd say wait a while, Jake, but you know
yourself, Willard wouldn't wander off. Says he'll do a
job, he's gonna do it.''

''I know. I'll get Ray to send out a couple of guys.''

Ray Bailey, normally unflappable, abandoned the report he was typing in midsentence. ''Vince is right, Willard doesn't mess around. We gotta find him.'' He called

Darrell and Rosie, his two youngest and liveliest detectives.

"Great Scott, Holmes," Darrell said, "a Santa caper."

"We haven't had one of those in some time, have we, Watson?"

"Willard Chase missing is no joke," Ray said, "you hear me? He was one of the best street cops we ever had in this department. So get your butts out there, look every possible place, call me as soon as you've made a sweep." He followed them into the hall and called after their retreating backs, "Willard Chase would not be missing without a good reason! Find him!"

They got plenty of help, they told Ray, half an hour later. "The manager of this mall knows him, everybody knows him, they all want to help," Rosie said. "But we've looked in all the dressing rooms, Ray, and behind the counters, and I even did a stall-by-stall search of the ladies' rooms. But we sure haven't found him."

He told them to start looking in cars in the parking lot. Then he came to see me. "The rest of my crew's calling hospitals, doctors' offices…you think of anything else?"

"I don't like this." I stood, because it felt wrong to be sitting. "We should have found him by now."

"I know," Ray said. "His wife is at the mall now. I think I'll run out there myself."

"I'll come with you." Ray and I are administrators, we don't really belong on the street. But this was Willard.

Ray rolled a department car up the ramp and edged into the icy, crowded street. Snow was falling faster now; we could barely see the stoplight two blocks ahead. "There's the salt spreader out again," Ray said. "Every vehicle in this town is gonna need a new paint job by spring.''

"We gotta live through the winter first," I said, watching the fishtailing car in front of us. "They're forecasting this snow to last all day and into tonight, you hear that?"

"Where's global warming when you need it?" Ray said.

TWO

WILLARD'S WIFE, ELVIRA, stood just inside the center doors of the mall, talking to Captain Lyman, who wore a red-banded hat and dark blue coat with epaulets.

"So I'm not alarmed, but I am concerned," he was saying, "because it's not like Willard—" Elvira nodded emphatically and began citing examples of the rock-solid reliability of her husband. We interrupted to say hello and assure them the department was working the problem.

"Oh, we know you are," Elvira said. "We've been talking to your other detectives."

A round, ruddy man with a handlebar mustache walked up to her and said, "Any news?"

"Not yet. Jake and Ray, do you know Mr. Lovejoy? Blair, is it?"

"Blaine," he said, shaking hands. He had a crinkly sort of fond-uncle smile, and his clothes suited the rest of him, baggy gray flannels and a tweed jacket.

"He's the manager of the mall," Elvira said, "and he's been so kind—"

"We're anxious to help," he said. "Anything I can do—"

"Good, we'll be in touch." I asked Mrs. Chase, "When our detectives come back in here, will you tell them we're going to split the mall between us and cruise it again? We'll start from the central display there.''

An immense Christmas tree dominated the two-story atrium space, its branches covered in glittering ersatz snow. It was hung with hundreds of lights and ornaments, festooned with miles of ribbon and tinsel ropes and topped with a lighted crystal star the size of a beach ball. Around its base, a shiny black engine pulled a toy train full of toys up a fake snowy slope and down the other side. Atop the slope was a workshop where an automated Santa figure stood in a doorway with a carpenter's apron over his red suit. As each car passed him, he bent to inspect its load of toys. On the sides of the slope, his elves worked hard at little workbenches, using hammers and saws, paintbrushes and looms, ostensibly creating the toys that were piled in the boxcars and heaped under the tree. All the figures performed a series of animated moves, sequenced in a complex choreography like some vast, berserk cuckoo clock. Christmas carols blared from several speakers, and colored spotlights played over the entire panorama.

A few yards away, the double entrance doors of Davidson's department store opened as we watched, to reveal another Santa, a live one, seated on a huge ornamental chair like a throne. The mothers and children surged forward, making a kind of herd noise. Just inside the door, they were captured in a posh corral formed by red velvet ropes, which opened at the far end into an aisle that formed them into a single line moving toward Santa. The rest of the crowd in the atrium space began to shape itself into a long, jostling line waiting to get in.

The people at the rear end of the line, backed up against the gaudy central display, passed their time watching the animated figures. Dozens of children pulled on their mothers' hands, shouting shrilly, "Look, Mommy, this one's got a—", and "Mommy, that one's making—" and "Can I ask Santa for one of those—" on and on, endlessly. The mothers had fixed, brave smiles, like people who've just heard that the tooth can be saved with root canal.

Ray yelled, "Maybe we oughta start from one end, huh?"

"Good idea," I bellowed back, and we began easing around the massed bodies, trying to escape the crowd without treading on any children. One boy near us, a healthy six-year-old with a penetrating voice, demanded of his mother, "What's that other Santa Claus gonna do?"

"He's going to talk to you," his mother said, "as soon as we get up there."

"No!" he screamed, and jerked on her hand. "Not that one! The other one!"

"Justin, don't pull on my hand like that," she said, "you're hurting me."

"Well, why won't you look where I'm pointing?" he bellowed, starting a tantrum. "Over there, in the tree!"

I bent to his level and looked across the train tracks to the base of the tree. Behind a jumble of piled-up toys, just visible within the heavily frosted tree branches, I saw what might be a pair of red-clad legs above two black boots. The legs didn't appear to be attached to a body; they disappeared into some kind of white drapery material. But higher up in the branches, barely visible behind many ornaments, I thought I could make out another splotch of red.

"Ray," I stood up and yelled in his ear, "bend down here and look in the tree."

Ray bent, looked, stood back up and said something that dissolved in the din but sounded like "Willard?"

"Call the paramedics," I screamed, "and get that mall manager to stop the train."

"You got gloves? Here," Ray said, pulling some out of his pocket. He turned and pushed through the children, getting glared at by mothers. I vaulted over the wall around the display and jumped across the train tracks just ahead of the engine. The nearest kids, surprised and delighted, began calling to their mothers, "Look, Mommy, look what that man's doing, can we do that?" as I laid down among the dolls and teddy bears, and skootched under the tree.

There was a great, "Oooohh," from the crowd as the tree went dark. The train stopped and the music died with a little groan. I was blind for a few seconds; then my eyes adjusted and found plenty of light from the surrounding stores. I rolled onto my back, spitting out the flock and glitter that rained down on my face, and looked up at the big man in a Santa Claus suit, tied snugly to the trunk of the tree with what appeared to be clothesline. A white sheet encased most of his torso, but his arms had been pulled out of the bundle and fastened to tree branches with plastic ties.

I got my feet under me and pushed up through the branches till I was standing in front of him. His hat was gone. The sheet was falling off, luckily, so that I had been able to see enough of his red suit to come in after him. His white hair, of course, blended nicely into the tree. Below it, his ruddy face was mostly covered by two strips of white cloth wrapped around his eyes and mouth. They were held in place by a strip of clear plastic wrapping tape that ran under his chin, up along both cheeks and across the top of his head. Two more pieces of tape ran around his head laterally, one over the blind-fold and another over the gag in his mouth. Both strips continued on around the tree, holding him firmly in place. His fake white beard–mustache arrangement hung on his chest by its elastic string.

I touched his face. It was warm. He made a sound, "Mmm."

"Willard?" I said.

"Mmm," he said again, and tried to nod.

"This is gonna hurt some, I guess," I said, and began ripping the tape off his cheeks. When I had most of it off, I untied the rag that covered his lips; he still couldn't speak because an extra ball of cloth was jammed into his mouth. He had dried out badly, so the rag stuck to his tongue and hurt coming out.

"I'm so sorry," I said.

"Ahhh," he said, sucking air gratefully, "Hooo."

Ray had come back and was sliding under the tree trunk on his back, saying, "Paramedics are on their way."

"Good. He seems to be okay, though."

He tried to talk. The words came out garbled because his tongue wasn't working very well yet, but the gist was, "...ged me ow?"

"Hang on," I said, "we're close."

Ray got out a jackknife and went to work on the plastic ties and the rope while I used my Leatherman and plenty of spit to get that miserable blindfold off his face and out of his hair. His original voice came back suddenly and he said, distinctly, "Just go ahead and pull!" He lost some skin and hair in the next few minutes. He squinted against the pain, but he never whimpered.

"Son of a gun," he said when I lifted the last of the cloth off his eyes, "Jake Hines."

"What happened to you?"

"Not sure." He made a shaving mouth, left, right, flexing his face. "Can you get me out of here?"

"You think you can walk?"

"I think so." He made fists, shrugged and stamped his feet, bringing down a small avalanche of fake snow. "Feels like everything's working. Do you see my hat any place?"

"Uh…here." Ray grabbed it off a branch where it must have snagged.

"Because I'd like to…I mean, all them kids out there—" He crammed the hat on his head, pulled the beard-mustache thing back up over his face and said, "That look okay?"

"Uh, fine," I said, not believing we could be having this conversation, "but—"

"This the best way out, ya think?"

We held branches and tinsel and lights for him, and he crouched and wiggled his way out of the tree. We kept asking, "You sure you're all right? You need any help?"

"I'm fine," he said, "just hot and thirsty and I need to take a leak." He stepped over the piles of toys with the two of us following, carrying the sheet and blindfold we had taken off him. He waved to the crowd of wide-eyed kids who by now were watching his every move and had forgotten entirely that their intention had once been to get inside the store and sit on that other Santa's lap. They could see that something much more interesting was happening out here; a somewhat messy but wonderfully agile Santa was wriggling out of the Christmas tree.

"Hey, cool," a boy near me said, and all around him kid voices said softly, "Yeah."

"Ho-ho-ho!" Willard shouted, "Merry Christmas, boys and girls! Ho-ho-ho! You be good now, and I'll come back Christmas Eve and leave you lots of good stuff!" He climbed over the wall, ho-ho-ho-ing at the top of his lungs, and set off for the North Pole through an utterly captivated crowd.

THREE

A SIREN SCREAMED closer and closer, then died abruptly outside the back door of the mall. Lovejoy hit the start button on the display, and the animated elves went back to work. Santa resumed bending from the waist every twelve seconds to inspect their work, and Bing Crosby's voice, triumphantly remastered for still another year, crooned on about a white Christmas. All the tree lights came back on and were revealed, in the blinding moments before everybody's eyes adjusted, to be punishingly bright.

"Manager's office is over there." I pointed.

"I know," Willard said, and strode toward it without looking back.

Lovejoy hustled us inside and closed the door, asking, "Willard, what do you need?"

"Rest room?" Willard said urgently.

"Right here," his secretary said, and got up from her desk to open the door and turn on the light.

"I'll go get Elvira," Ray said. In the doorway, he met two men in firemen's coats wheeling in a gurney. We explained that the patient was walking and appeared unhurt, so they stood at ease while Willard did a lot of flushing and running water and clearing his throat. He came out of the manager's bathroom carrying his hat and beard and belt, just as his wife arrived. She pushed past the paramedics and into his arms. Pieces of Santa gear flew onto the carpet as the two of them demonstrated that affection was still warm and lively in the Chase household.

"So worried," she murmured, and kissed him some more. Finally she pulled back and said, "Sweetie, what happened to you? Did you get hurt?"

"I'm fine." He hugged her some more. "Just stiff, is all. I'm not sure yet what happened. Oh, here's the captain, too." They shook hands. Then he turned to the taller paramedic. "Hey, Milt," he said, "What're you guys doing here?"

"We called them," I said. "We couldn't tell from outside the tree if you were gonna be okay."

"And since we're here," Milt said, "let's check your pulse and your blood pressure. Can we make some space here?" Darrell and Rosie were crowding into the tiny office behind Ray.

"We'll wait outside," I said, and the four of us detectives stood in the hall with Lovejoy and his secretary, all of us nervously looking at our watches and talking about the weather. It was either fifteen or sixteen minutes after ten, depending on whose watch you believed, and if there was ever going to be a whiter Christmas in Minnesota, none of us wanted to see it.

"If Willard's okay," I asked Lovejoy, "is there someplace in the mall where we could all sit? We need to ask him some questions."

"I bet you do. I'd kind of like to hear some answers myself," Lovejoy said. "Let me think. There's one small store upstairs being remodeled—"

"Why don't we use number twenty-six, right down the mall here?" his secretary asked him.

"Plumbers started in there last night."

"Are you sure? Because I thought they said—"

"Quite sure, Judy, thank you," Lovejoy said, and his bouncy secretary looked suddenly abashed and made a small gesture of appeasement. "We can use the one upstairs, though, I think, if you can all stand the smell of fresh paint?"

"That's no problem," I said.

Willard opened Lovejoy's door and crowed, "Blood pressure's 130 over 87! Pulse is 64! Anybody wanna go skateboarding?"

The paramedics wheeled out the gurney, grinning, Milt saying, "I don't believe we can do any business with this fella."

Back in Lovejoy's office, Blaine found the keys for the store upstairs, while Judy borrowed a white jacket from a nearby pharmacist and helped Willard replace his red coat, so he wouldn't be too conspicuous on the escalator. His red pants and high black boots combined oddly with the skimpy cotton garment that didn't quite cover his Santa padding, but we all walked close around him, carrying his hat and coat and belt. Blaine led us upstairs to a storefront with soaped windows, where he unlocked the door and turned on overhead lights, revealing an empty space with drop cloths on the floor.

We gathered chairs and benches in a circle. Ray and Willard had begun to sneeze.

"Sorry," Lovejoy said. "That's from all the air freshener we sprayed in here, I'm afraid. Trying to cover up the paint smell."

"Hey, we'll get used to it," Ray said. He got out his pocket notebook while I set up a fresh tape in my recorder. Willard stretched and groaned a couple of times, but he was ready to start as soon as we were.

"Why don't you just tell us what happened?" Ray said.

"I keep my gear in my minivan," Willard said, "the bell and the bucket. The suit I take into the house every night so it'll be warm in the morning, and I don't bring it out to the van till I've got the heater going good. You stand out in the cold all day, it helps to start out warm.

"This mall's got a nice free program for early walkers, stroke victims and so on that need a warm place to walk in the morning. They unlock one delivery door in the back by the rest rooms, and let 'em come in there as early as six o'clock.

"So during Christmas season I come down here in sweats every morning about eight-thirty, set up my wishing well out front, get my suit and Thermos out of the van and go inside and have a cup of coffee while I change in the men's room. It takes quite a while to get into this thing, the padding and all. By the time I'm ready, the merchants are getting their stores open, and I pour another cup of coffee and walk around the mall saying good-morning to everybody, ask 'em how business is going and stuff like that. It kind of reminds me of the old days when I first got on the force," he said, turning to Ray and me, "when we used to walk a beat."

Lovejoy's beeper made three soft sounds; he pushed the Off button, got up quietly and went to find a phone.

"But this morning, something happened?" Ray said, straining for patience.

"I came out of the stall in the men's room, all suited up and about ready to put on my beard, and somebody jumped on me from behind and put that blindfold over my eyes—"

"They did your eyes first?"

"And then right away, just as I opened my mouth to

yell, stuffed that ball of cloth in my mouth and tied the gag on tight. Twenty-seven years in the department—" he looked around in wonder "—I gotta tell you, I never been so startled. I mean, what the hell? Who attacks Santa Claus? It was the furthest thing from my mind."

"It's a wonder you didn't have a heart attack," his wife said, petting his arm.

"Guess my ticker's still pretty good, huh?" He nudged her elbow. "You wanna go dancing?" She chuckled and gave him a bump with her shoulder.

"Say?" Lovejoy said urgently, coming back from the phone. "Excuse me? That was Irma from downstairs in Davidson's. And I'm afraid they just found somebody else tied up down there."

"I'll go," I said. "Keep this running, will you?" I handed my tape recorder to Darrell.

"Maybe I should come with you," Ray said.

"You better stick with Willard. I'll take Rosie."

"Okay," Rosie said, jumping up. She loves being first on the scene. As we went out, I heard Ray asking, "Was it a man who jumped you, you think?"

"Musta been two of 'em," Willard said. "Big, strong buggers."

Rosie and I followed Lovejoy, who said, "Let's take the back stairs and stay out of that crowd." He led us down unpainted concrete steps to a landing, then in through a heavy metal door. We passed a time clock, two employee rest rooms and a stockroom where people were pulling garments out of boxes and hanging them on racks. At a door marked, "Manager," Lovejoy entered without knocking.

We were facing a long, low reception desk with a telephone console and a computer. Behind it was a paneled wall with two doors, which appeared to lead to inner offices. There was nobody behind the reception desk, so we followed voices through the left-hand door, which stood partly ajar. In a bigger second room, between a messy desk and a table strewed with metal drawer inserts, two young women stood with their backs to us. They were bending over a man with purple-flowered cloth covering the top of his head, his eyes and most of his nose. It was held in place with wide strips of clear wrapping tape, and his mouth was taped shut.

He wore yellow suspenders over a blue oxford shirt open at the neck. His tie was loosened and hanging crooked, and he was trussed up pretty much the way Willard had been, except he was tied and taped to an office chair instead of a tree.

"Yvette?" Lovejoy said. "Irma?"

The dark woman screamed.

"Yvette, come on, it's only me," Lovejoy said.

"Oh, Mr. Lovechoy!" She waved her hands distractedly. "I'm joss so estartle—"

"Calm down, okay? These are police investigators." Rosie and I stood there with our shields out, looking as harmless as possible. "Tell them what happened."

"We joss fine Mr. Garza like thees." Rosie and I leaned closer to her, trying to pick English words out of her agitated Hispanic accent.

"Yvette came up to me as I was unlocking the office door—" the other woman said.

"Are you the manager?"

"His secretary. Irma Bell." We shook hands. She was small and neat, with carefully tousled blond hair. "Mr. Fitzgerald should be here soon. Yvette came up to me and said, 'We don't have any cash drawers at the counters, how are we supposed to work?' So we came back here looking for Mr. Garza. Because he's the auditor, he works all night counting the money, and then he puts the drawers back out in the registers, ready for the next day.''

The figure in the chair made a noise. I said, ''This Mr. Garza?''

''Yes. I wanted to get him out of that, but I thought you'd better see how he was tied up,'' she said. ''I thought there might be fingerprints and, uh, fibers and things.'' The whole population watches *CSI* now, so we get plenty of advice on procedure.

Rosie and I pulled on fresh gloves and went to work. The purple flowered cloth turned out to be a pillowcase. The solid purple cuff had been torn off and used as the gag, stuffed into his mouth. After his lips were taped shut the rest of the pillowcase had been taped onto his head like a helmet, with wide strips of tape running over the top of his head, down his cheeks and under his chin. He presented a different pain problem than Willard had; there was no tape in his hair, but much more on the skin of his face.

He wasn't as stoic as Willard had been, either. The first few times he moaned, we stopped, but then he made an impatient sign like, ''Go on, go on.'' Finally we looked at each other, nodded and began ripping and chopping, regardless of noise, till we had him free. We were bent over him, trying to help him with the damage to his face, when a tall, good-looking man in an elegant blue suit walked in.

''Oh, Mr. Fitzgerald,'' Irma said, ''we're in such a mess—''

''Why are all the doors open?'' He stared around. ''What's going on?''

Irma started an anxious explanation but Garza, who had lost chunks of his mustache as well as all that skin,

raised the red face he was cradling in a damp towel and
snarled, "What does it look like, for Chrissake? I've
been assaulted and robbed, and I'm damn lucky to be
alive, and I'm thinking of suing the company."

"My God, Bernard," Fitzgerald said, instantly cowed
by the profanity, "how awful! What can I do?" He noticed Yvette standing there, and said, "Why are you
here?"

"She doesn't have a cash drawer, she can't go to
work," Garza said. "Be some use, will you? Make her
up one while I go to the john." He got up and limped
toward the bathroom, rubbing his back and groaning.

"Okay, sure... Well, God, they're all messed up,
aren't they?" Fitzgerald surveyed the mess of empty
cash drawers spread over Garza's desk and the floor. He
set one upright, peered into the open wall safe and said,
"I don't see any bills in here."

"Well, I suppose they took all the paper money.
That's what robbers do, Devon. Give her one roll of each
of the coins and get her some charge forms. And then
write a check and run to the bank. We'll need five thousand cash, twenties and fives and ones, to get started."
Garza went into the bathroom, closed the door hard and
started the flushing and splashing thing that was evidently de rigeur after being tied up.

I turned to Rosie to suggest we give the Davidson's
team time to regroup, but she was watching Fitzgerald,
wearing a bright, curious expression like a fly fisherman
watching a trout. She licked her lips, smiled and said,
"Good morning, Devon."

He turned, stared a minute and said, "Rosie? Is it?
Rosie Doyle?"

"Sure is," she said, beaming like a lamp.

"What in hell are you doing here?"

"I'm a police detective now. This is my boss, Jake Hines."

To me, she said, "Devon and I went to high school together."

"How about that," I said.

Fitzgerald let out a short bark of laughter. "Rosie was a real orangutan. She had the nuns on her case all the time, didn't you, Doyley?" He had deep blue eyes and light brown hair streaked with gold, and a bright, teasing manner. All three of the women in the room were watching him, looking turned on. His easy success with women probably accounted for some of Garza's hostility, I thought. Then he twinkled at me, too, asking, "Do you really think you can make a cop out of this outlaw?"

Rosie tossed her head. "You used to pull a few pranks yourself, I seem to remember." They laughed together then, that clubby laugh that old school chums use when they reminisce.

"Son of a gun," Fitzgerald said, "Rosie Doyle, a cop, I can't believe it! Your name still Doyle, by the way?"

Yvette cleared her throat and said, "Uh-scuse me, Mr. Fitzgerald—"

"You're busy," I said. "We'll talk to you later." I put my hand under Rosie's elbow and steered her firmly into the front office, where we were nearly bowled over by three more women in Davidson's uniforms, all looking grumpy. They crowded around the reception desk, hurling loud, rude questions at us. We pointed mutely to the back office, and they charged through the open door. As she passed us, the biggest, angriest-looking one muttering contemptuously, "Nobody but Irma ever knows anything useful, up here. I don't know what they pay the rest of them for."

"Rosie," I said, in the hall, "what are you thinking?

This crime scene is a mess already. We don't need you giggling and getting cute with the store manager.''

"Well, I'm sorry, Jake, I was just so surprised to see him because—never mind," she said quickly, seeing me start to grit my teeth, "I'll tell you later. You're right, there's a lot going on, isn't there?"

"They're all so busy, a lot of them are mad, and once word gets around about two people being assaulted, they'll be scared besides. Getting straight answers to questions is gonna be hell on wheels.''

"Yup. Gonna get our asses royally chewed out here today.'' She didn't look distressed, though; she still had that happy, engaged look she got when she first spotted Fitzgerald.

I called Ray and said, "Tell Willard we've got a major felony down here. This store's been robbed. He should be thinking about anything he saw or heard that connects him to that." I described the mess in the manager's office, including the pillowcase blindfold.

"Pillowcase? For sure?''

"Looks like it.''

"Weird. But a robbery. Willard's gonna be relieved.''

"You think he'll take comfort from a robbery?''

"Well, it's better than getting mugged for no reason, isn't it?''

"I guess. If you gotta get mugged.''

"Whaddya think, should I get a couple of fingerprint guys out here?''

"I don't see much use," I said. "Everything's getting pawed over by dozens of people, and there's no way I can stop it. They gotta keep the store open. We've got the tape and the sheet and the blindfolds. We can test all that. While we're waiting to interview the auditor,

Rosie and I will bag what we've got here and take a look at all the entrance doors to this store.''

The front ones were still too mobbed to get near, but we did a careful inspection of the two outside doors that opened on the back parking lot, and the inside one that led to the back hall and stairs, without finding any signs of forced entry. When we finished, we went back to Garza's office to see if he was ready to talk to us.

''I gotta stick with this for another half hour or so,'' he said. He had money stacked all around him and was cramming bills and charge forms into cash drawers, which Devon and Irma were shuttling to clerks all over the store. ''After that, sure, then we can talk. Till the insurance adjuster gets here, anyway.'' He was sipping a fresh cup of coffee and seemed energized by doing his job; his face was losing the red, scorched look it had when we first pulled off the tape.

''You know, I'm starting to worry about Gus,'' Irma said, coming in with her hands full of change orders.

''Who's Gus?'' I said.

''The night janitor. All the clerks are complaining that their stations weren't cleaned, their trash bins are full—did you see him last night, Mr. Garza?''

''Yeah, he was out on the floor when I first got to work—damn!'' He broke off and began recounting a drawer. ''Don't talk to me while I'm counting money!''

We moved away from Garza's desk and I asked her softly, ''Are you saying you think there might be another person tied up around here somewhere?''

''I hate to think so, but...Gus is reliable,'' she murmured, frowning. ''I've worked here eight years. He was here when I came, and I've never known him to leave work undone.''

"Have you talked to Mr. Fitzgerald? What does he say?"

"Well...Mr. Fitzgerald just replaced our old manager two weeks ago." Irma lowered her voice. "I'm sure he'll be fine but...it's hard for him to judge people just yet. And there's a lot of resentment...Mr. Kranz was our manager ever since this store opened, and some people felt he was kind of forced to take early retirement. Especially the old-timers—" she inclined her head discreetly toward Garza "—think Mr. Fitzgerald is just a joke because he's so young and, um, attractive. So they won't cut him any slack at all."

"Have you tried calling Gus at home?"

"No. I haven't had time."

"Can we have his number?"

"Sure. Come out to my desk." We followed her to the front office, where she put her change orders down carefully on the console by her desk, whispering to herself in fierce concentration as she did it. She found the number in a Rolodex and copied it for us. Rosie took it and began dialing, asking, "What's his last name?"

"Finseth."

Fitzgerald came in, empty-handed and smiling after his last round of cash register shuttles, and said, "Well, there, I guess we've got 'em all pacified, haven't we?" Seeing Irma Bell's tense, worried face he said, "What? What now?"

"We're calling Gus's house."

"Gus the janitor? Why?"

Rosie closed her phone. "Ten rings. No answer."

"Let me have his address," I said. "I'll send a squad to check." Irma read it to me and I wrote it in my notebook. "Has he got a wife?"

"She died last year."

"Children?" Irma had bent over her change orders, intent on picking them back up in the order she'd put them down in. When she didn't answer, I looked up from my notebook and met Fitzgerald's eyes. He shrugged and turned away.

Having ostensible command of a staff he didn't really know anything about must have been uncomfortable, but Devon Fitzgerald seemed to drift around the edges of the action in the store, cool and pleasant, undisturbed. As he started into his own office, he passed Rosie, smiled and asked her softly, "A cop? You sure you want to be a cop?"

She winked, showing him all her dimples, and raised her right thumb.

FOUR

STILL WAITING FOR GARZA, Rosie and I took the back stairs up to the empty store, where Ray and Darrell were standing just inside the door, talking to Lovejoy.

"I keep trying to think who that mall manager reminds me of," I muttered into Rosie's ear.

"A young Wilford Brimley?"

"That's it. I wondered why I kept daydreaming about oatmeal."

Willard Chase, costumed again, sat on a bench with his wife beside him. She was smoothing his coat and helping him put his beard back on.

"Willard," I said, "you're not thinking about going back to work, are you?"

"There's nothing wrong with me," he said, "and they got nobody else to collect those coins today."

"Well, I'm gonna ask you to let the coins wait awhile," I said, "because it stands to reason there's some connection between your assault and Garza's, and I need you to come down and help us figure it out."

"You saying it was Bernie? Bernie Garza got tied up?"

"You know him?"

"Ever since high school. Bummer. He's not hurt, is he?"

"He seems okay, but his office is a mess. Cash drawers and credit-card forms all over the place, and all the paper money gone.''

"How much did they get, do you know?" Old law-enforcement types are pretty predictable. "Help us figure it out," was still vibrating in the air between us as Willard pulled down the beard his wife had just so carefully arranged and began unbuttoning his red coat.

"We haven't got a figure yet, but...yesterday's deposits, all the bills out of the cash drawers and the contents of the safe...upward of ten thousand, I'd guess, maybe more."

"And Bernie got tied up just like I did?"

"Except he was tied to a chair and had a purple flowered pillowcase on his head for a blindfold."

"Seriously? Purple flowers?" His tried not to look pleased, gave it up and said, "I'd kinda like to have seen that."

"Garza's not a favorite buddy?"

"Aw, he's all right. Just...kinda sure of himself, is all."

"Maybe a little less so right now."

"The hell." He took off his hat. "Worth a walk downstairs to see that, too." Unbuckling his belt, he stopped thoughtfully and said, "Why me, though, I keep wondering? I didn't have any money."

"That's what we gotta figure out. Rosie? Darrell? Where'd you go?"

"Right behind you," Rosie said, and I turned and stepped on her foot.

"Sorry!" I said. "When you came out here this morning—is your foot all right?"

"It's fine," she said, massaging her instep. "What are you asking?"

"When you got here this morning, were all the stores open?"

"Hardly any of them were, at first."

"So where did you look?"

"Well, Vince took us in the back door and we found the mall manager." She smiled at Lovejoy and he gleamed back at her, a little less avuncular, I noticed, with Rosie than with the rest of us. "He gave us a list of stores and told us which ones opened first. We went through all the public areas for a few minutes, and then as fast as the merchants came to work we got them to let us in their stores. By the time the mall opened we'd been in everything but—well, what did we miss?" she asked Darrell.

"Uh—" he consulted his list "—Davidson's. And this place we're in right now, of course."

"You didn't go through Davidson's?"

"Well, no," Darrell said. "They were the last to get open. We were waiting to start on them when you told us to look in the parking lot. Then you found Willard under the tree, so—"

"And of course we didn't know about the auditor yet," Rosie said.

"Well, now we got a new worry," I told them. "It looks like Davidson's night janitor is missing."

"Why do some days get like this?" Darrell said. He looked at Ray. "You think there's any point in looking through Davidson's now? It's so full of people—"

"Yeah, but there must be lots of areas shoppers don't get into. Janitor's closets, storerooms, employee rest rooms...there might be cupboards or—get somebody to show you."

"The store's pretty busy," Darrell said.

"Betcha the manager has time to help us," Rosie said with a kind of Mona Lisa smile.

Ray looked at Rosie the way a rug merchant looks at backing. "Something you need to tell me about the manager?"

"Jake says forget it until later." To Darrell, she said, "Ready?"

"Stay in touch," Ray said. "We can meet—" He turned to Lovejoy. "Okay if we make your office headquarters while we're here?"

"Oh, I wish you would," Lovejoy said, "that way you'll be handy in case somebody ties me up." He tried to make it sound like a joke, but he was beginning to look a little stressed.

"Good!" Ray said, "Thanks. Darrell and Rosie, right now I'm going to Davidson's, to that suite of offices that's marked 'Manager' to talk to the auditor. If you run out of places to look, come there and find me. If I'm gone from there, page me and I'll meet you in Mr. Lovejoy's office. You got it? Go!"

When they were gone, he asked me, "Is Rosie on to something with the Davidson's manager?"

"Old school chums, is all I know," I said. "I told her to knock off the jokes with him till we finish this job."

My phone rang. Dispatch said, "Lulu's looking for you."

Lulu Breske said, "This is your reminder, you have a meeting with the chief at one o'clock, at which he expects to see your budget estimates for next year."

"Oh, damn. What time is it?"

"What, your watch is broken? It's 11:45." Lulu is the chief's secretary. She has great respect for Chief McCafferty and very little for the rest of us.

"Let me speak to him." I was pretty sure he'd agree to push it back a day.

"He's out of the building. Don't be late, now, he's got a full afternoon, I gotta keep him right on skej." She hung up without saying goodbye, a favorite ploy when she's moving quickly down a task list. I could see her drawing a black line through my name while she dialed the next number on her sheet.

I thought about calling her back and telling her if she ever hung up on me again I was going to come back to the station and set fire to her desk. I didn't, of course, because Lulu is the chief's good right arm and nobody messes with her. But I thought about it until the red bubble of rage stopped dancing in front of my eyes, and then called Dispatch back and asked her to send a squad to Gus Finseth's house and tell him to call me from there.

Ray said, "Everybody ready to go down?"

"I guess," Willard said, "soon as I get back into my sexy white jacket." He did a little vamping hip-wiggle as he stripped down to his long-john top and belly pads, and broke everybody up.

As before, the rest of us carried pieces of his extra gear and walked close around him. On the escalator, we could all hear how the noise level had risen since we went up. The sound of marching feet and the roar of voices from hundreds of shoppers rumbled through the mall like thunder in a worsening storm.

"It sounds kind of like a big hungry beast, doesn't it?" Elvira Chase said.

Lovejoy looked at her anxiously and said, "Don't do anything to annoy it, huh? We need this beast right now."

"Been a tough year, huh?"

"Two stores empty at Christmas? Better believe it."

Halfway down, Elvira suddenly said, "Willard, your back is starting to hurt, isn't it?"

"No."

"Yes, it is. I can tell by the way you're standing."

"My back is fine." He stood straighter.

"You know perfectly well you'll get cranky if your back starts to hurt and you don't—"

"Elvira," Willard said over his shoulder, "go home, will you?"

"See, you're starting already."

We reached the bottom of the escalator and everybody got off. Willard turned to his wife and repeated, "Go home, Elvira." He kissed her cheek. "I'll see you tonight."

"I don't feel right about leaving you," she said.

"Do it, anyway," he said. "You'll get used to it."

"Promise me you won't forget to eat something."

"I won't forget to eat something. Go." She left him reluctantly, turning back twice to wave before she got out the door. When she was finally gone, Willard said, "Okay, now let's go find Bernie Garza. Because the truth is my back is starting to hurt quite a bit, and I may not be good for a whole lot more of this fun."

"We can do this later if you—"

"Now don't you start," he said. "Let's go."

FIVE

"GARZA ABOUT READY to talk?" I asked Irma Bell.

"Let me check." She was seated behind her reception desk, with her hair in precise spikes, her white blouse unrumpled and all her pens and pencils in a neat row. The doors to both the offices behind her were closed, and canned music came faintly from some distant place. If I'd been meeting Irma Bell for the first time, I'd have assumed she was having a routine day.

When Garza answered his phone she said, "The detectives are back, are you—" She listened for a few seconds, said, "Fine," cocked an ironic eyebrow at me and reported, "He says he'll be ready to describe the crime scene in five minutes."

"Sounds like Mr. Garza is beginning to enjoy this," Ray muttered, as the three of us took seats against the wall.

"Well, that makes one of us," Willard said. "The more I think about it, the madder I get."

"Willard," I said, "why don't we let this wait and find you a doctor?"

"Will you forget about my back? I got a little arthritis, is all, and getting jumped on and tied to a tree didn't do it any good, but I was okay till I tried that cute little dance move while I was taking my coat off. Showing off to my wife, serves me right. I'll be fine as soon as I go home and take a muscle relaxant.''

''Then why are you so mad?''

''Because, dammit, Jake, you know as well as I do people don't go to the trouble to tie other people up without a good reason. And I'll be damned if I can think of a good reason to tie up a man impersonating a myth-ical red-suited saint.''

''You must have been where you could see some-thing—''

''From a stall in the men's room? You wanna go in there and see how excited you get about the view?'' Elvira was right; Willard was getting testy.

The console buzzed. Irma murmured into it and said, ''Mr. Garza will see you now.''

Willard grunted, getting up, but once on his feet his old cop stance came back and he walked into Garza's office looking sturdy and collected. Which was just as well, because a big guy in a too-small white lab coat over red fleece pants and knee-high black boots, unless he carries himself really well, could look undignified.

Not that Garza was any candidate for hunk of the month. He had on a worn suit jacket over his suspenders, now, and his tie was back in place; his desk and console were neat again and the safe was closed, but his earlier energy bump was clearly fading. His face had gone gray and mottled, his shoulders sagged and the hand he held out to Willard was starting to shake.

''Willard,'' he said, ''isn't this a helluva note?''

''Some deal, Bernie. The two of us tied up the same day. Who'd've thought?''

''I never heard a thing, did you?''

''No. I thought I was all alone in the men's room.''

''Putting on your Santa suit like always, right? This

time of the year I see this guy every morning," Garza told me, "when I make my deposit."

"Regular as clockwork," Willard said, "just before he goes home, he walks down the mall and drops the money in the night-deposit slot there at the bank."

"What time is that?" I asked Garza.

"Nine-fifteen, nine-thirty. Just about the time ol' Santa here—" he nodded ironically at Willard "—is making his grand tour of the mall with his last cup of coffee."

"It's my chance to visit," Willard said. "The rest of the day I'm out front by myself."

"But you don't see each other every morning, do you?"

"No, I just do weekdays," Willard said. "They've got another guy does weekends."

"What about you, Bernie?"

"Thanksgiving to Christmas, I work every night. The rest of the year, I spread my forty hours over six nights and skip Sunday. Sunday's lighter, the salespeople just lock their drawers and leave them, and I audit Sunday and Monday together on Monday night."

"So...you audit all the money the store takes in?"

"That's right."

"That's pretty unusual, isn't it?"

"Somewhat. Couple other stores in the chain have the same arrangement, where they have longtime employees willing to do it."

"Don't you get tired of such a tough schedule?"

He shrugged. "I get paid extra, I'm building a little nest egg for retirement. I like not having to straighten out anybody else's mistakes, and it works for them because I've shown I can save the manager a lot of headaches."

"It sounds hard."

"I'll be retiring soon, and then I can rest all I like."

"What time do you come to work?"

"Two a.m. Sometimes three, in the summer when business is light."

"You work all alone?"

"And that's another thing I like about it. I can concentrate, nobody hassles me. I audit the drawers in the same order every night and then make up the change in the same order. Some people will tell you it doesn't make any difference, but for me it's faster and more accurate if I always do everything the same way."

"So all the drawers were here on the desk when you got attacked?"

"Stacked up the way I always do them, four rows wide, three deep, two high."

"And the safe was open?"

"Sure. I work out of it, making change. When I'm done I lock it up, take the drawers out to the registers and lock them in, take my deposit to the night slot at the bank down the hall there, come back up here and lock this office and then go home."

"Any other employees work while you do?"

"The janitor. Gus. Once in a blue moon if I have trouble balancing I might still be here when Irma comes in. I used to see Mr. Kranz once a week or so when he came in early, but of course with this new twinkie—" he nodded toward the office next door "—I don't expect I'll ever see him. You saw for yourself, this morning, he came strolling in a little after ten."

"So you don't know any other employees?"

"I see them at the company picnic. If I go. Mostly I know them by their work."

"You can tell people apart by their cash drawers?"

"Oh, you bet. Eloise is slovenly, bills every which way and trash in the coins. Yvette does well enough with cash, but her charge slips are a disaster. Helen is anxious. She wraps everything in rubber bands so tight I have to cut them off."

"You're a good observer," Ray said. "You pay attention to details. So tell us, what was different last night from all the other nights?"

"Till some crazy bastard attacked me and taped a rag on my head? Nothing."

"What time was that?"

"Uh...lemme think a minute." He took a sip from a cold cup of coffee and winced.

Willard asked him, in a sort of choked voice, "Bernie, did they wrap you up?"

"Wrap me up? No. Whaddya mean?"

"I don't know exactly. But it was the spookiest part." He looked a little sick. "After they taped that blindfold over my head, they wrapped me up in something. Real tight. A sheet or a rug."

"It was a sheet," I said. "It was still partly around you, under the tree."

"It felt like a—" he looked around, oddly shamefaced "—it felt like a shroud. I wanted to say, 'But I'm not dead yet.' And then I thought, 'but maybe soon.'" He rubbed his face. "It's just things you think when you—you feel so helpless, don't you?" Garza nodded, looked away, picked up his coffee cup again and put it down without drinking.

"They must have wrapped you up to move you, Willard," I said. "How did they move you, by the way?"

"Picked me up and put me on something. I think it might have been one of those garment racks they use to move merchandise around the store. I was standing up, sort of. Propped up somehow with people holding on to me.''

"But you, Mr. Garza, you weren't moved, I guess?''

"Nope. They tied me up in the chair I was already sitting in.''

Ray thought for a minute and said, ''Let's talk about the time. Willard, we know you got tied up in the men's room between nine and nine-fifteen. But Bernie, you must have been attacked and robbed before that, right?''

"Uh...yeah.''

"How much earlier?''

"Well...I'm not exactly sure.''

"Think about it, now. You have to keep pretty close tabs on your time, don't you? So you finish before the store's ready to open?''

"Well, yes. But I've been doing this for so long, I kind of have a feel for it. I don't keep my eye on the clock every minute.''

"Okay. Just give us your best estimate of the time you got attacked.''

"Well, lemme think. I was auditing the last cash drawer. Soon as I finished that I was going to carry all the drawers out on the floor and set up the registers for the day. Then I'd come back in here and make up the deposit, see?'' He leaned back in his chair and looked at the ceiling. ''Must have been right around five-thirty.''

"The safe was open?''

"Sure. After I take all the cash and charge slips out of the drawers, I set the drawers up with the basic change and fresh charge slips for the next day. Have to have the safe open to do that.''

Willard leaned forward with sudden urgency. ''See,

Bernie, that's what driving me nuts. You were sitting
here with money spread out all around you—''

"It's the only way to do this job," Garza said defen-
sively.

"Well, right. And a damn good reason for somebody
to attack you, right? You had money and he wanted it.''

Bernie spread his hands, palms upward, and said
crossly, "What else is new?"

"Nothing. That's my point." Willard rapped firmly
on Bernie's desk with his knuckles. "Nothing whatever
is new in this scenario so far. One guy has money, another guy wants it. But if I was attacked by the same
fella, what did he want from me?"

Garza regarded him tiredly across the desk for a few
seconds and finally said, "You're the cop, Willard. I
can't help you with the mind-game stuff."

"Ex-cop," Willard said, "and it's not a game. There's
gotta be a helluva good reason why a person ties up
another person, puts a gag in his mouth and blindfolds
him." Looking suddenly, unexpectedly pleased, he said,
"Bernie, did you know they made your blindfold out of
a purple flowered pillowcase?"

Garza, not amused, said, "I expect the color was irrelevant, Willard."

My phone rang. I walked into the outer office, pushed
Talk and said, "Hines."

"I'm at Gus Finseth's place, Jake," Tim Casey said.

"And?"

"He's not here. He didn't answer the door and the
paper was still on the doorstep, so I got the landlady to
let me in. His bed hasn't been slept in."

"His car there?"

"No."

"Get her to describe his car, will you? And then get

on your MDT and see if you can find the license number.
Call me back, huh?"

"You got it."

"What's an MDT?" Irma asked me, as I closed my
phone.

"Mobile Data Terminal." She stared at me blankly.
"The laptop in his car."

"They have a—dear me." She eyed her workstation.
"I don't think I could work this thing and drive at the
same time."

"Sometimes they drive with their knees," I said, af-
flicted suddenly with an irrational desire to impress Irma
Bell.

Back in Garza's office, Ray was saying, "Let's talk
about access for a minute. Was your door locked, Mr.
Garza?"

"Yes. Well, the front one, the door to the outer office.
I don't bother with this inside one of mine. I go in and
out all night and that's too much locking and unlocking."

"What about the side door here, between your office
and the manager's?"

"That one has to be locked on the manager's side."

"And was it?"

"Yes. I mean it must have been. Always is."

"But you didn't check it last night?"

"To tell you the truth I forget it's there—"

"Let's check it now," Ray said. It was locked.

"Kranz always kept it locked," Garza said. "Our old
manager. When Tinker Bell started—" Bernie nodded
toward the other office and curled his lip "—I told him,
we always use the front doors, please keep the door between us locked. He said okay. I checked it a couple of
times right after he started and it was always locked, so

I quit thinking about it.'' He shrugged. ''Well, but even if it wasn't, the front door to the suite was locked, so it comes to the same thing.''

My phone rang again. Rosie said, ''We found him, Jake. On a lower shelf in the stockroom, wedged in behind a lot of pillows.'' Her voice was hoarse with strain. ''Call 911, will you? He's in bad shape. We're starting CPR right now.''

The paramedics hadn't even put their truck away, so they were back in just over six minutes. I waited for them by the back door and led them to the stockroom where Darrell and Rosie were working over Gus Finseth. The medics had an oxygen mask and an IV on him and were going out the door in a little over a minute. As soon as the gurney disappeared, Rosie sank down, exhausted, on the cold wooden floor and buried her head in her hands.

Darrell leaned against a wall, looking woebegone. ''I think I mighta cracked a rib.''

''Don't worry about it,'' I said, ''it just means you were doing it right.''

''Oh, not on the janitor,'' Darrell said, ''on me. Jeez, he was really crammed in that cupboard, wasn't he, Rosie? We had to pull like hell to get him out.''

''Listen—'' I touched Darrell's arm ''—was Gus blindfolded like the other two?''

''Yup. And had a gag in his mouth.''

''Where is it? The stuff—''

''Uh...over there on the floor.'' We walked over and he showed me; soft white cotton, maybe cleaning rags once. ''You want 'em bagged and tagged?''

''Yes. Soon as you're, uh, rested.''

''Aw, I'm okay.'' He looked over at Rosie, walked

back to where she sat and poked gently at her heaving back. "You all right there, Sherlock?"

"Mmph," she said.

"Better get up," he said, "and move around before your sweat gets cold."

She swabbed at her face a couple of times, took a long deep breath and stood with her red curls flying in wiry spirals all around her head, freckles showing clearly in her set white face.

"When we find the pond scum that hurt that old man like that," she said, "I want to testify against them in court, okay, Jake?"

"For sure," I said.

My phone rang. Lulu said, "Jake—"

My watch said three minutes to one. I had not thought about my appointment with the chief even once since Lulu hung up on me. "I'm on my way," I said, "I'm almost there."

"Will you listen? The chief is delayed, he wants to reschedule for Monday."

A new little bubble, of glee this time, formed and rose before my eyes. "Jeez, Lulu. After I drive all the way downtown?"

"Well, I'm sorry, Jake, I didn't know until just now. Is one o'clock Monday all right?"

"I'm not where my calendar is," I said, not wanting this pleasure to end. "Put a note on my desk, will you?"

She said something under her breath to herself and then, to me, "You bet," and clicked off.

SIX

DARRELL AND ROSIE followed me back to Garza's office. Ray was still there, and Devon Fitzgerald stood in front of the desk saying, "The insurance adjuster is here, Bernard, have you got a figure for me yet?"

"Oh...well, yes. But I'll handle the adjuster, Devon, just send him to me."

"No, no, you've been here too long already," Fitzgerald said, "time you went home. Just give me the amounts for what's missing and I'll deal with him." He stood there with his hand out, smiling his easy smile but looking, suddenly, a little more sure of himself. After a few seconds Garza wrote a figure on a scrap of paper and handed it to him.

"I guess I'll need the documentation too, though, won't I?" Fitzgerald said.

Garza opened and closed his mouth a couple of times, opened a drawer and pulled out a bigger sheet of paper with many tapes stapled on the back. "Be careful with this," he said, "it's the only copy I've got right now."

Fitzgerald smiled his handsome *GQ* smile and said, "For sure."

Garza watched him leave, shaking his head. "Lucky if I ever see it again. He's right about one thing, though," he said, turning back to us, looking suddenly exhausted, "it's time I went home. You boys got enough from me to get started?"

"Oh, sure. We can come back another time." I stood. "You've been very helpful. Thanks."

As we filed out, Garza, behind us spoke. "Is Gus okay?"

Rosie and Darrell were halfway out the door and kept going, pretending not to hear. Ray and I half turned, and I said, "We don't know yet."

"Whaddya mean you don't know? He's not hurt bad, is he?"

"You probably should ask the hospital," Ray said.

"Oh, Jesus." Garza's face took on a slightly greenish cast and his mouth quivered.

"Are you all right?" I thought he might be going into shock. "Do you need some help getting home?"

"No, don't be silly." He sat up straight and did his best to look insulted. "I'm fine."

Outside in the mall, Willard said, "I'm running out of steam, too. I'm gonna put all my gear in my van and go home."

"Good thinking." We helped him load up, all of us squinting into the worsening snowstorm. The wind had come up, and fierce little stinging tornadoes swirled around the cars. The buildings on the other side of the parking lot were becoming indistinct.

"Let's collect all our evidence bags and meet in the food court," I said as we came back inside. "We all need lunch, and I want to talk about this day before I forget what I know."

"You think you know something?" Ray asked. "What a grand feeling that must be."

"I'll have the bacon cheeseburger with everything," Darrell said, flexing his weight lifter's muscles happily in front of the food line a few minutes later, "and the large Caesar salad."

"You want croutons?" the counter girl asked him.

"No, but I'll take some of those little toast squares there," Darrell said, whereupon Ray quit scowling at the soup and looked, for a few seconds, delighted to be alive.

"Ethnic grease and salt," Rosie said, plunking down a paper plate heaped with tacos, rice and beans. "The most dangerous thing about police work is the way we eat."

We applied ourselves to the spicy food with single-minded concentration for a few minutes. When Rosie said dreamily, "Guacamole's actually better than ice cream, isn't it?" and Darrell was starting on his second salad, Ray pulled his little spiral notebook out of his breast pocket and flipped it open on the table. "I'm beginning to feel very curious about the timing of these attacks," he said.

"We don't know when the janitor got tied up," I said, "till we talk to him."

"I wouldn't count on talking to the janitor," Rosie said, "if I were you."

"Oh?" I looked from her to Darrell. They nodded grimly in unison.

"I never found a pulse," Rosie said.

Darrell said, "He didn't seem to be breathing."

"He might get lucky yet, you can't tell," Ray said. "I seen some pitiful cases get well. What I was mainly wondering, though, Jake, is why such a big time spread between Bernie and Willard?"

"That bothers me, too," I said. "If Bernie got robbed at five-thirty, why weren't the bad guys long gone before

Willard got here? What the hell were they hanging around for?''

''And where?'' Ray said.

''Another thing,'' I said. ''Gus and Willard both got blindfolded and gagged with those soft white rags—looks like they might have been Gus's cleaning rags. But Garza's head was wrapped up in a purple flowered pillowcase.''

Ray looked mildly skeptical. ''I think I agree with Bernie, the color's irrelevant.''

''Okay. But why did they switch?''

''They ran out of rags?''

''But then the pillowcase should have been on the last guy tied up.''

''Hmm. See what you mean.'' Everybody at the table ate a few more mouthfuls in thoughtful silence. Then Darrell neared the bottom of his big soda and began dredging the last few drops up through his straw, with sound effects like dinosaurs slurping. When I couldn't stand the noise any more I grabbed the cardboard container out of his hands and tossed it angrily into the nearest garbage container.

''Dunk from the forecourt,'' Darrell said. ''Nice one.''

''But can he jump?'' Rosie said.

''The two of you, go back downtown,'' I said. ''Rosie, here's four bags of evidence. It's the blindfolds and ties and tape from all three men, and the sheet from under the tree. Take them to the evidence room and check them in. Darrell, after you drop Rosie at the station, go to the hospital and check on Gus, call me on my cell phone with a report. Ray and I will talk to Lovejoy before we come back in.''

''But first, I bet,'' Darrell said, winking at Rosie,

"they're going to sit here and ask each other a lot more of those deep, searching questions."

"We will if there's time," I said, "after I kick your ass out the door."

"Maybe it's the weather," Ray said when they were gone, "they're not usually so giddy."

"They got pretty upset when they couldn't resuscitate the janitor," I said. "They're just working it out in their own way. Let's talk about Willard's question. Why do you think he got jumped?"

"Can't be anything he saw. Tying him in the tree wouldn't fix that."

"So it must be something he was going to see."

"Such as?"

"Well, not the robbery, that was all over. But maybe the robbers leaving?"

"Why would they have to go by him? There are half a dozen entrances."

"That's the other thing, access. If Garza was tied up at five-thirty, and the janitor even earlier—which he must have been, right?"

"You'd think so."

"Then somehow the thieves got inside the mall before the back door was opened at six. Who does that, by the way?"

"What? Opens the back door? Don't know."

Ray wrote a note to ask Lovejoy. "We keep saying 'thieves,' but do we know for sure there was more than one?"

"Had to be two, at least. Willard's a big man. It would not have been easy to get him under that tree and tie him there."

"In fact, how could they do it at all without everybody noticing?"

"The quick and dirty answer has to be very quickly, on a dolly, with a sheet over him."

"Yeah, that's right, there was a sheet around him, wasn't there?"

"Half off, but it was there. And he says he got wrapped up."

"Did you notice that part spooked him the worst?" Ray drank the last of his coffee. "He's still a helluva guy, isn't he?"

"Yup. Let's go talk to Lovejoy."

But Lovejoy was not in his office, and his secretary, whose dimpled smiles seemed to get even perkier when she had the place to herself, said he was out of the mall and might not be back for a couple of hours. In the end we asked her virtually all the questions we had saved for her boss, and got quick, confident answers. The back door was opened at six a.m. by the night cleaning crew, which was run by an independent contractor whose telephone number she gave us. She ran off a copy of the mall's hours for us, too, and another of the list of people with keys to the mall.

"So many?" Ray said.

"All the store owners have to have keys, because they often stock while we're closed. Many of their spouses have keys, too." She showed us. "And the three big department stores each have their own night janitors, so one for each of them. Directors of three city departments, fire and water and power—"

"And then there's all the ones that have been lost over the years and replaced," Ray grumbled as we left her office, "they might as well just leave the damn doors open, save time."

My phone rang. Darrell, uncharacteristically subdued, said, "Gus Finseth was DOA at Methodist."

"So now it's homicide," Ray said, driving downtown. "Autopsy Monday, probably. I'll call the coroner and the county attorney."

"I'll tell the chief," I said. "And Willard, I better call him."

"Right, we don't want him to hear it first on TV, do we?"

It took me some time to explain enough about the assaults and robbery so the chief felt he could deal with the media. By the time I called Willard, his wife said he was taking a nap. "I'll tell him when he wakes up," she said. "No hurry about this kind of news."

Just before five, I remembered to call Irma Bell. She said, "Poor Gus. Oh, poor Gus. I'll tell Mr. Fitzgerald."

"And ask him to notify Mr. Garza?"

"I don't suppose he'll do that," she said, "but I will. Oh, poor dear sweet old Gus."

Then it was finally time to check out of work and begin my yuletide celebrations. I fought my way to the hardware store in near-zero visibility, circled a nearly gridlocked parking lot for fifteen minutes before I found a space, mushed into the store and found most of the items I needed with zero help from staff. Ruthlessly grabbing the last two extension cords off the wall just ahead of the little old lady who was reaching for them, I waited ten minutes more in line to be checked out by a clerk who talked on the phone during the entire transaction. Finally I traveled the forty miles to Mirium, the small town where my house is located, on a snow-packed highway filled with would-be suicides driving high-powered vehicles at top speed.

Late as I was, I arrived home ahead of Trudy, who phoned as I was turning into the yard to say, "Forget the pizza, I'm on the south side of Eagan in a line of cars following a snowplow. If I make it through this mess, I'm not stopping for anything.''

"I'll put some water on. We'll have macaroni and cheese.''

"I'm not sure I'm up for the tree tonight, either.''

"What tree?'' I said. "Just try to get home.''

SEVEN

"IT'S LEANING a little to the left," Trudy said.

"That's not the tree. The wall slopes to the right."

"Very funny. Try rotating it clockwise, huh? Clockwise. Jake, have you forgotten which way a clock turns?"

"The longer I crawl around under this tree," I said, "the less I remember. Any chance you might settle for less than perfection?"

"We're very close. Here——" she passed me a folded piece of paper "——slide this under the leg nearest the door. The leg on the tree stand, silly——" She dissolved into giggles. I pulled the paper out from under my thigh and slid it under the tree stand as she ran to the kitchen, saying, "Oh, here comes Mama, I bet."

Ella Hanson's minivan purred to a stop by the side porch, as I backed out from under the tree and stood up. Trudy threw open the door calling, "Hi, Mama!" I heard Ella's boots stamp across the porch, and a rush of cold air hit the parlor. Trudy said, "Glad to see you! Were the roads okay? Here, let me take that."

"This stuff's all for the tree," her mother said, unbuttoning her fox-collared coat. "There's more in the car." Ella's third husband was a provider, so she now enjoys, as she says, "doing for myself a little." Her taste runs to velvet pants, big silk shirts in vivid colors and clear plastic slides with four-inch decorator heels, that she brings with her in their own carrying case, since they can't, of course, ever be worn outside in Minnesota. Add a determined blond bouffant sprayed to iron perfection, and Ella cuts quite an imposing figure.

Coming back in the parlor, Trudy looked at the tree. "Well, there, Jake, that's perfect now!"

"It's kind of small, isn't it?" Ella said. "I thought it would be bigger."

"It's just about right for the space," Trudy said. "This room's not very big."

"I just hope this ornament I got for the top won't be too heavy for it," Ella said, digging through a big bag from Wal-Mart.

"Oh, Mama, now, I thought we agreed you'd just bring the old ornaments you had at home," Trudy said. "Jake and I are going to string some popcorn—"

"Popcorn? Oh, for heaven's sake, Trudy, popcorn? Sweetheart, nobody's put popcorn on a tree since the Great Depression. You want everybody to think you're a pair of losers?" She held up a cardboard box with a picture of an elaborate ornament ablaze with lights. "Nineteen-light special," the big print said. "Here, Jake—" she passed it to me "—see if you can get this up there on the top."

"Ornament is easily attached by patent pending system—" I read aloud. The box pictured gold-spangled angels and many lightbulbs circling the top of a tree. The directions for installation were three paragraphs long.

"I think I'd better wait till all the other ornaments are on the tree," I said, "so we won't knock it off."

"It looks pretty complicated," Trudy said.

"Oh, well, don't worry about it," Ella said. "If Jake

can't figure it out, I'll get Bonnie to bring Mel along when she comes, and he'll fix it.'' Mel is Trudy's sister's buffoonish husband. His humor runs to Sven-and-Ollie jokes and whoopee cushions.

"I don't see any problem with it," I said. "Did you say there's more stuff in the car?" Trudy's mother was maintaining her unblemished record for arousing my inner thug; she had been in the house less than ten minutes and I was already longing to break her nose. I went out and stood in the snow by her minivan till my freezing ankles persuaded my brain to cool down a little. Then I brought in several bags containing Santa hats with leopard trim, a skein of eighteen-foot light strings guaranteed to blink forever, miles of tinsel rope in assorted colors and a four-foot-high fiber-optic snowman whose colors, the package assured me, would begin to change continuously as soon as I plugged him in.

"He's to stand by the tree," Ella said. "Isn't he cute?"

Some of the tinsel ropes had bells.

"Well, this is very generous of you, Mama," Trudy said, "but what happened to the old ornaments we talked about? Those carved wooden animals from the Old Country—"

"Oh, honey, I gave all that trash to the Goodwill years ago." She pulled off her gauzy scarf and inspected her otherworldly hair in the sideboard mirror. "You got the coffeepot on? Let's have a cup before we start."

Bonnie arrived shortly after lunch, bringing tall electric candles to stand on either side of the front door. The candles were adorned by angels blowing gilt horns. "Their wings have real feathers, see?" Bonnie said. "And these spangles catch the light real pretty at night."

"Bonnie, I kind of think it's too much—" Trudy said.

"No, don't worry about that. Mel won these in a raf-fle, and I already had my door ornaments up." Mel had stayed home with the children and the TV set, after I had assured Ella repeatedly that I could manage the tree-top decoration. "They're all watching cartoons," Bonnie said, rolling her eyes.

"Never mind, he brings his paycheck home, doesn't he?" Ella's eyes rested briefly on me, and I could feel her thinking, "And he knows who his parents are."

Bonnie had also brought wreaths for the windows fac-ing the road. They had lights strung in their branches, and a sleigh with eight reindeer galloping diagonally across their fronts. Each lead reindeer had a red nose that blinked on and off.

"Guess we'll need one more adapter," I said. "I can probably find one in Mirium."

"As long as you're going," Trudy said, "could you pick up some replacement lights? It says here these blinkers work in series."

"So if one went dead," I said, "they'd all stop?"

She saw me considering the possibilities and said hast-ily, "Or I can take care of it Monday."

"Never mind, I'll find 'em. Anybody need anything else?"

"Bring in that pint of vodka I've got in the glove compartment of the van, will you?" Ella said. "We'll have a little snort here after a while, to keep us going." She was up on a chair with her shoes off, clipping lights onto the top branches.

"Bottle of vodka. You got it," I said.

I fetched the bottle, went to town and bought supplies, went back again later and bought some more. By four o'clock, as the sun set behind the silos to the west of us,

Trudy and I stood in our yard, saying goodbye to her mother and sister.

Ella stood for a moment by her car, looking at the wreaths, the angels, the string of blinking lights she'd installed around the doorway. She rattled her car keys, gave a little sharp sigh and said, "Well, it's better than it was."

When they were gone, we stood in their tire tracks, watching the old place blink and scroll.

"I'm sorry about this," Trudy said. "It seems like it kind of got away from me."

"I'm trying to think of it as a test run for the new wiring," I said.

"Hey, you're right," Trudy said. "If this doesn't set the house on fire, we're good for another fifty years, aren't we?"

EIGHT

"TIME FOR THE BAKING FRENZY," Trudy said Sunday morning, tying on a big white apron.

"I'll do the donkeywork." I bagged the week's laundry and heaved it, along with a mountain of trash and garbage, into the back of the pickup, and set off on the first of several runs into Mirium. My morning settled into a closed loop of mindless tasks, with the garbage dump, Laundromat and two or three stores on the Mirium end, and vacuuming, pot-sink duty and put-away tasks at our house.

Whenever I had a spare minute, I detoured to the parlor and made another pass at putting Ella's ornament on top of the tree. Once I actually got the patent pending jaws to open and bite into the tree instead of my hand, but when I let go of the ornament, its weight bent the top branch sideways and it almost toppled the whole tree before it fell off. I put it on the sideboard. "I'll deal with you later."

"What?" Trudy asked.

"Never mind. I'm talking to the tree."

"Oh, good." She was in her own universe, as silent and focused as a laser, producing one crusty, spicy delight after another. By early afternoon our kitchen smelled like Heaven, Incorporated. "It's too dangerous to sit down here," I said, snarfing a cookie by the door. "I'll go nuts and eat everything."

"If you'll go get the last of the laundry and one more extension cord," she said, "I'll have most of this put away by the time you get back."

"Deal. What's the extension cord for?"

"Bonnie brought a centerpiece for the table." She waved a floury hand. "I can't describe it. You'll have to see it to believe it. Is that your beeper?"

I called Dispatch and got the message to call Bo at home. When I reached him he said, "You don't have to get involved in this if you don't want to, Jake, but it looks like this weed we been chasing might be part of the answer to those assaults at the mall."

"Then I'm involved. Does Ray know?"

"Yup. He's meeting me tonight. Darrell and Rosie, too." He told me where to go. "Mall closes at nine on Sunday. Quarter after will be soon enough. Dress warm. We can't run the engine in the van."

I finished my chores and took a nap. Trudy fed me a lot of chili and made a sandwich.

"We'll probably sit there all night and do nothing, you know," I said. "Surveillance is always a crap-shoot."

"I know. Why are you taking your flashlight?"

"Why not?" I pulled my Stinger out of its rack by the door. It's smaller than the Streamlight the guys in the squads carry, handier to pack and delivers almost as bright a beam.

At ten after nine, I parked my pickup in a brightly lit convenience store on the highway where they know me, walked three blocks and found the unmarked black min-ivan in the shadow of a defunct gas station, across badly lit Fillmore Street from the rear parking lot of the Iroquois Mall. Bo, in the driver's seat, slid the side door open and I got in without speaking.

"Your vest is on your seat. Put it on now, will you?" I took off my down jacket and got into the heavy, stiff, prickly bulletproof vest, put my own coat back on over it and sat still for a while, waiting to get used to the feeling of being in restraints. Jail without jokes, Vince Greeley calls a Spectra vest. I got used to it, slowly.

"DEA guy will be here soon," Bo said.

We watched late shoppers coming out of the mall, heard people calling to one another as they loaded their vehicles and started their frosty cars. When the last of the lights were going off in the stores, Ray slid into the seat next to me and Bo made the vest speech again, very quietly now because the world around us was closing down for the night. At nine-thirty, with the parking lot all but empty, we saw Blaine Lovejoy turning out lights in public areas and locking the back doors. Rosie arrived and then Darrell; they got in the two seats behind Ray and me and spent several squeaky, zippery minutes helping each other into their vests. As the last cars drove away from the mall, Lovejoy locked the front entrance facing the highway, leaving one dim light burning in the foyer. A minute later, we saw what must have been his car pull out of the front lot and onto the highway.

After that it was just us in the silence. We were looking through the smoked side windows of our van at the blank brick walls of the back side of the mall, punctuated only by half a dozen locked metal doors. Small floodlights on the roof at each end of the building bathed the walls in dim light that dissipated a few feet from the building. Watching paint dry would have created a lively diversion.

By ten o'clock we were getting on one another's

nerves in tiny, peripheral ways. Ray, beside me, had a
habit of rocking forward and back half a dozen times
every minute or so. Darrell had a postnasal drip.

"Quit sniffling," Rosie whispered.

"I can't," Darrell protested. "My nose is running."

"Here's a tissue," she said. "You know what to do
with that?"

"Shut up, Rosie," Ray hissed.

It's one thing to shrug off in advance the idea of sitting all night in the cold doing nothing, but in practice,
five people in an unheated vehicle in the dark, watching
snow and trash blow across an empty parking lot in
which nothing is taking place, quickly get so bored out
of their skulls they start wanting to blame somebody for
the fact that their bulletproof vests are uncomfortable.

There was no way to relieve the tedium; we could not
tell jokes or trade department gossip or even give vent
to inane chatter about Christmas. Silence was key. Using
murmurs, grunts and whispers, by eleven p.m. we had
offered one another snacks, checked the time and com-
mented on the weather until those subjects were, by
common agreement, closed.

By midnight, we had passed through the surly stage
and were all battling torpidity, breathing shallowly
through our mouths and staring with glazed eyes into the
darkness. So three minutes after midnight, when the right
front door of the van was yanked open, the group rate
of systolic blood pressure inside the van shot up about
two hundred points.

A black-hooded figure slid in beside Bo and said,
softly, "Hey."

"Howsgoin'?" Bo said.

"My lads say they're heading this way." There was
a ripping noise as he pulled open the Velcro closures on

his dark hood and slid it off his head. He turned in the front seat and smiled. "Everybody's here, I see."

"Ah, so," Rosie breathed behind me. "Devon Fitzgerald."

"Good to see you, Doyley." His gleaming smile reflected light from somewhere, and the two of them exchanged barely audible chuckles.

"Jake," he said, smiling his way around the van. "Ray. Darrell." Then he turned back to Bo, all business. "Should be seeing the man with the key any minute."

Four minutes later, a tan Camry pulled into the parking lot and stopped in front of the central glass doors.

"Anybody know the car?" Fitzgerald asked. Nobody answered.

Two people got out right away; both men, I thought, but couldn't be sure. In cold weather, virtually everybody in Minnesota looks like a blob of quilted goose down. The taller of the two unlocked one of the tall glass doors, and they went inside without turning on any lights.

"Anybody you know?" Fitzgerald asked again.

"All I could see was overshoes and car coats with hoods," Bo said.

"Jake? Anybody?"

"Same here."

"Okay," Fitzgerald whispered over the seat to the four of us in the back of the van. "Now we hope to see some traffic. Should be soon because the cleaning crews come on at two."

Another eternity passed while the numbers on my watch crawled toward 12:20, and the wind made a snowdrift around the Dumpsters at the south corner of the building and rattled the beer sign on the 7-Eleven store two blocks away.

"Heads up," Fitzgerald said. He pressed a speed-dial number on his cell phone and repeated the same two words into the mouthpiece, as a dark green Honda Odyssey rolled to a stop beside the Camry. Nobody got out for a couple of minutes. I couldn't be sure in the dim light, but it looked as if the person on the passenger's side made a phone call.

Presently a blur of movement showed behind the glass doors, and the left-hand one opened a crack. Two men got out of the Honda and walked quickly through the door that was held halfway open for them. We saw three figures silhouetted against the dim light in the front foyer, before they disappeared into the darkened mall.

We all stirred restlessly. "Wait," Fitzgerald said.

For something to do, I watched the time. In just under three minutes, the two men who had gone into the dark building came back out carrying two shopping bags apiece. One of them popped the doors on his vehicle with his key, and they jumped in without waiting to stow their bags. Ten seconds later, the big shiny Odyssey was pulling out of the lot.

"No offense," Ray said, "but aren't we going to do anything?"

"My guys'll grab 'em," Fitzgerald said, "when they get a couple of blocks away. We don't want to interfere with the flow here."

"We're kinda hoping for a little bit bigger fish," Bo said.

A Jeep Cherokee rolled up to the doors about five minutes later. Bo gave a small grunt of satisfaction and said, "Tilly Baines. I wondered if he'd show."

"Friend of yours?" Fitzgerald said.

"Heard he got out." Baines and his helper made their phone call, darted in when the door was opened and came out two minutes and forty-five seconds later with five shopping bags. They were evidently only medium fish; Bo and Fitzgerald sat as still as gravestones, not even turning to watch them leave.

After that we endured ten silent, nerve-lacerating minutes of nada.

"Sure hope we guessed this right," Bo muttered.

"That can't be all of it," Fitzgerald offered. "You know there's more."

A Lincoln Navigator came and went, repeating the rituals of the first two visitors, while Bo twitched in barely contained anxiety and the rest of us became virtually spasmodic from stress. Fitzgerald, as pleasant as ever, just kept making his abbreviated phone calls and enjoying the show. As the Navigator disappeared into the darkness, he looked at his watch. "Not quite one o'clock. We can wait a few more minutes for the big kahuna."

And three minutes later a shiny black Ford Excursion, looming over the landscape like some improbable rolling mansion, turned into the mall's front entrance and pulled cautiously around the building, crunching the brittle snow of the parking lot under its truck-sized tires. Fitzgerald, watching its progress toward the entrance doors, gave a tiny satisfied hiss, and Bo said, "Bingo."

"JoJo Jackson," Fitzgerald said. "That scamp."

He made his phone call while the men in the SUV made theirs. The shadowy figure appeared at the door, and three men got out of the Excursion. They went through the door a little slower than the earlier callers, as if they had lost the habit of hurrying. But the last one paused in the doorway for a quick scan behind. As soon as they disappeared, Fitzgerald said, "Okay, let's do it."

We all got quietly out of the van, arming our weapons

as we approached the building. Moving was agony for the first few seconds; I felt as though my legs and feet had been trampled by bison. I heard tiny stifled groans all around me, but we all scuttled quickly across the asphalt, and the exercise helped; my feet had quit hurting by the time we reached the entrance.

Fitzgerald's key turned the lock without making a sound. We filed through the half-open door one at a time and flattened against the walls inside, listening. The silence was so complete I could hear myself breathing. When a motor came on, somewhere, my heart jumped against my ribs.

We were in the central pod of the mall. The enormous bulk of the white Christmas tree loomed above us to the right. The one dim light in the foyer opposite, and a distant glow from an exit sign in the next pod, changed the interior from full dark to tricky dusk, in which shapes were barely visible, but details disappeared. We left the wall one at a time, covering one another, and made three long stealthy strides to the shelter of the first stairway to the south. When we were all bunched there we paused for a minute, peering around in the almost dark. Then I heard a low murmur of voices coming from somewhere on our left.

Suddenly I realized where we had to be headed. I met Ray's eyes and saw he had just figured it out, too. Bo and Fitzgerald had already left the sheltering dark under the stairway and taken four long silent strides across the empty terrazzo to reach the next row of storefronts leading south toward the junction with the next pod of the mall. As soon as they disappeared into a doorway, Ray and I followed, pussyfooting across the open space holding our breath. In a few seconds we were crowded into the doorway of a camera shop with the other three, waiting for Darrell and Rosie.

After that we hopscotched down the row, four of us covering each pair as they emerged out of cover and dashed silently toward the next doorway. The voices got more distinct with each move, and now we could see some light leaking through the soaped windows of the empty store.

We were three stores away from the lights, and Bo and I, in the lead this time, had just hopped out of the doorway of a cutlery shop and were scurrying fast toward the entrance doorway of a store that sold baby furniture, when I tripped over something I never saw and went sprawling. Bo jumped to his right to keep from falling over me, so we were both in the open when the soaped doorway burst open, and a man jumped out and fired a handgun at us. In the indoor space, it sounded like a cannon. I heard the bullet zip over my head and crash into something far behind me.

I rolled onto my back, raised my Stinger as high as my arm could reach and aimed it at the man with the gun. When I turned it on, Blaine Lovejoy, blinded by the sudden blaze of light, quit firing and stood still for one breathtaking second with his mouth open. Then Bo fired, and Lovejoy went down, as a second man jumped out of the storefront, aimed into my light beam and fired. I felt a searing pain in my left hand as my flashlight flew away into the darkness, smashing noisily into unseen objects as it tumbled away.

Bo yelled, "Stay down, Jake!" He didn't have to urge me, because by now everybody was shooting and yelling at the top of their lungs. A third man just coming out of the store thought better of it and ducked back inside, and the man who'd shot my Stinger followed him. Bo and

Devon led the way through the door after them; there was a lot more yelling for a short time, and then silence almost as complete as when we first came in.

More lights came on inside the store. Bo propped open the door and a streak of the corridor was suddenly illuminated, within which Blaine Lovejoy lay still on the cold tile floor.

Ray ran to him and knelt, felt the artery behind his ear and looked up. "He's alive." Darrell and Rosie were beside him then, Darrell putting cuffs on Lovejoy, Rosie calling 9-1-1.

Bo stepped around the group kneeling over Lovejoy and came toward me. "Jake? Where are you? You okay?"

I didn't answer him right away, because the pain in my left hand and arm was so intense it had made me nauseous, and I was busy trying not to barf. I realized I was still on the floor and that Bo would think I was hurt worse than I was, so I tried to get up, but that made the nausea much worse so I sat down quickly and put my head between my knees. When Bo knelt beside me saying, "Are you hurt?" I stuck my hand up and said, "Glah."

It turned out my hand was only scratched, but the bullet had knocked the flashlight out of my grip with such force that it broke my thumb. It swelled up to about the size of a baseball in the next few minutes. The paramedics who came for Lovejoy put an ice pack on it, and later that night I got a cast in the ER.

"Damn nice move, getting your flashlight on him so fast," Bo said, sitting in the ER with me while I waited for a doc to read my X rays.

"Glad it worked out," I said. I had a couple of nice pain pills working in me by then, so I was mellow. I smiled, remembering the part of the Famous Flashlight Lecture that had come back to me just when I needed it. "If you do have to turn the damn thing on," Willard had said that day, "hold it well away from yourself so you don't become the target."

My feeling of contentment wasn't entirely owing to pain pills. In between the ice pack and the cast, I had had a delightful few minutes, standing in that empty store in the mall, watching Bernie Garza try to wiggle off the hook. Despite being well and truly caught holding the goods, surrounded once again by money, and now surrounded by many glassine packets of marijuana as well, he protested over and over again that we were making a big mistake; this was all Lovejoy's doing; he was only the bookkeeper; none of this was his fault.

NINE

"THEY RIGGED UP A TRIP WIRE," Bo said Monday morning, "with an alarm. That's what Jake fell over."

The entire People Crimes investigative staff was gathered around the oak conference table in front of Ray's office. Property Crimes were sitting around the outside of the circle on extra chairs, because we had decided it would be more efficient to get the whole story out to everybody at once.

"If we don't," Ray said, "they'll be sitting around in cubicles telling each other about it for a week."

"Well, it is a pretty good story," I said. "Even the chief thinks so." McCafferty was attending this bull session, too, because Bo and I were begging him to take some of the media heat for us, and he said he would if he could ever master the details.

The drug bust was getting huge local coverage because print and electronic reporters had already been feasting all weekend on the story of the Santa who got tied in the tree. The *Times-Courier* had even featured pictures of a couple of small, delighted eyewitnesses above the fold in the Monday-morning edition, sending their newsstand sales to new heights. Now that it was clear the assaults in the mall had resulted in a homicide and then the discovery of a local drug ring, reporters couldn't get enough details to satisfy their editors.

Devon Fitzgerald's heroic profile and winning smile were appearing everywhere, now that his undercover role in the story had come to light, and the story had gone statewide. "The Spy Who Stayed out in the Cold," one Minneapolis paper had dubbed him. He was getting book offers and marriage proposals and needed to get out of town fast, but not, of course, before Rosie got him on the phone and uncorked a gigantic raspberry in his ear.

"Why didn't you tell us he was a Fed?" I asked her now.

"I didn't know, so help me."

"Then why were you so surprised to see him there in the store?"

"Devon Fitzgerald was one of the smartest kids who ever attended St. Catherine's. He got into plenty of trouble because even the accelerated classes weren't challenging enough for him. He was usually bored, waiting for the rest of us to catch up. That's why we got to be friends, because I wasn't exactly—" she cleared her throat "—a model of deportment myself. We helped each other dream up diversions." She shoved some stray hairs into place.

"I still don't see why you were so surprised."

"When Devon graduated he got scholarship offers from Notre Dame and Princeton and two or three smaller schools. We didn't keep in touch, but I heard rumors he went on to big things. I thought he'd joined the CIA." She shook her head, remembering. "When I saw him there—it just didn't compute, Devon Fitzgerald selling sheets and shoes. But things never slowed down enough for me to find out the truth."

"Okay. We're gonna have to be more organized how we tell this story," Ray said, "or we'll be here all day.

I'm gonna go around the table, starting with Bo.'' He started a tape, said the date and time and named the people present, and from then on we ran the meeting like a critical incident debriefing, except nobody cried.

Bo told about his initial contact from DEA, pointing out that they were just following street rumors at first, and that he had put scant credence in the story. "It was too much dope for Rutherford," he said. "Why would they bring it here instead of the Cities?"

In the meantime—Rosie and Darrell took turns with this part of the story—we got our call about the missing Santa. When they got the narrative to the point where they had begun searching through cars in the parking lot, Ray took over and told everybody how we'd found our very own Willard Chase in the tree. He took the story up to the empty store and the call from Davidson's. Then I told about going down and finding Garza tied up by his open safe.

"Okay, stop right there," the chief said. "Tell me again how they arranged that."

"It was the key to the whole plan," I said. "Garza had to get tied up and robbed to take any suspicion off himself. Then he planned to retire in a couple of months, Lovejoy could stay in place as manager of the mall and they could keep their original deal going as long as they liked."

"Which was what?"

"Running a neat little dope ring, just a couple of dozen favorite customers, not big enough to bother anybody."

"So this was just a one-time deal, this big shipment?"

"That's right," Bo said. "The wholesaler who was supposed to take delivery in the Cities got crossways with a couple of his dealers and ended up in the river.

The shipment was already on its way from Mexico, and the other big operator in the Cities had an oversupply and couldn't handle it. So the big boys in New Orleans offered Lovejoy this wonderful deal—seven hundred dollars a pound if he'd take the whole twenty-pound bale. For a little over fourteen thousand they could get product with a street value of a hundred thousand at least. He and Garza figured to make a one-time killing, fatten their retirement accounts and go back to being small-time. They couldn't raise enough cash on their own, though, so just this once they decided to tap the till at Davidson's.''

"In its way I suppose it was an ideal heist," Ray mused. "They didn't have to worry about fingerprints or DNA."

"Exactly. They'd be expected to be all over everything."

"All along they planned to tie up the janitor?"

"Right. The idea was to tie up Gus early so he wouldn't see Garza running around. The sellers had promised delivery by five o'clock at the latest. They'd only have to dodge the night cleaning crew that's employed by the mall—easy enough, since Lovejoy controls their schedule, knows where they are at all times. Once they had product locked in the empty store, they intended to stage the holdup—in reality they'd have robbed the tills and safe much earlier, of course. After they got Garza tied up, Lovejoy would disappear and not come back till his usual time.

"But the weather messed up everything. The shipment got off-loaded at the docks in Minneapolis okay, but the driver took a wrong turn in the blizzard and ended up on a back road south of Burnsville somewhere. He was afraid to call a tow, naturally, and by the time he dug himself out and got back on the highway he was four hours late.''

"Lovejoy and Garza were faced with bringing a bale of MJ into the mall after nine o'clock.''

"How could they possibly?'' Rosie said. "A bale— is it like a bale of hay?''

"Things have changed some,'' Bo said. "Now they put it in a trash compactor and end up with a very dense block about eighteen inches square and ten or twelve inches high.''

"But it would still be pretty smelly, wouldn't it?''

"Not bad. They shrink-wrap it three or four times, maybe pack some pepper or coffee between the layers. They're getting more high-tech all the time.''

"So they could get it past all those walkers in the mall? And the early storekeepers?''

"They weren't much concerned about the walkers— bunch of twinkies counting their laps, Garza said, talking about their insurance plans. And the storekeepers are used to seeing shipments, and they're mostly thinking about getting their stores open. Lovejoy figured to throw a rug over the stuff and just look like it was part of the routine, put it away fast in the empty store and spray a lot of air freshener around to cover the smell. But they realized right away their big problem was Willard. He's an observer.''

"Good cop.'' McCafferty nodded. "Always was.''

"Right. And he knew the morning routine in the mall. There was no way he was not going to notice Lovejoy wheeling in a taped cooler full of weed and locking it up in an empty store. And they knew he'd remember later if he saw Garza scurrying out to the truck with the money after he claimed to be tied up in the store.''

"So they had to get him out of the way,'' Ray said.

"They must have had to go like the devil, to blindfold Willard and get the dope inside and still tie up Garza before ten o'clock."

"God, yes. Busy, busy, busy." The chief stretched. "Heavy lifting, too, ol' Willard's a rock. I understand how they could blindside him, but how in hell did they get him under the tree?"

"The answer still seems to be just about what I said the first time," I said. "With great difficulty, as fast as possible, wrapped in a sheet."

"Kind of inspirational, in a way, isn't it?" the chief said. "Shows what you can do when you're motivated."

TEN

"MAMA CALLED ME at work today," Trudy told me on Monday night, "and said she had a couple more decorations for the front of the house. She asked if you'd call her tonight."

"Me? She wants me to call her?"

"She wants to ask your advice about something. You should feel flattered. I've known her all my life and she's never asked my advice."

"Wow. This is a challenge. I better get that ornament on top of the tree first."

"You think she can see through the wires?"

"I think she'll ask me about it, and I'm not sure I can lie so she'll believe it."

"I've always had trouble with that, too," Trudy said. "I wonder what it is with her?"

I got out the dowel I'd brought from town and slathered it with glue. By standing on a ladder and plunging my face and hands deep into the scratchy pine needles, I was able to press the dowel tight to the central spine of the tree, the top protruding two inches above it. I held it there while Trudy, perched on a chair and equally punished by the evergreens, tied the dowel to the tree with many wire twists, which, being a model of frugality, she saves from things she brings home from the grocery store.

"As soon as that's dry, up she goes," I said, when we were back on the floor wiping off needles and sweat. A few minutes later, I got back on the ladder and slid the jaws of old patent pending over the top of the dowel. It stalled, when it got to the top of the tree branch, so I whittled off some bark and tried again, holding the cuff open with my right hand while pressing downward with my left, gritting my teeth against the pain and sweating profusely.

"Your thumb—" Trudy said.

"What are casts for?" I said. "There, how does that look?"

"It's perfect," she said, "Come down."

It leaned only a little to right. I summoned all my courage. "Go ahead, plug it in." When the lights came on, the gold tracks revolved, the angels circled the stars and all the little bells tinkled. It completely dwarfed the tree.

"It looks like the Christmas ornament that ate Detroit," Trudy said.

"I keep waiting for the Rockettes," I said. I was happy, though. I watched the angels chasing the bells and thought, *Just stay up in that tree, you little bastards.*

"I've just got these two or three little things that I thought would look nice on the front of the house," Ella said when I called her. "Are there some outdoor plugs I can use?"

"Sure." I told her where to find them. "You want me to leave a ladder out?"

"Oh, well, maybe—yes. But I'll bring my own extension cords so I won't need a key to the house."

"Ella," I said, addressing her by her first name for the first time, "are you sure you don't need some help with this?"

"No, I don't want to be any trouble." There was a pause, in which she did some funny breathing, and then she added, "Jake."

It was a Big Moment. Since her daughter had moved in with me, she'd never actually spoken to me directly; she addressed her remarks to Trudy and referred to me, if at all, as "him." And I guess, now that I thought about it, I'd been treating her the same way.

Neither one of us knew where to go with this new-found warmth once we'd stumbled onto it, so I got off the phone quickly and told Trudy, "Your mom's gonna put some more decorations outside."

Trudy threw me a sideways look. "Is that okay with you?"

"Hey, long as everybody's happy."

Tuesday went by in a blur of phone calls, reports, interviews. I generally rely on the chief to handle the media, but this time there was simply so much story, it was so big and complex and loony in spots, that reporters were turning over rocks looking for more faces to put in front of the cameras. They were under unusual time pressure too, because tomorrow was Christmas, when church events would use a lot of newsprint and TV time. Even Bo was not able to dodge the microphones entirely; a local TV reporter insisted on an interview with him. He set a new standard for short answers to long, fascinating questions.

Lovejoy was off the critical list at Methodist, but his doctors said he wouldn't be able to talk for two or three more days. Garza's brain was being picked nonstop by our guys and Fitzgerald. The accountant was having wild mood swings, alternating between boyish boasting and craven denial.

"You local boys would never have figured it out," he

said once, sneering at me, "if the Feds hadn't been tipped."

"Actually we just about had it," I said, "because of the screwy time intervals and the pillowcase."

"I told Lovejoy to go find some more rags," he said bitterly. "But we were out of time and he said, 'Oh, what's the difference?'"

"That's what I realized," I said, "that somebody had been prepared to do two blindfolds, not three. But then it didn't make sense that the oddball one would be used in the middle. I was just gonna call Ray to suggest we go talk to you again, when Bo called me and said the deal was going down."

"Sure, sure. Easy to say now. It was really all Lovejoy's deal, you know," he said, retreating once more into his inner thumb-sucker, "I'm just the bookkeeper."

Bo worked hard all day to uncover the money trail on both men. He came and stood in my doorway Tuesday afternoon. "I'm kinda out of business till after Christmas, I guess. All the banks are closing early."

"Sure." I stretched, feeling good. "We've got a little R and R coming anyway, huh? Last two days have been crazy."

"I'll bring Maxine and Eddy tomorrow, huh?"

"Oh, good. The roads are pretty good out our way, but—that's great, Bo." Maxine Daley was my foster mother for the best six years of my childhood. She's a day-care provider for Bo's daughter Nelly, now, and has a foster son named Eddy. I lost Maxine out of my life for a long time and found her again last year. Suddenly, when I thought about having her come to my house for Christmas, it was as if roses had bloomed without warning in the snow. I told Bo, "Come about three, if you can. It's gonna be a funny mix of people, but—"

"Nelly's really excited."

Snow had stopped falling at midafternoon, and the plows had been busy, so the drive home was actually a pleasure. Fresh snow softened the outlines of everything; all the buildings looked thatched with foot-thick roofs, the fields sloped gently away from barnyards where every flaw had disappeared, and the fence posts had perfect white eight-inch biscuits perched on their tops. Turning into my yard out of all that quiet purity felt like losing my innocence; our mellow relic had morphed into a Vegas casino.

"Mama decorated the house some more," Trudy said, "as you see."

"Is that what happened? I thought maybe I'd wandered into a George Lucas movie." I poured two glasses of wine without taking my coat off. "Let's go out and have another look."

Ella had hung electric icicles across the entire front and both gable ends. And somebody must have made her a helluva deal on chasing rope lights; all the ground-floor windows, and the front door, and the entire porch outside the kitchen were outlined with brilliant red bubbles that chased one another insanely through the dark.

"It dims down the Rudolph noses some," I said.

"But the glitter on the angels shows up better than ever," Trudy pointed out. And suddenly we were both laughing, holding on to each other in the cold and yelling up at the frosty stars, clinking glasses and drinking and then leaning on each other and laughing again till we couldn't breathe any more and had to stop.

"How in hell did she do this all by herself?"

"I don't know," Trudy said, "except this is Mama when she takes a notion."

"Well, you know—it's beyond ugly, but it's awesome, too."

"You're good not to be mad, Jake."

"No wonder you're so dauntless," I said. "You come of sturdy stock."

"How about coming inside and I'll give you a big dauntless kiss." She did all that and more, and after that if I say so myself our Christmas Eve celebration was quite a success.

The next morning we cooked up an enormous ham and all the trimmings, put the leaves in the dining-room table and laid on a lace tablecloth, candles and the pretty red wineglasses Trudy had selected.

Finally, we tried to figure out where to put Bonnie's centerpiece. It was the size of a child's drum, all gold with many elfin figures on top. When Trudy plugged it in, they all began striking tuned bells that tinkled out Christmas tunes.

"That's gotta go on the sideboard," Trudy said firmly. "I'll save some space on the table for the one the kids made, though." Around midafternoon Eddy and Nelly came through the door carrying it as carefully as precious jewels. Maxine lifted off the dishtowel and we all stood around and said, "Beautiful! Beautiful!" It was a piece of cardboard wrapped in aluminum foil, with a lot of glitter pasted on the foil and a plastic crèche with many animals glued into the glitter. The special feature, Eddy pointed out, was the miniature trees around the edge, clippings from Maxine's fir tree set in Play-Doh, painstakingly hung with strips of tinfoil and dusted with more glitter.

Bonnie and Mel arrived soon after, with their two children about whom the less said, always, the better. They were no more amusing than usual, on Christmas, nor had any of Mel's Sven-and-Ollie jokes improved since the last time I heard them, but Bonnie contributed a beautiful moment by coming in with her arms filled with white plush bears in gold lamé jackets, which she perched under the tree and on windowsills, saying, "I had more bears than I needed."

We sat for a long time around the crowded table and ate too much, talking nonstop about nothing. We offered toasts; Ella recited a long Swedish one that may have made sense to the Vikings at one time, and perhaps did to her by then, too, since she'd had, as she pointed out, a couple of snorts. The centerpiece shed tinsel into the food and we picked it out and said, "No problem," which it wasn't because, as Trudy fortunately knew and shared with the rest of us, tinsel is known to aid digestion.

"Isn't it handy to have a scientist right in the family?" Maxine asked, and we toasted that.

When the guests were all gone home and we'd finished cleaning up, Trudy said, "How about turning out all the lights but the tree, and I'll show you how I look in one of those Santa hats with the leopard trim."

"You mean just the—"

"You could try one, too. It might bring out the beast in you."

Actually the beast in me didn't need any help once I'd seen how Trudy looked in that hat. So after New Year's, when we packed away the electric icicles and chasing rope lights, the Rudolph wreaths and candles with feathered angels, I took special pains with the leopard-trimmed Santa hats, which had earned a special place among our Yuletide traditions.

A Romantic Way To **DIE**

A SHERIFF DAN RHODES MYSTERY

Bill Crider

When a romance convention comes to Blacklin County, Texas, Sheriff Dan Rhodes is not quite sure what all the fuss is about—though his wife, Ivy, happily demands he use his badge to cut in line to get the autograph of the show's star: the very buff cover model Terry Don Coslin, a hometown boy turned hunk of the century.

But not even great pecs, gorgeous hair, kissable lips and thousands of devoted fans can protect Terry Don from the deadly intent of a killer. Now Rhodes must make his way into the breathless, steamy, backstabbing, sweet savage world of the happily ever after.

"Crider fans will welcome this..."
—Publishers Weekly

Available December 2002 at your favorite retail outlet.

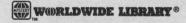

WORLDWIDE LIBRARY ®

WBC440

Take 2 books and a surprise gift FREE!

SPECIAL LIMITED-TIME OFFER

Mail to: The Mystery Library™
3010 Walden Ave.
P.O. Box 1867
Buffalo, N.Y. 14240-1867

YES! Please send me **2 free books** from the Mystery Library™ and my free surprise gift. After receiving them, if I don't wish to receive anymore, I can return the shipping statement marked cancel. If I don't cancel, I will receive 3 brand-new novels every month, before they're available in stores! Bill me at the bargain price of $4.99 per book plus 25¢ shipping and handlng and applicable sales tax, if any*. That's the complete price and a savings of over 10% off the cover price—what a great deal! There is no minimum number of books I must purchase. I can always return a shipment at your expense and cancel my subscription. Even if I never buy another book from the Mystery Library™, **the 2 free books and surprise gift are mine to keep forever.**

415 WDN DNUZ

Name	(PLEASE PRINT)	
Address		Apt. No.
City	State	Zip

* Terms and prices subject to change without notice. N.Y. residents add
   applicable sales tax. This offer is limited to one order per household and not
   valid to present Mystery Library™ subscribers. All orders subject to approval.
© 1990 Worldwide Library.
™ is a trademark of Harlequin Enterprises Limited

MYS02

HARLEQUIN®
INTRIGUE®

presents

~~NIGHTHAWK ISLAND~~

by award-winning author
RITA HERRON

On an island off the coast of Savannah doctors conduct
top secret research. Delving deep into uncharted
territory, they toy with people's lives. Find out what
mysteries lie beyond the mist this December in

MEMORIES OF MEGAN

A man has memories of passionate nights spent in the arms
of a beautiful widow—a woman he's never met before.
How is this possible? Can they evade the sinister forces
from Nighthawk Island and uncover the truth?

Available wherever Harlequin books are sold!

HARLEQUIN®
Makes any time special ®